MW01244632

The Missing Jackal Murder

(The Cora Chronicles)

R. M. Scott

R. M. Scott

The Missing Jackal Murder

It is 1926. Determined not to yield into the pressure to marry and settle down—like a proper lady should—Cora Gudmundson wants a life filled with adventure, so she saves her money and books a cruise to London on her own. Her mother is appalled, but in time her father agrees to let her go. On the cruise, Cora meets two young English archaeologists, Archie Thorogood and Brandon Williamson, who are returning to London with a valuable Egyptian artifact locked in a black case exactly like the one she is carrying. Her case contains two of the magical woodcarvings her family has been honor bound to protect for over 600 years. These two woodcarving Villagers have been her friends and confidants all her life, of course, they want to share her adventure.

Upon arrival in London, two ruffians steal their cases off the dock. As Cora goes on a mad chase through the streets of London, someone murders Brandon Williamson. Armed only with wits, Cora teams up with the remaining archaeologist, Archie Thorogood, to hunt down their cases with the priceless treasures stowed inside. Can she trust Archie? Can they avoid arrest by Scotland Yard for interfering in a murder investigation? Will they solve the murder without falling victims themselves, or worse, fall in love?

R. M. Scott

The Missing Jackal Murder is the first in the Cora Chronicles mystery series. Each standalone story features Cora's adventures around the globe and always includes a devious and twisting murder mystery.

This book is a work of fiction. Names, characters, places and incidences are the product of the author's imagination or are used fictionally. Any resemblance to actual events, locales, or persons, living or dead, is coincidental.

Copyright © 2021 R. M. Scott
Cover design by Russell Scott

All rights reserved. No part of this book may be reproduced, scanned, redistributed or transmitted in any form or by any means; print, electronic, mechanical, photocopying, recording, or otherwise, without prior written permission of the author.

Basswood Publishing

Table of Contents

Chapter 1

Cora Gudmundson sat on her bed with her back to the headboard as anxiety filled her mind. Now dressed in her comfortable pink flowered day dress, she contemplated her decision with her family over breakfast. She only shook her head in frustration. "Jeepers creepers, I'm twenty-four years old, and an adult. This is the twentieth century, for God's sake, and not the Middle Ages."

"But your mother still mourns over your brother Nils' death in France," Ola, Cora's magical six-inch village friend, said to help her understand. They sit side by side on top of the crocheted white coverlet on her bed, talking before breakfast.

"I don't care if mother thinks it's not lady-like for a young woman to travel without an escort."

"No one has said that you're not capable of traveling without an escort—I mean, perhaps if you had a friend to travel with you."

A June morning sunshine slipped into her bedroom and found her bookshelf filled with geographic books, including her complete collection of National Geographic magazines, with the latest May 1926 edition. Through the years, she decorated her sanctuary to reflect her personal interest in adventure. Two-winged model airplanes from the last great war hung from the ceiling in mid-flight. Small horses and cowboys stood on her bookshelf. Ethnic figurines from faraway lands paraded on any surface that would provide room to hold them. Toy automobiles, Tin Lizzies, raced across her bookshelf along with a ship floated suspended on a pedestal. "This is a boy's room," her mother often complained as her disappointment how her young lady turned out, so Cora made sure there were feminine touches such as live plants and flowers in vases and colorful art on the walls, though pleasant to her, but placed to deflect some of her mother's complaints.

Cora perused through the travel itinerary for her upcoming trip to London, England. The latest National Geographic's magazine featured the city of London led her to that decision to escape from her provincial life in Duluth, Minnesota.

Ola placed her fingers on her lips. "Perhaps that is a major reason your mother would not let you go. Perhaps you do need someone to go with you." Cora's disproving expression caused Ola to shift. "It sure would help your case if you brought a friend along."

Cora snapped to her papers and shifted through the pages. "But I'll have a friend, an assigned traveling companion. Here, for me to be able to afford this trip, I will be bunking with another woman throughout this entire trip––train, boat and hotel."

"Oh," Ola's voice fell off. "I was thinking… maybe…"

"I wonder if I could find a new stylish dress in New York before I get on the boat. Something more fashionable; more daring; more modern; nothing too flapper-like." Cora crinkled her nose. No overboard fashions that would create unflattering looks. "What were you saying, Ola?"

"Oh, nothing. Just thinking." Ola sat up and re-adjusted her yellow collar, then brought one of her thick long brown pig-tales to the front to rest upon her bosom. "Have you come up with a convincing way to tell your parents yet?"

Cora did not reply as she strolled to the open window and breathed in the scent of June lilacs and gazed out at the Duluth Harbor. The Lake Superior drawbridge lowered after the last iron ore barge passed through, and Model T's and horse-drawn wagons drove across.

She paced to the center of her room while she daydreamed about dancing in the ship's fancy ball room. With her eyes closed, she mimicked some of the dance steps she'd been rehearsing.

"I wonder how well Arve, and I would be if we danced on the dance floor," Ola said.

Cora bent forward and retrieved her travel papers and sat on the edge of her bed. She closed her eyes, took a deep breath, then read the schedule in rehearsal to convince her parents. "Our group will gather at the St. Paul Union Depot on June 14th. The train will go through Milwaukee, Chicago, Cincinnati, Pittsburgh, and on then to our last stop in New York City. From there, we will board the cruise liner 'The Brandenburg'. The voyage will end in London for a one-week tour of the lovely British city."

"That sounds adventurous." Ola walked to where Cora sat on the bed to peer at the document in her hand.

"In New York City, we end with a day of sightseeing before boarding the ship. I don't know if we get any extra time to do sightseeing in the other cities along the way, but I sure hope so."

Ola nervously picked at her fingers. "Oh, I'm sure you'll get off the train to see the sights one way or another."

Unaware of Ola's suspiciously uneasy nature, she went on. "That's part of the excitement. My travel mate will be another woman who yearns for adventure." Cora felt her pulse rate quicken as her mind conjured images of the woman she will share her trip with. "Or perhaps she'll be an elderly widow spending her inheritance to do something she dreamed of and couldn't. Either way, we'll be bosom travel companions, out for adventure." Cora sighed and closed her eyes.

The sound of creaking from the ceiling wrenched her thoughts away. The Fokker D7 biplane model strung high from her ceiling rocked back and forth as if the plane was in flight. Cora sighed. "How did they get up there?" Ola closed her eyes in disgust. With a disapproving shake of her head, Cora ignored the spectacle and re-inspected her papers.

"You've planned everything except for the part where you have to tell your parents."

Cora closed her eyes. "Oh yeah, except for that." She lay back on the bedcovers, then brought the confirmation sheet at arm's-length as she considered how to win her situation. She brought her right leg up, crossed it over the left and absentmindedly twirled her right foot. "Father may be easier to convince. He's brought me off on many excursions through the woods and to meet with his lumber jack employees, which I guess you could say is one of the many perks of having a father who owned the largest lumber company in Northern Minnesota. Still, my mother will explode."

Ola sighed. "I could ask Arve what he thinks what you should say. I'm sure he's around here. He is so clever and diplomatic. He may have an idea about bringing an extra friend?"

Cora stood, then walked to her dressing desk mirror and checked her image. This morning she had let her shoulder-length hair relax with a lazy wave, rather than plugging in her hot iron. The finger wave was her usual style, so maybe later. She hung her two hats on the corners of the mirror. One hat, a medium gray cloche hat, fit over her short wavy brown hair like a deep salad bowl. A wide pink ribbon band laced the edge. The other was a light tan wide-brimmed hat her father affectionately dubbed 'Cora's cowboy hat.' Both hats were mother-approved.

Now, the rocking biplane became wide, as if in a violent storm. The model came dangerously close to smashing into the ceiling. She got up to investigate. Before she reached the airplane, a knock on her bedroom door caught Cora's attention.

A small voice called out from the hallway. "Auntie Cora, mummy said breakfast is ready."

Cora turned to the door and found her four-year-old niece, Alice, standing in the hall. "Okay, Alice, I'll be down shortly." The scent of freshly cooked bacon reached her nose.

Alice smiled brightly as the precocious, straw-colored pig-tailed girl paused for a moment. Her talkative niece would fit perfectly into the colorful picture of children from Norway, their family heritage, that she had seen in her National Geographic magazine. Alice held out the skirt of her soft white dress and stepped into the room. At that moment, her cuteness ended when Alice's eyes flashed up toward the ceiling and focused on the rocking airplane. With a huff, she stepped further inside and stomped her foot. "Kel. You are being naughty again. How many times have mummy and grand-mummy told you not to be naughty?"

Cora watched as Alice imitated the gestures her 'mummy and grand-mummy' frequently used. She followed Alice's gaze back to the rocking model airplane. Cora sighed in exasperation at the sight of a familiar tiny blonde head peeking out of the plane. "It's okay, Alice."

"But mummy says it's not okay."

"I'll take care of it. Like I said, I'll be down for breakfast shortly."

Alice did not take the hint to leave.

The Missing Jackal Murder

Cora bent over, pulled out a pair of shoes from under her bed, then sat back down. She put on the first shoe with care.

Alice's tone changed brightly, without warning. "I memorized the story of 'Nicholas and the Villagers', Auntie Cora. Do you want to hear?"

"Not really." Cora pulled on the second shoe and chose not to give her any attention.

Alice ignored Cora's refusal, stood with her hands behind her back, and recited. "Six-hundred years ago our Nicholas' village, Nordlund, in Norway suffered a terrible plague. Shaman Agar used his magic to save the Villagers as wood carvings, to keep their spirits alive."

Cora sighed and sat back, now impossible to stop her little niece's recitation.

Alice droned on. "Nicholas and Astrid were the leaders and told the Villagers that Agar had a plan. When the plague came, the magic worked, but Agar became drained, and he disappeared. Isn't that sad?"

"Uh-huh."

"The wooden Villagers came to life. And as promised, Nicholas continued to deliver gifts to the Villagers and others from other towns, then soon to the whole world. It got too much, so Nicholas decided to only deliver on Christmas Eve Night. And because of the protective magic placed upon the village, no one knew it was Nicholas giving the gifts. Did you know that Auntie Cora?"

"Couldn't you tell me this while we head downstairs?"

"Agar's wife, Sigrid, who was still human, protected the little wooden Villagers from those who wanted to harm them. Do you want to hear about Oluf?"

"You did say breakfast was ready?" Cora opened her encyclopedia for Chicago.

"Apprentice Oluf did not believe Agar's premonition. That means prediction."

"You're sure about that?" Cora said sarcastically.

"But when the black plague came, Oluf had enough magic to keep himself alive while he watched his family die. That's the bad part. Oluf was angry and blamed Agar and wanted the Villagers to pay. I don't understand Auntie Cora. It wasn't Agar's fault that Oluf didn't listen." Alice stared at Cora with confusion clouding her eyes.

"What? Oh. I guess that's just how men are sometimes."

Alice nodded and continued her speech. "Sigrid used the last piece of Agar's magic to protect and hide the Villagers from the dangers like Oluf or anyone else who discovered the Villagers. Sigrid passed the protecting magic down from generation to generation through the oldest girl. Mummy said that girls should stay at home while men hunt and go to war. We know the protector as the 'Santa Keeper.' Do you remember what it meant in Norway?"

"Not off the top of my head."

"Mommy said it in Norwegian. But in English it means, 'Daughter who protects the Villagers.' Do you know the words in Norway, Auntie Cora?"

"No, I never even tried."

Alice took a deep breath and pushed on. "In 1856, the family brought the Villagers to the United States. The oldest son spoke English and help the family settle in and buy a man's lumber business."

"Sure, do trees eat breakfast, too?"

Alice giggled. "That's funny. And it's also funny nobody knows the real Santa Claus is our Nicholas and that he lives in our attic. Mummy told me the protective magic prevents people from talking about the real Nicholas and Lars's flying reindeer. If they see him and try to speak, nothing will come out. Some people tried to explain this and came up with ideas like the naughty and nice list and Santa Claus' workshop at the North Pole. Nobody knows that Nicholas' workshop is here in Duluth, Minnesota. Aren't you happy we have Nicholas here in our house? Aren't you?"

Before Cora answered, the airplane swung so violently the propeller hit the ceiling and broke off.

Alice stomped her foot and spoke to the airplane. "Kel, how many times do I have to tell you not to be naughty?"

"It's okay. I'll take care of it. I'll see you down at the breakfast table." Cora stood and nudged Alice toward the door.

Alice gave a snort through her nose, then stomped out of Cora's room.

Cora reached up and stopped the violent flight. She glanced inside the cockpit. A small wooden figure sat holding on for dear life. "Kel, what are you doing in there?"

"I'm delivering presents to London, England for Christmas, like Nicholas. But I'm using an airplane rather than those slow old reindeer."

Kel's words reminded Cora of her youth when she had begged Nicholas to take her on his Christmas Eve adventures. "But the presents the Villagers make are tiny but grow to normal size when you put them under the tree. Why can't you make me small so I can go with you to help you deliver presents and make me big again when we return?" Cora had pleaded. Nicholas finally convinced her that magic didn't work that way. It had been another disappointment in her quest for adventure.

"Kel, how did you get up there? No, wait, don't tell me. Where's Uda?" If Kel was causing mischief, his twin sister, Uda, was sure to be nearby making just as much trouble. Now, as an adult, Cora no longer saw the wonder of living with a village of living woodcarvings. The responsibilities of the Santa Keeper made her shudder. If anything happened to her mother and her sister, Anna, the dreadful job of Santa Keeper would fall upon her. She would forever have to relinquish her plans for travel. That thought made her more anxious than ever to go.

"We're racing." Kel peeped over Cora's shoulder toward the rocking model sailboat on her bookshelf. Uda held onto the rudder and made wind sounds as she pretended to sail across the ocean. Her yellow hair, blue dress and white apron flapped as she swayed to imitate the wind.

"Uda!" Cora shouted in warning.

"There's plenty of room," Uda said. "Climb aboard. Kel and I are racing to London, England. He'll run out of all his fuel so I will sail all the way to the finish line. I will win and he will lose. You are right, boys are dumb."

"Uda, you're breaking my…"

"I've landed in London, England. Now I'm going to drive." Uda jumped out. The model sailboat rocked, ready to tip. Cora rushed over to steady the model. Uda climbed inside a toy jalopy on the bookshelf.

"You did not!" Kel shouted from the plane.

"Did so," Uda said, making motor sounds. Her determined enthusiasm caused her to snap off the steering wheel. "Oops," Uda said, and gave Cora an alarmed expression.

"Ha ha, you're in trouble now, Uda." Kel laughed harder.

Cora closed her eyes, slapped her hand on her forehead. She snatched up Uda and gingerly placed her on top of her bookshelf in front of a mouse-shaped hole, a passageway that led to the Village in the attic. She turned and wrenched Kel from the biplane.

"Ouch."

She placed Kel next to Ola, none too gently.

"Here, Cora," Ola said. "I'll send them to the village."

Cora picked up Ola and placed her hard on top of her bookcase.

"Whoa, careful there."

"Sorry, Ola." As Cora walked out of her bedroom, she heard Ola say, "you two, now."

#####

The hallway grandfather's clock struck its bell for the eighth time as forks clanked on porcelain at the dining room table. Baby Agnes sat upright in her highchair and protested when her mother, Anna, had not filled her mouth fast enough. Alice giggled after her father, Hans, mimicked Agnes' angry face.

"Eat," Anna, Cora's older sister, said to Alice. She gave Hans a disapproving look.

Anna's reproach to Agnes prompted Alice to place her fists on her hips and wag a finger at her baby sister. "Now you behave and eat your breakfast, young lady."

Cora could not keep from laughing at her little niece's imitation of her mother and grandmother.

"Cora," her mother, Marit, said. "Are you listening to me?" Her not-so-gentle brown eyes stared despairingly at her youngest daughter.

Cora, her mind drowned in her upcoming London trip, returned to her mother's drone. Though her mother was in her sixties, she kept herself up in the latest fashions for women her age. But breakfast time in the family dining room was not the same as attending a social event with her successful husband and his influential friends. She preferred

15

her mother dressed as she was today and looking more relaxed, except for the frown.

"Oh, sorry mother," Cora lifted the platter of sausages and passed it to her mother. Marit looked down at the serving platter as if she was looking at horse manure. She took the plate from Cora's hand and passed it to Hans.

"Oh here, grandma, I'll get the eggs for you." Alice shot her hand out and picked up the platter. Her arms wobbled. Cora reached forward. "That's alright Auntie Cora, I have it." Before Cora could assist, the platter found its way safely to Marit's hand. Again, Cora smiled at Alice.

Again, she met her mother's frown. "Cora, where you not listening to me?"

"Oh, sure, mother."

"So, where was your mind this time, Cora?" Marit asked while she spooned scrambled eggs from the platter to her plate.

"What?"

Hans spoke before Cora explained. "Oh, I know. You were off to Fiji."

"What do you know about Fiji?" Anna said to Hans, followed by, "all right, all right," to Agnes as she pushed another spoonful into her noisy mouth.

"It's a feature article in last month's issue of the *National Geographic* magazine," Hans answered. "Am I close, Cora?"

Cora smiled and shook her head at Hans, her spirited and immature brother-in-law. She considered him for a moment. Though Hans worked in her father's lumber company, he did not have the muscular build of the other lumber jacks. His good nature suited Anna just fine. Their parents, however, only tolerated Hans. Her father had attempted to chisel in some woodsmen roughness by making Hans shop work supervisor near the big saw. Putting rough edges on Hans had not worked, but Anna constantly stood up for him as he always had a positive outlook on everything and tried hard to fit in. Cora grinned to her thinking Hans was a wonderful addition to the family and expressed genuine love for Anna and his children. He also showed great respect to her parents.

Thinking about 'suitable men', her mind shifted to how her mother paraded men in front of her as potential husbands, like an auctioneer, marched cattle onto an auction block. They ignored Cora's protests. Only Hans spoke up for her to explain she was not ready to settle down. Usually, her father agreed with him, and Marit would give Hans the evil eye.

Hans's voice brought Cora out of her thoughts. "Maybe it was a story about the Hawaiian Islands?"

"No, that's not it."

"I know. May's issue in London, England... is that it?"

Cora felt her face grow warm as his guess landed on the truth. But a glance at her parents revealed that, as usual, they had no interest in what Hans had said.

The 'London' subject would have ended rather swiftly if not for a small voice that shouted out from on top of the china cabinet. "When are we going to London, England, Cora?"

His mischievous twin sister, Uda, returned Kel's voice. "Yeah? Did you tell them the news about our trip?"

Cora gazed with an angry scowl at the tiny pests on top of the china cabinet.

Marit studied Cora. "What's this trip? What are they talking about?"

"Nothing. I don't know. Those two are always causing trouble."

"Didn't you tell them yet?" Kel said.

Uda jumped in front of Kel. "No, let me tell them."

"Go away," Cora said with a low hiss. She glanced at her mother.

"Tell us what?" Marit asked.

"Nothing."

"No, it isn't nothing," Kel's said. "If Cora is going to London, then we can go too."

"Shut up!" Cora's voice rose. Her eyes locked on her father at the other end of the table. His head remained buried behind the newspaper, as he apparently chose not to be a part of Kel's and Uda's usual shenanigans.

"What's wrong with London, England? I thought you said you are going there."

"Uda, shut up."

"You two go back up to the attic," Marit commanded. "I won't stand for your bickering during our breakfast."

"So, Cora isn't going to England?" Kel asked.

"Now!" Cora snapped.

"What about your plans to go to London? Did your mother say no?" Uda ignored the orders to leave the room.

Cora closed her eyes tight and slapped her right hand to her forehead.

"Don't be ridiculous. Cora isn't going anywhere," Marit said.

"Yes, she is. Cora has tickets, haven't you Cora?" Uda asked.

"She has what?" Marit asked, and stared at Cora.

Cora's shocked expression only confirmed the news.

"Can we go too?" Kel asked.

"Oh, boy. London, England," Uda said. She scowled at Kel. "Where is London, England, again?"

Kel lifted his shoulders in a shrug.

The Missing Jackal Murder

"Get out!" Cora shouted and stood with intentions to grab two tiny Villagers and throw them across the room.

Cora's mother cut in. "Cora, don't shout at them like that. And what does London have to do with this?"

Kel extended his arms to his sides. "Are you going to take an airplane, like mine?" Kel made engine sounds with his mouth.

"No, you dimwit, she will take a boat like mine."

"Oh, yah?"

"Yah?"

"What's going on?" another voice from the hole in top of the china cabinet spoke up. Ola and her husband, Arve, came into view.

Cora pointed at Kel and Uda. "Take those two rats back to the attic."

Arve pointed to the small doorway that led to the stairs to the attic. "You two, get in there."

Ola put her hands on the waist of her green dress. "What trouble are you causing now?"

"Nothing."

"We are just—"

"Go!" Cora snapped in a loud, angry voice.

The two troublemakers gasped and entered the hole that led to the attic.

Cora sighed, first in relief, and then prepared for the explosion.

Anna put her fork down. "Are you really thinking of a trip to London?"

"She absolutely is not," Marit said.

Anna gazed intensely at Cora's face. "Mother, I think it's a good idea for Cora to get out and see the world."

"Two of my boys went out to see the world, and one of them didn't come back. Have you forgotten that?"

"That was from the war," Anna and Cora said in unison. Cora didn't know whose face was redder, her mother's or little Agnes's.

Hans sprung up, took the spoon out of Anna's hand, scooped up smashed potatoes and eggs and crammed it into Agnes' wide, screaming mouth before her little head popped off.

"Cora should be home and—"

"Trapped, like you?" Cora completed the sentence.

Marit sat up straighter and glared at Cora. "Being a wife and mistress of your own home is hardly a trap." Marit spotted her husband across the table.

Knude was busy ignoring the discussion entirely.

"Knude, say something."

"Hmm, what?" Knude said as he peeked over the newspaper held in his large, work-roughened hands. At the sight of his wife's glare, he slowly lowered it to the table.

Cora gave her father an imploring expression. Though in his late sixties, he remained a tall, muscular man. Despite the decades he had spent working hard at the lumber camp, his face, covered with a white mustache, was that of a thoughtful and kind man of business.

Hans lowered his eyebrows to Knude. "What are you reading?"

Cora knew this was Hans' attempt to divert the lightning bolts flashing over the breakfast table between her and her mother.

"It's this week's crop report."

"Crop—" Marit sputtered. "Why are you reading the crop report when you're not a farmer? We are having a serious discussion here."

"Well, in a way, I'm a tree farmer. And I was thinking of my Uncle Ed, you know, who took on a piece of land."

Cora laughed out loud.

"You think this is funny?" Marit's voice rose in tone and volume as she glared at Cora.

"No, I think you're all just swell," Cora said in a sarcastic tone.

"You, now you little–" Marit's mouth opened and closed like a fish out of water. "Are you going to help me with this or are you going to stay buried in your paper and not see your youngest daughter make a huge mistake?"

"Calm down," Knude said as he folded and set his newspaper aside. "Let's hear what Cora has to say."

Cora took a deep breath and prepared to face the music. "I've been thinking about this for a long, long time. It's time for me to get out and make my mark on the world."

"Get out into the world?" Marit snapped. "You are a lady, and at your age, your place is at home with your husband and children."

"Are you kidding?" Cora shouted back. "I never intend to get married."

Marit's face grew redder. Her mouth opened and closed several times as if she were searching for words.

Cora continued, "One day I might get married, probably. But not today. Not for a long time. You should know this by now. You've been shoving boys in front of me since the day I graduated high school. That's why I went off to college."

Marit's eyebrows rose as if it shocked her.

"Don't look at me like that. We've talked about this before, but you keep pushing and pushing. Yes, I wanted to learn new things, meet new people, but I mainly wanted to get away from your constant pressure to marry so young."

Marit sat stunned.

Cora feared she had insulted her mother. She didn't know whether to apologize or insult her further. She pressed on, carefully. "When I came home, I was afraid you would continue your onslaught of 'woman should be married.' I was afraid. That is why I asked Eric to let me work at his automobile dealership."

"Interesting. What does this have to do with you working with Eric?" Hans asked.

"Shh," Anna said.

"Oh, never mind. I got it," Hans said.

"I wanted to be with people, well, originally. Eric thought I was a great salesperson because I always tell the customers about the adventures they can have with a new automobile. But then I was sad watching them drive off the lot, knowing I had to stay there. Some turned left, some turned right. Where were they going? How come I couldn't go where they were going?"

"What does this have to do with—"

"Everything," Cora interrupted.

"I've got it," Hans said, and counted on his fingers. "High school plays full of adventure. High school clubs with people to share their ideas and plans. College to learn there are other things besides a simple domestic life. Eric's car dealership was to meet adults who shared your sense of adventure. With a life like that, we should have seen that Cora had been planning this trip all her life. It's obvious Cora is ready to go. Today London, tomorrow—who knows?"

Agnes' scream for more food brought Anna out of her trance and lifted the spoon, scraped up some eggs and shoved them into her child's mouth.

Marit gave Hans a scathing stare. Her nostrils flared. The morning sun that peeked into the dining-room window reflected off the sweat from her forehead. She then turned to Knude. Her eyebrows arched. "This is your fault. You took her along with you, here, there, everywhere, filling her head with adventures and other wild dreams. It is unnatural for a young lady."

Hans stood up and pulled Agnes out of the highchair. "I think she needs changing." He tilted his head at Alice, then tilted his head to the living room. "Come along, Alice, and help me with your sister."

"But I want to hear," Alice whined.

"Out, now," Hans commanded, and walked her upstairs. Her long cotton dress bounced as Alice followed in whispering protests.

"Mother," Anna said, "it's not father's fault. Women have been making great strides lately. Women can be doctors and lawyers and even run for Congress. Who knows, Cora may be the next famous explorer. You know Cora has been roaming since—"

"You stay out of this!" Marit snapped at Anna.

"Fine." Anna lifted her hands in defeat and rose from the table.

Before she left, Anna moved behind her mother and signaled to Cora to keep up the fight and stand up to their mother.

"The only reason you want to keep me from going is because of what happened to Nils. This is not the same situation."

"What does Nils' death have to do with this? God rest his soul," Marit said. Her eyes flashing into Cora's.

Knude removed his glasses and placed them on the table next to the folded newspaper. "Perhaps Cora is right."

"What?"

"Elmer and Nils marched off and fought in that senseless war and our son Nils did not return."

"Yes, he did. He returned in a casket." Marit's voice ended in a slight sob, and she covered her mouth with her hands.

Knude took in a deep breath. "You believe the world is a dangerous place because of what happened to Nils. But that was a time of war. Now people are traveling all over. I read about it in the newspaper every day."

Marit faced Knude. "First, it has nothing to do with Nils and the world and everything."

"Yes, it does," Cora interrupted.

"No, it does not. It's about you being a single, young lady—"

"—with no business being outside in the world," Cora finished her mother's sentence.

"Well," Marit took a breath and her voice took on a softer tone of encouragement. "What about Oscar Benson? He is a nice young man and really took a shine to you. I thought you were considering him?"

"What? I have absolutely no interest in… you were the one who took a shine to him. I want more in my life than being a wife to some stuffy man who can barely string two sentences together."

"Knude, aren't you going to back me up on this?" Marit waited.

He lifted his glasses, wiped them on his shirtsleeve, and said nothing.

"Umph," Marit huffed. "Well, I guess I'm going to lose on this one. Her welfare is on your head." She stood and waited as if they would change their minds.

"Now, Marit," Knude said after several moments of silence.

"No, go, if you must," Marit said, and left the dining room in a near run.

Cora and Knude remained seated on opposite sides of the table, and she smiled in triumph. She gazed up at the top of the china cabinet where Ola and Arve had listened in on the discussion. They gave her the thumbs up sign. She glanced at her father.

"I assume you have a plan?"

Cora smiled, rose from her chair and danced to her father's side to kiss him on his forehead. "Of course, I have a plan. You taught me well."

"Okay. Before you leave, we need to talk over your plans, in detail, of course."

"Yes, father, you will see I have everything in order." She kissed his forehead again and prepared to leave the room.

"Excuse me?" her father's voice stopped her departure.

"Yes, father."

"Aren't you forgetting something?"

"What?"

"Since everyone is out pouting, these dishes will not fly into the kitchen by themselves. Let's see how well you can plan this task."

Both laughed. As Cora stacked the dishes, Knude stacked his and other close by, then slid them to Cora. She lifted the batch, and he returned to his newspaper.

Chapter 2

Cora returned to her bed and sat with her back against the headboard. The new May 1926 edition of the *National Geographic* sat on her lap, opened to the article called, "London, From a Bus Stop". Focused on the aerial view of Trafalgar Square and the mall, she imagined herself standing at the base, reading the inscription about Nelson and what part he played in history. She put the magazine down and inspected the brochure, which mentioned a one-day stay over in New York City.

The quiet sound of a throat clearing brought Cora out of her fantasy. She found Arve and Ola staring down at her from the top of her bookcase.

Arve started the conversation. "Cora, I hope we're not disturbing you?"

"We don't want to interrupt your packing," Ola said.

"No," Cora said absentmindedly and got up to shuffle through the clothing stacked in neat piles on her bed, chair, and vanity. She picked up a blouse and a skirt, one in each hand, and held them up for inspection. "I don't even know where to start. I have no idea what to bring along."

"Congratulations," Arve said. "So, you really are going to London then, aren't you?"

"I imagine you'll have a great time over there—by yourself," Ola said.

"I can't wait to leave. I wonder if I should bring along some of my books." She put down the clothing to pick up a couple of books, only to put them back down again. She laughed. "I suppose that's ridiculous. There will be plenty of books over there to read, if I have any time to read. Besides, with all the treasures I plan to bring back home, I will need a lot of room. Don't you think I should travel light?"

"Traveling light is a wonderful idea," Ola agreed.

"Cora," Arve said, "do you really think that you should go alone? I mean—I mean, shouldn't you have a traveling companion or two? You might get lonely traveling by yourself."

"I won't be by myself. I'm going with a tour group, and I'll have a traveling companion."

"Nevertheless, they will be strangers."

Cora stopped, whipped her head around, and stared at the two. "Did my mother put you up to this?"

"No," they both said and shook their heads.

Ola shifted from one foot to another. "It's just — well, we hoped you wouldn't mind bringing something else along…"

Cora frowned. "What? Who?"

Before Arve and Ola could respond, a knock on the door disrupted their conversation.

"Come in."

Knude walked in with a large black suitcase in hand. "I thought you might need something sturdier on your trip."

Cora squealed with delight and reached out to take the case in both hands. "Oh father, it's perfect. I hope you didn't spend more on me. Paying for the rest of the trip was more than generous enough."

"Not at all," her father grinned. "I bought this case a year ago, in case Elmer needed me to go along with him on his business trips." Knude sighed at the case. "I wanted a good suitcase. Interesting, if you look at the manufacturer's tag on the inside, you see that this case comes from London. How ironic."

Cora studied her father's face. Did he regret retiring and passing the lumber business down to Elmer, her third brother? His voice had sounded wistful when he mentioned the possibility of going on a business trip. He changed the subject before she raised the question. "I am quite proud of you, my dear, for doing thorough research, along with planning and purchasing the tickets. But I'm also proud of you for doing this all by yourself."

"Well, I'm a grown woman, father. Women are striving into so many things today. We're not just a pile of domestic fluff, you know."

Knude smiled. "You have grown into a fine woman." He studied her as if to memorize her face. "Well, I'll leave you to pack now—oh, I almost forgot. Look inside the case."

"I thought I heard something loose inside." As she opened the case, she found and pulled out a soft cover book with the words— 'My Journal' inscribed on the cover.

"Anna bought that for you. She wanted to present that to you later, but thought I'd bring it up now so you can pack it properly."

"A journal, for my trips. How thoughtful of her. Yes, I will jot everything down I see and do." She thumbed through the empty pages. She looked around her room for a pen or pencil.

"Here." Knude pecked a ball-point pen from his shirt pocket. "Take this along with you to London."

"Thanks." She opened the to the first page and thought. To be clever, she wrote on top 'The Cora Chronicles', followed by the date, then wrote: 'Two things are for certain: I'm off to a grand adventure and I have the most wonderful dad.'

Knude smiled, kissed Cora on the forehead, and left the room. "Don't forget to thank Anna."

"I won't." She paused. "I've got to get packing."

"Yes, you should finish packing," Ola said.

Cora jumped. She had forgotten Arve and Ola were in the room. "I still have two days. However, when father went on business trips, he often made a mad scramble to remember things before he ran out the door." She smiled and shook her head.

Ola stepped forward. "So, what do you think about what we were talking about before your father walked in?"

Cora didn't answer as she opened the case and inspected the inside, wondering what would fit where. When the two Villagers stood silent, she realized she did not know what Ola was talking about. She turned to them. "What was that again? Something about me bringing something along on my trip?"

Ola shifted back and forth but said nothing.

"Ola?"

Arve stepped forward and blurted, "We were wondering if you would take us along."

Cora stared at the two as they stood motionless, staring down at her. Her mind worked slowly, trying to comprehend what Arve said. "You want me to bring—what?"

"Us," Ola blurted out. "We could be your traveling companions—see the world and talk about it, you know, we would be with you—on your trip—you know, in London..." Ola trailed off.

"You're kidding?"

"No, we're not," Arve said.

"We expected this response," Ola said, "but hear us out."

R. M. Scott

Cora shook her head. "Do you honestly expect Mother and Nicholas to let you come along? Do you have any idea what they would say, if I even dared to ask such a thing?"

"We'll convince Nicholas."

"Do you honestly think Mother or Anna would consider letting you leave this house?" Her voice rose at the end.

"Like we said, all we have to do is convince Nicholas as we leave. He'll convince them later." Before Ola gave Cora a chance to speak, she continued to explain. "We'll sneak a ride and pretend we're stowing away. By the time we're long gone–"

"And mother and Anna will find out, send Nicholas, and he'll bring you two back."

Arve put his fingers to his lips. "We know they will, but then we hoped by then Nicholas would convince them to let us stay with you."

Ola dove in as if to keep the conversation going. "I made this for you. Do you like it?" She stepped back to lift a large handbag they hid behind them. She moved forward to hold the pouch out for Cora's inspection and smiled at her as if it was the greatest thing Ola had ever created.

Cora paused and remained stunned, then stood silent with a confused expression. Ola opened the pouch and held it out for Cora to see inside. "Look here," Ola said, waving her hand inside the main compartment. "It appears to be like any other purse, so when you go shopping, you can put your items in here. But see here." She opened a little pocket in the front and poked her fingers out. "This is where we would be, looking through these two small sets of holes so we could see the sights with you." Ola closed the pouch and waited for Cora's approval.

The Missing Jackal Murder

Arve placed his arm around Ola. "Genius, don't you think? She thought of it all by herself."

"Oh, thank you, Arve." The two kissed, then waited for Cora's response.

Cora watched their hopeful faces. She tried to think of a reply to explain how ridiculous and dangerous it would be to take two Villagers along on her journey.

The silence stretched on until Arve cleared his throat and motioned toward the purse. "Well, it will be your size when you take it along, of course. You know how the magic makes the small objects we create human-sized once touched by human hands, of course." He stopped rambling and waited.

Cora sighed at her two favorite Villagers. She considered Ola to be one of her best friends, which was weird since Ola was 600 years older than her. "Look, I don't think taking you along is such a good idea."

"If we feel a situation is dangerous, then remember, we can always call Nicholas and he will instantly come to our aid. Even if we were to fall into the ocean, though I know we would never would, Nicholas would rescue us," Arve said.

Cora sighed. "I can see you've spent a lot of time thinking about this and creating the purse pouch," she said, trying to think up another argument to discourage them.

She had hoped mentioning the danger and her mother's and sister's anger would have been enough to change their minds. But then, saying, "I don't want you with me," would devastate them, but she truly wanted to do this trip alone. She knew what to say. "What about your work in the village? Ola needs to create sweaters, hats, and other woolen things. Arve, you need to package them and provide supplies for

Ola's work. If you come with me, how will the Villagers keep up with the supply of sweaters?"

Arve ignored her question. "We don't want to be a nuisance in your travels, merely companions," he said, as if he had rehearsed the speech. "But then, if you feel we are a nuisance during your tours, you can call on Nicholas and he will take us back to the village."

Ola handed her the pouch. "Here, try this on."

Cora thought to at least give the traveling pouch a look; they'd spent time making it, after all. She pinched the tiny bag as it grew to her full size. She swung the strap over her head where it rested comfortably across her shoulder.

Ola clapped her hands and laughed. "Wonderful, Cora, it fits you perfectly."

Cora looked inside. "There *is* plenty of room to carry souvenirs, food, or anything I would need for the day." Cora ran her fingers inside the hidden space that was large enough for Arve and Ola with the small holes for them to look out. On the outside was a decorative wide strip of black woven fabric that hid the holes.

"So, what do you think?"

"Nice, very nice."

"And the small pocket inside. Do you think there's enough room for Arve and myself?"

Cora smiled.

"There's only one way to find out. What do you think?" Arve said as he winked at Cora.

Cora recognized the manipulation, like how her father negotiated a successful sale. She smiled and placed them in the secret pockets.

"Splendid," Arve's muffled voice said from inside the pouch, "you did a good job, Ola. Plenty of room."

"Everything's looking great and now we can see the sights too," Ola said.

Cora stared in the mirror at Ola's handbag draped over her shoulder, then looked down at two sets of imploring eyes.

"I know we can convince Nicholas and he can convince your mother that we will be safe and can handle any difficulties along the way."

Cora gazed into the mirror and imagined herself as a tourist walking the streets of London. She closed her eyes. Maybe it would be fun to take them along. But then again, perhaps Nicholas would say no. If he didn't allow the two to come along, the disappointment would be on Nicholas rather than herself.

#####

As Cora opened the creaking door to the small room housing the village of living woodcarvings, she ducked as eight small four-legged wooden figures flew past her face, missing her nose by inches. The figures flew around like large, brown gliding spiders.

"Sorry Cora." Lars, keeper of the eight tiny reindeer, stood at the edge of the village platform. "I like to give the little beasts a chance to stretch their legs every now and again."

She approached the village that sat upon a waist high platform. Cora remembered the hours she spent in this room as a child watching the Villagers do their work in complete awe. The row of Viking style huts and primitive workstations always fascinated her. But, as for all children, time changes everything. What once was a delight had faded into a mix of practical realism and simple logic. Her mother taught her that the magic of the village did not apply only to children, but to all who possessed the magic inside. Cora no longer felt the wonder which Nicholas's magic gave to the world. Today she had only her trip on her mind and tried to figure out a way to talk with Nicholas. "That's all right, Lars. I'm here to see Nicholas. Is he around?"

"It seems that's all anyone ever wants to see," Lars said.

"I'm sorry. I didn't mean to offend you."

"I'm only kidding." Lars gave a whistle. The flying reindeer turned, reentered the attic, and landed near the pen at the back of the village. "Not too sure where Nicholas is, I believe he went down to the storage area to fetch supplies."

"Thanks, Lars."

She smiled and panned the village to her left to the staircase that led down to the open area where Nicholas had supplies stored. Below the front of the village platform, two doors would pull open and reveal a storage space for the supplies. Her temptation was to swing the doors open, but decided that would be rude and she'd have to wait.

Keeping supplies became one of Nicholas's primary functions, along with his role as leader and the whole Christmas Eve gift delivery process. The rest of the Villagers had their own specific tasks and talents. Cora reached into her new pouch and placed Arve and Ola next to their hut near the front. Baskets with wool materials overflowed near the door. Weaving brackets of different sizes and shapes leaned against their hut.

The short, squatty villager, Stian, Ola's father, approached the two. "Where have you been?" Stian sported a Viking-like attire much like the others.

"Cora and we have business to discuss with Nicholas."

"You're not planning to abscond with the wireless?" Stian asked.

"No, it's something personal."

"Good, the Cubs are playing the Cardinals and I have a bet with Hans that–"

Nils stomped into view. "What's going on here?"

Cora considered Nils, who was a sort of Nicholas's head elf—a description he hated endlessly. He was Nicholas's right-hand man and ensured everything stayed on schedule.

Nils placed his hands on his hips. His brown beard seemed to point at Cora as he looked up. A utility belt holding chisels and hammers held the wood maker's brown shirt together.

Every time Cora saw Nils, she thought of her brother, whom her mother had named after this Villager. This Nils had taken her brother's death hard. Aside from that tidbit, though, Nils was her least favorite villager. He was not mean, but stern, because of his heavy responsibilities and strict time schedules.

"You're not falling behind on those deep green wool sweaters, are you, Ola?"

"No, in fact, I'm a bit early with those, as well as the maroon hats and gloves."

As her previous encounters with Nils, Cora, and the others looked to Gunda, Nils's wife, to smooth out his gruff outbursts. Fortunately, Gunda walked up.

"Oh, hello Cora, did you come here to help paint today?"

"No, Gunda, we're here to see Nicholas."

"Oh, I really do miss your artwork, Cora. You used to have so much fun."

Cora smiled. She had enjoyed painting in her youth, especially when Gunda was next to her gossiping.

"Nicholas is down in storage. I'll go get him for you." She walked away.

Nils approached with his familiar stern face. "Gunda, if you don't get those train cars painted, we may get out of schedule."

Gunda sighed and walked on. "Nils, don't worry. As I always say, don't worry. Oh, never mind."

He returned to Cora. "Just don't take up too much time with Nicholas." He frowned at Cora and then walked away.

From the corner of her eye, Cora saw another female figure stare up at her. Liv quickly looked away and walked towards her husband, Vidor, who pounded a piece of metal on his anvil. Vidor created beautiful silver jewelry and useful tools. Liv was extremely shy, especially around her. But, as Anna pointed out, Cora's robust personality was scary, not only to Liv, but sometimes to others.

Nicholas entered the room. "Cora?" He held several beams of wood over his shoulder, followed by his wife, Astrid, who also carried an armful of wood.

"Is that Cora?" Astrid asked, with a broad smile.

"Oh, hello Astrid. I hope I'm not interrupting."

Nils grunted. "I told Cora you were busy."

"Nonsense," Nicholas said. "I always have time for visitors. What can I do for you, Cora?"

"I have a rather large and unusual request."

"Does this have to do with your trip to London?"

"Well, yes, as a matter of fact, it does."

"Let me see," Nicholas said, and dropped the wooden beams near his hut. Nils lifted them over his shoulder and turned, barely missing Liv's head. "The best part of London to visit—as a matter of fact, one of my favorite neighborhoods is—"

Ola interrupted, "No, Nicholas, Cora wants to ask you something, something about us."

Arve nodded his head, clenched, and unclenched his hands.

"What Arve and Ola are trying to say is that they want to come along with me to London."

Nicholas studied the three but said nothing. The entire village stopped, except Vidor, who continued hammering.

Cora looked around and sighed. Kel and Uda were not around to make things more difficult than they already were.

Liv grabbed his bicep to get her husband's attention. "What?" Vidor held his hammer in midair.

"I know this is very irregular, but I thought it would be fun to bring Arve and Ola along on my trip."

Nicholas stroked his beard. "Has your mother approved?"

"Well, I haven't asked her yet. I thought if it was all right with you, then mother would agree."

Nicholas folded his arms over his chest. "You did, did you?"

Cora nodded.

Nicholas turned to Arve and Ola. "Whose idea was this?"

"It was mine," Cora lied.

"Was it now?"

Cora nodded again.

Nicholas put his hand on his mouth as if giving the idea consideration.

"They would be safe," Astrid spoke up, "you know Cora is very responsible."

Again, Nicholas said nothing while he stared at Cora.

"I think they should go," Astrid said, speaking up again.

"Yes!" Ola said.

Nils approached Nicholas. "Are you considering letting them go when you still need to finish your quota? If Ola is

out gallivanting around, how is she going to keep her
production levels up?"

Cora ignored Nils's comment. "I think Arve and Ola
would make excellent traveling companions. They work hard
and deserve a break. Don't you agree, Nicholas?"

He smiled. "So, you're finally seeing us through adult
eyes. Yes, they do work hard."

Cora gave Arve and Ola an appraising look. "Yes. I now
see them as a young couple, still in the prime of their life
with the same yearning for adventure that I feel. I see them
through adult eyes."

Nils jumped in front of Nicholas. "Wait, wait. You're
not considering this, are you?"

Nicholas smiled.

Cora smiled back.

Nils jumped in again. "But what about your quota, Ola?
What about your knits for the gift giving?"

"Like I said, I'm early in my quota. I can catch up when
I get back."

Nils crossed his arms in defiance. "But what about
Marit and Anna? They certainly will not let you go."

Nicholas placed his hands on his waist. "Nils is right,
Cora. Your mother will not let you take Arve and Ola along
with you. Not all the way to London."

"But, but…"

Astrid chuckled. "I believe the key word is 'let'."

Arve rose his hand. "What if, what if we do go with
Cora? And when Marit and Anna find out, after we leave,
you can say we stowed away."

Nils put his fists to his waist. "They would demand
Nicholas to go and fetched them."

"What of it?" Gunda said to Arve.

He paused. "When Nicholas approaches, we could, we could tell Nicholas how Cora. Yes, Cora is taking care of us."

"And remind them how she is a responsible adult," Ola added.

Nicholas stroked his light brown beard. "That could work."

"As long as the two little monsters don't get wind of this," Berthina, Kel and Uda's mother said as her husband, Buldar, nodded his head in agreement.

"Now, can we get back to work?" Nils grunted out, shook his head, and walked away.

"Yes, and I got to get back to packing. Let's see. I need to put my pouch, the one Ola made for me, on my bed and go downstairs. I think I have other things I need to gather."

"We're packing," Arve whispered with a smile. He grabbed Ola's hand to pull her into their hut.

As most of the Villagers bid Cora, Arve and Ola a 'bon voyage', Stian popped his head out from behind his hut. "Are we going somewhere?"

Cora left the village with a small smile.

Chapter 3

As the train conductor announced their imminent arrival at St. Paul in the coming half hour, Cora sat back in the cushioned seat and closed her eyes. Arve and Ola sat at the table in front of her, hidden behind a standing menu. By now her mother had definitely discovered the two had stowed-away with Cora and no doubt had become enraged. She could imagine poor Nicholas explaining to her mother that they would be fine in Cora's care.

She could hear Ola exclaiming at each site outside the train window as they passed from open country to urban concrete. Every once-in-a-while Arve grunted when Ola nudged him away from reading his book on London to look at some interesting sight.

A familiar man's voice spoke in Cora's ear. "Cora. Cora, wake up."

Cora expected his visit since their departure from the Duluth train station. "How's mother? Did she raise the roof?"

"We need to talk."

Arve, Ola, and Nicholas yelped as she snatched them up, dumped them unceremoniously into her bag, stood and walked down the train's hallway to a bathroom. She shut the door behind her, slammed the toilet seat down, and sat. She placed the three Villagers on the nearby sink.

Arve glanced around the cramped compartment. "Cozy."

Ola sat down on the edge of the porcelain sink so as not to slide off from the sway of the train. "What do you mean? This looks like a mansion to me."

The Missing Jackal Murder

"Speaking of mansions, how is everything back home?"

Nicholas folded his arms and lowered his eyebrows. "Your mother instructed me to return with Arve and Ola immediately."

Ola stomped her foot. "You can't do that."

"We're alright with Cora. We will be alright throughout the trip. And you can tell Nils we will catch up once we get back. If he doesn't like it, he can knit Ola's quota himself."

Nicholas's eyes focused on Cora. "Hmm, Gunda said the same thing to Nils."

Arve and Ola turned to Cora and waited for her to speak.

Cora's eyes shifted between the three. "I don't understand why my trip is such a problem. The entire village has been on a boat on the Atlantic long ago, and on trains and wagons before that. Why should this trip be any less safe?"

Ola held on after another shift on the track. "We can take care of ourselves. Right, Cora?"

"Is that so Cora?" Nicholas said.

Cora's mind raced. She understood Nicholas was looking for a reason to allow Arve and Ola to continue their trip. Her mother's bashing of irresponsibility came to mind, but she was not irresponsible. She enjoyed Arve and Ola as traveling companions. Cora's spine tingled as she looked at them. "What if something bad does happen to you two?"

"Well, you can call on Nicholas and—"

Arve nudged Ola, then turned to Nicholas. "Nothing will happen to us."

Nicholas looked into Arve's eyes.

Arve continued, "We're all in this together. We made a promise that we won't get into trouble."

"And if something catastrophic does happen beyond our control, Cora, Arve and I will call on you. And that will never happen—the catastrophic part, that is."

"But then, if you're still not comfortable with Arve and Ola going with me to London, maybe you could replace them with Kel and Uda."

Nicholas raised an eyebrow. "Don't push it."

"Look," Cora began, "I'm a responsible adult and can take care of other people. And if anything bad happens, I will take care of it myself—no Nicholas, unless it's a huge emergency. I want to take care of it myself. Every time a slip-up happens, I don't want Nicholas to come charging in. Then my mother will have more reasons why I can't make my next travels. I have to learn how to take care of such things on my own, anyway."

"Absolutely. We're here to stay. We're going to stay," Ola said.

"And we'll work everything out together," Arve agreed.

Nicholas gazed into Cora's eyes. "Cora?"

Her mouth opened as the train conductor's voice boomed through the door, "St. Paul—ten minutes, St. Paul—ten minutes." She stood, grabbed Arve and Ola, and placed them in her pouch. "If you'll excuse us Nicholas, we have another train to catch."

Nicholas smiled and gave what sounded like a sigh of relief. "That's just what I wanted to hear."

"What about mother?"

"Leave that to me. You know she'll come around once I talk to her. Everything will be fine."

Arve peeked up, passed the pouch rim. "What about Nils?"

"Hmm, well I'll never hear the end of it from Nils."

They all laughed. After saying goodbye, Nicholas disappeared with a pop. Cora flushed the toilet just in case someone was waiting outside the door. As she left the bathroom, her pouch bounced in the air as two careless children ran down the hallway.

Arve peaked out over the edge, then fell back in. "Damn kids!"

"Arve!"

Cora readjusted the strap on her shoulder. "I hope Nicholas didn't notice that."

#####

"Excuse me," Cora said through clenched teeth to a woman who had bumped into her in the St. Paul train station. Her pouch, with Arve and Ola tucked safely inside, swung dangerously—nearly flying off her shoulder with every bump. Cora heard them gasp as she pulled the bag sharply into her side and placed her hand on top to prevent further jostling.

"Oh, excuse me," the woman said without making eye contact with Cora. The harried woman looked over her shoulder and continued her trek. Her frightened face concealed from the low white rim of her grey hat, while her head swiveled like a woman fearful of being followed.

Cora panned the station nearby but saw nothing unusual. She inspected her pouch frantically. "Are you alright?"

"We're fine," they both whispered.

Cora sighed, and she searched for the tour guide. "Good." Since they departed Duluth at 6 a.m., she had expected to nap on the train. But the terrain scenery became too exciting to ignore. She wanted to take out her camera and try to snap a picture of the sunrise, but conserved her film supply for New York and London.

"As I was saying," Arve began, "the construction of the St. Paul Union Depot came around..."

Cora did not interrupt Arve's presentation as she listened to the hustle-bustle atmosphere of the station. Conversations echoed against the marble walls and pillars added to the experience. Another rush of commuters dashed by Cora, also with harried faces determined not to miss their next connection. The sounds of people rushing around, luggage carts being pushed by freight handlers, and announcers calling out departures and arrivals made her head spin.

"Oh," Arve said, as a man bumped into the pouch.

Cora scanned the station again. "Let me find a quieter spot." She moved in a hurry to a pillar. She felt like a fish moving behind a large rock to get away from the strong current. "I barely remember this depot. Father took me to Hudson, Wisconsin, once long ago, but I don't remember all these people being in the station at the time." The warm June sunlight streamed in beams against the haze of cigarette smoke rising from the bustling crowd. She bit her lip and looked from one end of the long marble-pillared corridor to the other. "My travel agent told me there would be a man holding a sign showing where our group should meet. Too bad I was the only one who signed up in Duluth. I wished my traveling companion was there too, so we could've talked all the way down."

There were several groups of people standing next to signs as gathering points to each activity. Cora sighed in relief when she found hers, at least. A loudspeaker announced instructions for the train bound to Los Angeles that will leave soon. "Los Angeles. Wouldn't that be a great place to visit next? I'll keep that in mind."

Ola giggled from inside the bag.

Cora hurried to join her group to hear the man continue his announcement. "And as the pamphlet shows, you will have double occupancy on the train, the boat and the hotel in London. If you have come alone, I will assign a partner to you. The train will leave on time at 10 a.m." He gazed at his watch. "That will be about fifteen minutes from now and so I suggest you climb aboard as soon as possible. Gather here and I will direct you to your car and the berth."

"An hour," Arve said, "just enough time for you to take a quick stroll outside."

"I'm not sure," Cora said as she glanced toward the train and felt the nervous commotion all around her. "Nicholas can pop in and take you back, but won't be able to pop me on the train if I miss it. She took a causal stroll around the depot, then found her way to the passenger car. She watched people take choice seats while children argued about who got the window spot.

The tour guide motioned for the group to sit next to him to receive more information a half hour after the train departs. Cora waited anxiously for her traveling companion to show up. She scanned the slip of paper given to her by the tour master and focused on the name Wilhelmina Benson, scrawled out as her partner. Strange. No one named Wilhelmina came forward when the guide had called her name. Cora grew anxious. *Did she get on? Is she going to miss this trip?*

She made her way toward her sleeping compartment to stow her suitcase. The cramped walkways made it almost impossible for two people to pass. The constant buffeting left her alarmed for Arve and Ola's safety. She dragged her suitcase behind her, which felt like an anchor. Holding the pouch in front was not much of an improvement.

The train made noises as it prepared to leave the station. Cora hurried forward to stow her case and return to the club car before the train jerked forward. She found her assigned upper compartment and felt some of the tension slip away as she entered. She pulled the privacy curtain to block its entrance to the sleeper. When she reached her bunk, Cora grabbed a handful of curtain and yanked it open.

"Oh," a woman said in alarm, bolted up and smacked her head on the ceiling. Her white rimmed grey hat fell forward to cover her face. With haste, she grabbed the hat and pulled it back to reveal her frightened appearance.

"I'm so sorry," Cora said. "You appear to be hiding.

The woman rubbed the top of her head. "I'm sorry. I thought you were someone else." Again, the hat slipped down over her face. "Well–" she said, pulled the hat off and quickly placed it aside. She reached for the top of her smoky blue dress and pulled it up as if a man were gawking at her appearance in an unsuitable manner.

Cora looked around her in the walkway but saw no one close by, then studied the woman's frightened expression. She then recognized her as the woman who had bumped into her at the station.

The woman said as she leaned forward and glanced up and down the aisle. "Are you alone?"

"Of course I'm alone. There's only room for two people in these berths, and not much of that as is."

The woman took a breath as if trying to regain her composer.

"My name is Cora."

"Oh, I'm Willie, I mean Wilhelmina, but you can call me Willie."

The Missing Jackal Murder

The train jerked forward, Cora jerked to her left, and Willie lurched forward to keep Cora from falling.

The sound of the metal wheels masked Arve's exclamation of surprise.

Willie's eyes scanned near Cora. "Are you sure you are not being followed?"

"Ahh—I'm not sure, but why would anybody follow me?"

"Well, I…" the train jerked again and gathered speed. As if she could read Cora's mind, Willie took a deep breath, closed her eyes for a moment and blew out a cleansing breath. "I'm very sorry," she sat up on the edge of the berth. "I believe I need to explain myself."

Cora set her suitcase up on the berth. "I believe you do."

"I'll explain everything in the… in the club car. I'm starving. How about you? I haven't eaten all day," Willie said as she jumped off the berth and led the way to the club car.

"Me neither."

Willie glanced over her shoulder as if to make sure Cora followed. "The quick explanation is that I'm running away from my abusive husband."

"Oh, that's terrible." Cora grabbed the pouch on her berth and both made their way to the club car as Willie occasionally paused and scanned her surroundings. They entered the club car and found a seat, then within moments had coffee and sandwiches in front of them.

Willie took a sip from her cup. "I've not done anything like this before."

Across the table, Cora noticed the tremble in Willie's hand. She ignored the clacks of the tracks, the rolling and rocking of the club car and the sounds of other conversations as she listened to Willie. The sunny green scenery passed without a glance from the two.

Willie gave Cora a forced smile. "Leaving by myself to go on a tour overseas. It may be irresponsible, but I feel free."

"Free from what?"

Willie paused, took one more look at her surroundings, then faced Cora. She took another sip of coffee before starting again. "It wasn't always like this. I mean, before the war, Roy wasn't overly attentive, but never violent. After, I thought, if we went ahead with our wedding, he would change and not be so moody and angry. If anything, he got worse. I was foolish to think love would change him."

Cora leaned forward. "Did he hurt you?"

Willie looked away and bit her lip. She did not answer the question, but continued. "He refused to have children. And I've longed for as long as I can remember to raise a family."

"Did you discuss your desire to have children with him?"

Willie nodded. "Several times. I was a schoolteacher while I waited for Roy to come home. When we got married, he refused to let me work. I quit teaching and stayed home, dutifully attending my chores. But I longed for children of my own. Roy finally allowed me to resume teaching, but it wasn't the same. I believe he thought teaching other children would stop me from wanting my own. But I craved having a baby even more day after day."

"Why didn't you?"

"What?" Willie asked with a startled expression.

"Why didn't you? You really didn't need to ask his permission to—to have a baby," Cora lifted her cup to her lips as she observed Willie over the rim. She suspected this line of conversation was inappropriate, but she didn't believe a woman needed to ask permission for everything.

"I couldn't have done that," Willie spoke rapidly. "I couldn't bring a child into the world with Roy so angry. I mean, I couldn't do that to a poor, innocent child." Her eyes shifted, and she glanced out the window.

"I'm sorry," Cora touched Willie's hand. "I shouldn't have said that. Men like your Roy make my blood boil. Its 1926 and they need to realize that women have rights too."

"That's what my mother said."

"Did you have the support of your parents?"

"They live in Moose Lake, where Roy and I grew up. After we married, it was Roy's idea to move to Minneapolis. It wasn't until later I realized he had wanted to get me away from my family."

Cora frowned. "He sounds very possessive."

"Very. He would not let me out of his sight. If I even looked at another man, he would—" Willie bit her lip in silence and glanced over her shoulder. "I couldn't handle it anymore. I had it. The only thing I could do was to go back to my family at Moose Lake and start the divorce proceedings."

"Oh boy, how did your husband take that?"

"He went crazy. He destroyed everything I left behind and did everything he could to drag me back. I've heard he has gotten so violent he started fights with strangers and spent time in jail."

"It's good you left him. No telling what he would have done had you stayed."

"It was my father's idea to leave the state, even the country, at least temporarily. Til things ease a bit."

"Were your parents able to help you with the resources for this trip?"

A devilish grin crossed Willie's face.

"What did you do?" Cora leaned forward, eager to hear Willie's deception.

"Roy was not very smart with our money, or investments, at all. Just about everything he touched failed. However, one of his investments paid off..."

Cora bolted up in her chair. "You didn't."

"It was father's idea. Normally, he doesn't believe in interfering. He is an alderman at the mayor's office. He knows how to get around loopholes and, in this case, decided the end justified the means." Willie lowered her head. "My father believed things would cool off before I got back." Her subdued tone warned Cora that things had not gone as planned.

"Did Roy find out?"

"I'm not sure he found out I took half the money, at least not yet, but he knows I left town." Willie looked hard at Cora and took a deep breath.

"Does that explain why you ran into me at the station and why you were hiding in our berth?"

Willie nodded. "He found out about my trip. Father thinks someone let it slip. Roy learned I was leaving today and tried to get information about it from father. He warned Roy not to follow me or he would call the police and have him arrested. Father lied and said I was departing from the Minneapolis Depot. Hopefully Roy went there instead. But I worried he would figure it out and come to St. Paul and find me, especially if the train didn't leave on time."

Cora sat back. "Whew. What a mess." She looked around. "Well, if he had got on this train, he would have found you by now."

"That's another reason I waited to come to the club car now. I knew there would be a crowd in case he did show up." Willie finished abruptly and reached out to grab Cora's hand in a tight grip. "I'm so sorry."

Cora jumped.

"I didn't mean to drag you into this. I didn't mean to put you in danger."

"Don't worry about me. My father taught me how to defend myself." Cora patted Willie's hand.

Willie looked confused.

Cora smiled. "My family has been in the lumber business for forever. We learned to be tough when we had to. Father took me along on business trips, which fed my quest for adventure. As I got older, men looked at me differently. Father knew I might be on my own someday, and so he taught me some things. You know, where to hit, where to kick. I know that sounds unladylike, but you know things could happen."

Willie smiled. "Are you sure you'll be all right with me? I may be a nervous Nelly, always looking over my shoulder."

"I think we will get along just fine. And you don't have to look over your shoulder here, unless there are men who find you interesting, if you know what I mean?"

"Why would anyone want to look at me in that way? I'm an old lady," Willie said.

The words shocked Cora. "You are still beautiful and young." It was then she supposed Willie to be about ten to fifteen years older than her. Though a slender, shapely woman, Willie's face showed the tracks and traces of depression and fear, but if a man were to look closely, he would see an attractive woman nonetheless.

Willie smiled and made a short, dismissive sound.

"You are. And any astute man would agree."

Willie giggled. "Let me know if you see any 'astute men' lying about the cabin."

Cora laughed.

"I suspect you have an interesting story of your own. In fact, since you are seeking adventure, I would wager you have a stack of *National Geographic* magazines at home," Willie said with a grin.

"How did you guess?"

Willie laughed. "We may not be so different after all." She reached into her bag to pull out a worn copy of the magazine that featured London. The same edition Cora had back at home. "So, tell me your story," she said, setting down the magazine. She lifted her cup of coffee to take a sip.

"And I brought along two of my favorite traveling companions." She reached down into her pouch and pulled out Arve.

Confused, he froze in his wood carving form.

"This is Arve. And this is Ola."

After she placed the two on the table, Willie reached for them. "They're darling—oh, and they look old. Are they antiques?"

"Yes and no, but they are rather valuable to me. Let's just say I knew they wanted to come along. We'll let them stand here to watch the scenery go by." Though the two had their backs to them, in time Cora placed her coffee cup between them and Willie's eyes. It was a risky move. Somehow, she thought Willie would find out eventually the two had come along. They wanted to join Cora's adventure, now it was up to them to stay motionless.

Cora pointed down an electric lit, cable car-filled street from where she and Willie sat on a bench near Chicago's Union Station. "Over in that direction is Wrigley Field. I believe it is only a couple miles down. I wonder who the Cubs are playing tonight. And over that way is the Chicago Theatre." She pointed in another direction while reading a small tour book. "I wonder if they're playing a Rudolph Valentino movie right now."

Willie adjusted her spectacles and turned each time Cora pointed. "I know we don't have time to visit all these places. Even so, being out and away is lovely. It was a great idea of yours to stroll outside the train station and glimpse the night life of the big city."

Unbeknownst to Willie, Cora brought her pouch containing Arve and Ola to catch a bit of that nightlife as well. Or probably Arve had his nose in one of Cora's books, reading about interesting spots in the Windy City.

Cora repeated the description of downtown Chicago facts that Arve had told her earlier. She found a chance to peek into her pouch to see Arve observing a Rolls-Royce driving by. Ola looked up at the tall buildings lit up against the dark sky.

Willie snapped her head back to Cora. "You do remember that we have less than an hour stop in Chicago, right?" She brought in a huge breath of air and slowly blew it out. "Just to remind you."

"I know, I know. I just want to soak in as much as I can and get a feel for the city, to find the pulse of Chicago," Cora said as the streetcar stopped to see if they wanted to board. Cora waved her hand, and the streetcar moved along. Jalopies honked their horns at the momentary delay. Cora found the bustling of traffic and city sounds intoxicating.

Willie chuckled, then looked over her shoulder.

"That's the millionth time you've looked over your shoulder now."

"I just want to make sure we don't miss our train."

"But the train station is that way," Cora pointed in the opposite direction. "You know it would be next to impossible for him to find us—oh," Cora's words ended abruptly when an automobile honked and stopped in front of them.

"You copacetic dolls are positively Jake. Want to see the town? Hop in my breezer," a nattily dressed man called out to them through the open window.

Cora glanced up to see two men sitting in the front seat and leering at them. She used modern lingo to show her disinterest. "Scram, bank's closed."

Willie sat in stunned silence.

"Oh, come on."

Cora stood up. "Hey, do you know who the Cubs are playing tonight?"

"Don't know. Hop in and we'll find out together."

She gazed down the street and placed her fingers to her chin. "Tell you what, you find out, then come back, and we'll hop in."

Willie stood.

"Why waste time? We'll all go together." The men lingered.

"Sorry, we're not interested in gentlemen who are not up to date with the Cubs, sorry. My Uncle Stian would be quite disappointed in you," Cora tsk-tsked.

"Wait!"

Cora put her hand on Willie's elbow and led her away.

Willie looked over her shoulder at the jalopy as it drove away. "You sure know how to handle men."

"When men have only one thing on their minds, they're easy to steer. I've learned a lot about that in the lumber camps. You would think some men have never seen a woman before. Sometimes it's flattering when men fight for you, but it gets old after a while. I think we should return to the station."

"You think they'll come back and try again?"

"Oh, I'm pretty sure they will. In Duluth, they'd get the message, but here in Chicago... What?"

Willie had halted.

"What?" Cora exclaimed when she saw the horrified look on Willie's face.

From the dark pillars of the station, a man scanned the crowd as they entered. He spotted Willie and dashed across the street towards them, out dodging cars that honked.

"Run!" Cora said.

"You stay right there, you hear me?" The man shouted and pointed his finger at Willie. His eyes seethed with anger and his disheveled dark hair bounced as he ran toward them with heavy steps.

"Run!" Cora repeated, but Willie was rigid with fear as her ex-husband Roy approached and grabbed her wrist. He pulled her violently towards him.

Cora tugged his sweaty hand off of Willie. "Hey, get your hands off her, you brute."

"You stay out of this. This is no business of yours." His alcohol breath sprayed on Cora's face.

"Yes, it is. You keep your hands off her."

"Listen, you little bitch, this is my wife. You stay out of this." He turned back to Willie and grabbed her again. "As for you, when I get you home, I'll make you sorry for this."

"So, you're the bastard who's been abusing her," Cora said, with no intention of backing down.

"How dare you talk to me like that?" He slapped Cora with the back of his hand.

Cora stumbled back but did not fall. She gasped and put her hand up to her stinging cheek.

"No, don't hurt–"

Roy slapped Willie with the back of his hand. "Don't you tell me what to do. I'll tell you what to do." He reached back to slap Willie again, but Cora lunged forward and blocked his hand.

"So, you want another?" Roy swung at Cora, but she moved out of the way.

"Cora, don't, he'll–"

"I said shut up!" and he moved his arm abruptly to push her away. Willie fell to the ground.

"Now, to deal with you," he said to Cora. "I'll teach you not to meddle."

"No, I'll teach you," Cora cut Roy off. "This is something I've wanted to try, but I had to wait for a baboon like you to come along."

"Oh, what is a little girl like you going to do? Cry for your father?"

Before Roy completed his threat, Cora grabbed the collar of his coat, shook him back and forth and screamed. "Help! Help! Somebody save me! Help!"

Roy grabbed Cora to shake her loose, but she held on and shook and screamed louder.

People watched in shock at a man attacking two women while they tried to get away. "Oh my," a female on-looker said.

"Those poor girls," another woman said.

"A slug like that should get the Billy clubbed and thrown in the slammer," a man said. He stepped to Roy with his hands clenched. What seemed two police officers came from nowhere and dashed to their aid. The man stepped back and watched the officers at work.

The first officer took out a Billy club and cracked it over Roy's left forearm. "Oh, no you don't."

She broke away. "Oh, he came after us." Cora babbled as she reached for Willie and clutched on to her while being helped up by the second officer. "We were minding our own business. He dragged us here. He was going to take us away. I thought we were goners." Cora held on to Willie, who wobbled but remained silent.

"That woman is my wife," Roy hollered and pointed to Willie.

"Oh, no she isn't," Cora snapped back at Roy. "That's what he said, and he dragged us here. He was going to take us away. He's drunk."

"Not you, just her. She's my wife." Roy grew more agitated.

"Is this man your husband?" The first officer asked Willie as he clutched Roy's elbows from behind.

Willie's mouth opened and closed, but no words came out. Her eyes were wide with terror as she stared at Roy.

Cora checked her pouch to see if Arve and Ola had survived the big shake up. They were sitting with their arms outstretched, holding onto the wall as if trying to survive an earthquake. Relieved for their safety, Cora looked back at the officer. "I need to take Willie back to her room where she'll be safe from thugs like this."

"You'll have to come with us to file a complaint," the officer said.

"She's my wife," Roy said again.

"Come, Willie." Cora helped her to regain her balance.

The crowd continued expressing their anger. The police officer waved his hand. "Alright, we can handle this. Go about your business." The crowd dispersed before it formed. The police officer looked at Willie and Cora. "Do you ladies want to press charges?"

Cora vigorously nodded her head and wiped the dry tears that did not appear on her cheek. "Yes, definitely. They should lock up a man like that away for attacking us poor, helpless women."

"I said she is my wife. Tell them or I'll smack you." Roy threatened Willie.

The second officer raised his baton in threat. "You shut up."

"Listen," Roy struggled to break free, "if you don't get your hands off of me, I'll call the mayor and he will can you two."

"Yeah, right buddy," the officer replied.

"You ladies will need to come with us to give a statement," the first officer said to Cora.

Cora stuttered and looked at Willie's stunned face. "We, we have to go back to our hotel to, to change, to change our clothes."

"Your clothes look fine."

"No officer, you don't understand. It's not the outside clothing that's—He frightened us and—I—wet myself." Cora said with a play of embarrassment.

"Oh. I see." The officer looked uncomfortable and shifted in his stance. "Well, you go change and meet as at the second precinct. Tell the cabbie and he'll know how to get you there."

Roy struggled. "They're not in a hotel, you idiot. Those little bitches are—"

"Oh my," Cora placed her hand on her heart as if appalled by Roy's swearing.

"Shut up you," the second officer hit Roy on the cheek with his club.

"Do you need a lift to your hotel, ladies?"

The Missing Jackal Murder

"No, we're right here." Cora pointed to the nearest hotel she saw next to the station.

"Very well." The officers nodded and dragged Roy off.

Cora felt woozy over-doing her false panting. "Oh, thank you officer, thank you."

"I'm telling you she is my wife!" Roy again attempted to wrestle his way out of the officer's grip while swearing and yelling.

"Do you want another clubbing?" Their voices drift away as they rounded the corner.

Cora grabbed Willie's hand and pulled her into a run across the street. "To the station, now." Like with Roy, they weaved between cars as they honked at the ladies.

When they were safely inside, Cora laughed.

Willie only managed a gasp and tried to catch her breath. "What will happen to Roy?"

"Do you really care?"

Willie paused. "No, no, I really don't. But he is going to be angrier than ever now." She took several deep breaths and stood taller, as if shaking off her fear. "You know, I hope they give him more of the same. In fact, I hope they give him the chair... Oh, my!" Willie's eyes widened at what she had said, and she put her hand on her perfectly round mouth.

Cora laughed, and they boarded the train. Willie went in first, then turned to Cora. "Why did you tell the police we were staying in a hotel here?"

"So that when Roy gets out, he'll spend time here looking for you there. I know he probably found out about the trip to London, and seemed to protest what I was saying, but just in case he didn't."

Cora checked on Arve and Ola once again. Arve wiped a hand across his forehead as a sign of relief. Ola clenched her fist and jabbed it into the air to show she was proud of how Cora handled herself.

"Did you bring your woodcarvings along, Arve and Ola?" Willie asked with a raised eyebrow as she looked back at Cora.

"You bet. I did not want anyone stealing them from the train."

"That was probably a good idea."

She gave a false explanation that since this was her first trip alone. They were like a good security blanket. Willie had accepted the explanation.

Willie continued, "After what we just went through, caution seems to be the order of the day. I'm glad they didn't fall out after that shaking you gave Roy. That image will burn in my brain for years to come." She chuckled.

"His face did turn a peculiar shade of red, didn't it?"

Cora joined in Willie's laughter. She paused when a sudden thought occurred to her and she looked over her shoulder and around the terminal. "What are you looking for? Do you think Roy got away?"

Willie had stopped laughing. "No. It's not that I—never mind."

Cora took a deep breath, paused, then realized despite the dangerous situation they had encountered, Nicholas had not popped in to rescue her or Arve and Ola. Did he know it was an act? Or does Nicholas realize Cora is now mature enough to handle any situation? She smiled and led the way back to the club car and convinced herself to ponder on that later.

Chapter 4

Cora paused on the granite steps to the entrance of the New York Museum to marvel at the marble statue of Theodore Roosevelt. He rode his horse majestically on a granite base with his name and dates etched into a brass plate. The carving looked so lifelike, she wished he would offer her a ride. The guide marched the tour group into the building, leaving Cora to straggle behind. Willie, mesmerized by the artifacts and artworks, and appeared unaware of Cora's absence.

As Willie and the tour group moved on out of sight, Cora walked towards the entrance. Alone, she intended to explore. She walked up the stone steps, gazed up at the tall granite pillars and pretended the marble went on for miles. "Magnificent."

Arve sighed. "It is, but you know there is more inside."

Ola put her hand on Arve's shoulder. "Let Cora savor the moment, like I told you in Cincinnati. You can't rush her like this."

Cora observed Arve, who sat and inspected the New York City guidebook. She smiled and entered the building. The spacious entranceway with high glass ceilings allowed the morning sunlight to bathe the entire room. She walked around the skeleton dinosaur displayed in the center, never taking her eyes off the beast's eye sockets as if afraid it was ready to attack. She had to get a photo of this to show to her niece Alice. "Excuse me, Arve," Cora said as she lifted the Kodak camera that Arve's back rested on from out of her bag.

R. M. Scott

"Oh sure," Arve said, never taking his eyes off the book.

She lifted her camera, advanced the film, and took a picture of the skeletal monster.

Occasional gasps from Ola and Arve emanated from her pouch. "I've only seen pictures of such a sight, Cora. Could you move closer," Ola said.

"Shh," Cora said.

Other visitors walked by and observed Cora with raised eyebrows. She dropped her pouch, then swung the pouch over her shoulder. She got into the information desk line, ready for her brief visit with questions.

A set of three screaming kids caught her attention and planned to go there in the opposite direction. Screams dissipated as they moved away from the Norwegian display. She will revisit this stop again. During her journey, stuffed animals filled the natural habitat exhibit. An open display of larger animals sat in the center of the room. Her heart pulsed as she gazed at the fearsome tigers staring back into the crowd, ready to come to life and charge at the patrons. These exotic animals would be worth another look after her visit to the display of her mother country.

Next stood displays from various countries. The Egyptian exhibit was first. An Egyptian Pharaoh bust carved in stone caught her mind's eye, as if her prose from the *National Geographic* magazine had come to life. The harshness of time washed away its beauty. Other pieces had a smooth, chiseled surface, as if these works of art now finished by the sculptor. Without touching the surface, her tactical memory felt the cold-smooth surface to keep in her mind. Their pupil-less eyes stared out at the incoming crowd. The headdress came down and spilled out upon his chest, with ornamentation on the forehead. Cora stood motionless.

The Missing Jackal Murder

Arve began his speech on the history of Egypt while she listened absentmindedly. The art was more interesting to her than the history, at least for now. She stopped near a statue with two figures of a man and his wife sitting down on a stone chair. He crossed his hands in front of him and the woman's arm wrapped behind him; as if to show that he belonged to her. Both looked forward as if to gaze into the crowd. The well-preserved condition of the statues amazed her, now caused her to reach out and touch them. Her memory brought her back to the lumber camp and fresh cut wood moved through the planer. The sound of throat clearing of a stern-looking man caused her to force her hand back and sidestepped to an area with missing objects.

Arve lifted his tiny copy of a museum book. "They sometimes send the artifacts to the basement for cleaning. Maybe they broke through mishandling. But then, I believe they're gone because-"

"Shh," she said as she observed three men had gingerly stepped up to the Egyptian display. There were more artifacts missing. They spoke in loud voices. The two younger men waved their arms with inanimate motions. They appeared to be in a heated argument with the third and older gentleman. She moved closer to eavesdrop.

"Cora, I really don't think—" Ola started.

"Shh. If their discussion is private, then why are they quarreling in public?"

The older balding man gave the impression of a round large beach ball. His hands gestured and his round head shook as if to calm the men.

"Jeepers, something really upset that man."

The two younger men dressed about the same, in light gray suits and pants with white shirts and smoky blue, thin neckties. Both had dark hair slicked back. Cora thought the

R. M. Scott

two men might be brothers, but then the younger of the two called the taller man 'Mr. Thorogood' with a return to the younger as 'Mr. Williamson'.

Cora tilted her head and whispered, "I think they might be colleagues who have offended the older man." She did, however, notice both men's handsomeness, even though the tall man's face flushed with anger. The younger appeared disappointed. His eyes shifted between the other two.

"I cannot believe what you're saying," Mr. Williamson said, with an obvious English accent. He shook his head and looked away, giving Cora his profile. However, his facial expressions did not match his words, his eyes moved around as if bored by the conversation.

The older spoke with a New York accent. "It's not so much that I believe it myself, but the museum staff refuse to have any further contact with your display."

"Poppycock," Mr. Thorogood said, also in an English accent. "You Americans are so superstitious. Every time you turn around, you claim to see a ghost doing one thing or another." He passed his hands through his dark hair, then put his fists on the hips on his suit coat. The thin dark brown necktie came to a crease near the knot and stuck out, appearing as a man who withstood harassment.

Mr. Williamson lifted his hands as if to smooth over the tension of the other two. "Let us settle this like gentlemen. If you are afraid—"

"See here, Americans are not the only people who get the heebie-jeebies from a bump in the night. However, as a museum curator myself, I do not believe in such hokum. However, it is my staff that I am concerned about."

"These are just plain ordinary objects made from wood and clay and metals," Mr. Thorogood said. "They are dead things. I'm surprised you are acting in such a way. You, an

64

educated man, along with your staff allowing yourself to be so easily afraid does say much about you. I assure you these pieces come from human hands and were not acquired by ghostly means."

"I don't care what you think. I certainly want nothing looming that will spook our employees or our patrons. Too many unexplained things have happened while your artifacts have been here." He spun and walked away.

Mr. Thorogood clenched his fists. "Mr. Williamson, do please follow the curator, account for everything, and check they package these appropriately."

"You know they have been, Archie. You stood there when—"

"I want to make sure, so please follow him. I'll check around here to make sure we left nothing behind."

Cora watched the man called Archie glare at Mr. Williamson until he followed the curator.

Archie shook his head in disgust. "Americans! Idiots. They are frightened of even the simplest—" A glance at Cora made him stop. His face turned red. His hand rose to his hair again in frustration and straighten his collar. "I do apologize for the outburst. I did not mean to imply that all Americans are idiots." Archie took a step back and shook his head.

Cora folded her arms over her chest, and one eyebrow lifted. "I see. And what exactly is it that you do mean, about Americans, that is?"

Archie stepped towards Cora. "Again, I apologize." He looked over his shoulder, then back at Cora. He took in a deep breath. "Please allow me to explain myself." He gave a slight bow.

"There doesn't seem much to explain. You have voiced your opinion rather clearly," Cora said as she moved further into the room for a closer and inspected the items that remained. She tried to ignore him, although that was difficult as she confirmed he was quite attractive on closer inspection, through her peripheral sight.

He took another long breath. "Well, yes there is, and if you would permit me. First off, allow me to introduce myself. My name is Archibald Thorogood." Again, he gave a slight bow.

"Yes, yes, Mr. Thorogood. You're from merry old England and you think your people are smarter and more sophisticated than us. Is that correct?"

He straightened his back. "Now see here. And please call me Archie. I do not think the English are smarter than the Americans. It's just a particular curator who is an idiot. You see… ahh, I'm sorry, I had not allowed you to introduce yourself. I do apologize, again." Archie stopped and waited for Cora to respond.

After a few moments of staring into Archie's beautiful green eyes, Cora collected herself. "My name is Cora Gudmundson, and I am from Duluth, Minnesota. In fact, I am on my way to London, England, with a tour group."

"You are?" Archie beamed a smile. "How splendid. I hope you will enjoy London."

"Thank you. I intend to do so." Her annoyance with him faded as she noticed how flustered and embarrassed he appeared.

"Well, Miss Gudmundson, I am trying to do my job as best I can. I may not, shall I say, as seasoned as some," Archie said and looked in the curator's direction. "But it seems the older don't respect the younger in my profession. They think we're too young to understand. That's why I became upset. I have great respect for Americans, especially those who are as beautiful as–" Archie stopped abruptly and his face flushed again.

Cora turned to him with raised eyebrows as she tried to suppress a grin. His accent was irresistible, as was his handsome boyish face and charm. "Oh, so you think we are beautiful." She unfolded her arms and placed them behind her back. "But you must've seen many beautiful women in your travels from other countries."

"Yes, I have," Archie stuttered. "How did you know I have traveled abroad?"

"Lucky guess. You're a long way from home and you appear to be a gentleman who has seen much."

Archie nodded. "Much. You see, I am an archaeologist. In fact, I was the archaeologist who uncovered these artifacts we were… discussing."

"So, you've been to Egypt?" Cora asked with a note of reverence in her voice.

"I have many times."

"Tell me what it's like?"

He smiled. "Let me show you through the exhibit instead. What is it that you want to know about Egypt? The pyramids, the Sphinx, or the digs?"

"All of it. But mostly tell me about the people."

"Few speak English. Their language is Arabic or Masri. Most Egyptian religions are with the Islam faith, which means people of the tradition of Mohammed. Most small communities live in the desert regions of Egypt and most cluster around oases and—"

"No, I don't want a geography lesson. What are the Egyptian people like?"

"Oh, I see, right, the Egyptian people are quite friendly, and many times, helpful." He led her to a diorama with a painted scene of a river on the wall and manikins and artifacts displayed in front. The scene gave the impression they were looking at an ancient Egyptian town.

Cora gestured at the mural with the painting of the wide river. "Tell me about the Nile."

"The Nile is not only the largest river in Africa, but it flows north, not south, like most rivers. When one looks at a map and sees a river, they assume that… oh, right, you're not interested in the geographic aspects. You want me to describe what it was like standing on the shores of the Nile."

Cora smiled. "Oh yes, I wish you would."

"The Nile is like no other river. I cannot do justice to the atmosphere with mere words. When you have a chance to visit Egypt, you must visit the people along the Nile. To stand on the bank of the Nile or in front of the pyramid of Giza or any of the other splendid wonders truly takes your breath away." Archie smiled, then stopped and gazed at Cora as if there was something wrong with her.

Cora's eyebrows creased. "What's the matter?"

"I apologize," Archie brought his right hand up to his chest. "For taking advantage of you like this."

"What do you mean?" Cora asked as she straightened her hat and inspected her dress to make sure her appearance remained proper.

Archie panned the vicinity where they stood. "Where is your escort? It is improper for a lady to be alone without an escort."

"Are you serious?" Cora asked with a soft chuckle. "Applesauce, this is the twentieth century. Do you think we are in Renaissance England or something?" Cora pointed over her shoulder. "I am not exactly unescorted. I was with a tour group, but we became separated. And I assure you that you are doing nothing wrong by talking to me."

Archie sighed. "You don't believe I am taking liberties?"

The Missing Jackal Murder

Cora folded her arms. "If I thought you were taking liberties, Mr. Thorogood, I most certainly would have let you know by now. You spend little time with women, do you?" She gasped and put a hand over her mouth. "I shouldn't have said that. Now I need to apologize."

Archie smiled.

Cora sighed in relief. "I am curious, and if I am not overstepping my bounds, why were you arguing about an Egyptian artifact with the curator?"

Archie paused if to consider her request. "These artifacts have been on loan from the British Museum. Now the curator of this museum wants me to take them back because he thinks they're haunted. I tried to reason with him that they're only pieces of wood and clay and stone, meaning dead objects. But he insists I remove them. I believe it relates to the unfortunate events surrounding the discovery of the tomb of Tutankhamen."

"Interesting," Ola spoke from inside Cora's pouch.

"Excuse me?" Archie said, looking confused.

Cora patted her pouch. "I read about that case. What evidence makes the curator believe your artifacts haunt them?"

Archie shrugged. "It doesn't matter. What frustrates me is that we are men of science. This gives the heebie-jeebies of his untrained staff. If you ask me, I'd say they have imbibed a little too much, you know." He finished by pretending to drink from an imaginary bottle.

"But what did they see?" Arve spoke from inside the pouch.

Again, Cora patted her pouch. "Did they say the object in that box did anything specific?" She pointed at the near empty display.

"There you are," a woman's voice interrupted from behind Cora before Archie replied.

Willie approached her. "Willie, this is Mr. Thorogood. He is an archaeologist. Mr. Thorogood, Wilhelmina Benson, is my traveling companion."

The two shook hands.

Willie smiled at Archie then turned sharply at Cora. "When I discovered you left the group, I looked for you endlessly. I thought maybe Roy had–" she paused as she looked from Cora to Archie.

"Don't worry about me, Willie. I get along fine by myself." Her attention returned to Archie. "Mr. Thorogood, thank you for the brief tour of Egypt."

"It has been a delight, Miss Cora. I hope we meet again."

"I suppose it depends on how big the British Isles are."

He smiled. "I hope not too big for us to meet again. Miss Cora, Miss Wilhelmina. Have a pleasant journey." Archie bowed and walked away.

Willie again turned on her. "Cora, of course I'm concerned. Roy should be out of jail by now and–"

Her voice seemed to disappear as Cora peeked over her shoulder to give Archie one last look, to find he had done the same to her. "What's that about Roy?"

Chapter 5

Cora leaned against the cruise liner railing basking in the surrounding view. "The Statue of Liberty looks different from this angle," she mused. She observed the New York skyline and took a couple of shots with her Kodak camera. Since the Brandenburg had left port, most of the passengers had settled in and took a stroll on the deck. Other passengers appeared to find the New York skyline as fascinating as Cora and lined up along the rail for a last-minute peek before the ocean swallowed the view.

"This is so picturesque," Willie said, mirroring Cora with her head hanging over to scan the horizon. "Can you believe it? We are really sailing the Atlantic Ocean." She took a deep breath. "Just smell that salty, fishy air. Feel that ocean breeze. And what about those massive waves?" She put a hand on her stomach. "I sure hope those waves won't be a problem when we get further out to sea."

"Me too. It seems like only hours ago we walked to the top of the Lady Liberty to the observation room and—oh wait, it *was* a few hours ago." She chuckled.

"I'll never forget New York. The city is full of life, full of people, so many things to do. I wish I could have spent more time here." She looked Cora up and down and smiled. "You sure made a good purchase with that new outfit. I love it."

Cora glanced down at her dress and grinned. "My mother, of all people, handed me some cash before I left and insisted I buy myself a cruising outfit for the ship. I was so surprised by her gesture you could have knocked me over with a feather. It's really not like her, but I love my new outfit." She tugged on her white collar, then smoothed down white fabric on her chest to lie against the dark blue dress that clung to her shapely figure. Then she shrugged and opened her pouch hanging from her front right side to check on Arve and Ola. They were peeking out, also getting their last view of New York.

"Here, Cora, let me take your picture so you can show your new dress to your mother with the New York skyline in the background." Willie stepped back and snapped a shot of Cora. "I don't think I've ever seen anyone shop as fast as you." She laughed.

"Speaking about not wasting time, have you thought about your future? Do you plan to marry again?"

Willie looked startled.

Cora thought she had overstepped her bounds and prepared to apologize.

"We haven't settled our divorce and I really haven't thought about it. But I suppose I'm glad that we didn't have children after all."

"After your experience with Roy, I suppose you are not eager to get into a relationship with another domineering man."

Willie looked over her shoulder.

"And we will not worry about your abusive husband. We checked the ship. And if he were here, he would have found you before we left and have dragged you off by now."

Willie sighed.

"You were also a bit agitated during our tour of New York. Are you going to let the thought of him ruin your trip to London?"

She sighed again. "Certainly not." She gave a devilish grin. "I am happy and free. And, like you said, I do look forward to meeting other people, other men."

"That's the spirit. That's the spirit and good for you, Willie. Good for you." Cora peeked into her side pouch. Most of the onlookers had left the deck. Arve and Ola still had their eyes glued to the New York skyline, their hands interlaced.

"So," Willie said, "what are your plans for romance, if I might ask?"

Cora thought for a while and cleared her throat, wondering what to say.

"How about that dashing young man from England that you became fond of?"

"Well, I suppose he's... but we'll never see him again."

Willie's smile widened. "And what about his dashing friend?"

"I suppose his friend—wait, I didn't say he had a friend with him. How did you know he had a friend with him?"

Willie pointed behind Cora.

She turned. Her mouth fell open.

"Miss Cora? Miss Wilhelmina? What an unexpected pleasure."

To Cora's shock, Archibald Thorogood and Mr. Williamson approached and stood in front of the ladies. "Mr. Thorogood, what a surprise. I didn't expect to find you on this voyage to England. I thought you would travel on a freighter alongside your artifacts."

Mr. Williamson said nothing but gave Willie an appraising look.

Archie took her hand and gave a slight bow, then bowed to Willie. "It was the only vessel available. I am—we are eager to return home. The next ship would have left in three days. That would have been most disagreeable. And please call me Archie. Mr. Thorogood is my father." He smiled.

"Is your precious cargo locked down, Archie?" Cora's eyes bounced between Archie and the man standing next to him, who she recognized as his assistant from the New York Museum.

"Yes, I have stored everything away in the cargo hold. Oh, and yes, please forgive my rudeness. This is Mr. Brandon Williamson. Brandon, this is Miss Cora Gudmundson and Miss Wilhelmina Benson."

Willie placed her hand on her chest. "You remembered my name."

"Oh, of course." Archie gave a slight bow to Willie.

"A delight to meet you," Brandon said with a slight bow. "Please call me Brandon. Since we're sailing mates for the next few days, I see no point in remaining formal. Don't you agree, ladies?"

Cora and Willie both nodded.

"I overheard you also gave that narrow-minded curator a throttle at the museum," Cora said to Brandon.

"Indeed, I do apologize for my behavior. That man was, as you said, at the best, narrow-minded." Brandon took Cora's hand, then his eyes shifted to Willie.

"Wilhelmina is my traveling companion for this trip. And please call me Cora."

Willie smiled. She shook Brandon's hand. "You may call me Willie, if you please."

Brandon gave Willie a bright smile as he held her hand for a moment too long. "Miss Willie, it is a pleasure to meet you."

Willie smiled warmly at him, and Cora thought she saw a spark of interest. She estimated Willie was approximately fifteen years older than him. But why not? Age should not be a barrier between two people. This was a new era with new ideas.

The Missing Jackal Murder

Archie looked toward the New York skyline, which was now only a mist of unrecognizable buildings. "Would you care for a cup of coffee or perhaps a spot of tea?" Archie said and motioned toward the dining area.

They agreed, and he led the group inside to a table and they placed their orders.

"Are you comfortable, ladies?" Archie said after they were all seated.

Cora paused. "I beg your pardon?"

He observed her with a face of confusion. Then his face snapped. "Oh! What I meant was, are you all settled in for our long journey across the ocean?"

"Smooth with the ladies, old man," Brandon said under his breath.

Cora chuckled, "I knew that's what you meant. I guess it's our American sense of humor." Both eyed each other with expressions which they understood the inside joke.

Brandon leaned back. "Ah, a spot of fun. Good for you, Miss Cora. Fun is what this old boy needs." He motioned his head toward Archie.

"Excuse me," Archie said with a note of affront. "I'm as jovial as the next."

"Of course you are," Brandon said as he rolled his eyes.

Cora fumbled through her pouch for some papers inside as an excuse to find Arve and Ola, who appeared to enjoy the conversation.

Archie sipped his tea. "So, Miss Willie, are you also from Minnesota?"

"Yes, I was born and raised there."

Cora observed Willie stealing quick glances towards Brandon as she described her hometown. It seems, with that, Brandon appeared to keep moving his chair toward Willie, his hands on the table pointing at her. His eyes on her were strong, without interruptions. After a few comments about 'how quaint' and 'simply lovely' from Brandon, Cora wondered about a matchup between the two. However, she suspected if Brandon discovered Willie was divorcing an abusive man, the romance would die on the vine before it had the chance to bloom.

Cora decided Brandon was a braggart. Yet Willie mirrored Brandon and leaned against her chair toward him, her hand on the table, inches from Brandon's. He spent most of the time giving details of his life, born in Liverpool, schooled in Oxford and had a passion for archaeology with big excavation plans. He described his work in the British museum and his desire to go to exotic places.

Thoughts of a matchup between Willie and Brandon quickly died when Brandon discussed his engagement with a woman named Eve. Willie had appeared enthralled with his conversation until he mentioned Eve. Her face changed and her lips formed into a phony smile.

Brandon lifted his teacup. "Yes, I suppose I will take that plunge into marriage and hope for the best."

"She's a lucky woman," Willie said, her hand slowly found its way from the table to her lap and lowered her head.

"I'm the lucky one." His eyes remained locked on Willie.

She then turned to Archie. "How about you, Archie? Have you made the proverbial plunge—if it is not too impertinent to ask?"

Before Archie would answer, Brandon spoke up. "Heavens no, he is a bachelor, through and through."

"Not everyone is as lucky as you are, Brandon," Archie said with an annoyed expression.

Brandon smiled at Cora. "Speaking of romance, I heard—"

"Were we speaking of romance?"

Brandon laughed. "Well, if not romance, then a rhythmic ritual that could lead to romance. To be more precise, I understand there are dances every night of our journey. I think it would be splendid if we danced." He smiled at the two women.

"Now, Brandon," Archie said in a disapproving tone, "it was somewhat forward to assume Cora and Willie would—"

"I believe it would be grand," Willie interrupted, looking between Cora and Archie. "I mean, what else would we be doing tonight? Just moping around in our staterooms. Do you dance, Mr. Thorogood?"

Cora suspected Willie was trying to play matchmaker for Archie. True, he was a handsome man, probably a few years older than her, and a man of the world. But romance was not part of her trip. However, she decided there would be no harm in being friends with someone who could discuss his travels and exploits.

Archie rubbed his chin. "It would be prudent to join in some, if not all, of the festivities this vessel offers. And with that, It would be an honor if you would join me in today's and this evening's dances." Archie bowed his head at Cora.

Cora laughed. "I hope my dancing skills, or lack of, do not disappoint you. They may not be up to the King's standards."

"I am sure they are. And I will regale you my exploits during my excavations in Egypt, unless that would bore you, Miss Cora."

Cora held out her hand to him. "Archie, it's a date— rather, I will dance with you and learn more about your work as we do so."

Archie took her hand and gave a slight bow. "And you may tell me more about Minnesota, Miss Cora, if you please."

Cora raised one eyebrow. "Only if you drop the 'Miss' part."

Archie smiled and nodded.

As if on cue, Brandon turned to Willie. "It would also be delightful if you would join me in a dance or two, Miss Willie."

"What about your fiancée?"

Archie chuckled at Brandon. "What she doesn't know won't hurt her, correct?"

"Quite humorous, old boy." Brandon smiled at Willie. "A few dances between friends are quite acceptable. You can tell me what you know about the native tribes in Minnesota. Perhaps I shall bring a research team to excavate long-lost Indian villages."

Cora saw the smile return to Willie's face. It would be good to see Willie have a little fun with the man, despite her age and his engagement.

They ordered drinks and prepared to dance.

Brandon lifted his hand to Cora, stopping to say, "And your story, if I am not incredibly impertinent."

Cora took a deep breath. "Well, my father owns a lumber mill in Duluth and took me everywhere as his traveling companion when I was younger. I had three brothers, now two, as my brother Nils did not return from the war. He was with General Pershing's unit and, well–"

"I'm sorry," Archie said, touching her hand in a comforting gesture. "Dreadful war."

Cora paused, sighed, and went on. "Eric owns a large auto dealership, the first in Duluth. Elmer started a refrigerator company, also in Duluth. But recently my father gave him the lumber company. Now Elmer must decide if it is worth his while to balance two companies, or rather, if he has the energy to do so. I have a sister named Anna, and she's married with two daughters. As for myself, I was born late in my parent's life when they thought that their baby days were long over. One day my mother had pains, saw a doctor, and he said, 'Oh, applesauce you have another baby coming.' Since my brothers were all grown and off on their own, my father asked me to be his traveling buddy in their stead."

"You were lucky you got to travel," Willie said.

"Of course, though we did not travel far. We traveled in my father's old jalopy through Minnesota, Wisconsin, and a bit of Canada. Watching the miles go by, going from town to town, was intoxicating for me. Since then, the traveling bug has bitten me and there is no turning back."

Brandon rubbed his chin. "Lumber. Must be big money in that."

"I suppose," Cora shrugged.

Willie's eyes widened. "You said you visited lumber camps and saloons. Didn't it frighten you to see all those big men?"

Cora laughed at Willie's expression. "The 'big men' in the camp thought it was adorable having a little girl running around. It was a change of pace."

"But when you got older, when you began to... you know," Willie said as her face turned pink.

"Things didn't change with the old veterans, but the new employees were a different story. However, I was never afraid."

Brandon chuckled. "I suppose you have had several marriage proposals."

"That and other proposals. But, as I said, my father taught me how to take care of myself, especially from a man's unwanted attentions."

Willie laughed, then put her fingers on her lips. "You should've seen what Cora did to my husband in Chicago."

Both men gaze upon Cora as if they wanted to hear how the spectacle took place. But she only smiled.

Willie gave them an abbreviated version of the story and explained that she was getting a divorce.

Both men reached out in sympathy.

The drinks arrived, looking mightily refreshing to Cora.

Cora nodded to the servers, then turned to the men. "So, tell me about this precious cargo from Egypt that you are carrying back to England."

"Yes, please," Willie said, "Cora told me about the Egyptian cargo. She said you discovered some of those artifacts in your excavation. What are they specifically?"

Brandon grunted, shifted his seat away, and crossed his legs. "A spot of luck is all," he said in a huffy voice.

Archie gave Brandon another look of annoyance. "I must admit, it was a spot of luck."

"How so?" Cora asked.

"To make a long story short, a farmer in Egypt was plowing his—"

"In Egypt, of course," Brandon interrupted sarcastically as he took a sip from his drink.

Archie continued as if Brandon hadn't spoken, "—field and brought up a bronze cylinder. Fortunately, the cylinder appeared in fairly good shape. It contained a role of parchment that was intact and easily readable."

Willie leaned forward with a look of fascination. "What did it say?"

The Missing Jackal Murder

Brandon laughed and sarcastically interrupted Archie. "If you're looking for the tomb of Tutankhamen, this is not the place."

"Hardly." Archie raised his eyebrows. "It claimed to be the burial site of a very interesting Egyptian artifact, and an unusual find."

"What was the unusual artifact?" Cora asked as she leaned forward on the edge of her seat.

"The Jackal of Prince Iknokman."

The two women looked at Archie with open mouths in amazement.

Brandon took a sip of his lemonade and coughed. "Wait till we're at least fifty miles out at sea before we order some adult drinks, indeed."

Cora ignored Brandon and leaned forward. "Was the Jackal of Prince Iknokman in that box at the museum? What the museum curator was so afraid of?"

He nodded, glanced at Brandon, then leaned in towards the women. "The story is quite complex, but I'll try to make it short. To our amazement, the cylinder acted as a sort of beacon. Instead of a treasure map where 'X' marks the spot, the cylinder rested about six feet above the Jackal of Prince Iknokman's figure. That figure placed in a small box inside a larger box-like small child's coffin. The coffin preserved the box and the jackal perfectly."

"What does the Jackal of Prince Iknokman look like?" Cora noticed that Archie's face had taken on a look of excitement and his eyes sparkled as he described his discovery.

"When we reach England, I will unpack the crates at the museum. You must have a look at the display as to understand my disagreement with the New York Museum curator. In short, it is a simple thin black dog, sitting, with its long sharp ears perked up."

"Is that all you found at the site?" Cora asked. "Were there more artifacts?" She waited to watch the excited expressions cross his face. He obviously loved his work.

Archie sat back. "That's a peculiar thing. This dig yielded only this one artifact. However, the writings gave clues to a small city nearby that had disappeared into history. After that excavation, those artifacts found there would be a part of the set."

"How fascinating." Willie's eyes may have been on Archie, but she had leaned forward, but her head on her hands with elbows on the table to face Brandon.

"Now if I had been there," Brandon interrupted again, "I'm sure we would've found many more artifacts..."

Willie's eyes returned to Brandon. "What kind of digs have you done, Brandon?"

Brandon fidgeted in his chair. "Though I have not been to any sites, I feel confident I will be on a major expedition the next go-round." He looked sharply at Archie as he lifted his glass and sipped again.

"Oh, I'm sure you'll find many wonderful things. I can't wait to see all the treasures you will find." Willie patted his hand in a gesture of reassurance, as if he were a petulant child. "Speaking of treasures, look at what Cora has brought along in her pouch."

"Have you brought antiquities, possibly rare Indian artifacts?" Brandon said in a teasing voice.

"No. They are just woodcarvings." Cora ignored Brandon's sarcasm and reached in to pull out Arve and Ola who had resumed wooden form. She set them on the table and the men reached for them.

"Very nice," Archie said as he handled Arve. "Most definitely Scandinavian in form and extremely old, from the little I know of the region."

Brandon rubbed his chin as he inspected Ola. "Why have you brought these along? If Archie is correct, they are quite valuable."

"They remind me of home when I am so far away. They comfort me. I've only recently grown to appreciate them. They are proving to be great traveling companions," Cora said with a chuckle. She watched Brandon handle Ola.

"Are you sure they are old?" Brandon asked Archie.

"They are over 600 years old," Cora said before Archie could reply.

"They seem so clean and well kept." Brandon rubbed his finger along the knife cuts and ridges originally made by the woodcarver.

Cora watched as Brandon's thumb rubbed on Ola's bosom. She feared either Ola would come to life and say, 'Excuse me,' or Arve would run over and punch Brandon in the nose for his impertinence. However, they remained frozen as Archie and Brandon set them back on the table. Cora left them there so they could be a part of the group. "And of course, they are only two of an incredible set. The leader is—" The protective magic prevented to reveal Nicholas or any other clues to show they were alive. Cora almost forgot that fact, cleared her throat and pretended nothing happened.

Brandon sat back and changed the subject as he described his comprehensive plans to find treasures to Willie as his obvious attempt to impress her. Cora thought Brandon was a big blowhard.

#####

Early the next morning, Archie checked on the Egyptian artifacts in the cargo hold for security. As he neared the stack of crates and boxes labeled for the British Museum, he spotted Brandon standing in front of them, reading a sheet of paper. It appeared to be a telegram. Brandon looked up at the small box Archie knew held the figure of the Jackal of the Prince of Iknokman.

The hair on Archie's neck stood up immediately. Why was Brandon in the cargo hold? He had excused himself from breakfast, claiming he had an appointment to play table tennis. But this was not the first time Brandon's behavior caused unease. Back in London, he had been at several unexpected times and places at the museum when Archie had been working on exhibits. He wasn't exactly sure why the curator Mr. Mitford had sent Brandon along with him to America. He had planned to bring his assistant, Freddie. But Mr. Mitford had informed him at the last minute that Brandon was to travel with him instead. It had been most unexpected.

Archie considered the black suitcase that house the Jackal. Brandon's desire for fame and fortune was strong. The Jackal of Prince Iknokman would certainly command a high price.

Archie shook his head and cleared his throat as he stepped forward.

Brandon recoiled, quickly stuffed the telegram into his pocket and turned a red face toward Archie. "You startled me."

"I didn't mean to. I'm quite surprised to see you here, though."

"I was checking the luggage."

The Missing Jackal Murder

"Oh, were you?" Archie moved forward to check the tension on the ropes holding the crates in place. "Is everything shipshape and Bristol fashion?"

"Tiptop," Brandon said as he slapped a hand against a crate. "What are you doing down here yourself, old boy, when you have a lady upstairs to keep company?"

Archie recognized the quick change of subject and again glanced at the box. He frowned as he looked at Brandon's pocket where the telegraph rested, then met his eyes. "And what about you? I thought it was your plan to keep Miss Willie occupied to provide more opportunity for me to get to know Miss Cora, I mean Cora?"

"Oh, you picked up on that, did you?"

Archie smiled weakly but did not reply.

Brandon turned squarely on Archie. "By the way, how is that coming along?"

"Not too well since you are spending your time down here, alone, rather than distracting Willie." Archie folded his arms.

"I wanted to make sure everything was 'shipshape and Bristol fashion' as you said." Brandon adjusted his tie, though it didn't need adjusting.

His nervous response did not ease Archie's suspicions.

Brandon moved closer to Archie and leaned against the chain rail that divided stacks of secured luggage and the small walkway, as if to assume a casual pose. "You really do like this girl, don't you, Archie?"

To momentarily put his suspicions aside, Archie allowed Brandon to change the subject. "Cora is just an American tourist in a tour group. We will spend most of our time with the group, thus we will say our goodbyes as we ramp off, nothing more."

"Goodbyes? You, certainly you find her attractive, right? Are you going to let her slip away so easily?"

"What do you expect me to do in such a short time?"

Brandon raised his eyebrows. "You're an absolute dote with women."

Archie frowned. "Now see here."

"Now you see here. You know I'm right."

Archie said nothing.

"In our brief acquaintance, she has talked about her desire for adventure."

"Yes?"

"So, since Cora is interested in seeing London's inner works, she would be far more interested in a personal tour from you than in the regular tourist places. Then, after a long day of going here and there, you can show her what the nightlife of what London offers. You could take her out for a romantic dinner."

"I hardly think—"

"And you do know, they have their blasted prohibition there," Brandon interrupted.

"So?"

"So, a little gin, a little romantic dancing." Brandon lifted his arms as if to dance with an imaginary woman. "And there you have her."

"Oh," Archie said, folding his arms and nodding, "I see, and there I have her."

"What could be easier?"

"So, you think it would be easy for me to—to steal her heart?"

Brandon's smile vanished when Archie said 'steal'. He straightened from his casual leaning pose, peered toward the Egyptian crates, then back to Archie and cleared his throat.

The Missing Jackal Murder

Archie's suspicions grew, but he did not want to overplay his hand and changed the subject. "So, old boy, how are you getting along with Willie?"

"Getting along with Willie?" Brandon looked alarmed. "You know I'm engaged. Happily so. I was merely showing an old lady a good time while on board this ship."

"Old?"

"Well, older lady. I am not into anything like that, even if I were not engaged."

"But she certainly perked up when you showed an interest in her," Archie said.

"Perked up? I hardly noticed that over her paranoia."

"Paranoia?"

"Whenever I'm with her, she is looking over her shoulder."

"You know of her horrible marriage."

"Yes, yes, I know. I have assured her it would be impossible for her husband to be on board. And if he were, he would have come out by now and given me a thrashing. She's even got me paranoid," Brandon said, looking over his shoulder.

"How so?"

"You know Eve would kill me if she saw me with Willie, innocent as it is."

"Innocent, you say."

"Excuse me," Brandon said, raising his eyebrows again.

"So, you would do nothing deviant or underhanded?"

A flash of panic crossed Brandon's face but quickly changed to one of defiance. "I love Eve. She loves me. We'll marry and live happily ever after." His voice had risen.

Archie patted him on the shoulder. "I'm sure you will, chap. And I hope you have many children from your happy union."

"Indeed." Brandon calmed down.

"And with that," Archie put his hand on Brandon's shoulder to steer him out of the cargo hold. "I think we should return to our lady companions, less they think we've jumped ship."

Archie and Brandon ascended the steps. "I was thinking," Archie said, "for better security I will take the Jackal of the Prince of Iknokman's black case and carry it off the ship myself."

Brandon stopped dead in his tracks and Archie ran into him. He stared at Archie. "Do you think that's wise?"

"Why yes, as long as the statue gets off the boat and arrives safely at the museum, what of it?"

"I could take it?"

Archie laughed. "No, no. I would think it might impede your romantic reunion with Eve."

"But—"

Archie ignored Brandon's sputter as they climbed the stairs.

######

Archie breathed a sigh of relief when the ship's lounge band slowed the frantic tempo from a Charleston to a slow two-step.

"Whew! That was fun," Cora said as she glided smoothly into his arms for the slower dance.

Her cheeks were flushed, and wisps of chestnut hair had escaped her bobby pins to cling to her damp temples. She brushed them aside with one hand while keeping a tight grasp on Archie's hand with the other. He noticed she was careful to maintain a respectable distance between them while they danced.

The Missing Jackal Murder

Archie wanted to remain with Cora. To do so was to keep the conversation going. "It was quite an athletic dance, wasn't it?" His heart rate returned to normal.

Cora giggled. "Definitely athletic." She looked around the dance floor. "Willie seemed to enjoy her dance with Brandon as well. I'm glad she's having fun. I'm afraid life hasn't handed her too many joyful moments lately with a husband like Roy."

"He certainly sounds a cad," Archie said as he guided them across the floor and changed the subject after a few betas. "Were you allowed to attend a major university?"

She paused and took a few more breaths. "I wanted to go to the University of Minnesota in Minneapolis, but my mother settled on the Duluth Normal School, not a university, but it was college nonetheless." Her breath seemed to return to normal.

"What courses did you attend? What, let me think. Of course, there would be creative writing to express your desire for travel and places to go. Then there is sociology to study people and their culture in far way lands. Hmm, I suppose classes associated with domestic living were not on your list."

Cora frowned. "Unfortunately, they were. Mother insisted. I said yes to satisfy her. My marks were always beyond satisfactory. I burnt nothing on the stove and my sewing is grand. But when I attempted to create the latest fashions from the magazines, this did not impress the teachers. I did my best and graduated with honors. But then, what good is that while stuck at home?"

He grinned. "Yes, I see your point. What about your friends? Did they attend college?"

"Some, but most of my friends got married straight away. I see them now and again, but I then dare not tell my family about my friend's family life. They would jump on the 'Cora, you need to get married too,' bandwagon."

Archie noticed the note of irritation in her voice about becoming forced to settle down. True, he imagined her in a simple wife's dress, but the image drifted into an excavation jumper with dirt scattered about. His heart skipped a beat to see Cora with him on an expedition. He realized his expedition fantasy cause him to miss several lines about her life. Archie refocused on her.

"... we got together to do volunteer work for the soldiers. It was a comfort to share our grief."

Archie looked down at her face and caught the fleeting shadow of sorrow that drifted through her eyes. "That's right, your brother Nils did not return. You mentioned that earlier. I am sorry."

She fell silent for a moment, then looked sharply back at him. "But, goodness, the war must have been much worse for you in England. It was practically on your doorstep. Did you suffer loss?"

"Not in my family. Many of my chums and classmates joined up right away with misguided dreams of adventure and glory. Many did not return."

"I'm sorry. Did you join up?"

"Oh yes, but not for the battlefield. I was quite young. They recruited me for map making and interpretation. I've always been quite adept with topography and languages."

"Really? How did you come by those skills?"

Archie realized they were no longer keeping up with the tempo of the musicians. They had drifted off to one side of the dance floor and were barely moving. "We had an excellent tutor growing up. My brother, Marcus, and sister, Evelyn, did not commit to their studies as I did. Our tutor, Mr. Pritchard, was a keen collector of what he called specimens. We trampled through back alleys, rural lanes and wooded areas for historical treasures and rummaged through old attics, and what have you, searching for items to add to his collections."

"You've seemed to have adventures throughout your childhood."

"Yes, however, there were other studies. I don't know how he did it, but he got me interested in learning deferent languages including French, German, Latin, Spanish, a bit of Farsi and even Russian. I'm not sure how much I remember of those languages, though."

"Say something in Farsi."

The sparkle in Cora's eager eyes made it hard to focus, to grant her request. He shook the image of her enthusiastic presence that he kept fighting not to become intoxicated with; he mustered the strength and tell her how happy he was to be with her in a clumsy form of Farsi. After he spoke, he hoped she didn't understand.

"I wish I could have understood. I bet you spoke something that the ancient people would have said. What did you say?"

Archie coughed. "I said something about—about, how much does paprika cost today?"

Cora giggled

Did she know what he really said? He shook his head and returned to their conversation.

"You were so fortunate to have this Mr. Pritchard. Where is he now?"

Archie stopped grinning and blinked several times before he cleared his throat. "Unfortunately, Pritchard was one of the first to join up and one of the first to return home wounded."

"Oh, Archie. I'm sorry. Did he pass away?"

Archie nodded.

"Oh, that's terrible." She hugged him for several moments in a comforting gesture.

Archie held her close, enjoying the warmth of her arms, but then she stiffened as if she had remembered propriety and pulled away.

"I believe the musicians are taking a break," she said as she glanced over to the band, where several were setting aside instruments and standing to stretch.

"Oh, right." Archie dropped his arms and almost came close to cursing the band. He looked around the room at the other dancers and guests. "I don't see Brandon or Willie, do you?"

Cora searched the room. "No. I don't see them either. Willie did say she wanted to make it an early night. I'm afraid she suffered a touch of seasickness this afternoon."

"That must be it," Archie said as he once again searched for Brandon. Were you hoping to make it an early night as well, Cora?" Archie asked, thinking again about keeping the conversation going.

"No. I'm not even a bit tired," Cora said. "Are you?"

"No. Not at all. Since our companions seem to have abandoned us, we needn't wait for them. Would you care to join me in a stroll on the deck?"

"Yes. I would love that. I overheard a sailor saying the stars are amazing from sea. Let's decide if he's right."

Archie held out his arm. She took it, and they walked toward the door. He noticed her eyes locked on a lit room down the deck. "Is something wrong?"

"I don't know. I thought I saw Brandon in a conversation, possibly an argument with Mr. Crawley. I believe it is his name, the communications officer. He charged off in a hurry. What do you suppose that was about?"

"I'm not sure. Which way did he go?"

Cora pointed toward the opposite end of the ship from their staterooms.

Archie looked in that direction for several moments as he considered Brandon's actions.

"Should we investigate to find out what he's up to?" Her eyes remained on Brandon's path.

"I suppose we could stroll in that direction to see if we encounter him on deck."

"Are you concerned about Brandon?"

"About what?

"I noticed he seemed irritated and perhaps jealous that you have gone out on excavations, with success, and he hasn't. Is there a reason for that?"

"I believe the governors don't trust him to go on anymore expeditions."

Cora stopped their walk and looked into his eyes.

Without asking, Archie explained. "I want you to keep this between us, but the museum invited Brandon along on a dig in Greece by a colleague of ours, and I'm afraid it did not go well."

"Oh, what happened?"

"In haste, Brandon damaged some artifacts and compromised the integrity of a part of the site. My colleague was beside himself."

"What did he do?"

"He unearthed a very rare and valuable statue of Hercules. In his eagerness to claim it, he pulled it out roughly and broke off an arm. Then he tried to hide his error and blame it on some hired locals who were there to assist in the dig. Now, I am saying this in confidence, bad form of his, but…" Archie took in a deep breath and moved on. "They would have none of that and denied the claim vigorously. My colleague believed them. He sent Brandon back to London in short order."

"Oh dear. Why was Brandon allowed to stay at the British Museum after such a disastrous outing?"

"The Board of Governors interviewed him, and as you have witnessed, he can be very charming and animated when he wants to be. They chalked up his error to youth and inexperience and have given him more time to prove himself." Archie gazed out over the railing at the moving waves in deep thought. "I'm afraid the Board rarely realizes the serious nature of our work. They are more interested in obtaining objects than in studying and recording history."

Cora stood nearer to Archie. "How will Brandon prove himself if he's not invited on another exploration?"

"Mr. Mitford, the curator, has been working with Brandon to train and coach him on handling antiques. They have spent many hours together." He paused. "I believe Mr. Mitford sent Brandon along with me to America to retrieve our loaned artifacts as a sort of test."

Cora turned to Archie. "A test? How is he doing?"

Archie shrugged. "I found Brandon in the cargo hold doing what appeared as though he'd been inspecting the cases."

"Appeared?"

Archie paused again. "I certainly don't want to give you the wrong impression about Mr. Williamson. You see, several items from the Museum had gone missing as of late. Our curator, Mr. Mitford, dismissed many questions regarding to the whereabouts of the missing items."

"You're now calling him Mr. Williamson? So you do suspect Brandon. Is there any proof?"

The Missing Jackal Murder

Archie raised his shoulders. "I certainly have no grounds to press Mr. Mitford about him. Again, I have pressed our curator on these missing items, but his explanations seem, I'm not sure, suspicious."

"Fascinating." Cora said and gazed out into the dark ocean. "Tell me about your assistant—Freddie, is it?"

Archie laughed, then stopped. "He's young and has absolutely no social life, and it shows. However, his work is exemplary. I suppose his dedication is to his work more than anything; he spends most of his life down in the museum's basement where we clean the artifacts and stored them. He has a meticulous record keeping and tracking system and, no, I cannot see Freddie would say nothing about his record keeping. No, he has been around for years now. And these thieves began about the time…"

"Brandon showed up."

"Hmm, again, I have no proof."

"His character is, at least, enough for you to monitor him."

Archie grunted in a sign of agreement.

Both stood silent and gaze out into the nighttime ocean waves. Cora broke the silence. "So, tell me the story behind the Jackal of Iknokman."

Archie smiled. "I will. It is a long and tragic tale, but not one to share on such as beautiful…" He became interrupted by the sound of shrill giggles coming from a short distance away. They turned in unison to look in that direction. Willie, leaning heavily on Brandon's arm, was weaving her way toward them.

"Cora?" she hiccupped. "Archie?" she hiccupped and laughed. "What are you two doing out here?" She stumbled as she let go of Brandon's arm and hurried forward.

Cora dashed forward to grab her. "Willie? I thought you had gone to bed early."

Willie giggled. "I didn't." She giggled again and looked at Brandon. "Me and Bran—Bran— Brandon went for a stroll."

"Willie, have you been drinking?" Cora asked as she sniffed the air near her.

"Yup. Brandon told me it would help my seasickness, and he was right. I don't feel a thing."

"Where have you been?" Cora asked Willie but stared at Brandon.

He cleared his throat and shuffled his feet but would not meet Cora's gaze. "We strolled the deck for some time."

"But I just saw you arguing with Mr. Crawley a few moments ago and Willie was nowhere in sight," Cora said with a frown.

Brandon looked startled by her comment. "Me? You must have been mistaken. Why Miss Willie and I have been together for most of the evening?"

Willie giggled. "Uh ah," she wagged her finger at Brandon. "That's not right. You went to get some more gin, remember, and I waited for you by that door. You were gone a long time… I think." She hiccupped again and shrugged. "But I don't remember too well."

"What door?" Archie asked.

"I wasn't gone long," Brandon interjected before Willie could reply.

"Yes, you were," Willie said. "I waited and waited by that door."

"Which door?" Cora asked as she held on to Willie to keep her from falling.

"The door to the luggage place. You know. The place with the crates."

The Missing Jackal Murder

Archie looked sharply at Brandon.

Brandon waved his right index finger. "Miss Willie had too much to drink and isn't thinking straight. I shall escort her to her room." He moved forward toward Willie.

Cora moved in front of him. "That won't be necessary. I will take her back to our room myself and assist her into bed." Her voice was sharp and gave Brandon a reproachful look. "Good evening, gentlemen." She took hold of Willie's arm and guided her.

Willie waved at Brandon. "You're a good kisser, Brandon." She giggled and hiccupped.

Archie looked sharply at Brandon again. "What were you doing in the cargo hold tonight?"

"What? I wasn't. Miss Willie is drunk. You know how these American women are."

"And whose fault is that? You kissed her? And what about your precious fiancée, Eve?"

Brandon cleared his throat. "You know how it is, Archie, ol'boy. A man has needs. Miss Willie has needs too. There's nothing wrong with two adults indulging in a bit of fun, now is there?"

Archie frowned. "Yes, there is when one of the two is drunk and not capable of making proper judgment."

Brandon scowled. "You're always so high and mighty, aren't you, Archie? As always, the proper English gent. Everything works out in your favor. We can't all be as lucky as you. Some of us have to take things into our own hands to get ahead in this world." He abruptly strode off in the opposite direction.

Chapter 6

Cora shook her head and gave Arve her most serious voice. "No, this is not a bad idea. I am placing you and Ola in my suitcase because I don't want the other passengers to jolt you out of my pouch as we off-ramp."

"But," Arve began.

"How could you forget that almost happened in the crowd, especially when we got on the ship? I had to look down every five seconds to make sure you were still there. I'm sure it's going to be worse as we disembark. When I leave the ship and before I get onto the bus, I will let you out before the tour people put my suitcase on the bus. The boat will be in London in less than an hour. And no, Ola, I will not call on Nicholas to help because—remember, we're on our own. And if I call on Nicholas, my mother would—"

"Yes, yes, I understand. We won't call on Nicholas. Even so, I don't think this is a good idea," Arve said. He sat up, clutched onto Cora's blue dress, and shifted his eyes in terror.

"Would you rather I put you in my steamer trunk? I won't open that till we get to the hotel. Would that be more to your satisfaction?"

"It will be alright," Ola said. "The suitcase will be fine."

"I don't think we will fit," Arve said. "And besides, you know I don't like dark places."

"No, I didn't know that," Cora said as she rolled her eyes. "You can tell me about it when we get to our hotel. The key thing is not to panic. You know we don't want you to call on Nicholas to pop in and spoil everything."

"I know, I know. It's just that I still think this is a bad idea."

Cora looked down at Arve. "Just think of a good memory. I know. Remember the day you and Ola met?"

A look of panic crossed Arve's face.

Ola looked at Cora as if she had said something horrible. "I know," she said quickly to Arve, "think of the day we fell in love."

"What?"

"You heard me. Wasn't it one of the best days of your life?"

Arve paused. "How about the day we got married?"

"That's the spirit," Cora said. "I will place my suitcase next to my steamer trunk in the baggage hold. They'll place the luggage on the luggage cart. I'll try to open my suitcase on some pretenses, if anyone is looking, and then pull you two out. If not, they will load the luggage onto the bus and the bellhop at the hotel will bring you to my room. Either way, we'll be back together before you know it."

"Are you sure we can't go along with you?" Arve asked.

Just as Cora closed the case, she saw Arve take a deep breath and close his eyes as he repeated, "There are no wolves, there are no wolves."

#####

Cora held onto the suitcase in her right hand with the chain-link handrail down the metal steps that lead to the cargo hold. She stopped on the last step when she saw a man's back. Recognizing who the man was, Cora spoke out and startled him. "You sure are paranoid."

Archie spun around and gasped at her presence.
"Blimey, you frightened the… what are you doing down
here?"

"Same as you. We don't want to lose anything. I put
Arve and Ola in my suitcase to prevent any buffeting from…
did you see Brandon down here?"

"No," Archie said, "But like you said, I am a bit
paranoid. I've left everything here as it is and just keep a
constant eye on Brandon." Archie finished as he patted a
black suitcase among the stack of luggage.

Cora placed her suitcase on the cart next to Archie's
suitcase. "I can't believe it. Our cases look identical."

"Perhaps both came from the same manufacturer here
in London."

"Yes. My father mentioned his suitcase came from
London. I guess you and my father think alike with your
luggage choices." She paused, then sighed.

"Is something wrong?"

"I can't wait for my tour of London, but these last few
days and nights seem to disappear so quickly and, what am I
talking about, it's been a full seven days on our journey to
England, it seems just a few days." Cora turned and walked
up the steps before Archie could respond.

The last few hours also seem to fly as they watched the
wide ocean shrink to the River Thames as the Brandenburg
found its way to the docks for departure. Archie and
Brandon pointed out points of interest to Cora, Willie, and
anyone else nearby them to care to listen.

Often, Cora's interest in London's scenic view lost to
the interest of the connection between Willie and Brandon.
Yet, it is her life. But going from one bad man to the next
would not be wise. That, and Willie's late return to their
compartment along with them standing close together with

his arms around her waist. Does that mean they're just friends?

As the ship docked, Brandon stepped further away from Willie. At least she appeared to be mature about the end of their ocean-bound affair. As for Archie and his problem with Brandon, they engage in a lively discussion about what to expect at the museum and how to explain their conversation with the New York Museum curator to their London Museum curator. After Cora watched their conversation, occasionally receiving Willie's input, she added to the discussion, believing it was Archie's way to monitor Brandon and keep him occupied. This seemed so as the dock luggage staff opened a hatch on the ship, enter and began removing luggage and placing the lot on the dock to return for the next portion.

Archie stepped back and gave Cora the signal to look down. They saw what look like their cases from the latest lot of luggage now landed on shore. It now became the time to depart, Archie and Brandon to the museum and Cora and Willie to their tour group. A lump in Cora's throat told her this is 'goodbye' with a possibility of never meeting again.

Cora smiled as she tried to think of something else to say to extend their time together. But as the crowd of people pushed against her to get a better view of their waiting loved ones, she thought of the safety of Arve and Ola. A large, well-dressed woman pushed onto Cora's right as she waved frantically to people on the dock. Her colossal frame rubbed against the pouch and made the contents come dangerously close to spilling out. She looked down at the deck, reassured herself she made the right decision and not given in to Arve's worries.

Archie reached for Cora's elbow and stood practically on top of her. "I do hope you plan to visit me, I mean, my Egyptian display, at the British Museum."

Cora and Willie each held one of Archie's elbows. A quick look behind her told that Brandon had disappeared, perhaps to greet his Eve and stay as far away from Willie as possible. They walked through the crowd of passengers towards the plank

Archie lifted his right arm to look at his watch. "9:22 a.m. I hope there will be enough time today to unpack, clean and set up the collection at the museum. Freddie is quite efficient, so I believe we will make do. The collection would display upstairs by tomorrow morning, undoubted."

The gang plank dropped, and the passengers frantically disembarked. One harried woman briskly dashed by Cora. The woman's belt buckle grabbed Cora's pouch. It swung violently to the side and dumped the contents onto the deck. Cora's travelogue book of London fell dangerously close to the lifeline and into the water. Another scrambling passenger's long stride accidentally kicked the book overboard.

"Sorry," the woman said with hardly a glance.

Cora, Willie, and Archie fell to the deck to retrieve her belongings. Willie picked up a handkerchief and cotton gloves. Archie retrieved her note pad and reached for her rolling pencil before a woman's hard heals landed on his hand.

"Oh, no," Willie said in a panic-laced voice as she looked down.

"What?"

"Where are Arve and Ola?"

"Oh, I put them in my suitcase. I worried that something like this would happen."

The Missing Jackal Murder

"Is that everything?" Archie asked as he straightened and assisted Cora and Willie back to their feet. He looked down, "Oh, is this...?" He picked up the thumb size copy of the *National Geographic*.

"Oh," Cora said and snatched the micro-sized magazine out of Archie's hand.

"You must have to read that with a magnifying glass," Archie said with a smile.

"It's just a novelty."

"Now, is that everything?" Archie said as he looked around for anything left behind.

"Yes," Cora said. "Well, except for the travelogue. I'll ask the tour guide if he has another, if I can find him of course."

Archie offered each woman an elbow again as he steered them through the buffeting crowd. Most walked forward, like cows led to pasture, others walked against the flow to return to retrieve what they had left behind.

Cora found walking down the gangplank not much better. The disembarking passengers fought their way against dock hands and family members who walked up against the flow like salmon against the river. Even though Cora held her pouch in front as if clutching a baby, her pouch buffeted against the crowd. When the three made their way to the docks, the crowd thinned out. They their feet landed on solid ground. A shift to the right and they were out of the violent stream.

"Welcome to London, ladies." Archie chuckled and gave a slight bow.

Cora adjusted her cloche hat. "I'll celebrate when I am able to catch my breath."

Willie adjusted her wide brim hat. "You know, I believe a trip to the British Museum is a part of our tour. We look forward to seeing you there, Mr. Thorogood." She smiled and gave Cora a wink.

"Of course it would be pleasant to meet you again," Cora said in an offhand voice, as if she were disinterested.

Willie scanned the area. "And where is Brandon?"

"He's waiting on the cargo deck next to the crates of artifacts." Archie looked over his shoulder. "In a moment, I will join him to supervise the unloading."

"Where will we find our luggage?" Willie asked.

"I thought that the tour people have luggage people to put all your cases on your bus. Oh, I believe over there." Archie pointed toward a growing number of carts congregated on the dock. "I hope they don't upset the Prince."

Cora chuckled. "I hope they do not upset Arve and Ola. I see our cases on the top. They do look alike. I hope we can tell which one is—HEY!" She hollered and pointed at two badly dressed men who had picked up both of their cases and looked at each other in confusion.

"They certainly don't look like passengers from our ship," Archie said. He and Cora pushed on in a gallop towards their cases. The men's appearance seemed disheveled. They had miss-matched suits and pants, wrinkled ties around necks of unshaven faces, and unkempt hair.

"Those are ours!" Cora shouted and pointed her finger at the men. The men looked at her and their eyes widened.

One man turned to the other. "Beat it, Clyde." Both dashed off. Each had an identical case in his hand.

"Stop!" Archie shouted and pursued the man.

Cora wasted no time. Arve and Ola were in her case and were probably bouncing around inside. She ran after them.

Willie called out. "Cora, wait."

The Missing Jackal Murder

Cora shouted to Willie, "I've got to stop them. Arve and Ola are in that case." She used all her energy to catch up with Archie.

"Stop, please, someone, stop those men!" Archie pleaded to the crowd. Not one Good Samaritan stopped the thieves. By the time anyone had the chance to understand what was happening, the two men passed with no chance of anyone to make a tackle.

The two men zigzagged around dock hands and automobiles.

"Why? I never." One well-dressed woman said as she clutched the front of her dress.

The man named Clyde ran straight onto a dock hand pulling a crate. The crate wobbled, but the dock hand spun around as the suitcase hit him and made him fall to the ground hard. "You son of a-look out then." He sat up, then put his arms around his head when Archie passed by.

"Sorry," Cora said a few feet behind Archie.

A whistle sounded, and a police officer picked up speed to join the chase. The two rough-looking men sped up to keep ahead of their posse. They ran with the cases held high in the air, their coats flapping in the breeze and the soles of their shoes slap loudly on the concrete.

The taller man looked over his shoulder and shouted to his partner. "Clyde, that way, meet at you know where."

"Right," the squatty man said, and the two men split up. The thin man went left and the squatty man, Clyde, dashed off to the right.

Cora, now a mere ten feet away, saw the police and Archie follow the thin man. She watched them dash around the corner, but saw Clyde cross the street. Cars honked as she followed Clyde into the street. Cars screeched and avoided hitting her. Her eyes looked forward, and she was not aware of the oncoming traffic while focused on her prey. She did not comprehend the shouts from nearby drivers and passengers. She ignored the laughs of those to see a woman chasing a man.

"He's not good enough for you, miss!" the cockney voice of an old woman said.

"You'd never have to chase me. I'd stay at home," a large old man shouted.

An old woman across the street shouted, "Leave him be. He's not worth it, dearie."

Cora growled and mustered all her energy as the man turned left. She stepped up her pace, her stride grew wider and faster. She caught up to almost two arms-reach from him. Her hand reached for the case, flapping in the wind. The man did not slow down as he approached the busiest street yet. He plunged in and did not stop. A car slid, smashed into another. Honking, more cars crashed when Cora cautiously entered the street.

Her eyes found Clyde and picked up steam through the screaming, motionless traffic. She dashed into the street, but could no longer see him in front of her. Her peripheral vision spotted him to her left. She swore, halted, and followed in pursuit.

She bumped into a middle-aged man. "Here now, that's not how a lady should behave."

Cora ignored the jeers and saw Clyde headed towards an alley. At the corner, his flapping coat rubbed against a wall advertisement for the local theater and pealed it off. He flung it off, and the bulletin hit Cora in the face. She flung the dirty paper off her face and spit out the loose glue. Before he turned right, he placed his hands on the top of an old wooden barrel and pushed off to tip it over. The barrel teetered as if to decide whether to fall or stand. Cora shifted her hip to miss the barrel. She heard the barrel fall on its side; the lid popped open and let loose the oozy contents.

"Oy, you get back here and clean this up."

Cora kept pace and followed him down the alley and under an archway. A business building sat on top of the archway. Echoes of footsteps filled her ears. Clyde jumped over wooden boxes. Before she could hurtle and give pursuit, the footfalls grew louder. She saw the thinner man, with a black suitcase heading straight toward her. Without thinking of the danger, she held out her arms as if to catch him. He zigzagged around her, then she screamed when the police officer followed the thief and zigzagged around her.

She screamed again as Archie suddenly appeared in front of her. When he saw her at the last minute, he could not stop and slammed into her. While in mid-air, Archie reached his arm around and grabbed Cora. They turned halfway around and fell to the ground. Archie took most of the impact. The force was so great that she flipped over and landed in a seated position.

Archie sprung up. "Are you alright?" His left hand gripping his right elbow.

Cora peeked over her shoulder and saw the second man leap over boxes. He pushed them aside with his hands as the officer fell over, got up and returned to the pursuit. "What?"

"I said, are you alright?"

"I, I think so." Cora looked down at her exposed upper legs spread apart to reveal her underwear. She quickly snatched her dress down to cover. "Yes, I am alright, are you hurt?"

"Nothing too serious." Archie sat back in the mud. "Not to worry, Cora, that officer will catch the two thugs, and we'll get our cases back."

"I certainly hope so. If I lose that case, I'll—"

"Not to worry, we have many dress shops where you can purchase new clothes."

She glared at him from her spot on the ground. She could mention her steamer trunk on its way to the hotel.

"Oh heavens. I forgot you put Arve and Ola in your case."

"I did, and they are far more precious to me than any dress." Cora closed her eyes. The image of Nicholas's face came to mind. Then she quickly erased it. She knew Nicholas could locate and retrieve Arve and Ola in an instant. But that would be the end of the little trust her mother had of her. And if Arve and Ola call on Nicholas, Cora would be sure to keep this incident quiet, but she only guessed. "No, I will handle this. I'm not irresponsible. I am independent and—" The thoughts of what was happening to that case and Arve's and Ola's faces contorted in terror filled her mind. She had not forgotten Arve's terror of being locked up in the dark case. "No, I will find them."

"We need to let Scotland Yard find our cases. I have complete faith in them."

Cora's mind shifted gears again. "Yes, yes, Scotland Yard. Of course," Cora sighed.

Her resolve to handle all problems erased thoughts of Nicholas's face. If Arve and Ola were in danger, they would call Nicholas and he would rescue them. She just hoped they were not in danger.

Archie rubbed his elbow. "I say, Cora, I've never seen a woman run as fast as you did in pursuit of that fellow."

Cora's mind remained focused on the present conversation. She let out a cleansing breath and found him staring at her as if she were some rare specimen. She smiled. "As I've said, I grew up with three older brothers. I either had to learn to run fast so I could keep up with them or resign myself to staying in the house playing dolls and having tea parties with my older sister." She wrinkled her nose. "Running was much more fun." Cora took another deep cleansing breath.

They got up, wiped off as much dust as they could, and walked out of the alley. Cora inspected her carrying pouch to see if Arve and Ola had reappeared. It was empty. Did Arve and Ola know they were in danger? But then Cora remembered their resolve to help her remain independent... They also wanted adventure. Arve was the Villager's statistician, the one who kept his head. But what about Ola? Why hadn't she called Nicholas by now? She looked again into her pouch in case they had reappeared.

"Did you lose something from your pouch during our pursuit?" Archie asked as they walked back in the direction they had come.

Cora frowned at Archie. "You don't seem upset about those crooks stealing your Egyptian artifact."

"I am as mad as hell," Archie said as he gazed in the thief's direction that he lost. "Pardon my language, but I do have faith in Scotland Yard. Simply put, the Jackal of the Prince of Iknokman is extremely distinguishable. That, and my report on other museum pieces missing, could all lead to the same trail. If we find the Prince, we'll find Arve and Ola."

"Yes," Cora said, "I suppose that is true."

Archie looked at her. "Again, welcome to London." This time his voice held a note of sarcasm.

"Thanks." Cora hoped he was right about the ability of Scotland Yard to find their cases. On the other hand, she has no intention of just sitting around and doing nothing. Her mind shifted to other rescue operations that did not include magic. The image of Brandon came to her mind.

The police officer returned empty-handed. Archie suggested their first course of action was to return to the dock to find Brandon as they both agree as him being held as their first suspect. That, and Archie wanted to make sure the rest of the Egyptian artifacts were en route to the museum. "Why don't you join your tour group and allow me to contact you after I've spoken with the constable?" Archie motioned to the officer, who was still trying to catch his breath.

"No, I'm coming with you. Willie will ensure that my traveling trunk arrives at the hotel. I will not stand by and wait. I'm going with you to see Brandon. He may have seen something that could help us find those two thugs. Wasn't he behind us as we were leaving the ship?"

"Yes. I believe he was," Archie said, rubbing his chin.

As Big Ben chimed its ten bells, the officer finished jotted down the descriptions of their cases and the descriptions of the two men. Cora and Archie gave their contact information if they find the stolen items. The officer walked off.

"I understand the value of your woodcarvings and what they mean to you, but those men could be dangerous."

"Have they considered how dangerous I am?"

"Look Cora—"

"No, you look. I'm coming with you. Don't worry about me. By now you know I'm not some piece of fluff or a frightened kitten. I am going to look for Arve and Ola. If you want to come along with me, you're more than welcome to." She picked up her pace, left Archie behind, walked under the arch and looked toward Big Ben through the combination of morning fog and sun.

"Wait," Archie caught up with her. "We'll talk to Brandon and go from there."

Cora nodded, "As long as you're not in my way."

"Oh, I will not do such a thing. But if it's not too impertinent of me, the dock is this way."

"Oh, I knew that. I just thought this would be easier to, oh, never mind." She and Archie re-entered the archway and put Big Ben to their backs. Cora again glanced at her empty pouch. Still no Arve and Ola. She took a cleansing breath. They made their way through the traffic and through the crowd. The dock came into view. "This did not seem like a random theft. Did you see how they looked?"

"How did they look?" Archie asked, glancing at Cora with a puzzled frown.

She lifted her right hand. "Confused. If it was a random theft, they would have snatched and run. Also, there were other larger cases for them to take. Why take just ours, or rather, yours? I'm sure they weren't interested in my case. It mainly contained clothing and toiletries. Well, along with Arve and Ola. To anyone else, those carvings have no monetary value. Could they have been after your case?"

Archie remained silent as they approached the ship.

"Your silence obviously means 'yes'."

Archie stopped abruptly and looked at Cora. His expression was not encouraging.

#####

Cora and Archie climbed onto the dock when they saw five constables and what looked like a detective, standing over a prone figure. Most of the cargo and passengers had left the ship.

"That was quick. It appears Scotland Yard is already here," Cora said.

111

Archie and Cora approached the group, and an officer lifted his hand to stop them.

"What's going on here?" Archie said. "I'm here to see if my crates are bound for the British Museum. We just came back from -"

"Archie," Cora gasped and pulled on his arm as she got a better look at the prone figure. "Is that Brandon?" She pointed to the body lying on the dock near the crates, then put her hands over her mouth.

Archie looked in the direction she pointed and gasped. "It can't be." He moved closer. "I say, it is... That is my assistant," Archie told the officer, who raised his eyebrows and let them pass to approach the scene.

Cora gasped as they drew closer, and she identified Brandon Williamson lying motionless in a pool of blood. Tears pricked her eyes and her voice wobbled. "Is he dead? How did this happen? We just saw him a moment ago."

Archie did not reply but continued to stare with a dazed look on his face.

Cora noticed a woman standing over the body. She nodded her head, then put her hand to her face to wipe tears from her eyes. "Yes," she said to the large short suited man, "that's my Brandon. He's—he's dead."

Cora observed the woman and the officer as they spoke, then leaned towards Archie. "Who is that?"

"That's Brandon's fiancée, Miss Eve Tomlinson." Archie whispered.

She observed what she considered the phoniest attempt at crying. It reminded her of a high school drama class when the students tried to ham it up during a play.

Eve Tomlinson wore a floppy, beribboned hat tilted to one side and laced with silk flowers around the brim. The fur around her neck appeared to have been dead for many years

112

and was not well kept. The fur dropped to the side as if to display her half-exposed breasts with a stance to give the officer a better view of her bosom. Her makeup was light and simple, though she wore more lipstick than necessary. One eyebrow rose in what looked like suspicion, or perhaps stayed there permanently. Her dress may have been the height of fashion years ago, but did not improve her appearance today.

Cora suspected Eve was putting on an act. Instead of being distraught at the death of her beloved fiancé, she appeared annoyed at having to waste her time identifying the sap's body. Her snuffles only happened when one officer looked her way or asked her a question. "Oh, my!" Eve said to an officer, then looked back toward the bloodstained body.

Archie approached the plain-cloth officer. "What happened?" Cora following closely behind.

The man swiveled his head to Archie and glanced at Cora. "And who are you?" The man had a large white mustache and white, well-kept hair. He gave the appearance of being in charge yet mixed with pompous finesse.

The surrounding officers scanned Archie and Cora as if suspicious they would attack their leader. Cora carefully examined the scene. Brandon was lying face down, the blood pooled on his left side. His body lay a few feet from the stack of Egyptian artifact crates that were the only cargo remaining. Three dock hands watched the commotion as two officers approached them.

"My name is Archie Thorogood, and this is Miss Cora Gudmundson. I am Mr. Williamson's associate. What happened?" Archie said and motioned toward the bloodstained body.

"I am Inspector Bevan of Scotland Yard. Mr. Brandon Williamson appears to have been stabbed and has died from his wounds. When was the last time you saw the victim alive, Mr. Thorogood?" Inspector Bevan appeared to be a man not to be trifled with. He stood straight with his husky frame, ready to attack if provoked. The inspector looked as though he had no sense of humor, nor ever wanted one. He first focused on Cora, as if to understand these could be two viable suspects.

"Stabbed? By whom? How?" Archie asked.

"I will ask the questions," Bevan replied in a voice that commanded authority. His narrowed steely eyes bore into Archie as if to get into his brain. "I repeat, when did you last see the victim?"

"Of course," Archie replied and nodded. He explained his professional relationship with Brandon and described the time the four of them had spent together during the voyage. He described the theft of the cases from the dock and their pursuit of the thieves after they departed the ship. "We were unsuccessful in retrieving our cases and are just now returning to the dock."

Eve Tomlinson listened to the conversation with a vacant expression. Cora thought why Eve did not appear upset or curious over the news that her fiancé had spent the last few days with another woman. Eve also failed to respond when Archie nodded a greeting in her direction: It was as if she didn't know him, or didn't care to.

Cora frowned. Surely Brandon had introduced Archie to his fiancé at some point. They were colleagues. She wrinkled her brow and gave Archie a furtive look as she felt a moment of concern.

"And who is Miss Wilhelmina, and where is she now?" Bevan asked when Archie finished speaking.

The Missing Jackal Murder

Cora spoke up. "Miss Wilhelmina and I are members of a tour group from America, Inspector Bevan. She must have gone to the hotel with the group. I am sure Willie had nothing to do with this."

"And you know this how?"

His tone annoyed Cora. "She was with me and Archie and our entire tour group as we departed from the ship."

"Is that so?"

"Yes, that's so."

"Did either of you see Mr. Williamson interacting with other passengers on the ship?"

Cora shook her head.

Archie also shook his head. "I didn't, but then again, we weren't together all the time."

"I see," the Inspector said. "So, it was possible that Mr. Williamson and Miss Wilhelmina had interactions you were not aware of?"

"What?" Cora said, shocked by his innuendo. "Are you asking if Brandon and Willie had a sort of fling?"

"You did say they spent time together. It may have been innocent on Mr. Williamson's part, but perhaps Miss Wilhelmina believed there was more between the two of them. Perhaps they met here on the dock after the two of you left and he told her it was just one of those things. Perhaps she was not happy and sought revenge."

"What?" Cora said sharply. "Why would she follow him into the cargo with such intents—Willie is not that kind of woman? Her interest in Mr. Williamson was completely casual, as was mine. We were merely passing time with Mr. Williamson and Mr. Thorogood during the ocean voyage and nothing more. Willie was entirely aware of Mr. Williamson's fiancée."

The Inspector called to one of his officers and motioned him over. "You will kindly tell this officer here about your tour group and where you and Miss Wilhelmina will stay tonight."

Cora nodded her head curtly. She watched as another officer with a camera took pictures of the dead body.

"And for her sake, she better have an explanation for her whereabouts after departing the ship." Bevan spoke to Archie. "Do you know anyone who would have wanted to harm Mr. Williamson?"

"No, but I have had some concerns about his integrity, especially regarding this cargo." Archie tilted his head towards the crates.

"Oh?"

Archie explained how Brandon acted suspiciously around the artifacts and how some artifacts had recently gone missing from the museum. He described how both his and Cora's identical cases had been stolen off the luggage pile and how they gave chase while accompanied by an officer.

"An officer also gave chase, you say?"

"Yes."

"Kindly give the time and location of this chase, so we may find this officer to verify your claim."

"Our claim?" Cora repeated with raised eyebrows as she heard his condescending tone. "Those cases contain *our* valuables. What are you going to do about finding the criminals who took our valuables?"

"My concern is surrounding a murder, Miss Gudmundson, "Bevan said." You must take your complaints about stolen cases to the head office."

"And what will they do exactly?"

The Missing Jackal Murder

"Cora, we must not interrupt the inspector right now," Archie said as he touched her arm. "He needs to focus on Brandon's murder."

"But what about—"

"We can discuss it when we get to Scotland Yard," Archie said as he interrupted her.

Cora pursed her lips in irritation at Archie's calm acceptance of Bevan's authority. Did he imagine she was some shrinking violet, incapable of speaking up for herself?

"Now, may I continue?" Bevan said in a pompous voice as he gave Cora a disdainful look.

"Yes, Inspector," Archie said, "but I do need to add one more thing."

"Oh?"

"Speaking of suspicions, I spotted Mr. Williamson in the cargo hold earlier this morning with no cause to be there." Archie said as two officers covered Brandon's body. "I had told him I planned to carry the Jackal of Prince Iknokman off the ship in my black case."

"What is this Jackal of Prince... whatever?" the Inspector asked with a frown.

"The figure I mentioned, which was in my stolen case," Archie explained. "I suspected Brandon of planning to take the case. I tried to outmaneuver him when I placed it on top of the cart so the luggage handlers would take the case out with other passenger's luggage while assuring Brandon remained in sight as the ship entered the London harbor. Unfortunately, Miss Gudmundson's case was practically identical to mine."

"Are you suggesting my Brandon would steal something?" Eve blurted out.

"Yes, I would." He cleared his throat and fidgeted as he glanced at Cora. "That's why the thugs took both of the

117

cases. I apologize, Cora." He looked at Bevan. "Miss Gudmundson's case contains two very rare and valuable woodcarvings. Her case and mine should be located immediately."

"You said the figure in your case is valuable and belongs to the British Museum?"

"Yes. The piece is quite valuable, monetarily, and historically. The Jackal of Prince Iknokman is a small black statue of a long thin dog sitting down."

"The Jackal is valuable to you," Cora said to Archie and then to Bevan, "but Arve and Ola are precious to me, and dollarwise as well."

"Arve and Ola?"

"My wood carved figures." Cora lowered her head and realized she shouldn't have given him their names.

He raised his eyebrows. "Very well, tell the officer here everything about your property. Now you mentioned something about Mr. Williamson being suspected of stealing museum property. Was this reported previously?"

"No. Unfortunately, my colleagues and I discussed the matter, but I have no evidence."

Eve Tomlinson interrupted and pointed her finger at Archie. "It was you." Her eyebrows up on her forehead, yet one higher than the other.

"Me what?" Archie looked startled by her outburst.

"Brandon wanted to go on an expedition, so he could find treasures. But you stopped him."

"Miss Tomlinson, it is the curator and the governors of the Museum who grant excavations and expeditions. I have no say in such matters," Archie replied in an even tone.

"But you have influence we both are aware of such. You could have convinced the governors to let him go. But you told them lies about him and insisted he travel with you on this wasted trip to America," her voice rose. "It's your fault he's dead. Now you are lying about him and calling him a thief when it may have been you who stole the priceless artifact." Her chest rose and fell as she grew more and more agitated and spoke to the inspector. "He's the murderer," she pointed at Archie. "Arrest him."

Archie straightened his spine. "I assure you, Miss Tomlinson, that I did no such thing. I could have easily walked off the boat with the statue and disappeared instead of coming back and making this fuss. Besides, Brandon was my professional colleague. I certainly hoped I was wrong about his intentions."

"But you didn't help Brandon. You didn't care," Miss Tomlinson accused. "If you truly cared, you would have helped him."

"Miss Tomlinson, I am merely stating the facts to the inspector as I saw them. No one from the museum forced Brandon to take the actions he did."

Miss Tomlinson sputtered with incoherent words.

Bevan stepped up to place himself between Archie and Eve before their argument became violent. "If you two don't mind, we're in the middle of an active murder investigation."

"I do apologize, Inspector," Archie replied. "But it is important that I find the Jackal. I believe Williamson's murder had something to do with those stolen artifacts."

"What makes you think the murder relates to the theft?"

Cora stepped forward. "I'm surprised that you don't see the connection. Archie placed his case next to mine. Two suspicious looking thugs took and ran away with our two cases in broad daylight. The murdered killed Brandon right next to the pile of crates and boxes where the stolen goods originated. There is an obvious connection. So, you see

Inspector, if we find the cases, we will find the killer. Where will we start?"

Inspector Bevan did not look impressed with her recitation. "'WE' shall start nowhere, Miss Gudmundson. This is a Scotland Yard matter. I suggest you and Mr. Thorogood give your information to the officers and get on with your day."

"But—" Cora sputtered. "I need to recover my case, and of course, to help Mr. Thorogood find his precious artifact as well. We can help you solve the murder." She was practically in the inspector's face as she tried to make her point.

"Come along, my dear," Archie said and stepped to Cora's side. He put his arm around her and pulled her away. "Let's allow the Inspector to do his job."

She tried to protest, but then noticed the frown lines between Bevan's eyebrows were growing deeper. She stopped talking and stood quietly next to Archie. Bevan took a deep breath and signaled the men to carry Williamson's body off the dock. He nodded to the dock hands waiting to load the Egyptian artifacts onto a truck for transport to the museum.

Bevan nodded in their direction and then led Miss Tomlinson off, away from Archie and Cora.

Eve glared at Archie as they passed.

Archie and Cora gave their stolen suitcases information to a police officer standing by.

Cora whispered, "Was I too adamant?"

"I believe the proverbial word 'overboard' would fit," Archie said with a half-smile. "Buts mostly understandable."

As the officer closed his notebook and left them, Cora observed the crime scene. "Someone stabbed Brandon with a knife. It would be quieter than using a gun, but messier than using a rope. I feel the murder was a spur-of-the-moment passion rather than premeditated. Brandon and the killer were standing close together, thus they knew each other."

"Person? Not a man? Do you think a woman could have done this?"

"Why not?"

"It's just not, I mean—a lady doesn't—"

"A woman is equally capable as a man of committing a murder, premeditated or otherwise?"

Archie sighed. "I do not understand the fairer sex completely. However, I'm not sure equality applies in this case."

"Why not? You saw his fiancée. I don't care where she's from. If a woman sees her fiancé dead, she will show at least some anguish. All Eve could manage were crocodile tears."

"Perhaps their relationship was not as close as Brandon led us to believe," Archie reasoned. "I do not see what would lead Miss Tomlinson to murder Brandon or to steal my—I mean, our—cases."

"Perhaps not completely, at least right now," Cora agreed with a heavy sigh.

Archie opened his mouth to speak but paused when Cora lifted her finger and said, "Yet anything is possible."

They paused as the remaining police officers departed.

She touched his arm and motioned back in the dock's direction. "We need to look for clues. We may find something they've missed."

Archie's eyebrows lifted. "What? You heard the inspector. He told us to go home and leave this matter up to the police."

"Nonsense. They're outsiders. We knew the victim, we saw the robbery, we have the best chance of solving the case," Cora said. She grabbed his arm and led him back toward the area where the dock workers were loading the artifacts.

"So far, the only connection I see now is that you and Brandon worked for the museum."

"Are you suggesting that I had something to do with this?" Archie stopped in his tracks and stared at her.

"I'm not suggesting anything. The museum is a shared victim or shared perpetrator in this case. We need to look for clues."

Archie sighed. "Cora. We really should let the inspector do his job and not interfere. He didn't appear to be a patient man."

"Yes, yes, he can do his job and search for the murderer. But I'm not giving up my search for Arve and Ola." Cora paused and looked inside her side pouch to make sure Arve and Ola had not returned, and that Nicholas's face was not looking up and her, waving a disapproving finger.

"But you're here with a tour group. They will be concerned about you."

"I don't care. If I have to walk all over London, I'm going to find Arve and Ola. Now, if you are interested in coming with me and talk to the deckhands, then you may follow. If not, get out of my way." Cora brushed Archie aside and walked toward the dock.

"Wait!"

Cora stopped, folded her arms, and leaned on one leg as she paused.

Archie focused on her for several moments. "Cora, you are a very determined woman. I admit the possibility of cracking this case and finding our possessions on our own is quite stimulating. Don't forget our chances of finding them are highly unlikely. So, don't get your hopes up too high. Be prepared to accept the fact that we may not retrieve our cases."

Cora's mind filled with the image of Nicholas' face. She shook her head. I need to do this on my own. This is my chance to prove I am responsible, she thought. Cora focused on Archie. "I'm not giving up yet, and we have much to investigate. I believe we will find your Jackal and my Arve and Ola."

"Very well," Archie said with a sigh, then straightened up. "Let's try it."

"Of course, yes, of course. This will be like—like an expedition."

######

Cora and Archie approached a dock worker who had a clipboard in his hand. "Pardon me," Cora said in a loud voice above the sounds of boat whistles and dock machinery. "Were you responsible for unloading the baggage from the Brandenburg?"

He glanced up briefly, then looked back at the clipboard. "If you're missing luggage, you need to take your complaints to the central office."

"Someone stole our bags. We want to get your thoughts on the type of characters who would have grabbed them and ran," Cora said.

The deckhand looked at her with a confused expression, as if she were some oddities.

Archie stepped forward and smiled at the man. "What is your name?"

"James, though you can call me Jimmy."

"Jimmy, now, I understand this is an unusual question, but it is important to us. We are interested in your thoughts and your experience seeing snatch and run characters. Surely you have seen this happen in your time here on the dock."

Jimmy took a step back and raised his eyebrows. "I hope you're not suggesting I lifted your baggage and ran."

"No, no," Cora said as she stepped forward. "We are not accusing you, sir."

Archie raised a hand. "I believe the lady is asking your thoughts about who would do something like this. Perhaps you have previous experience."

"As long as you're not accusing me, mate."

"No," Cora and Archie said in unison.

"Let me see. First off, this sort of thing happens all the time. There are a lot of shady characters that hang around the dock, even though the companies have hired blokes to keep an eye on things. Second, it is next to impossible for us to monitor everything. If the ticket gets ripped off a package, we don't know which bag belongs to which people." He shrugged his shoulders. "Could another passenger have taken your bags instead of theirs?"

"No. Unfortunately, we saw our bags lifted by two suspicious looking thugs. We tried to run them down, but we only got dirty and bruised," Cora said.

Jimmy laughed. "Oh, that was you? You ran fast, Miss. I thought you had him."

"Thank you, but unfortunately, not fast enough."

Jimmy stared at her for several moments. "It was probably for the best that you didn't catch up. A dirty dress would be the least of your problems. More than likely, you would have ended up in a hospital or casket after he was through with you."

Cora shuddered at his words. She hadn't considered the consequences if she had caught up with the thief.

The Missing Jackal Murder

Archie drew closer and put his hand on her arm. He looked back at Jimmy. "With your expertise in shipping, how would a person on board a ship goes about arranging a theft of luggage?"

Jimmy cocked his head back. "That's easy. The ship has a telegraph system. A passenger could have sent a message to an accomplice to let them know the when's and where's of the items to be nipped."

Archie looked at Cora. "Just a minute. I saw Brandon with Mr. Crawley, the communications officer. Could he have been in contact with someone on shore to arrange the theft?"

"That's right. Those two thugs went straight for our cases, as if they knew in advance what to look for and when we would arrive."

Archie nodded. "Thank you for your help, Jimmy."

Jimmy nodded and returned to work. Cora stopped him. "One more thing. Do you know a man named Brandon Williamson?"

"I never heard the name Miss." Jimmy walked away.

"So, Brandon may have sent a telegram to arrange for the theft," Archie said. "But that doesn't explain who killed him. We were in pursuit of the thieves, so it wasn't them. Who else would have wanted him dead? And why?"

"Good questions," Cora said. "Now we need to find the answers. Oh my, that reminds me I need to go to a telegraph office."

"Oh?" Archie said.

"I need to let my parents know I arrived in London safely."

Archie raised his eyebrows at the word 'safely'.

Chapter 7

Strong cockney accents of two men grabbed Arve and Ola's attention. They could barely comprehend what they were saying. First, they experienced the rough jostling of the case. Then they lay in wait, but they hadn't heard Cora's voice for a long time.

The case swung open. By instinct, Arve and Ola froze. Two rough hands reached in and lifted them out. He brought them close to his face. The fat wart-faced round nose almost brought Arve out of his protective state. But his horrible alcohol-laced breath blasting between crooked, yellow teeth proved unbearable.

Another man, thin, unshaven face, nearly collided with the first. "Whatcha got Clyde? What the blazes are those?"

"Get off," Clyde said, and pushed the man aside.

"That's not what we were supposed to steal."

"Ach, those are two of the ugliest things I've ever seen." Clyde dropped the two onto the floor.

Ola landed on her side and remained a wood carving.

Arve rolled across the floor with the sound of wood tumbling on wood. He rolled under a dresser but came alive as he reached for the dresser leg. He looked around his surroundings, then searched for and found Ola. She came to life but lay still on the floor as if to appear ridged. Their eyes met. He reached the edge of the dresser underbelly and found the two men's back towards them. As they reached for another case, he signaled Ola to get up and dash under the dresser.

Ola shook her head in fear.

"Now," Arve mouthed.

She got up, paused, and turned her head towards the men.

"Now," Arve whispered.

She took a step to Arve, but the men gave a gleeful expression that caused Ola to lie down and turn into her protective state again.

"Here," the thin man said. "This is what we wanted." His pants leg did not reach his well-worn shoes, but he kept his socks up to cover his ankle.

Arve looked at the other, his baggy pants legs draped over his large thick-soled shoes. His bottom half seemed to wobble as he spoke. "Blimy, Jerry, what do ya suppose that thing is?"

"Da' know."

"I know what it is."

Jerry snapped to his friend. "Clyde, you don't know nothing."

"Blimey, what is that painted with? It's as black as midnight."

"It's not painted, you maggot. It's made of Ebenezer wood."

"Oh. What's e-eb… wood?"

"It's some black wood, you dope."

"Look how smooth the—"

Jerry slapped his hands. "Get your bleedin' paws off. You want to wreck it?"

Clyde snapped his head at the thin man. "You get your bleedin' paws off me." He gazed at the object in his hand. "Look how black it is."

"A' course it's black. You don't think I have eyes to see with?"

"I wanna hold it." Clyde reached out to touch the object.

Jerry recoiled, preventing Clyde from grabbing hold. "Ya, crazy, you might drop it or break it, then he'll kill us, you want that to happen? It's going back in the case."

"Ahr," Clyde exclaimed.

"You'll have a chance later."

Clyde stomped away from Jerry. His foot came dangerously close to Ola. Though a short man, his round girth gave the impression of a heavy man. His dark gray suit coat was only held together by one button. His face, round, with a round pug nose with saggy graying sideburns and eyebrows.

Jerry took a few steps toward Clyde, then stopped. His dark brown suit coat fit close to his thin frame with all three buttons connected. He wore a flat medium brown hat tilted back. His smile looked sinister with his yellow teeth. He stopped. His light grey eyes looked down at Ola. "He's been a real crybaby. His entire life, he has." He walked across the room and kicked her out of his way. Arve readied to dash after Ola but paused and looked up.

"How long do we have to wait?" Clyde asked.

"As long as it takes," Jerry looked at the door. They walked to the table, pulled chairs out, and sat down. Jerry's foot kicked Ola, and she spun around. Her back was now to Arve.

"What do you suppose it's worth, Jerry?"

"I don't know, do I?"

The two men said nothing for a while. Jerry tapped his knuckles on the table.

Ola took the chance to turn around slowly and see Arve under the dresser. Arve shook his head.

"How long did you say it was going to take, Jerry?"

"Clyde, how many times do I have to tell you no? If he doesn't get here soon, I'll go out and find another buyer."

"We don't want to upset him this time. He's always been good to us, paid us all the time."

"Yeah, but he hasn't been this late before. He never kept us waiting."

"You suppose he got caught?"

"Nah, no one ever suspects him."

The two men paused.

Clyde broke the silence. "Let's have a drink while we wait."

Jerry grunted, and Arve could hear them pouring liquid.

He motioned for Ola to stand up and run to him under the dresser while the two men looked away.

Ola stood, looked up toward the bottom side of the table, then looked at their shuffling feet.

Arve waved Ola to run, swinging his arms vigorously to encourage her.

Ola took a deep breath and ran across the room and under the dresser. "Where's Nicholas?"

"Shh, later." Arve observed the two men.

"What was that?" Clyde said as he plunked his glass onto the table and looked toward the floor.

"What was what?" Jerry asked.

"I thought I heard something scurry across the floor."

"Probably another bloody mouse. You want a drink or not?"

"How much longer do we have to wait for him?"

Jerry sat back. "If you ask me one more time, I'm going to give you a thump. Why don't you take a nap?"

"Yeah, that run done tuckered me out," Clyde said. "That crazy bitch nearly caught up to me."

Jerry sat down with a yawn. "I'll just rest here."

The two men became quiet.

"What is going on?" Ola whispered to Arve.

"Shh," Arve placed his fingers on his lips.

"Where's Cora? What are we doing here? Who are they?"

Arve gave out a deep sigh. "I don't know. There must have been a mix-up with the luggage. We need to be patient. Cora probably already knows and is in progress to get her suitcase back."

"What are we going to do?" Ola asked in a high-pitched voice.

"First, we're going to stay calm down and take a deep breath. We'll figure something out. As I've said, I'm sure Cora is looking for us."

Ola pulled on Arve's arm. "What if she doesn't find us?"

"She will—and we need to have faith in her responsibility. Remember, we told Nicholas if we get into trouble, we'll figure it out ourselves. Think about it. If we call Nicholas and he brings us back to the Village, and her mother finds out about this mix-up? What do think would happen to Cora's next desire to travel?"

"But I'm scared."

"I know you are, but here's nothing to be afraid of right now. They aren't interested in us. As long as we stay hidden under here, we should be alright."

"What's that sound?" Ola said, hearing soft growling toward the other case.

Arve scanned from the case, then to the men. "It's that Clyde person snoring."

"Are you sure? I've heard nothing like that before."

"Shh, calm down."

Ola paused and gazed at Clyde as Jerry's breathing got deeper and louder. "Do you think Cora is in danger?"

"How can she be? She's with her tour group."

Ola grabbed Arve's arm again. "What's that? I heard something move by the other case."

"I'm sure nothing moved by the case. It's got to be one of those two men."

"It wasn't over by the men. It was over there," Ola said, pointing as her voice rose with terror.

"You're imagining things."

"Are you sure?" Ola said, staring at the opened suitcase. She quivered in Arve's arms.

#####

They dashed down the museum basement steps, with Cora's hand in Archie's, to locate his assistant.

Distracted by the objects lying higgledy-piggledy on tables and crates, Cora listened half-heartedly to what Archie had to say. It's like pictures from her history books or the National Geographic magazines come alive. Cora marveled, like to see history in person, something she longed for and believe possibly never would happen.

"Why aren't these treasures on display?" Her question ignored as Archie called out for his assistant. She beheld the clothing boxes stacked near mannequins ready to become ancient or modern people from faraway lands. Tables with pottery from ancient tribes with signage that described the origins of Nigeria and a brief description of where and when of their creation. A large stuffed brown bear stood in a ferocious stance, as if ready to pounce, but now pathetically silent and covered in dust. Cora's heart went out for the beast till she beheld skeletons partially constructed. Some stood, and others laid on tables. She searched her brain to understand if they were human or apes. As she rounded the tables, her shoe stubbed on the pile of rocks, some colorful while others looked like they could be volcanic lava specimens of different sizes. Deeper through the collection, she found herself in front of a table with microscopes and stacks of books standing between bookends and charts of different languages labeled on the wall, all ready for the museum staff to explore.

Archie stood next to Cora, his eyes in the opposite direction. "He probably has his nose in a book, or summit."

"Did someone call my name?" a voice sprang from Archie's left. Archie jumped at the sudden and surprising arrival of a young man who had descended upon him. "Jeepers. You gave a start."

"Sorry." Freddie pushed back his dark-rimmed glasses and swept back his mussed hair.

Freddie was quite a young man, appearing to be in his early twenties. His clothes seemed mismatched and thoroughly worn. Freddie's long neck shot straight out of his woolen sweater to his face with small protruding ears that did not touch his coarse, shaggy brown hair. His black rimmed round glasses wore crooked at the bridge of his long nose. He did not stop and acknowledge Archie's discomfort, nor allow Archie to offer a greeting to him despite their several weeks' absence.

Freddie launched into a rapid-fire report. "The artifacts of the Prince of Iknokman that Mr. Mitford wanted those quickly categorized and sent upstairs. But there was no Jackal of the Prince of Iknokman. What happened to the Jackal of the Prince of Iknokman? Do you have it?"

"No, men ran off with it."

He paused with his mouth open. "Stolen. Who stole it? Is that why Mr. Mitford was so upset? I was in the middle of the mastodon artifacts. I'm going to categorize and organize each of them and place them in drawers B7 through B14."

"Freddie, Scotland Yard is on it."

"That's the most important piece of the collection. The Jackal of the Prince of Iknokman is what the story is all about. It is the entire meaning of the hieroglyphs."

"Freddie, I told you Scotland Yard is on it."

"Oh. Very well, then. Yesterday I wrote the synopsis on the history of the reign of King Clovis during his stay in Rome, but I'm not sure of the actual date. Do you remember?"

"Freddie."

"No matter. I could look that up. I'm still working on reorganizing the library so that at least I can find the books on—"

"Freddie."

"You don't want me to organize the library?"

"Freddie, Mr. Mitford, had you open and categorize the artifacts of the Prince of Iknokman when they arrived? He wanted you to bring them up and for display already?"

"Isn't that what I said? Most unusual, most unusual. He wanted me to rush the artifacts up. I told him this may take time. I certainly do not want to rush it and possibly break something. He was most persistent, and this is highly irregular. This is unusual and irregular and..." Freddie suddenly stopped and gazed at Cora as if one of the museum's Egyptian mummies had come to life and stood next to him.

"This certainly is unusual and irregular," Cora repeated his words in a teasing voice.

"Oh, you're American. You have cowboys and Indians everywhere, I do believe. Fascinating. I've always wanted to excavate and study Indian artifacts and their culture and also the cowboy culture. Now that would be an interesting feature."

"Freddie."

"And the strange varieties of animals you people have there, especially those that we do not have here."

"Freddie."

"You have an interesting black mammal with a white stripe as well."

"It's called the skunk."

"That's right, a skunk. And the little beast protects himself with a pungent—"

"Freddie, stop, stop, pay attention." Archie paused, surprised by the two seconds of silence. "First, this is Cora Gudmundson who, of course, as you said, is from America."

"Oh, welcome to Great Britain, Miss Cora Gudmundson." Freddie vigorously shook Cora's hand. "I hope you can tell me about—" Freddie paused. His eyes bulged at Cora. "Wait, you're a—" Freddie quickly let go of Cora's hand and gazed up and down her figure and stopped as he locked his eyes on her chest.

"Eyes up here, Freddie," Cora pointed to her eyes.

"Oh," Freddie said and rocked uncomfortably.

"You must not get many women down here."

"No, not at all, to be truthful. I never, I mean I don't know girls. I mean, women have never been interested in artifacts and things."

Cora sensed Freddie's discomfort as she addressed him. "Yes, yes, we do have a rich Indian heritage in America and many museums have many artifacts that you would be interested in."

"Of course, yes, they do. One day I would like to go there and see."

"Freddie."

"But I would prefer to excavate on—"

"Freddie, for heaven's sakes, stop."

The Missing Jackal Murder

"Have I been rude again?" Freddie said to Archie than spoke to Cora. "I asked Archie to let me know if I'm being too rude and—"

"Yes, you are. Now pay attention."

Freddie stopped and watched Archie. He closed his mouth.

"Now Freddie—"

"When are you going to stop calling me Freddie? My name is Frederick." He then spoke to Cora, "Archie has called me Freddie since I've been here. I've been trying to get him to call me Frederick since God knows when."

"Freddie, I mean Frederick, I'll call you Frederick when you learn to stop babbling on and listen when I want you to listen. Do you understand?"

Freddie silently nodded his head.

"Now tell me briefly how Mitford acted before, during, and after he told you to expedite the artifacts of the Prince of Iknokman to the museum displays."

Freddie shook his head. "Most insistent, most insistent. As I told him, this is highly irregular. But he didn't listen. He was most insistent."

"Yes, you have mentioned that he was most insistent, but what else?"

"I tried to tell them how irregular it was, but he was—" Freddie stopped. His mouth opened and nothing came out as he gawked at Cora once more.

"Most insistent," Cora concluded.

Freddie nodded his head. "He also asked me if Mr. Williamson had arrived. I said no. I said he and Mr. Thorogood have not arrived yet because—oh that's right, you left to visit the United States museum to bring the artifacts back... How was America?"

"Freddie, stay focused. Keep going."

"Wait, why was he interested in Mr. Williamson and not you as well?"

Cora put her fingers to her chin. "How highly irregular and how most insistent of Mr. Mitford." She turned to Archie. "Why would he be?"

"Mr. Mitford got furious and stormed off. Why does he get so angry and so often? Could it be me?"

"I can't see why you would think anyone would want to be angry with you, Freddie," Cora said. "But I know this will be a long shot, but, amongst the artifacts that Archie brought back. Did you see two small flat plane wood carvings about this big?" Cora separated her thumb and finger about six inches.

"Why would there be two modern woodcarvings with the Egyptian artifacts?"

"It's a long story. Actually, they're not that modern. They were carved in Norway 600 years ago. They've been in my family since then, so you can see how important this is for me."

"600-year-old Norwegian wood carvings. How fascinating. That means your origins are Norwegian."

Archie took Cora's elbow. "We need to go upstairs and talk to Mitford, now."

Cora spoke to Freddie. "Yes, my heritage is Norwegian. It was nice to meet you. Sorry we have to run off so fast."

"Oh, Norway, the land of the Vikings." Freddie's eyes widen, almost maniacally. "An excavation to Norway would be lovely."

"Of course that would be—" Archie paused. "I'll tell you what, you look for possible Viking village sites to research. Then come up with a plan for a possible excavation. We'll present your data and your recommendation to the governors and other financial backers, and we'll go from there." Archie reached for Cora's wrist and pulled.

As Freddie walked away, he mumbled to himself. "Splendid, I'll get on that right away."

"You do that," Archie said with an out-of-view eye roll.

As he brought Cora into motion again, she stopped and looked over her shoulder. "Oh, Freddie."

Freddie stopped, turned and focused on Cora's chest and then moved up to her eyes. "Yes Cora, I mean Miss Gudmundson?"

"If you come across a small town, an ancient, extinct town called Nordlund in Northern Norway, I would certainly appreciate your findings."

"Excavation to Nordlund, Northern Norway," Freddie said with his right hand in the air as he walked away.

Cora and Archie threaded their way through tables full of opened crates and boxes in the basement of the British Museum. "Don't you find it a bit odd that your Mr. Mitford wanted to unpack the Egyptian artifacts so quickly?"

"Exactly. We need to find Mr. Mitford and ask him what the meaning of this is. Many of these Egyptian pieces are priceless. We would need to catalogue and register carefully. I don't understand what's going on," Archie replied as he led Cora up a staircase and down several hallways until they arrived at the Egyptian exhibit.

At the open doorway they stopped just outside, stunned to see Mr. Mitford and an assistant talking with Inspector Bevan. "... and Inspector, we are sticklers to make sure everything is in its place and there is a place for everything." Mitford tapped the end of his pencil on his cheek while he looked down at his clipboard.

Archie put his fingers to his lips and motioned for Cora to remain silent. She nodded. This gave Cora time to get a good look at Mr. Mitford. His figure reminded Cora of an illustration of an old college professor from her many books. Though medium height, Mr. Mitford wore a brown tweed coat, vest, and pants. A chain watch fob extended from his middle vest button and ran into a vest pocket. The chain wobbled with his pompous animation as he talked to Bevan. His black bowtie danced with his tight white collar as he spoke. His round face sported a sharp nose and bushy gray eyebrows, and he swept back his long grey hair.

Inspector Bevan cleared his throat. "Speaking of being a stickler, how would you describe Mr. Williamson's performance at and around the museum?"

"Oh, quite energetic indeed," Mitford said, animating his words with his hands. "Although I must admit, he could be full of himself."

"In what way?"

"He boasted about his ability to get out into expeditions and bragged about how skillful he was for finding treasures more quickly and efficiently than the others. He was constantly haranguing me with requests for me to send him out on excavations. But, as I had to keep reminding him, we have to choose carefully what and where to excavate, and his lack of experience was a key factor."

"How did he respond to your denial of his requests?"

"He asked how he could get experience if I didn't send him out to excavate. But it was not my position to provide opportunities for him to practice. We have several other, far more experienced archeologists to rely upon."

"Did he ever threaten you if you did not let him go on an expedition?"

"For heaven's sakes, no. At least, not that I ever knew of. But I cannot speak to the governors. I suppose they would have mentioned it to me if he did such a horrible thing. I am responsible for the employees here at the museum. If any word of ill-treatment had reached me, I would have discharged him immediately."

"I would like a list of these governors. I will need to speak to each one. Do you have any suspicions of wrong-doing here at the museum by Mr. Williamson or anyone else?"

"Oh, heavens no, we are most fortunate to—no, no, no," Mitford interrupted his assistant about placing an artifact. "That is where the Jackal of Prince Iknokman will sit when Scotland Yard returns the statue." Mitford said to Bevan. "I will have the names of the governors and employees for you shortly."

Bevan nodded as he looked at the empty stand. "What about Archie Thorogood? Do you have any suspicions about him?"

Cora saw Archie's back stiffen.

"Oh, he is one of our top excavators. Yes, he is a good chap."

"How did the relationship between Mr. Thorogood and Mr. Williamson seem to you?"

"I've heard no complaints. I am sure Mr. Thorogood would have informed me of any wrongdoing. But I did sense a bit of competition between the two."

"Enough competition for Mr. Thorogood to cause harm to Mr. Williamson?"

Mitford opened his mouth to speak, but Archie answered the question as he and Cora stepped forward into the room. "Certainly not!"

Bevan appeared annoyed. "Mr. Thorogood, Miss Gudmundson, I didn't see you there."

"We have just arrived after having visited the basement. Again, Inspector Bevan, I hope you're not accusing me of murdering Mr. Williamson."

"I am not forming any opinions just yet, merely collecting facts."

Before Archie could open his mouth, Cora interrupted. "What facts, Inspector?"

"None to give out at this time, Miss Gudmundson."

She pointed to Bevan. "Did you not find it peculiar that Miss Tomlinson did not seem overly distressed to see her fiancé's bloody body lying on the dock?"

"I did sense deception on Miss Tomlinson's part, but again, I am not ready to form any opinions."

Archie waved his hand. "Mr. Mitford, why have you unpacked and setup the Egyptian artifacts in such great haste?"

"Nothing odd about it." Mitford did not meet Archie's eyes. "I wanted to make sure everything was there."

"But the cleaning and cataloging process usually takes time to do a thorough job."

Mr. Mitford smiled and shrugged as if to dismiss Archie's concern.

Cora looked at Bevan and spoke in a louder voice. "Don't you think it was odd that the theft of our cases seems too precise to be random? Those thieves knew exactly what they were looking for and when it would be there. My case contained two priceless woodcarvings." She leaned forward. Her eyes roamed around the room and wondered if Mr. Mitford had Arve and Ola hidden somewhere. She hoped she would get their attention and try to come out. There was no response. She sighed and straightened.

"Hmm, I will make a note of that," Bevan replied, and he frowned with a suspicious look as he watched Cora. "Mr. Mitford, I believe I have everything I need for now."

"Is there any additional evidence about our missing cases, Inspector, that has come up?" Cora spoke loudly again. Her eyes darted from left to right.

"No, I'm afraid not," he gave Cora a fake smile and left.

Archie drew closer to Mr. Mitford. "I need to have a word with you, sir."

"I don't have time for chitchat at the mo—" Mitford replied.

"But you had time for the Inspector." She stepped to Archie's side and whispered, "Did I go too far again?"

"Actually, not far enough," Archie whispered, then returned to his normal voice. "Mr. Mitford, I really need to know why you had these artifacts on display so quickly. This isn't the usual practice of the museum."

"When the police informed me about the loss of the Jackal, I unpacked the remaining crates to determine if everything was there. Efficiency, I always say."

"Admirable, however, before I left for America, I discovered several other items missing and I fear, may have been recently stolen from the museum. I'm curious what you think about the stolen artifacts, and why you did not bring those to the Inspector's attention."

"Stolen artifacts? Nonsense. I think you mean 'put in storage'. Who have you been talking with?" Mitford responded too quickly for Cora to agree.

Archie sighed. "As you have taught me, we must be efficient. So, I looked through the storage for the specific missing artifacts. They are not on display, nor in storage or anywhere else. What would you deduce from this?"

Mitford folded his arms. "You need to look more carefully, Mr. Thorogood." He handed his clipboard to his assistant. "If you will excuse me, I do need to speak to one of the governors."

Cora jumped in before Mr. Mitford walked away. "What about the Jackal of Prince Iknokman? What do you think about that?"

Mitford glanced at Cora. "Most regrettable, but we do need to let Scotland Yard do their job." He walked away.

As soon as he was out of earshot, she moved closer to Archie. "Do you suspect Mr. Mitford would have the missing artifacts with our missing cases?" she whispered so the assistant would not overhear.

Archie nodded. "With what happened on the dock and what's been happening in the museum, he either has something to do with it or knows who does. He and Brandon were always together."

"Do you think someone murdered Brandon because he knew too much?" Cora said, looking at the empty stand where the Jackal should now sit.

"As Bevan said, we need to gather all the facts before we can form an opinion."

"Count me in," Cora replied.

"But what about your tour group?"

"Oh, I forgot about that. I'm sure Willie will cover for me for now. Alas, I hope she will cover for me for the rest of the day. First, this is an adventure, and furthermore, I'm off to find Arve and Ola."

Archie folded his arms. "Very well then, where do you think we should begin?"

"How about with lunch? I'm starving. Do you think we might find some of that tea and crumpets you Brits are famous for?"

Chapter 8

Despite Jerry and Clyde's snores, Arve turned as they heard the sound when the other black case magically opened. Ola lay fast asleep next to him. He removed his arm wrapped around her shoulders in an attempt not to wake her.

Arve realized Ola had been right about something else being alive in the room. He listened carefully, expecting to hear animal grunts and groans. Instead, the sound of mumbling, like a man's voice, came from on top. But then the voice spoke with a perfect English accent, "Where the bloody hell am I?"

Arve stood slowly and moved in the direction of the sound to investigate.

"What? What's the matter?" Ola said in a sleepy voice.

"Shh," Arve walked to the side of the dresser and looked up toward the table, the second case now wide open. Black, angular parts of a body were visible and rose over the edge of the case.

"What is it?" Ola whispered behind Arve.

Arve looked toward Jerry and Clyde, but they remained asleep.

"What is that?" Ola said again, grabbing at his arm.

"Shh," Arve said.

Ola's voice did not stir Jerry or Clyde, but the beast stopped his rant and moved to the edge of the table. Arve and Ola gazed upon the creature in its full form. A figure with a thin black head, long ears, and angry eyes stared back at them. The long snout mumbled something inaudible. The creature moved and appeared to be looking for a way off the table. He rose to full height, walked to another edge, and jumped off and landed on the chair seat. He climbed down the chair leg to the floor.

Ola gasped as the doglike figure walked towards the middle of the room. He observed Jerry and Clyde back in their seats, snoring away, then walked back toward Arve and Ola.

She tugged on Arve's arm again. "Should we get Nicholas now?"

Arve place his hand on her hand. "No, wait. I, I believe he's made of wood too. Maybe he's like us." The jackal walked to the dresser and approached Arve and Ola in front of them and looked down at them. To Arve and Ola, the jackal stood as high as a Clydesdale horse or probably a small elephant.

"Oh my," Ola exclaimed.

The jackal's head snapped towards Ola. He stretched his neck closer to sniff her.

"Are you—lost?" Arve said, and moved to draw his attention away from Ola.

The jackal sniffed Arve, then cocked his head back. "What evil did you do to become cast in this hideous form?" he said in an Eastern yet British voice.

"Our form is no more hideous than yours," Ola sputtered.

"Ola," Arve warned. "Don't rile him."

They stared at each other. The jackal shook his head and walked away muttering. "I'll not stand for this. Why have they taken me?"

Arve glanced up when Clyde gave a loud snort. They watched as the figure made a journey around the outside corners of the room. His figure disappeared into the shadows, then reappeared in the light. His tiny footsteps were silent as he walked along the perimeter of the room. He reminded Arve of a rat scurrying around to look for a way out.

"What is he?" Ola whispered.

"I'm not sure, but I believe he's an Anubis,"

"A what?"

"The Anubis is a jackal-headed figure associated with mummification and the afterlife in ancient Egyptian religions," Arve replied in his matter-of-fact tour guide voice.

"Anubis?" Ola said. "Does that mean he's dangerous?"

Before Arve could reply, the figure made his way back underneath the dresser. "Are you responsible for my incarceration in this room?" he demanded.

Arve paused and studied the smooth black figure. Though made completely of wood, the jackal moved as if it were a real dog. His long, thin snout pointed at Arve. When he spoke, the long lower jaw did not bounce like a barking dog, but his mouth formed to pronounce each word. His solid black pupils converged and stared at Arve. His eyes were decorated with a gold eye liner that trailed back like the shape of a fish with golden eyebrow lines above. The abnormally long black ears with gold interior pointed up to create an almost evil appearance. The figure wore a matching gold ribbon around his neck, with both ends draped to his front legs.

"Well?"

Arve stepped forward. "No, we're kidnapped, just the same as you."

"We shall see about that," the jackal said and strode out from under the dresser towards Jerry's chair.

"Wait," Arve said in a louder whisper. "Don't wake them. I don't think they've ever seen anything like you—or us—before."

"Arve?" Ola said nervously.

"I don't think he means us harm. If he did, he would have attacked us by now."

Jerry snorted and raised his head. The three figures remained motionless. Jerry put his head back down and snored again. The jackal looked at Arve and returned and stood next to them under the dresser.

"What is the meaning of this? Why did they take me?" the figure said with more confusion than anger in his voice.

"We don't know, not to be overly clever, but we are just as in the dark as you. From the conversation between these two, the best we can surmise is that you were their intended target. I believe we're here because our carrying cases are identical. It seems they did not know which case to take, so they took both."

"Why do you think I was the one they were after?"

Ola peered over Arve's back. "That's because you're a museum piece. They said you are worth a lot of money, while we, evidently, are not."

"I'm not interested in your lack of value. You must have done something serious for someone to curse you like this."

Ola stepped to Arve's side. "What do you mean? If anything, we're blessed."

He grunted and looked away. "I'm not interested to hear of your crimes. I have my own to think of." He walked to the opposite side of their hideout under the dresser, sat down and put his head on his paws.

"We did nothing wrong." Ola's outburst caused Clyde to stop in mid-snore and say, "Heh?" After a moment, Clyde resumed his snoring and Ola walked towards the jackal.

The jackal lifted his head towards Ola. Arve stepped up and stood beside her as she spoke. "It's because of Agar, a wonderful shaman in our village, saved us from death. It was his plan to keep us alive during a devastating plague. We all did this. Yes, sometimes I wish we were human again. Arve and I were just married before—well, I'm glad he saved our village from the plague."

The Jackal only stared back in response.

Ola explained how the Village is passed from generation to generation and how they now lived in an attic somewhere in America. By the time Ola explained how Nicholas distributed gifts each year around the world, the jackal had sat up on his hindquarters to listen. Ola finished with the story of how she and Arve convinced Cora to take them with her to London.

"What is your story?"

"There's nothing to tell truly."

"There's plenty to tell, I'm sure," Arve said. "You are a magical creature, just as we are. Please tell us. We'll listen."

"Is it something you're ashamed of?" Ola asked.

The jackal bolted up and growled.

Ola flinched. "Oh, my," Ola whimpered, hiding behind Arve.

The jackal became silent, dropped his jaw, and widened his eyes in fear, or possibly embarrassment. He shook his head and turned around, then dropped again to put his head on his paws. "I do apologize," he said, "I—I just don't have time to tell the story."

Arve chuckled. "We appear to have a lot of time."

"My name is Ola. This is my husband, Arve." When the jackal remained silent, Arve escorted Ola to the far side of the space and they sat with their backs against the wall. Arve put his arm around her shoulder. Ola leaned into Arve.

"Prince Iknokman."

"Excuse me?"

"I suppose we can drop the 'Prince' part. My name is Iknokman, just Iknokman."

It was his tone of embarrassment that warned Arve not to press for more details.

#####

"Are you sure you want to do this?" Archie asked and examined the short flight of brick steps to the door that led to the loud, dodgy bar. He looked up to the round weathered wooden sign that was suspended by two rusty chains on a rusty pub, with the sign that read 'Charlie's Establishment.' A grimy brick wall formed an archway that led to the weathered wooden door. The door latch hung precariously, as if the next patron who opened it would pull it off. The indented shoe marks on the door presented the reason for the condition of the door latch.

Cora shrugged. "I'm not sure, but it beats doing nothing. You said this one is by the docks."

"I still say we should go through all the pawn brokerage shops to see if anything has shown up."

"We found nothing in the last three, again like I said before, I don't believe anyone would bring a priceless item to a pawnshop," Cora said.

"Agreed, but those thugs might bring your wood carvings to a pawn brokerage shop."

Cora looked sharply at Archie. "As I've told you, if we find Arve and Ola we find Prince Iknokman. These, what you call, dodgy bars would be a great place for people like those who lifted our cases will be. I feel it and it makes sense."

"Yes, I know Arve and Ola are quite valuable, but those two did not look like men who would be knowledgeable as to the true value of the items they stole."

"Exactly. Someone had to have hired them to do the job. They needed a place to deliver, not in the open public, behind closed doors, not where families gather, but with their lot. They would blend right in."

Archie looked down the concrete steps. "The problem is, there are too many of these drinking establishments in the city. We don't know which one of our thugs might end up in, or if they will even visit one at all tonight, to say nothing about us missing the exchange already. This is much like searching for a bloody needle in a haystack—oh, sorry for my language."

"Well, I'm bloody going to do something about it. If Bevan appeared more interested in our missing cases, we wouldn't have to do this—at least on our own."

"Inspector Bevan assured us he will fully investigate. It has only been a few hours. We need to give him more time."

"Do you really believe he is giving any attention to this matter? His focus is on solving the murder of Brandon, among his other cases."

Archie sighed. "Quite right, he did seem to have a typical 'what's gone, is gone' attitude about it."

"And that's why I want to do something." Cora inspected the door again.

"I wonder what your tour group is doing right now."

"I'm not sure, but I'm fairly sure they aren't visiting any dodgy saloons."

"Seriously, Cora, you don't have to throw away your chance to have a grand tour of London."

"Do you want to find your Jackal or not?"

"You also have to understand how dangerous these people can be. They're like sharks on a shallow beach."

"I don't see it that way, Archie."

"Oh, and how do you see it? Do you think we can just walk in, tap someone on the shoulder, and ask if they know who stole a priceless Egyptian artifact? Or better yet, would they tell us why it is they stole our property?"

"Archie, you're not seeing this as an opportunity."

"Opportunity, Cora? You see this as an opportunity to drink watered-down whiskey and walk out feeling less than blissful?"

"Archie, you're so full of meaningless metaphors. How about this obvious metaphor? Look at this dodgy pub as an excavation site digging for information about this primitive culture. You do remember how to excavate, don't you?" She raised one eyebrow as she looked up at his face.

"Yes, I do, but how do you see this as an excavation? By the way, what do you know about an excavation?"

"I read *National Geographic* magazines. We find a dig site, we dig. If what we are looking for is not there, we go somewhere else. We use the proper tools to dig, and we document all findings and details, important or not, at least for the time being. If the time spent yields nothing, we use the knowledge of what we learned to come up with a better plan on how to excavate or to move to a more plausible site. Or better yet, to dig deeper to the next level till we yield something."

"I understand the part about going elsewhere. What I don't understand is what type of information are we expected to find on an upper level to dig deeper at this particular site?" Archie said and tilted his head towards the door.

"I was thinking about role-playing. If a direct question yields nothing, we play the role of people who are looking to buy or sell items… to warrant off suspicion. Perhaps we can ferret out the people Brandon would have delivered it to and get information from them. If they won't tell us directly, we can use the information as clues to the whereabouts of our cases."

"As far as I'm concerned, I suspect Mitford is the one whom Brandon was to deliver to," Archie said. "So far, he is our only lead."

They were both silent for several moments until Cora spoke. "Tell you what, if this dig site yields nothing, we'll go back and dig further at the museum."

"I'm sure we'll find more there," Archie perked up, but then looked at the disappointed expression on Cora's face. "But since we're here, we might as well go take a peek inside." Archie looked at the door with an expression of anxiety.

She smiled. "So, if you believe Mitford and Brandon are responsible for the thefts, then I suggest you think like them while we interrogate... or dig, rather."

"You know Cora, I like how you think." Archie stopped. She ran into him. "I think you'd make a great archaeologist. Maybe I should take you on my next dig."

Cora chuckled. "Oh Archie, I like the way you think, too."

Before he could take a step, the door opened and expelled two intoxicated men. They stumbled their way up the stairs.

One drunk looked between Archie and Cora. "Oh there, now missy, is this ugly bloke giving you a hard time?"

"No. Go away and take your formaldehyde breath with you."

"Now see here, missy," the other said. "Your bloody parents need to turn you over their knees and spank you for your insubordination."

Archie stepped back to let the men through. "Listen, you two, move along."

Cora stepped farther back to let them pass. Instead, the two men moved closer to her.

Archie pulled Cora away from the men. "See here, you maggot, or I'll have to teach you a thing or two. Now move along and leave the lady alone."

The drunk man belched. "That's it. I've taken all I can, and I will teach you a lesson."

The other drunk man stepped next to his friend, nearly bounding off him, and held out to catch himself. "I fully concur, Thomas. Let's give him a thrashing."

Archie easily blocked his slow, wide cross. The man stumbled to the steps.

"Now see here, you hit my friend Tom, now I have to—"

Archie did not let the man finish his threat before he punched him straight in the nose and knocked him to the steps.

Cora pointed to the men. "Wait a minute, which one of you is Tom?"

"Now you did it. you got us both mad. Two against one."

Before the first got up, Cora kicked him in the side. "Are you Tom or Thomas?"

"That's it," the man said, "kick a man when he is down, will ye?"

"Ha, Tom, you let a bird kick you."

"Cora, I really don't think that's necessary," Archie said.

"Yeah, you should mind your men-folk when they— ouch," Cora kicked the second man in the groin. He grabbed hold of his injuries and stumbled back to the steps.

"Cora!"

The Missing Jackal Murder

Cora sneered down at them. "Oh, you two step on a piece of fat and slide, or I'll kick your tail feathers off."

"Now there miss, no need to get your bloomers in a pinch."

"Now!" Cora stepped towards the men. Both got up and ran up the steps, laughing. When they reached the top, one fell. The other help the man up and laughed again.

"Did you catch the gams on that one?" the first said.

"What a chassis," the other said, "but she kicked me."

"Now I know we can handle ourselves in these situations," Cora said to an astounded Archie. "We do what we must do."

"What goes on in those logging camps of yours?" Archie asked, astounded.

"When big men drink lots of alcohol, they often say stupid applesauce and are easy to knock over." She glanced in her pouch to see no other belongings had slipped out, and to make sure none had returned since her last evaluation. They walked down the stone stairs and opened the door. Cora didn't know what was worse, the sight, sounds or smells. The only spots available through the raucous crowd were two stools at the bar. She pretended to fit into the environment when she took Archie's elbow and led him straight to the stools without looking across the room. They sat down. They both scanned the room.

An out of tune piano attempted to play above the loud conversation with little success. Mismatched sets of chairs and tables were all occupied. Cora tried not to retch at the stench of body odor masked by heavy clouds of tobacco smoke and alcohol.

A large man lifted an obnoxious customer and threw him out.

"What will you have, miss?" a firm voice came from behind the bar. The voice also brought Archie's attention forward.

"I'll have a ginger ale."

The barkeep stared at Cora as if she had told a joke that was not particularly funny.

She glanced at Archie. "I'll bet if I asked for a Coca-Cola, he'd kick me out of the bar."

Archie gave Cora a sympathetic smile and spoke to the barkeep. "Two gins please." The barkeep nodded and left. Archie placed a few coins on the countertop. "I suppose you've never had alcohol in your life."

"Only once. It's not that we grew up in the Bible Belt or anything like that. My father had a taste for spirits now and then when my mother wasn't watching. I remember one evening when my father wasn't watching, I snuck a drink. Then, I thought my mouth was going to catch fire. I have never quite acquired the taste for alcohol since then."

The bartender delivered the drinks. Cora took hers. "But when in Rome…"

"Careful with that." Archie put his hand to her glass before she could drink it all in one gulp. "They may have water these drinks down, but still be careful. Remember why we're here."

"Gotcha," Cora said and brought her glass to her mouth. She took a tiny sip, then slammed the glass back down. "Wait a minute," her eyes widened as she watched Archie take a drink.

"What?"

"I thought we were in the middle of a prohibition. What are we doing? Isn't it illegal to serve alcohol?"

Archie placed his glass back on the bar and grinned. "Cora, my dear, it's prohibition in America, not in Great Britain."

"Really, not here?"

The barkeep tossed his wiping rag on the bar. "There you Americans go again. Whatever you do over there, you think the entire world must do entirely. Just because you came late into the war, you think—"

"She's our guest," Archie interrupted. "This is her first time out of the Americas, and we should show some hospitality. It's not her fault about the war, or anything else."

The barman grunted, picked up his rag, and moved away.

"Are we really that uppity in America?"

"Drink up, Miss Gudmundson. Here's to our success." They clinked glasses. Archie took another swallow. Cora held her breath, took a sip, then set her glass down and put her elbows on the counter to stare into the large mirror above the bar that reflected the crowd behind. "So, how should we locate any possibles?"

Archie put his glass down and looked in the mirror.

Cora gestured at the mirror as she spoke. "I assume the people we are looking for would not engage in casual conversation. It'd be more like two or more men huddled together, talking quietly to not cause suspicion."

Archie took another sip. "You still think it could be a woman?"

"Why can't it be a woman?"

"She possibly can, or could, but then—"

Cora saw Archie focus on something in the mirror and she looked in that direction. A man and a woman sat at a table. Their heads were close, nearly touching, as they carried on a conversation.

"There, they could discuss the exchange of goods or services for money," Archie said sarcastically.

"You think so? You don't think they he'd be interested in anything else? I mean, why else would they–" Cora caught a gleam in Archie's eyes and realized he was teasing her. "Archie, you think she is a woman of the evening."

"Why not?"

Cora watched the man take the woman's hand, then reach forward to kiss her on the lips. "Oh well, maybe he's after genuine romance."

Archie raised eyebrows. "In a place like this? Hardly."

"Hmm," Cora said, and changed the subject. "Maybe the person we are looking for is here alone? One of these drinkers might wait for a contact to show up."

"Well, let's get on with our excavation, shall we?" Archie said as he continued to examine the clientele.

Cora signaled for the barkeep.

"Anything else, miss?"

"Yes," she said in a louder voice. "Where may I find someone who would be interested in, say, certain Egyptian artifacts?"

"Cora! Beg your pardon!" Archie stared at her as if she had sprouted horns. He spoke to the barkeep. "Excuse her. She's not handling the gin well. She's been listening to too many detective programs on the radio."

The bartender grunted again and walked away.

"Cora, for heaven's sake, are you trying to get us into trouble?"

"Pardon me, miss," a confident speaking man asked. "Did I hear you mention you are in possession of Egyptian artifacts that you wish to part with?"

Cora looked the man up and down. "For the right price, of course." His coat and vest were clean. His shoes were polished, and he wore a watch fob that led to his watch pocket. This could be a possible suspect who would have the means to purchase stolen art.

"Yes, of course, my name is Mr. Swan, at your service." The man shook Archie's hand and moved next to Cora. "The right piece, the right price, of course."

"Of course," Cora said.

Swan took a deep breath through his nose. "Now, I understand there's a particular piece floating through town, one that I'm quite interested in."

"Which piece?" Archie asked.

"A dog made of ebony wood that sits on his hind legs?" Swan said.

Cora sensed Archie's back straighten.

"Yes, that sounds about right. Mr. Thorogood here is more knowledgeable about the piece," Cora said and sat back in her stool to let Swan and Archie talk.

Archie opened his mouth, closed it, and looked at Cora with an expression that warned of caution.

Cora looked at Archie with an expectant smile.

Archie cleared his throat. "It's called the Jackal of Prince Iknokman, a sitting jackal made of—"

"Just what I have been looking for," Mr. Swan mused.

"So, tell me why you want with this particular piece?" Cora stopped talking when she noticed a small pistol concealed in Mr. Swan's hand aimed in their direction.

"What is this?" Archie asked when he also spotted the weapon.

Cora waved her hands. "Look, we just want information, is all."

"What's going on here?" the bartender said when he moved closer and also spotted the pistol.

Swan held his pistol close so as not to cause attention. "We need to leave now."

"But, what if we don't want to?" Cora said as a shiver of fear raced down her spine.

"Listen, I'll go with you." He motioned his head in Cora's direction. "She's not part of this."

"Not part of this?" Cora said to Archie in a raised voice.

"Shut it, you two."

The barkeep folded his arms and motioned toward the door. "Get out and stay out."

Cora lifted her hands.

"Put your hands down, you want to get shot?" Swan said.

"Not particularly."

"Outside, now."

"What if I don't want to?"

Swan cocked the pistol. Cora's legs, planted on the floor like a stump, found enough energy to move, and the three left.

Chapter 9

Clyde's snore could peel paint, Arve had decided. While Jerry had gone out to search for their contact, Clyde slept.

Ola approached Iknokman. "We told you our story. I don't understand why you're not happy to be alive after all these years."

"Why should I be happy?" Iknokman snapped.

"As I understand it, the great princes and pharaohs of Egypt lived centuries ago. They are dead, yet you're still alive and well."

"Alive? You call this a life?"

Arve and Ola looked at each other, confused by Iknokman's anger.

She took yet another step. "I'm sorry to offend you. I won't ask about it again." She looked away.

After several moments of silence, Iknokman spoke. "Life like this may be a blessing for you, but is a curse for me. And the worst part is that I did nothing to deserve this. Someone betrayed me."

"What happened?" Ola said as she and Arve sat next to him.

Iknokman paused. "I couldn't tell this to anyone before. In fact, I could not talk to anyone. Recently, I came close to speaking with that Thorogood chap, Archie. But I thought he would lash out and smash me or run and never approach me again if I told him all the truth. I tried to speak to some museum people in New York, but they did not stay long enough to listen."

Clyde gave another loud snore and rolled over with his back to the dresser.

R. M. Scott

"Life in Egypt was different from here. A king required strict obedience from his subjects, and loyalty was absolute. Disloyalty brought instant, and often violent death. My death was cruel. You believe this a blessing. To me, it's a curse."

"Oh?" Ola asked.

Arve motioned to Ola to remain quiet and let Iknokman speak.

"Perhaps I should start at the beginning." Iknokman closed his eyes. "I am Prince Iknokman, second son of King Aktenhotep, Pharaoh of all of Egypt. I had the potential to become King by his decision. My mother, Ankhesenpaaten, was the second wife of my father. His first wife, Neferneferatun, gave birth to Smenkhankur, making him first in line. But during my childhood, I presented myself as a better choice to succeed my father. Not only did I attend to my studies, but I thought about my people and their welfare more than my elder brother had. I also grew to be a formidable warrior. My brother believed that being first in line was all he needed to become the next in line."

"We grew. We fought, as brothers often do. As we became older, I tried to encourage my brother to love Egypt, to grow, to become a better leader. But he lashed out. He did not listen to our father. He did not study. He was rather lazy and cruel to those around him. So, I looked to myself to become the next king. My brother knew my ambitions, and he plotted against me to fail. He played tricks to show I was not suitable as King. This infuriated my mother. She told our father about my brother's pranks, but father would not listen."

Iknokman paused. Arve and Ola sat waiting.

"I was fortunate to have a good friend; rather, one that I believed was a good friend. His name was Haromaheb, and he was one of my many tutors. I thought since he was

160

young, he understood my predicament. I confided in him. He kept me from lashing out in rage and instead to focus my energy inwardly, to focus on what was good for the kingdom. I ignored my immature brother and focus on my tutor's teachings. Then everything changed."

Ola put her hand to her mouth. "What happened?"

Iknokman looked over his shoulder as if being watched. "There were many attempts made on my father's life. He trusted in no one, including me. It seems my brother tried to convince father I was responsible for this. I feared for my life. Several times, I saw my trusted friend talking with my brother. When I asked what they talked about, he said he was trying to get through to my brother, to stop whatever terrible tricks he wanted to play. They told him it would hurt Egypt. It would hurt him. But I wasn't sure if he told the truth.

"There were attempts to take over, but father repelled them and slaughtered the perpetrators. This enraged him. He questioned everybody's loyalty, even mine. Then," Iknokman sighed and paused. "The last attempt on his life placed all guilt on me, as if I was the one responsible. My brother claimed I did these things. The priests, guards, all, they said that I had planned everything. They accused me of trying to raise an army to kill my father; to tarnish all he had done for my people. They all lied. How could they all lie? I told my father this was not true. About how I could not have done such a thing because it would hurt Egypt if I had. To kill the King would be a disaster for me and for our people.

"Though he didn't believe me. He was in such a fury that he would not listen to me. I searched for my friend, the only one who would believe me, but he had fled. Even my mother told me he fled because he told the priests and the guards to lie. My mother tried to talk to my father. But I couldn't believe what I heard. My mother spoke not in my defense, the truth I was innocent. She said to my father that my punishment should be swift and merciful.

"I could not believe my ears, so I ran to my father and threw myself at his feet to beg him to listen to me. Someone else did this. When my brother shouted of my guilt, I knew it had to be him. I knew he had conspired with my friend, my only friend. I tried to tell my father, but he would not listen.

"The guards took me away. And I laid in prison for longer than I could've ever imagined. My pain overtook my rage because I was innocent. I wished nothing but the best for Egypt. They would execute me for this lie. The one who squandered his time and his life on selfish pleasures and ignorance would squash me like a beetle. The guards pulled me from my cell and threw me at the feet of my father to await his punishment. I tried again to plead my case, but he silenced me. Even my mother believed I was guilty by that point. My father called me a jackal. He said, 'A jackal you are, a jackal you will always be.' My empty flesh would be thrown to the jackals, but my essence would rest in the image of a jackal forever." Iknokman stopped, looking in the distance for a moment.

"How could they do this?" Ola asked.

Iknokman closed his eyes tight. "I am not sure. It's all a blur. The guards tied me down, the priest chanted. They laid the figure on my chest, the figure you see before you. I remember pleading of my innocence to deaf ears. Then all went black. I have only fleeting memories of enormous hands around me, putting me in a box, the box closed, and then darkness. The box moved, sounds of dirt thrown on top. I was afraid I would lie in darkness for all eternity, so I prayed to the gods for mercy.

The Missing Jackal Murder

"What seemed only moments later, the lid had opened up, and someone lifted me. There was bright sunlight, then eyes stared at me. I couldn't move. I didn't know if it was the magic, or fear. I heard talking, I did not understand such language though. Who were these people? What did they want with me? They seemed like giants. Was this the afterlife?"

"I thought for a moment they were the gods, Osiris, Anubis, and Horus, but they were all human. They sat me on a table among some things I was familiar with, but most I was not. I saw the man again. Other men called him 'Archie'. It was the first word of their language that I learned. I tried to learn more as time passed, but it was rather difficult. Archie would pick me up and stare at me often. I always wanted to say something, but I couldn't. I thought maybe I shouldn't until I found out who the people were and where exactly I was.

"Each time he lifted me, he put me down in a different place. One time, he put me down in front of a reflective surface, like a mirror. I saw the reflections of things in front of me. I remembered the jackal figure placed on my chest. Then was the shocking realization, the magic was successful, I had become the jackal figure. I couldn't move."

"It seemed hours I was alone with Archie. He lifted what looked like a cylinder. I saw him pull out a rolled parchment from that cylinder. He mumbled the words. I could not understand what he was saying to even the smallest degree. What he was saying seemed like our language in a way, but sometimes it sounded rather strange. But that didn't matter at all. It was not how he was reading, but what he was reading."

Ola put her hands to her face. "Why?"

"I'm still not sure. Something came over me like someone understood, someone knew I was innocent. The curse lifted, at least the part of the curse that kept me bound. I looked in the mirror. I could blink and move my eyes. Then I saw the cylinder on the table in front of Archie. It had markings on the side, but I could not make out what it said. He reached for the container. I remained motionless and pretended I was just a piece of wood. After he left for the night, I found I could move. I could stand, walk, and roam around to investigate my surroundings.

"My surroundings were vastly different from my home in Egypt. This Archie had moved me to a foreign land, stripped me of all I had known. He placed me back in the box, back into darkness. I wanted to shout out, but I saw light through the box lid, and I knew he wouldn't bury me again. Instead, I felt the motion of rocking, like a boat. I lifted the lid, and I saw other cases. I found myself at what they call the London Museum, where I was cleaned and set on a pedestal. During the day, people would come and look at me, but I stood still until I understood what was going on. At night when no one was around, I strolled out. I needed to know my surroundings, to know what my purpose served."

"To my shock, I saw many of my people's objects. Their sad condition, like many centuries, had passed. During the day, I listened to conversations, memorized them, and repeated them when everyone had left the building. At night, I found and read anything I could find to learn the phonetic language. I found I could understand and learned the language quickly"

"That's incredible," Arve said.

"You think that's incredible, Arve? Try holding a book and going through the pages with flat feet like these. It seemed like one or two years later, he placed me back in the box again and found myself in what they called the New York Museum. The crude American dialect seemed easier to master. I decided I would try to communicate with these humans after only a short while staying there. After all, I talked only to myself, so I wanted to see if I could hold a conversation."

"How did that work out?" Arve asked.

"I guess they hadn't talked to a live wooden figure before. They ran away hysterically. Why? Did they think I would bite or that I would curse them?"

"I know how you feel," Ola said, "every time a family member becomes engaged, they introduce us to them and well..."

Arve laughed. "Talk about hysterical."

"Most of the time they faint straight away with the shock. But what about now. Do they still act as though you want to hurt them?"

"I'm not sure what the people from London would do or say if I spoke to them. Look what happened. I tried to be friendly in America, but they literally threw me out. I wanted to talk to Archie for some time, but if he rejected me, and after his words had freed me—"

Ola stood and patted Iknokman's front quarters. "Look, when we get back with Cora, we will explain all of this to her. She won't scream and run."

Arve smiled. "In fact, I think she would find you intriguing."

"Intriguing?"

Ola chuckled. "Cora is an adventurous woman and comes from a magical family and knows many things. I don't know what women were like when you were last in Egypt, but here women have the freedom to do whatever they want, at least somewhat."

"I know we have plenty of time to discuss this," Arve interrupted, "but I think we should spend our time figuring out an escape."

Iknokman peeked over his shoulder at the two men. "It would be best to stay close. But I think I may have an idea that-" Iknokman stopped when the door opened, and Jerry walked through.

Jerry reached for Clyde and gave him a shake. "Asleep in the middle of the day? I'll have to put a stop to this."

Arve turned to Iknokman. "I'll leave this all in your capable hands." They watched the two men argue.

Iknokman smiled. "I do believe it's going to be quite easy with these two idiots."

"Ab-so-lute-ly," Arve said.

Ola put her hands on her hips, pressed her lips and shook her head and said, "Ab-so-lute-ly for sure."

Cora inspected the concrete walls that held her and Archie prisoner. Her elbows were on her knees as she sat on the iron bench and her hands cradling her chin.

Archie leaned forward against the bars, one hand up, holding a bar and his head supported by the two jail bars. "My family would find this appalling."

"I suppose I could tell my family that sitting inside an English prison was part of the tour itinerary," Cora said. The outer cell door opened, and two men walked in. Archie and Cora did not move from their pathetic positions.

"Well, well, well, now what do we have here?" a familiar deep voice asked with barely contained mirth.

Cora stood straight. "Like I tried to tell your so-called 'Mr. Swan', and the rest of the buffoons that we were trying to—"

"—play cops and robbers," Inspector Bevan finished her sentence.

"I know, I know. We have listened to too many detective programs on the radio, it seems." She pivoted her head to see Bevan smile smugly. "I'll bet you're getting your amusement for the day."

"Yes, I am," Bevan agreed, then nodded to the police officer next to him. "And I suggest you leave the 'cops and robbers' to us in the future."

"We would if you would do your job and find our cases," Cora said with a smug grin.

"We have enough on our plates without spending our time on your problems, Mr. Thorogood, and yours too, Miss Gudmundson."

Cora got up and Archie detached himself from the bars as the officer opened the cell.

"You running into one of my best men should have been hint enough that I am doing the best I can to find your possessions." Bevan finished as they walked to the lobby.

"Wait," Archie said to Bevan, "you said you had no time for a simple robbery and yet you have your best man on the job... Of course, you've got Mitford, and the museum governors on your back, haven't you?"

Bevan said nothing.

"Oh, I'll bet the governors are pushing you to find the jackal. But Mitford is not doing it for the museum, I'll wager."

Bevan shook his head in dismissal. "I don't have time to listen to your suppositions. As I said, I'm far too busy for this."

Archie grunted in reply.

"Inspector?" Cora said, her eyebrows lowered in deep thought, "why do I have the feeling that all of this has to do with the murder of Mr. Williamson?"

Again, Bevan said nothing, but Cora answered, "Find the jackal and you find the murderer."

"Possibly. Something like that."

Archie stopped. "Are you sure you're not being pressured by Mitford alone?"

"What have you found out so far about the murderer, Inspector?" Cora said, cutting off Archie.

"None of your business, Miss."

"I thought you agreed that if we find the jackal, we find the murderer. Would it not work in reverse?" Cora persisted.

"First, I did not say that. You did. Second, I want you both to stay out of this," he said with his hand raised, as if to show no more interference.

"Could we have at least a hint?" Cora asked while Archie grabbed her elbow and dragged her away from a sputtering Bevan. "What about Mr. Mitford? And what about Miss Tomlinson? They both look suspicious in my eyes."

Bevan said nothing.

Archie escorted Cora out. "I think we both need freshening up and a good night's sleep after today's ordeal." He looked at the late afternoon sky through the window bars. "Looks like they had us in here longer than I thought."

"What do you have in mind? I could go back to my hotel, but it is rather late." She rubbed her hands down her dress. "I do need a change of clothing. I think I've been sweating, especially with all the running and drinking we've been doing today." Cora lifted her arms and then let them drop to her sides. "Plus, I'm exhausted."

"The best place I know where we can both freshen up is my parent's home. I'm sure you could borrow a dress from my sister or mother."

"Oh, perhaps a pair of pants from your brother or your father," Cora said as they left the building and observe the long late day shadows.

"A lady in trousers? Maybe in America, but not here. We'll tell them I got a flat tire and had troubles changing it instead of our dodgy pub and jail debacle."

"What dodgy pub and jail debacle? I thought we were doing an expedition dig." Cora gave him a cheeky smile.

Archie returned her smile and reached for her arm. He placed her hand on his elbow and said, "Cora, you and I should get along quite nicely."

"Do we have to tell them that, too?"

Chapter 10

"Clyde, we are in a pickle, we are," Jerry said as he dashed in, unaware that the door had not closed behind him.

"What the bleedin' hell now?" Clyde asked.

Arve, Ola and Iknokman moved to the corner to listen.

"I heard from one of the dock blokes that someone murdered our contact."

"*Murdered?*" Clyde repeated.

Arve and Ola looked at each other, then at Iknokman, who stared at Jerry with his ears perked.

"That's what he said. Some coppers were all down there to carry his body away. They were takin' photos and everything."

"Who would bump him off?"

"Oh! Hey, did you—"

Clyde put his hand on his chest. "Me? Why would I do anything like that? But then we split. You didn't... did you?" He screwed up his face in fear.

"Hey, don't you put the finger on me. Why would I kill him if he is the one that was meant to pay us?"

"How do I know he didn't already pay you and you're fixed on a way to bump me off?"

"I would have bumped you off by now—while you were sleeping. Listen, we shouldn't squabble. We will end up killing each other and get nothing."

"Yeah, but since he is a goner, how are we going to get paid?"

Jerry paused. "Listen, with the news of the murder hitting the streets, so will the news about our little doggie here. I'm sure his contacts are out and about sniffing and looking for it."

"He's the only one that knew we live here on Fuller Street. How would anyone know where to find us?"

"I will have to go and find the right bloke, you idiot. He will pay us the same as what's his name would have...and this way we don't have to split it with him, and we'll get the full payment. It'll be much more than we would originally have got."

"Hey, yeah," Clyde said.

Jerry motioned to him with his hands. "Sit down and let's figure this out."

They sat at the table and discussed likely places to find a buyer.

Arve and Iknokman listened and strained to figure out a plan of escape. Then Ola interrupted and pointed to the cracked door. Iknokman stepped back under the dresser. Arve and Ola followed. "This is our chance," Arve said.

"But how are we going to contact someone?" Ola asked. "Even if they don't faint, or chase us with a broom, they won't be able to tell anybody about us."

"Then I should be the one to make contact," Iknokman said.

"But we can't contact anyone if we stay here," Arve said, as he tilted his head toward the door.

"Right," Iknokman said, "We have to improvise. We will use what we find."

"Are you sure this is safe?" Ola asked.

Iknokman shook his head. "Probably not, but we're getting nowhere sitting here."

Arve and Ola nodded, and the three quietly scurried to the door.

"What was that?" Clyde asked in a hushed tone and looked around.

Jerry thumped on the table to get Clyde's attention from his gaze near the dresser. "Stop listening to the bloody mice and listen to me for a damn second."

"Alright, Jerry, but I still say this place gives me the creeps."

Arve, Ola, and Iknokman passed through the door and into the hallway. No one stirred between the narrow walls. Arve found the hallway to be just as dingy and dank as Jerry's and Clyde's room. Dirty doors lined both sides of the hallway, with a cracked window down the long end. On the far side, there were no doors, but an open stairway that led down. Jerry's and Clyde's room was the first room on the floor.

They walked with caution towards the next door and listened through the crack at the bottom. A man's and a woman's voices argued about money and the sound bounced against the walls. Across the hallway, the door was also shut. No sound came from that one.

Arve ventured out to the middle of the hallway and searched for an open door. Ola and Iknokman waited.

"What are you doing?" Ola asked. "We don't want to get caught."

He looked back. "If there are no other doors open, this may not work."

Iknokman walked down the center of the hallway, Ola followed.

"I see what you mean, Arve, how are we going to—hold on," Iknokman said, stopped and stared at a door propped open like Jerry and Clyde's door. Iknokman trotted to the door. Arve and Ola followed. They looked in.

The Missing Jackal Murder

An elderly woman sat comfortably in an old easy chair. Her pronounced hooked nose and large ears gave an annoyed profile. In front of her was a radio playing orchestral music.

Iknokman looked back at Arve and Ola. "This is it, but we've got to be careful," He sniffed the air. "I think she may have a cat."

"A cat? Won't that be dangerous for us?" Ola whimpered.

Iknokman shrugged. "Possibly, but this may be our best chance to get help from a human."

"I have an idea," Arve said, and whispered his plans, so the woman or any other creature could not hear.

"Splendid," Iknokman said. Arve and Ola passed through the door and scurried around the corner and under a dresser where the radio sat. When Arve and Ola were safe, Iknokman squeezed through the door and the door creaked. The woman stirred as Iknokman scurried along the same corner to join Arve and Ola.

"Charlie?" the woman said and looked toward Iknokman's path. The woman scanned the room, still unaware her door was open. She looked under the dresser. She grunted, then closed her eyes again and smiled at the soothing sounds of the orchestra.

Arve, Ola and Iknokman quickly dashed behind wide legs that held the dresser. The two climbed the power cord to the radio. When Iknokman attempted to climb, his smooth wooden feet made him slip back to the floor. Arve signaled for Iknokman not to climb but to hang on while they pulled on the power cord to bring him up. This only worked to bring him halfway up when the slack in the cord ran out.

"What are we going to do?" Ola whispered.

Iknokman looked down, then looked up and said, "Get
ready to pull me up, and fast."

Iknokman kicked once, twice, but on the third time the
plug pulled out of the wall socket, the radio fell silent. Arve
and Ola quickly pulled him up.

"What the—" The woman sprang to the edge of her
seat and blinked. Arve and Ola hid behind books stacked
against the radio. Iknokman stepped behind the radio,
cleared his throat and exclaimed, "I do apologize for the
interruption. However, I now have news that I must report
immediately. Earlier today, someone murdered a man who
was a passenger of a ship called the Brandenburg,"
Iknokman repeated the story that Jerry had told Clyde about
the death of their contact. "The constables are on the
lookout for two men who are possible suspects. They are
also responsible for the theft of a valuable Egyptian artifact
from the British Museum. The authorities said they are
hiding out on Fuller Street. These men are dangerous and
must be—what?" Iknokman looked at Ola and Arve for help
as he ran out of things to say.

Ola pointed to Arve, who pointed down. Iknokman
stepped next to Arve, behind the books. An old tabby
looked up at the three, licked its chops and squatted, ready
to leap.

"Well?" The woman stared at the radio. "What about
the two hooligans? I live on Fuller Street."

Iknokman signaled for Arve and Ola to slide down the
cord. As they began, Iknokman growled at the big cat to
draw his attention away from Arve and Ola. But the cat
leaped up without intimidation, scattering the books to the
floor.

"What the bloody hell?" The old woman blinked. Arve
slid down the cord. The cat could not move around the radio

174

as the woman fumbled her hand on the table and lifted her glasses.

Arve and Ola made their way through the door as Iknokman slid to the floor. The cat jumped down, ready to pounce on Iknokman when the woman got her glasses on. She saw Iknokman and the cat square off. The cat lashed out and Iknokman snapped his jowls and missed the cat's paw.

"A rat! You get him, Charlie. Here, I'll help."

Arve stood outside the door, watched the woman grab something and he called out. "Iknokman. Now, run!"

Iknokman made his way past the door into the hallway with the cat on his heels. The three ran back to the room they had started with. They could see Jerry's and Clyde's door still ajar and ran toward it. When they were halfway to the door, the cat caught up and knocked Iknokman down with his paw. The cat slowly approached Iknokman. "Go, get in the room," Iknokman called out.

Arve and Ola dashed forward while looking back. Iknokman snapped. The cat jumped back, and he ran another five feet. The cat snapped again. This dance went on as Arve and Ola got to the open door. Iknokman and the cat were now only a few feet away from one another when they saw the old woman stumble out of her room with a straw broom held over her head.

Iknokman looked up into the old woman's screwed-up face, her silver dollar sized eyes focused on him. He made a last run to the door with the cat and old woman at his heels. Arve and Ola dashed inside and under the dresser as Iknokman made his way into the door, dashed in while the cat pushed the opening wider. One last snip from Iknokman and he made his way under the dresser.

"What the bloody hell!" Jerry said as the cat hissed behind him, followed by the old woman with her weapon in hand. "What the bloody hell?" he repeated.

"My cat chased a rat into your flat," the woman replied.

"Get out, you old berk," Jerry said.

"Oh look," Clyde said, "it's just a nice kitty." Clyde reached and lifted Charlie. His eyes glued towards what was under the dresser.

"What look. Give her the stupid bloody cat back." Jerry said as he pulled the cat away from Clyde and thrust it toward the woman.

"Charlie is not a stupid cat," she said defensively as she cradled the cat in her arms, cooing at it. "Did that nasty rat hurt you, sweet'ems? Are you bleeding?" She spoke to the cat as if it were her child.

"Out!" Jerry yelled.

"Alright, you don't have to shout. Come, my precious little kitty," she said and walked to the door and stopped. "Are you the two men who killed that bloke and stole a museum artifact?" she said, her eyes narrowing on the men.

Arve listened with anticipation.

"What, us?" Jerry said, "We wouldn't hurt a fly."

"You are the two, I know it. You killed that poor man. When I get a hold of Scotland Yard, they'll carry you off."

"Listen, you old coot," Jerry started.

Clyde interrupted. "Scotland Yard was already here, you see."

Jerry, the woman, even the three under the dresser, paused at Clyde's claim.

"What?" Jerry and the old woman said in unison.

"Yeah," Clyde said, "yeah, that's right. Yeah, that must've been—yeah, the scuffle we heard out the window, our window, from the first floor, just a while ago, right Jerry?"

"Oh, oh, oh yeah," Jerry said unconvincingly. "That must be what you mean. So, there were murderers, you say?"

"Good thing they caught them now, isn't it?"

"Downstairs?" The woman glanced towards the window.

Jerry put his hand to his heart and said in a relieved voice, "Thank goodness they're gone. They could have done us all in."

Arve took a step out from under the dresser. "No," Ola said and pulled him back.

Jerry put his hand on the old woman's shoulder, spun her around, and directed her to the door. "See now, all is fine."

"Thank goodness for that," she said.

Jerry closed the door behind her. And smirked. "Thank God for that. Good thing I thought of that story about the two murderers picked up downstairs."

"I thought of it."

"Now, you are thinking about it, too. Are we going to argue over my smart thinking or are we going to get back to our planning?"

"Oh, I suppose. Maybe this time I should go, or maybe both of us. You know I hate being here alone. There's something creepy about this place." Clyde scanned the room again.

"Don't be silly, now sit down and listen."

Arve stalked his way back to the wall.

"Don't get so down, Arve," Iknokman said, "we'll try again."

Ola put her hand on her chest. "Yes, Arve, this time we'll find someone who doesn't have a cat."

Arve put his hand to his chin. "Yes, but next I will have to search more."

"What do you mean?"

Arve walked back to the edge of the dresser and looked hard at Iknokman. "Where Jerry goes, I'll go." Arve concentrated on Jerry's coat.

The cab stopped in front of what Cora thought was possibly the largest house in London. She stepped out but was surprised when Archie dashed around the front and opened the door for her.

"Being gentlemanly, Archie?"

"Yes, opening a door for a lady is the proper thing to do."

Cora left the cab, stunned. "Wow, this house is bigger than the Glensheen Mansion back home. So, does your family work as servants here?" Cora looked up at the front of the gray brick building and tried to count the number of chimneys that protruded from the endless roof, to say nothing about the endless number of widows just on the front of the building alone. They approached. She gazed at the massive ornate front door.

"Hardly," Archie said with a startled expression as he paid the cabby and the taxi drove off.

"Seriously, you needn't lie. I understand that—wait, are you trying to tell me that your family owns this house?" Cora stood with her mouth agape as the truth occurred to her. Archie was from a wealthy family? Why didn't he say so? But then, what would they think of her in her filthy, bedraggled traveling outfit?

"Yes."

The Missing Jackal Murder

"Archie, you should've prepared me for this. I feel so unprepared." Cora closed her eyes for a moment. When she reopened them, she found him watching her.

"I suppose I should have warned you," he replied. "I'm sorry, but it didn't occur to me. You did say you came from a family who owned a logging company."

Cora sighed and took hold of his arm. "Yes, but. Well, yes, my father owns one of the largest homes in Duluth. And yes, most of our friends are wealthy. But this is… you have from here to the front door to fill me in on your family's history, rags to riches and all. I certainly do not want to sound ignorant in front of your family."

"I know you can handle yourself intelligently enough, my dear. And if you do sound ignorant, it's my fault." Archie chuckled. "Right. My father is in precious metals commodities. My mother, to my understanding, brought in the wealth. Father's business skills had multiplied that to what you see here. Obviously, my father does quite well."

"So, I see," Cora said as she gazed up at the tall mansion.

Archie appeared to take his time to climb up the steps to the door to tell his family story. "Both he and my mother attempted to press me into his business. It was quite a disappointment to them that I'm not interested. I ventured into archaeology. My snobbish mother was even more disappointed in my, what she calls, 'waste of good time and energy' or is it 'putting good into bad'? Also, let's not forget my brother Marcus, whom I believe you Americans would call a 'playboy', 'a ladies' man' during the night, and a lay-about during the day. My sister Evelyn is much like my mother, or the way my mother tried to shape her. Evelyn spends most of her time with her fiancé, Roger. She may not be at home at the moment, though I'm not entirely sure. And lastly there is—"

"Master Archibald," the butler said as he opened the door in the middle of Archie's conversation. "I thought I heard your voice. Splendid, you are right on time for dinner."

As the three walked into a large hallway, she first took in the butler's appearance. A tall, distinguish gentleman with a crisp servant's outfit on his tall, medium, beyond middle age frame, yet strong enough to carry his own portly figure. He directed them in. Cora gawked at the long staircase and banister that led up to an open second floor, much like a balcony. Exotic wood carved designs graced the beautiful, stained oak doors.

"Jefferson, this is Miss Gudmundson," Archie introduced her.

Jefferson bowed. "Will the lady be dining with us this evening, sir?"

"Yes, she will. I'm sorry I could not give you time to appropriately prepare for us. Plans do change and all."

"I understand, sir. Your family is currently in the drawing room. They would be most pleased to see you."

Archie sighed. "I doubt it, Jefferson. But I have always admired your optimism."

Jefferson smiled and walked away.

"Archie, we can't greet your parents looking like this," Cora said after catching herself in an ornate framed mirror. "We need to freshen up." She tore off her hat, fumbled through her side pouch—again with there being no Arve and Ola—and found a comb. Despite her efforts, her hair only looked half presentable if she marched into her Duluth house.

"What?" Archie said, his eyes nervously glued to one door.

"We need to freshen up," Cora repeated as she waved a hand toward her bedraggled dress.

"Oh. Right. This way." He led her up the stairway and took a left down a hallway. He stopped, cracked the door, and peeked in as if not to surprise someone. "This is Evelyn's room. There, pull on that rope and her maid, Miss Hobbs, will help you."

She stepped in.

"I'll just change and meet you back here shortly." He closed the door.

"Wait, I just can't walk in and—what do I say to her—this looks—you get in here." She grabbed Archie's wrist, pulled him in, and close the door behind him. "I'll pull the cord and when the maid comes in, you explain—Archie, what's the matter?" He stared at her as if she were naked.

"I shouldn't be in here, alone with you in a bedroom," Archie said with the last word to a whisper.

"We won't be alone when the maid comes in. Jeepers creepers, Archie. I want you here to explain to her. I don't want her to think I'm some stranger from the street and walked in by myself." Cora walked over and yanked on the cord.

With Archie's back pressed against the closed-door, Cora folded her arms. "Jeepers, you think I want us to…" she drifted off as she admired the elegant bed. "This bed is so comfortable."

"Cora!" Archie snapped as she first placed her hand on the daintily bed spread, then sat and bounced on the mattress.

Cora stood. "Oh, Archie, you're so 'all wet.'"

As Archie opened his mouth, there came a knock. He swung the door wide open. "Hurry, get in." The maid entered. Her expression of confusion changed to disdain at Archie then finished with near disgust at Cora. "Don't look at me—at us—like that, there's nothing here, just, this is Miss Gudmundson, Cora Gudmundson and as you can see, she needs tending to. I will adjourn to my room and—Cora, this is Miss Hobbs. Miss Hobbs, perhaps one of Evelyn's nicer dresses for our guest? Yet one she's not particularly fond of. I'll just change and meet you back here shortly." He slipped through and closed the door behind him.

Without a word, Miss Hobbs opened a closet and pulled out a modest blue dress and placed it on the bed and stood before her. Cora understood that meant for her to disrobe, she did. She put the pouch on the bed. Miss Hobbs inspected her undergarment. "I believe these are fine," Cora said.

Hobbs first gave her a disgusted look, then move to a dresser, pulled out a drawer and removed white ladies' undergarment, then approached her. Cora sighed, stripped down naked, and kick them next to her dirty dress.

As Hobbs bent down to put on the panties, like a mother helping her two-year-old put on an underwear, Cora snatched the panties out of her hand. "Oh, for heaven's sakes, give me those." She stepped in and pulled them on. Before Hobbs could reach for the bra, Cora snapped, "I can put them on myself." As Cora had problems reaching back to snap the ends, Hobbs sprang forward and finished the job. She found it improper to mention that Evelyn did not fill the bra that was uncomfortably snug on Cora; but at least she could still breathe.

After Cora slipped on the blue dress, with Hobbs' help, the maid directed her to sit in front of a mirrored desk and worked on her hair. After a few swipes with a brush and application of hair products, there was a knock.

"Cora?" Archie's light voice seeped through the closed door. She approached and swung the door wide open. "Better?"

Archie gasped, what Cora thought he expected her to be naked. He recovered. "Are you finding everything to your satisfaction, Cora?"

"Yes. Thank you. Miss Hobbs was very helpful."

"Splendid."

"And you look splendid as well."

"I shall bring this to the laundress," Miss Hobbs said, finding her voice for the first time. With her clothes in one arm, she lifted the pouch by the handle and gave an expression like she picked up a dead cat.

"I'll take that." Cora snatched her pouch out of her hand. She gave another look inside, then swung the handle over her shoulder.

She felt refreshed, but she needed to stretch and rotate her shoulders with the slight discomfort of wearing a smaller brazier. Archie escorted her back downstairs. "Now, I must warn you, please do not allow them to offend you by what they say. You will see they are one of the reasons I decided not to go into the family business." Archie led Cora to an open doorway.

Upon reaching the door, she admired the intricate woodcarvings of cupids and other mythical creatures that adorned the hallways. Two nude statues, also carved in wood, stood at the base of the stairway. Her mesmerized stare led her to reach up to touch the craftsmanship and spoke to herself. "This magnificent woodwork in your home would impress Nils."

"Who's Nils?" Archie asked.

"Oh, he's, he's—an uncle." Cora walked to the table near the front door and put her pouch down. Archie pass through the doorway and followed. She found three sets of eyes staring at her as if they wondered what the cat had dragged in.

Cora straightened her spine, adjusted her shoulder again, took a deep calming breath and placed her hands behind her back to wait for introductions. She thought of home and her mother's insistence on granting courtesy to all, no matter how they treated her. The three people stood.

"Archibald," his mother said, "I thought you were going to wire us upon your arrival in London."

"I'm sorry, mother, I became distracted."

Archie's mother looked at Cora as if she was a poor distraction for him.

"Mother, father, Marcus, may I present Miss Cora Gudmundson from Minnesota, an area in the United States of America. Miss Gudmundson, this is my father, Mr. Robert Thorogood."

Cora walked to the center of the room, reached out her hand to clasp Archie's father's hand. He took it briefly and gave a slight courtesy smile by pressing his lips together and raised his cheeks.

"And this is my mother, Mrs. Gwendolyn Thorogood."

When Cora extended her hand, Archie's mother looked at it as if she was presenting the tail end of a dead walleye. She slightly touched Cora's hand and gave a halfhearted courtesy smile.

"And this is my brother, Marcus."

Marcus slightly resembled Archie. However, he appeared to be a man who was thoroughly comfortable with his family's wealth. Dressed in the latest fashion, he wore a smug smile, ready for the joke, to give one or to receive one.

Marcus seemed pleased to meet her. He gave Archie a devilish smile. "My, my, Archie brought home a girl. Now that is peculiar."

Archie frowned at his brother.

"I am so glad to meet you all," Cora said, only to see no change in their expressions, except for Marcus, who looked between her and Archie as if this was a joke.

Gwendolyn's face gave the impression that Cora didn't live up to her standards for her son. "Where did you meet this person?"

Cora was not sure if that was her way of pointing someone out or her way of snubbing.

"Her name is Cora; Cora Gudmundson, Mother."

Cora decided she would be both direct and to have a spot of fun with the conversation. Archie's mother's comment proved she was a snob, but Cora decided she would not allow Archie's mother to bully her. "Oh Archie, I'm not offended. I understand that your mother wants to make sure that you associate with the right sort of people."

Marcus gave a quiet snort, and Archie's father smiled slightly. His mother showed no amusement. Her narrowed eyes watched Cora like a hawk ready to pounce on her prey.

Archie touched Cora's hand as if in warning her to be careful.

Jefferson entered the doorway. "Dinner is served."

"I have invited Cora to dinner, that is all." No one gave a negative response.

As they walked to the dinner table, Cora pressed her lips and raised her cheeks to mirror his father's smile back at Archie. Archie could not suppress his grin. They sat down and the room grew silent.

Cora found the lack of conversation gave her the opportunity to scan the dining room, which was well lit by crystal chandeliers. The drapes were closed. Two large gold-framed mirrors on either side of an enormous fireplace reflected the light from the chandelier in the room.

It was Archie's mother who spoke first. "That is correct. Archie, you seem to be a wayward child who is apt to bring home, shall we say, undesirable ladies, those who may not measure up to our standards."

"Mother!"

"Oh, I see what you mean," Cora answered immediately and studied Archie's mother at one end of the table, seated in a brocade covered chair. "Once I brought home a stray dog. I begged and begged, but mother said no. Of course it was impractical to have a dog around in the house because a dog would–" Cora stopped. She had nearly mentioned the Village. Though the magic protected the Villagers, it would have prevented her from doing so to anyone deemed unsafe. Archie's family fit that description. "Well, you know how dogs are? They get into everything. And, of course, as you know, they shed."

Marcus laughed and leaned towards his mother. "I hope you were not suggesting anyone you know would shed, were you, Mother?"

The room fell silent.

Cora opened her mouth to elaborate when Jefferson brought in the soup tray.

"Ah, finally," Archie said.

"I know, I'm starved too," Cora said.

Again, a quiet snort came from Marcus and his father slightly smiled. The soup was served.

Robert touched his soup bowl. "These may not be dishes you are accustomed to back in the states. Which state did you say you were from again?"

The Missing Jackal Murder

Cora scanned toward the other end of the table where Robert sat. "I'm from Minnesota, northern Minnesota. A town called Duluth, named after a French explorer who ventured to the area. Duluth rests on the North Shore of Lake Superior and–" Cora stopped. "I seem to quote from either the *National Geographic* or some other local historical document. But Duluth is much more than that." She looked down at the soup that Jefferson had presented. "Oh my, this looks wonderful," Cora said to Jefferson. "It smells good too. You must thank the cook for her wonderful efforts."

This time, Marcus's snort was the loudest. Even Jefferson looked surprised.

Again, Archie reached for Cora's hand.

Cora ignored and continue. "In Duluth, and in also most of the United States, we are very grateful for those who feed us, those who take care of us. Preparing food such as this bounty takes great care. If it is not impertinent of me," she smiled at Jefferson, "please tell the cook thank you and her work is much appreciated."

"Here, here," Marcus said and reached for his glass, "give a jolly splendid show from me as well, Jefferson."

"Here, here," both father and Archie said and raised a glass. Cora suspected they were making fun of her, and the glare from his mother was not reassuring.

"I take it you have no butler," Marcus said.

Robert frowned at Marcus.

Archie groaned.

Gwendolyn's face remained stony.

Cora continued, as if this was a perfectly natural conversation. "No, we don't, never needed one. I must admit we are not as well off as you are," Cora admitted freely. "But we live comfortably in a large house. My father owns a large lumber company. As you can imagine, there is

187

proverbially an ocean of trees in northern Minnesota, and in the surrounding Wisconsin and Canada." Cora stopped to sip the soup. "Oh my, this is good. It reminds me of when I laid in bed sick as a child and my mother would bring me soup. Sometimes I would pretend to be sick just to enjoy the attention."

Robert's head snapped up to Cora and interrupted, "Your father owns a lumber company, you say?"

"Oh yes. My father has often taken me along on his sales and lumber trips."

Gwendolyn sneered at Cora. "Surely it was inappropriate for him to bring his daughter to visit lumber mills where unsavory men were laboring."

"I suppose so," Cora said, ignoring Archie's mother's implied criticism of how Cora's family raised her. "But I had no problems with the men, as far as them acting out inappropriately towards me. In time, I became part of the company and the lumberjacks accepted me and took my presence in stride."

"I suppose when you were a child, but as an adult woman, your presence would be unseemly," Gwendolyn said.

"Mother!" Archie interrupted.

"Oh, I understand. My mother felt uncomfortable about our recent trips as well. And yes, things could have happened, but I formed a trust with the people I met after years of traveling to see them." Cora scanned the room. She changed the conversation in mid-sentence. "I also enjoyed working alongside my brother Eric, who owns the first automobile dealership in Duluth. Then there is my brother Elmer. He owns one of the first and largest refrigeration companies in the surrounding area back home. I believe my family has a head for success in business."

The Missing Jackal Murder

Marcus grinned. "I suppose you plan to start up a business of your own, say, in washing machines and cleaning supplies."

"Oh heavens no, I don't want to be tied down. I am afraid the adventure bug has got a hold of me. I plan to travel and see the world."

Gwendolyn gasped. "But suppose when you travel by yourself, you may run into unscrupulous men, especially without an escort."

Cora swallowed another spoonful of soup. "My father taught me how to defend myself, which is why I could give a good chase when those two thugs stole our cases today."

"What?" the three said in unison and stared at Archie.

"No, Mother, Father it…"

"Oh my. I'm sorry, Archie, I didn't mean to let that out."

"It's alright, I was about to get into that."

Robert straightened his shoulders. "How much did they take?"

"Oh no," Marcus said. "You didn't lose any of your precious artifacts now, did you?"

Archie explained the theft and the murder to appalled reactions from his family. "I want to keep the theft and the murder as quiet as possible, at least for now. Scotland Yard decided not to let out any information to the public as yet."

"I don't understand," Marcus said to Cora. "Why did you give chase and risk danger for a suitcase of clothing and toiletries? I'm sure as shop here in London could replace those items. Archie can loan you the money if you need it."

"Marcus," Archie interrupted as soup bowls lifted and become replaced with plates of roast beef, potatoes, and vegetables.

"Thank you again, Mr. Jefferson." Cora turned to Archie. "I'm not bothered by your brother's remarks. The case is important to me, rather its contents."

Archie smiled. "Yes, tell them about - Arve and Ola."

Marcus straightened his shoulders. "Who are Arve and Ola?"

"They are two wood carved characters passed down from generation to generation that I was carrying in my case as reminders of home. Though they are inanimate objects, they are special to me." Cora paused and felt another moment of panic at the loss of Arve and Ola. But she knew they would reach her. "I know it's hard for you to understand. I know you think I'm like a little girl who lost her teddy bear. But it isn't like that. I miss them and I will do what it takes to find them."

"No doubt Archie told you about our family business," Robert said.

"Archie mentioned a metals commodity business."

Archie's father delivered a nonstop recitation about his business as Cora carefully cut a piece of roast beef and maintained the proper table etiquette her mother had worked hard to teach her. She found plenty of time to finish her meal and pay attention. As what she assumed the conclusion of his recitation of his business, Cora gave advice. "How would iron fit in your business?"

"Iron?" Robert said in confusion.

"Yes, just north of Duluth is the Masabi iron range that produces most of the world's iron consumption."

"Indeed," Robert said. "I should look further into that." Robert smiled and continued, "Archie has a good head for business but prefers to dig up old bones for a dusty museum. Perhaps, as a lady of business, you can persuade Archie to reconsider and join the family business."

The Missing Jackal Murder

Archie sighed. "Father, I am happy where I am. There are so many stories these so-called old bones can tell us; where they were, where they are, and give us a sense of where we are going."

Archie's father winked at Cora and pointed his thumb as if he found it all amusing and thought Cora would agree.

"I'm afraid I will have to disappoint you, Mr. Thorogood."

Gwendolyn made a disapproving grunt.

Cora continued, "I agree with what Archie is doing and why. History is important to keep and preserve. Yes, business is important, to keep us in warm houses and put food on the table. But at the end of each day, its history as well as family that matters the most." The work of the Villagers, as well as Nicholas' flight make people happy, came to Cora's mind. She paused as Jefferson lifted her empty plate. "Again, Mr. Jefferson, you and the kitchen staff outdid yourselves with an excellent meal."

"Here, here," again, Cora was not sure the men's toast was sincere or to mock her for her praise of their staff. Again, Archie's mother sat stony and remained silent.

"Perhaps we should adjourn to the drawing room to discuss both Archie's noble quest for unearthing antiquities, as well as for us to excavate our splendid dessert," Marcus said.

Gwendolyn excused herself. "I am afraid I have another one of my dizzy spells and I must lie down."

Cora stretched her back and rotated her shoulders again. "Oh, does this happen often?"

"Yes," Marcus said sarcastically, "just about every time other people come to visit."

"Now Marcus, that is not so," Gwendolyn said.

R. M. Scott

"I remember one time my brother Nils felt a bit faint after simply too much of Mr. McGregor's homebrewed maple syrup. We had to—"

Gwendolyn waved a hand. "I will do as my doctor has ordered and lie down for some time. Thank you. I have no interest in such hillbilly voodoo."

Archie grabbed Cora's elbow and led her out. "Please don't mind rude remarks from my mother while she is having one of her spells."

"Not at all, Archie. I find it amusing that she would use the term 'hillbilly,' which does not refer to the northern states and the term 'voodoo' which comes from somewhere near New Orleans." Cora stopped and looked up the stairs, startled to make eye contact with a wispy old woman in her bed clothes on the balcony. The woman's stare locked with Cora's. Archie's mother reached the top of the stairs, saw the woman, and gave an annoying sigh.

"Come now, Mother Elizabeth."

Archie sighed. "That's Grandmother Elizabeth. She is no longer quite right in her mind." Archie looked up at his grandmother and sighed again.

"Come now." Gwendolyn yanked Grandmother Elizabeth sharply from the banister to pull her into a walk. The old woman's eyes again fixated on Cora. There was nothing frightening in grandmother's expression. Her eyes glistened as if she and Cora were best of friends. When grandmother disappeared around the corner, she saw Archie had remained in the hallway.

"Nana, rather Grandmother Elizabeth, well, she means no harm."

"You were rather fond of her, weren't you, Archie?"

"Were? I still am. She was the only ray of light in this dreary household."

The Missing Jackal Murder

Marcus cleared his throat. "Have you forgotten us already?" He stood in the doorway of the drawing room.

"Oh, sorry, brother." They entered the room.

Jefferson had brought in dessert and coffee to serve them.

"Still splendid," Marcus said after finishing his dessert.

"And shall I inform the kitchen staff of your delightful encounter with this delightful dessert, Miss?" Jefferson said as he gathered the plates.

"Ab-so-lute-ly," Cora said, not sure if he was being sarcastic or sincere. When Cora watched Jefferson carry the plates away, she saw him turn, smile, and wink at her.

Marcus filled a glass with brandy and offered one to Cora, who declined.

"So, who do you think murdered this Williamson chap?" Marcus asked.

Archie gagged on his sip of coffee as Robert spoke sharply. "Marcus, really, that's hardly proper conversation with a visitor here and all."

Cora's eyes brightened. "Oh, that's alright. As a matter of fact, Archie and I discussed the possibilities all day."

Marcus gave a satisfying smile. "Did you then? Do tell us your thoughts."

Cora put her coffee down and looked at Archie. His expression did not alter. "Hmm, according to the detective programs on the radio and the novels, there are three possible motives for murder. If we do research, one of these could locate the murderer."

"Oh," Robert said, "and what might they be?"

"Well, number one is 'jealousy', you know, another man or woman or person in the way of romance. Number two is, of course, money to take from the victim or kill anyone who stands in their way of money."

"That pretty much covers all," Marcus said. "What could be the third?"

"If the victim was an out-and-out despicable scoundrel and, through his wicked deeds, people would want to do him in."

Marcus was looking at Archie, making a face.

"Why are you looking at me like that?" Archie asked.

"Oh, dear brother, I certainly am not accusing you of—doing him in. I'm merely suggesting that you knew Williamson better than anyone else in this room."

"That's true," Cora replied as she also looked at Archie. "Archie, did anyone have cause to kill Williamson out of anger or spite? True, the first two possibilities are more probable, but I have no information to form an opinion on the third possibility."

"I only knew Williamson for a short time. The museum assigned us to make the voyage to New York and bring back the Egyptian artifacts. All he talked about was his desire to go on digs and become famous like Howard Carter."

"Howard who?" Marcus asked.

"He was the one who discovered the tomb of King Tutankhamen four years ago. As for Williamson, he unceasingly recited every detail of his precious Eve. Their engagement and their honeymoon became annoying. Frankly, listening to his constant drone made me want, to—but I didn't, so don't look at me that way, brother. The only time I saw Williamson argue with someone was at the New York Museum when he called the curator a fool for believing his superstitious staff."

"What did his staff say?" Marcus asked.

Archie laughed. "They thought the Jackal of Iknokman was alive. Can you imagine a wooden figure coming to life?"

This time Cora sputtered on her sip of coffee. *"If only he knew,"* she thought, *"about an entire village of woodcarvings coming to life in her attic."* She smiled. "I remember I heard them arguing. But did their discussion become heated?"

"No, Williamson laughed at him. The curator was quite angry."

Marcus sat back. "Ahh, the curator could be a suspect."

Archie shook his head. "I really don't believe he traveled the ocean to kill Williamson. I believe he was happy to see the back of us with the jackal in hand. And don't forget we saw Williamson quarreling with the telegraph operator on the Brandenburg. At least he was definitively on board when Williamson was murdered."

"He could be a suspect. The next time we see Inspector Bevan, we should mention that."

As Marcus opened his mouth, they heard the front door open, and a woman entered the drawing room.

He lifted his glass to the woman. "Ah, dear sister, just in time to help us solve a murder case."

Archie quickly introduced his sister, Evelyn.

Evelyn's appearance surprised Cora. Her attire was modern. Unlike her mother's conservative subtle makeup, Evelyn sported a short, straight, pitch-black hair cut into a bob with her bangs curled forward. Her makeup was bold with shockingly red lipstick. Cora wondered if there was such a thing is a rich, snobbish flapper. Cora's eyes shot to her bosoms, then rotated her shoulders from the discomfort. Despite her modern appearance, it took only moments for Cora to realize Evelyn was a miniature version of her snobbish mother.

Evelyn made eye contact with Cora as she looked her up and down, then crinkled her nose as if she smelled something foul.

Cora and Archie returned to their seats. "Please join us," Archie said to Evelyn.

"Not now, I'm exhausted. I will turn in and see you in the morning."

"Wait," Marcus asked. "Aren't you curious about the three causes for murder? Such discussions are right up your alley."

Evelyn's eyebrows raised, and she paused.

"To the point. The first cause is jealousy, the other a woman, or dare I say—for sex."

Evelyn rolled her eyes at her brother's usually inappropriate behavior.

"Wait, let us consider for a moment, if you caught Roger having an affair with another woman, would you murder him?"

Evelyn looked at Marcus with a stunned expression.

Robert shook his head. "You know Evelyn would kill no one."

"Oh, you think she would not? Alright, maybe that's not her personality. But another woman who was engaged to a man and caught him with another woman would at least consider killing him. Right?"

Evelyn sighed. "You are correct, dear brother. If I ever found my fiancé with another woman, I would think of many ways to, shall we say, make things very unpleasant for him, to which murder would be unnecessary." Evelyn moved toward the door. "Now, if you are through with your ridiculous rants, I am off. It was nice to meet you." Evelyn finished, nodding her head to Cora as she walked out.

Again, Marcus raised his glass. "Now there you have it. A jealous woman would kill her fiancé. Now, do we know if another woman dilly dallied with this Williamson chap?"

The Missing Jackal Murder

Archie looked at Cora. "He did spend a lot of time talking with Willie during the voyage and she did mention they kissed."

Cora lurched forward. "What? You surely don't suspect my friend Willie."

Marcus' eyes bounced between Archie and Cora. "Willie? Who's Willie?"

"A woman from Cora's tour group who spent time with Williamson during our voyage."

She eyed him with raised eyebrows.

"Cora, you needn't look at me like that. After all, you haven't known Willie for long."

"Ah, another love interest," Marcus said and put his glass small round table next to him.

She gazed at Marcus, opened her mouth, and just shook her head. "I know Willie would not do this. She was merely being polite to Williamson. She is in the middle of getting a divorce."

"A married woman? Now, if that isn't a prime suspect, I don't know what is," Marcus said with the shake of his head.

"Willie did not kill Williamson," Cora repeated. "She could not hurt a fly, let alone commit murder. If she was capable of such a thing, she would have gotten rid of her husband years ago. Trust me, I've met him."

Marcus rubbed his chin. "Perhaps she killed Williamson for practice. Her husband will be next."

Cora shook her head. "It is true I do not know her completely, but I can't see her doing such a thing from the short time I've known her." She lifted her hand to her lips and considered Marcus' suggestion. "Roy did go to great lengths to find Willie in Chicago. True, the police arrested Roy, but how do we know Roy is still there? We don't."

R. M. Scott

"You have obviously read too many detective stories yourself, dear brother," Archie said.

"Just trying to help."

"Now that we are on the subject, it is confession time." Archie set down his coffee and brought his fingers together on his chest.

"Oh, what naughty things have you done this time?" Marcus asked.

Archie regaled to his father and brother with the story of their misadventures in the dodgy pub and how they discussed the jackal with an undercover police officer which landed them in jail.

Robert gave Archie a disgusted look. "You are lucky the inspector only ridiculed you and did not keep you locked up. Why would you do such a stupid thing?"

"I'm afraid it was my idea, Mr. Thorogood."

"In that case," Marcus quickly replied, "I think it was a grand idea." He winked at Cora.

"You would," Robert said.

Marcus lifted a hand. "I am not joking. I admire their spunk for being out and about, searching for those shifty blokes, like in those detective programs on the radio."

"Yes, Bevan did say something like that," Cora said.

"No, I mean you're out and about in the human world instead of in the dirt, digging up bones, or worse, sitting home, in a dusty house. That reminds me, I'm off." Marcus put down his drink.

"Where to this time?" Robert asked sarcastically.

"With friends."

Archie dropped his head back in disgust. "Questionable lady friends as usual I presume."

The Missing Jackal Murder

"Archibald!" Marcus folded his arms and narrowed his eyes and turned to Cora. "I am a ladies' man and a lay about as Archie has described me, no doubt."

"Well, he didn't say that exactly."

Marcus laughed. "Oh, I suppose in a way I am." He got up, bowed to Cora and said, "A pleasure. I do hope you pop in now and again. You are perhaps the brightest star that ever graced our doorstep." He reached for her hand, lifted it to his lips and kissed it, winked, and walked out.

"I suppose I better get back to my tour group at the hotel," Cora said after he left.

"Nonsense," Robert said. "We have plenty of room here in this dusty house."

"I must return if you please. I suspect Willie must be worried about my whereabouts."

They stood. Robert found the butler's cord and pulled. "I do need to agree with my wayward son, Miss Cora. You certainly are a ray of sunshine and are most welcome to visit again."

She reached for Robert's hand. "Thank you. And then I'll tell you more about my father's business in wood commodities, with a few antics from the lumberjacks, of course."

Robert smiled as Jefferson arrived. "Miss Cora is leaving us now. Will you inform Mr. Hilliard to bring the car around front?"

Jefferson nodded and left.

"And Archie will accompany you," Robert said to Cora, "to make sure you arrive safely."

She thanked him as the three made their way into the hallway towards the door.

Archie looked over his shoulder at the place where the old woman had stood. "I hope Grandmother Elizabeth didn't startle you into leaving."

"Oh no, that's not it at all. Willie will be worried if I don't return, especially when I ran off like that. I'm sure I'll be up late tonight telling her all about our day's adventures."

"Of course," Archie said.

Robert walked with them to the door. Cora rotated her shoulders again and picked up her pouch, smiled and said good night, and allowed Archie to lead her to the car, her right hand on his left elbow. "Archie, your grandmother was not creepy, just—interesting. And I do look forward to seeing her again."

Chapter 11

Streetlights shone through the car windows illuminated Archie's quiet face as they drove on the rumbling cobblestone road. Cora leaned back with her pouch on her lap. She glanced inside again. No Arve, Ola, or Nicholas. *Am I being selfish by not asking for Nicholas to help? Am I leaving Arve and Ola out on their own so I can save face, so I can prove myself to be independent?*

"I hope nothing else fell from your pouch," Archie said as he glanced in her direction when she opened her pouch to look inside a second time. "Rather, if you've forgotten anything, we–I–could go back and retrieve it."

Cora smiled. "No thank you, it is alright. I have my trunk at the hotel." She tried to shift her shoulders slightly and not cause any concern for Archie. She changed the subject. "Meeting your family was a very interesting end to a very interesting day." His long-fingered hands tapped his knee as if trying to find something to say. *Perhaps now eager to finally get rid of her.* It had been a long day, not for her, possibly for him. She sighed.

"I do apologize for my family. They can be eccentric, at best."

She snapped her head at Archie. "Jeepers creepers, I enjoyed spending time with your family, you should meet mine."

"I would like to," he answered quickly, then cleared his throat. "I mean, they can't be half as bad as mine."

"My family is alright, and they would welcome you. You might find some of them to be a bit surprising," Cora said as the Villagers came to mind. *True, the villagers would love*

Archie, ab-so-lute-ly. Her mind filled with family stories of outsiders who plan to marry into their magical family, but her brother-in-law, Han's reaction when Anna introduced the Villagers to her fiancé—He fainted. That's why a vile of smelling salts rests on a front room table.

"This certainly can't have been what you expected for your first day in England and the start of your grand holiday. I'm sure things will get better once you have rejoined your tour group."

Cora felt a heaviness in her stomach. Did he want to get rid of her? "This day has been much more than I ever expected and not at all disappointing. A theft, a murder, an arrest and meeting your family may not have been on the itinerary, but adventurous, nevertheless. There aren't many adventures available back home, certainly not of this manner. Again, I'm glad I met you." Cora sighed. "You have traveled throughout Europe and the Middle East. You have seen things I have only read about. So, you see, this day has been eye opening for me. However, I'm afraid I forced you to get involved in something you would have preferred not to."

Archie was quiet for several moments. "My life is probably not as exciting as you imagine. Archeology is not all about finding grand objects."

"So, what is it about, and why be an archaeologist?"

Archie chuckled. "I do enjoy the endless questions relating to the unknown. How did an ancient community survive? What did they make? What did they eat? How did they live? Why did they...? When did they...? Who were they...? To answer these questions would be by exploring through layers of earth and debris, bits and pieces, evidence of habitation, bones, human and otherwise. I've processed my finds for days and days, scrubbing away with a toothbrush until my hands are numb from the cold water."

Archie laughed. "I've been bitten and stung by insects. I've sun burnt the back of my neck so badly I could hardly bear to move my head for a week. I've slept for weeks in an old, musty, leaky canvas tent. I've slept in a cave when the sandstorms were directly above us. My life isn't as exciting as you imagine."

Cora shook her head. "It may not sound exciting when you explain it like that, but I still think what you do is fascinating. Perhaps this day has been a grand adventure for both of us, after all."

Archie put his fingers on his chin. "It wasn't what we expected, but I think we made progress today. You may not think so after our time in jail, but I believe it was a good idea to case out shoddy bars."

"How so?"

"If the two learned of Brandon's murder, they need to unload the Jackal of Prince Iknokman and look for another buyer."

Cora creased her eyebrows. "What if they went to the museum and delivered it to Mitford?"

"I don't think those two would know who Brandon worked for, curator Mitford, for example. Those key people certainly would not want to be involved with those screwy characters at the dock." Archie stopped talking and gasped.

"What's wrong?"

"I've just remembered seeing Brandon talking with some shady characters one day before we left for America. I didn't ask him about them, as I thought it was his business. Funny not remembering that earlier."

"What did they look like?"

"I didn't have an unrestricted view, but I believe I saw the gentleman who looked fairly well-dressed and clean-shaven. I wonder if I should have told this to Detective Bevan."

"You did tell Brandon you planned to take the Jackal of the Prince Iknokman in a case. Then those thugs stolen our cases that tell me he did contact those two characters while on the ship to arrange the theft."

"A heist in haste," Archie said with a grin, then continued. "No, Brandon must have hired those thieves, not Mitford. Associating with shady characters would be beneath Mitford. Besides, they would see what a pompous fellow he is and turn on him in a flash; blackmail and all. I think we should continue looking in dodgy places tomorrow. That's if you are still interested in continuing the search, with me." He cleared his throat and swallowed.

Cora caught Archie's hesitation and felt a small thrill of pleasure knowing he wanted to see her again tomorrow. "I am."

"Excellent." He grinned again. "I'm glad I didn't scare you away with that long monologue about archeology. I'm not usually so long-winded. It's rare to meet a kindred spirit who is even remotely interested in hearing about the actual whys and wherefores of my profession. The likelihood of excavating something truly astonishing is actually quite rare."

"You haven't scared me away. I am flattered that you shared your feelings with me," she said, then glanced out the window at passing buildings to avoid saying more. She feared her feelings for Archie were becoming more intense than she wanted. After all, she had no interest in any forms of infatuation at this point in her life. "Oh Archie, I would like to stop at a telegraph office, the one we just passed, to let my family know I'm alright if you'd please."

"Wasn't this afternoon's message good enough for the rest of the trip?"

"It's because, well, it's my mother's request. I mean, in order for me to go on this trip I need to keep in constant contact," Cora lied.

Archie lifted an eyebrow but had Mr. Hilliard drive back to the telegraph office.

Cora's thoughts were churning as she ran into the telegraph office. Should she get Nicholas involved? Archie believed they had made progress. Was it true? Or was he saying that just to be with me? *"I do like being with him. In fact, I do like being with him, and how—wait—concentrate. One more day,"* she thought. *"If I am not any closer to finding Arve and Ola, I'll contact Nicholas. I will have to come up with an explanation to mother in a way that will not destroy her trust."* She returned to the car and thanked him for stopping.

Archie instructed the driver to move on. "Everything's alright?"

"Just thinking of the family back home." Though she thought of Arve and Ola, Nicholas entered her mind. She grappled with the realization it may soon be time to call on Nicholas. She took a deep breath and removed him from her mind. As she settled back into her seat and desired to resume their conversation, she turned to him. "Do you believe in magic?" The words came out without thinking.

"Do I believe in magic?" He raised his eyebrows as if startled.

Cora was not sure to retract her question but waited for his response.

He frowned. "What kind of magic? Do you mean a wand and hocus-pocus? Not at all. That is all a bunch of smoke and mirrors."

She paused, then became intrigued by his response. "What kind of magic could you believe in?"

His eyes shift in confusion, then spoke slowly. "I'm not sure."

"You've been around. I'm sure you've seen magic with your findings and your research."

Archie merely grunted.

Cora continued, "What about Egypt with their beliefs and priests and all?"

"Now that you've mentioned it, there are words written about the Jackal of Prince Iknokman, ridiculous of course."

"What about the Jackal of the Prince of Iknokman?"

"According to some of those ancient texts I found, magic was, allegedly, performed on him." The driver stopped the car in front of Cora's hotel. "But I didn't see any evidence that..."

"What?"

Archie shook his head and used the stop to change the conversation. "Same place, same time?"

"What?" Cora noticed they had stopped in front of a hotel. "Oh yes, ab-so-lute-ly."

Archie jumped back in. "I know why you changed the subject to a discussion about magic. You're worried about your case. You're worried about Arve and Ola."

Cora stared at Archie with an open mouth.

"Well, to answer your question, I do remember when I was young. I may have seen some things that were unexplainable. But I was a child then and believed in anything. Now I'm an adult and I don't believe in magic, hocus-pocus or otherwise."

"Oh," Cora said and rearranged her face as if the conversation meant nothing. But in doing so, something warm flushed through her body as she looked into his eyes. He stared back with no apparent intent of breaking the connection. Cora took a deep breath and leaned forward to kiss Archie on the cheek. She pulled back. "Thank you for all that you have done for me. I'll meet you tomorrow morning, right here."

Archie inhaled sharply and stared back at her.

As Cora turned, the door opened automatically as she found Mr. Hilliard there with the outer door handle in his hand.

"Shall I walk you to the door?" Archie said.

"There's no need for you to do so. Goodnight." She left the car. "Goodnight, Mr. Hilliard." The man gave her a warm smile and tipped his hat. The walk to the hotel felt endless. She felt Archie's eyes on her back. She heard a sound of the car departing and watched it drive away from the reflection of the hotel door glass.

She looked up at the round cornered four story gray marble building in front of her. Above the front door a sign read 'Copper Street Inn', then opened the door, and walked inside. A cloud of discomfort hung over her, for the first time in a strange place. She hoped this was the right hotel. The thought of abandonment in a strange country made her heart skip a beat. She closed her eyes and took a deep breath. 'Forward', she told herself.

Cora walked towards the worn red marble stairs but stopped when she realized she didn't know which room she was to stay in and walked to the reservation desk. The clerk gave her a stern look down his nose as if she were disturbing him. After her recent encounter with Archie's formidable mother, his patronizing look didn't bother her one bit. Besides, it was his job to help patrons of the hotel. "I'm sorry, I stepped out for a breath of fresh air," Cora lied. "I don't remember my room number. I'm with the tour group from America."

"That is highly irregular," he said.

"My name is Cora Gudmundson. I have a room with Wilhelmina–" A moment of panic ran up and down her spine, "I don't remember her last name." All this time I have been defending her and I don't remember her last name. Maybe I don't know Willie is much as I thought. She chose not to listen to the clerk's stern lecture that ended with, "You're in room twenty-four, second floor. Don't forget nosh is at 6:30 AM tomorrow morning."

"Thank you." Cora gave another rotation of her shoulder at the enjoyingly constricting brazier and walked up the stairs. I've forgotten Willie's last name, but I just know she did not kill Brandon. She does not have the killer instinct, but then she did find the courage to leave her husband. No, I won't believe that she could—oh, Benson, that's her last name, Benson. Cora knocked on the door.

The door flew open. Willie, in her nightgown, grabbed her arm and pulled her inside before she knew what was happening. "Where the hell were you?"

"I believe the statement here in England should be, 'Where the *bloody* hell were you'?" Cora replied with a barely suppressed grin.

Willie stood with arms folded. "That's not funny. Do you know how worried I was? And sick about you. The last time I saw you, you were chasing a dangerous man and disappeared."

"Willie, I'm alright."

Willie stood motionless.

"I'm sorry. There was no way I could contact you. Did you cover for me? You didn't tell the tour guide about my absents, did you?"

Willie paced the floor. "Maybe I should have. What if you were dead in the streets because I said nothing? I worried about you all day. There are a few times I was ready to tap on the tour guide's shoulder to tell him they lost you. And thinking about you alone in the city! Oh!"

"I was with Archie. I was alright."

"How was I to know?"

Cora thought the way to calm her was to tell her about the day's event except for Brandon's murder. They sat on Cora's bed. She spoke with occasional interruptions and outbursts from Willie. "Bars with dangerous people?" "At Scotland Yard, behind what?" But Willie's breathing calmed down when Cora spoke of dinner at the Thorogood's.

"And it was an actual mansion? Archie's family is rich?" Willie demanded.

"Put the brakes on girl, his family wasn't that great, well, his mother, that is."

"Why not? Did they have a butler and all?"

"Yes, but they all seemed a bit–"

"Eccentric?" Willie interrupted.

"Crazy is more like it," Cora stood from her bed.

"Was Brandon there?" Willie asked with her eyes opened wide as if in eager anticipation.

"No, no, Brandon was not there." With that question, Willie verified the news of his murder had not reached the general public, at least not to the tour group. Cora quickly changed the subject. "I hope we will not be going to his house again tomorrow."

"Tomorrow? Wait, you're planning to go with him again tomorrow?" Willie stood.

"Can you cover for me for one more day?"

"But, Cora…"

"I've thought about it and promised myself one more day of searching, then I'll let Scotland Yard handle it."

"I think you're making a mistake," Willie said. "You are in a strange town and don't know the customs or the dangers."

"I'll be careful," Cora promised.

Willie sighed. "Fine. I'll cover for you, but only one more day," she agreed halfheartedly.

"Willie, I really am sorry for this. I should have tried to contact you."

"Don't worry. I guess I'm getting better at deception. I wish I was more in control like you."

"Willie, you have more control than you think you have." Cora opened her trunk and pulled out her pajamas.

Willie let out a cleansing breath. "Thanks. I think we should get to sleep."

"And with that, I have one more favor to ask you."

"Oh, great. Now what?"

"Here," Cora said as she spun her back to Willie.

"Oh." She unbuttoned the top of Evelyn's dress. "There."

"No, not that." She dropped the dress to the floor, then pointed to her upper back. "Will you please get this bloody thing off of me?"

"Good evening. Sir, Master, and Mistress Thorogood are in the parlor. They would like a word with you."

"Of course, don't they always?"

Jefferson took Archie's hat.

Archie took two steps and stopped. "Sometimes I envy you Jefferson. I mean, Mr. Jefferson."

The butler smiled and nodded.

The Missing Jackal Murder

Archie was not sure which was worse, to stay in the dark hallway in hopes his parents would forget, or to enter the well-lit drawing room to witness his mother's usual 'ready to scold' face and his father's usual benign 'ready for good entertainment' look.

Archie stole himself and opened the door. His mother sat on the sofa and his father sat in one of the two wingback chairs separated by a small round table. A tray with a square decanter of brandy and two crystal cut glasses sat on top.

Archie chose the chair opposite his father. As he sat, he watched his father reach for the square bottle. "I suppose these are for us," he said as his father filled the first glass.

He looked at Archie, then tilted his head toward Gwendolyn. Archie followed. "Please, do continue, mother."

"I hadn't started," she said, shaking her head in irritation.

Archie grinned. "Oh, I thought these little fireside chats never ended."

Robert cleared his throat and frowned.

"I do apologize. You wish to have a few words at me— I mean, with me." He couldn't suppress his grin.

Gwendolyn shook her head. "I fail to see the humor in the midst of this tragedy."

Archie watched her eyes flick between him and his father, noting his father also tried to hold back a smile, unsuccessfully. "And what tragedy is that, Mother?"

She shifted to the front of her chair. "Don't play your silly games with me, young man."

"Young man? Father, do you have a clue what she is talking about?"

"You upset. Your mother, you see."

"Of course I'm upset," Gwendolyn interrupted.

"You displease your mother with the, how did you put it, 'despicable creature' you brought home," Robert said in a comical voice, lifting his glass.

Archie sprang from his seat and faced his mother. "Cora is not despicable. I thought I made myself clear I will make my own decisions, for myself, for my career, and for the ladies I choose to become acquainted with."

"You will cease this relationship, or I shall be forced to—to—"

"To what? To what, mother? Haven't we been through this, God knows how many times? Furthermore, there's nothing wrong with Cora."

She leaned back and folded her arms. "So, you are on a first name basis."

"Yes. I'm happy you have figured that out."

"How dare you speak to me like that?" She unfolded her arms and leaned forward again.

"Like what mother? You bring this out in me. I am thinking you find great satisfaction in our brief discussions."

Gwendolyn opened and closed her mouth several times, then glanced at her husband. "Are you going to just sit there and—"

"No," Archie snapped at his mother. "This is between you and me."

Before allowing his mother to continue, Robert spoke up. "Archie, sit down."

Archie glanced at his father.

"Please sit down."

Archie did as his father asked.

Robert continued, "We want to know your intentions with Cora—I mean, this young lady."

Archie took several moments to consider his words. He had no desire to continue the hostile conversation with his mother, so he chose to lie. "I do not have any intentions with Cora. We got caught up in our search for our stolen property and I have now left her alone and let Scotland Yard handle the situation." He had gotten proficient at lying to his mother to finish these discussions.

"Very good, I cannot believe you wasted time with that woman which led you to a jail cell, like a common criminal. You must forget this woman." She was staring intently at Archie, as if waiting for him to agree.

Robert spoke to her before Archie could reply. "You look tired, Gwendolyn. Why don't you turn in for the evening and I will take care of the residue of this matter?"

"Very well," she rose from her chair. Archie and his father both stood. "I am tired and please do not hurt your mother so." She paused beside Archie and waited. He bent and kissed her on the cheek, as expected, before she left the room.

The two said nothing until Archie's mother was out of earshot.

Robert filled the second glass. "You are becoming quite skilled at handling your mother."

Archie sat. "I learned from the best." Archie picked up the glass and tilted it towards his father. They clinked their glasses in a toast.

"You do know she loves you and is concerned about your welfare."

"The love part, possibly, but not concerned. I've concluded she is more concerned about herself and what her so-called inner circles would think."

"Did you know your grandmother was against me marrying your mother?"

"I only find that mildly surprising."

Robert sipped his brandy.

R. M. Scott

"So, why did you bring that up?"

Robert paused and gazed at Archie. "I am a successful businessman. It is my business to understand what is on someone's mind." He put his glass back on the table.

Archie narrowed his eyes. "Let me hazard a guess. You are wondering why I did not address my feelings for Cora. You're concerned with my love life, thinking that I am afraid to start and hold a relationship with the woman based on mother's lack of approval of the young lady. Now, I brought someone home, someone which I believe you do like. You are afraid I will botch this fledgling relationship and end up with a miserable life. How am I doing so far?"

"Good deductions," Robert said. "For starters, after this evening's events, I wanted to explain to you why I married your mother. To be honest, it was out of greed. Yes, for greed. I was a young man, ambitious, and I wanted to show my father that his business was in expert hands, that I would take the company to new heights. And so I did marry your mother. I once thought a bit like your brother Marcus to have fun, freedom, and romance, but I squashed all of that to impress my father. Your mother, of course, was the daughter of a wealthy man. Again, it was for greed."

"That is despicable," Archie said, with a sudden stiffening of his posture.

"I didn't think so at the time. Oh, how your grandmother pleaded and pleaded that I would not go ahead with the marriage. But I knew that, along with the money, your mother would use those inner circles you mentioned helping the business even more. As your American friend would say, 'I hit the jackpot.'"

They both sat silently, sipping their drinks.

"I suppose you are telling me not to make the same mistakes," Archie said, looking at his father and waiting.

"I know what you want. I know you work hard in your career. That's why I gave up my attempts to sway you to join the business. Of course, I stopped mostly for the benefit of the business. I would not want to share it with someone who doesn't care about it. You went down a path that made you happy."

"Are you happy, father?"

"Of course I am. Yes, I do realize that, as you said, I was despicable about how I achieved our wealth, but I adapted."

"Adapted?" Archie said with a chuckle as he lifted his glass to his mouth.

"Yes," Robert continued, "let me make one thing perfectly clear. I love your mother, now. And so, you and your mother, not seeing eye-to-eye, leads me to the reason I wanted to talk to you about Cora."

"To whom you called—God-send."

"I did, didn't I?" he said over the rim of his glass.

"Yes," Archie said, "So why do you like her when mother doesn't?"

"Oh, many reasons."

Archie arched one eyebrow. "One of them wouldn't be that she is an exquisite woman?"

"That certainly doesn't hurt, and I'm pleased to hear you noticed that."

"I may be a man of science, but I'm not dead, you know. What else?"

Robert looked up in the bedroom's direction and grinned. "I admired how Cora handled your mother. She did not cower. She stood up for herself. That takes more doing with your mother."

"Well, that's nice, but when she spoke to the help like equals, didn't it flabbergast you? Mother was, of course, appalled."

"I admired that. It means she looks beyond herself. That's how I knew she would care for you, for who you really are, and not for your wealth. As for that, this is one less thing for me to worry about. But then I'm not sure that for her securing your wealth would be good for her, for you. For Cora, your wealth will be more of a burden to her than, 'hitting the jackpot', when she marries you."

Archie gagged on his drink and coughed uncontrollably for a few moments.

Robert merely chuckled at his calamity.

"Marry? I've only known her for a few days!" Archie got the words out with effort.

"Again, I have the ability to know people quickly in business, as well as out of business. You, on the other hand, have known her for several days onboard the ship and during today's adventures. You can't tell me you don't already feel attraction and affection towards her."

Archie sputtered. "I'm not sure. I mean, I certainly haven't thought of marriage. I'm busy with my career—excavations, research, and writing. You do know I'm never been in one place very long. The places I travel are not always the most comfortable or safe, and that certainly is not a good basis for marriage or anything else."

"Take her along. Isn't that what a wife should do, follow her husband?"

"But—"

"She did say she wanted to travel and have adventures. Be honest. You would like to see her in one of those one-piece jumper suits diggers wear with a handkerchief tied around her head with the knot in front. Yes, covered in dirt.

And yes, she might not look too pretty then. But her smile, she does have a beautiful smile, doesn't she?"

Archie narrowed his eyes in suspicion. "Alright, alright, I know you're doing this for a laugh."

"You really think so?"

"I'm not sure that if I ever do decide to marry, Cora may not be the one."

Robert sighed. "Maybe you're right. I am doing this for a laugh, but it would not be at your expense. I saw how you acted with her, despite your mother's presence. She is at least a prospect."

"Alright, I like her, but that doesn't mean that I—"

"Answer me this. Who had the ridiculous idea to go to one dirty, disgusting saloon in the lame hope to pick up information with the possibility of getting hurt, and who was the one who decided to—to follow her?"

Archie said nothing as he searched for something to say in his defense. "The worse part of all this is that with a man contemplating a woman, the son should have this conversation with his mother," Archie said as he tried to change the subject.

"Ouch," his father said and took another sip. "But I didn't do so badly for a greedy, despicable father, did I?" He put his glass down.

Archie lifted his glass and said, "You did quite well, but be honest, no funny business. Do you like Cora? Do you really think she could be a prospect for me?"

"There's a time for humor, for humor's sake, and there is a time for the man's father to be forthright and truthful. If I wanted humor for humor's sake, I would have had this conversation with you with your mother present. Your mother's reaction to all this—well, now that would be good comedy."

Archie smiled and poured the last of the brandy into both classes. "I have always thought of you as a smart man." Archie lifted his glass in salute.

"Don't forget that and you will go a long way." They both drank.

"Then how about giving me some more advice now?"

"Very well, what about?"

"When I drove Cora back to the hotel, well, when we stopped in front of the door—"

Robert waved his hand. "Now, don't give me too many details. Your mother truly is tired tonight..."

Archie first rolled his eyes, then thought seriously about what he wanted to say.

Robert took another sip and waited.

"Cora asked the most extraordinary question. She asked if I believed in magic."

Robert lowered his glass and said nothing.

"I'm not sure what that means. She says it's nothing to do with hocus-pocus or—"

"It means she loves you, my boy."

"What?" Archie gazed into his father's face. "Why do you say that?"

Robert only smiled. "She loves you *ab-so-lute-ly*," his father replied, stretching out the word in a very close imitation of Cora. "Well, now I am done in for the evening," Robert stood up. "You told your mother that you will no longer have contact with Cora, so I assume you are meeting her again tomorrow. Perhaps you will take her on another tour of the underbelly of our fine city? Am I correct?"

Archie stood and replied in a monotone voice, "I am to meet her in front of her hotel at 8:00 a.m."

"You will, of course, be prompt?"

"Is there any other way?"

The Missing Jackal Murder

#####

Arve climbed onto the darkened table to join Ola and Iknokman. They gazed out onto the moonlit street. There was enough light to see that no human or animal stirred. This gave them an opportunity to get the lay of the land for an escape. Fuller Street led out to another busy street.

Clyde rolled over on his side and snored softly. Jerry lay motionless with a slight buzzing sound.

Arve sat next to Iknokman. "Any thoughts?"

The wooden jackal grunted. "Just the same, only darker and quieter. But if we did leave this building, where would we go?"

"That street over there may have more people. More people means more chances to get someone's attention."

"And anyone who does see us can't tell anyone about us because of the magic," Ola said.

Arve rubbed his chin. "I was thinking more about writing a message. Someone would read it and send help. It worked with that old woman and her radio. Maybe someone could get the police. If we get them here, all they need to do is to see you, in your wooden form, of course. If you talk to them, they will take a Billy club to you."

"And hopefully Archie informed Scotland Yard about me so they would know what it means when they do see me, in my wooden form, of course."

Iknokman sat down. So did Arve and Ola. Arve again gazed at the moon and imagined wolf cries and had to stop himself from shivering.

As if Ola knew what Arve was thinking, she said, "It was a night just like this when you first came to our Village. The moon was just like this."

Arve said nothing.

Iknokman looked at him, pondering for a brief moment.

"I wish Agar could've washed away that part of my memory."

"Why?" Iknokman said. "Was your meeting so horrible?"

After a few moments of silence, Iknokman apologized.

"But then," Arve said absentmindedly, "I wish Agar could've helped me remember where I came from." Arve saw Iknokman staring at him. "It seems my life started when I got up from the rocks, when I wiped the blood from my head. Best they knew was that I was out hunting. I must've fallen and hit my head. When I came to, it was dark. I remember wolves were moving in. I got scared, and I ran."

"Shh," Ola said, and put her arm around his shoulder. "You got out of that mess alright, didn't you?"

Arve smiled. "The funny thing was that when I ran and tried to figure things out, I came across some animals. I thought they were wolfs, but I wasn't sure because it was dark. I aimed to kill when a voice rang out and a man ran in front of his sheep. He certainly gave me the business."

Ola chuckled. "You're lucky you didn't kill any of my father's herd. He would've given you more than the business."

Iknokman smiled.

"Stian, Ola's father, brought me home. Ola tended to my wounds."

"And you fell in love," Iknokman said with a smile.

"No," Ola said comically, "I felt sorry for him, so I married him for that."

"Oh, ha, ha," Arve said.

The Missing Jackal Murder

They sat in silence for a moment until Arve spoke. "It was the first time I met the Villagers of Nordlund—Agar, Nicholas, Astrid, Gunda, Nils, and all."

"And then you lived happily ever since?"

"Ever since," Ola said with a small smile that faded quickly, "except today." Again, they looked out into the street, saying not a word. "I know you still remember you and the Villagers packed in a trunk on our way to America. But at least we were all with you."

This time, Iknokman broke the silence. "Tell me about this Nicholas bloke. If he has the power to rescue you, then why hasn't he? Are we out of his range? Is it something about this place that prevents him from showing up?"

"No, it's not that."

"Then what?"

Arve looked into Iknokman's eyes and knew he would not understand. "It's because we don't want him here to rescue us."

"What?"

"It's hard to explain."

"We seem to have all night."

"It's for Cora."

Iknokman looked between Arve and Ola, waiting for an explanation.

"Arve thinks Cora does not want us to call on Nicholas either," Ola said.

Arve looked out at the moon. "I don't know too much about your culture, but here and now, women like Cora are not allowed to be independent." Arve looked at Iknokman. "I know that's not much of a reason, but we, the Villagers, have always been fond of the Keeper's family—and especially of Cora."

"I don't follow," Iknokman said.

"If we called on Nicholas, the entire family and the Village would know. They would claim Cora is not ready to be responsible on her own and that we are not safe in her hands." Arve continued as Iknokman opened his mouth. "I think we are relatively safe, for now at least, and so is Cora. She wants to find us on her own and likewise, for us to find her. I know you don't understand our position on this, but it is very important to us."

"I do understand. It shows bravery and responsibility. It shows you will let this Cora prove herself and to prove yourselves as well." Iknokman frowned. "Wherever I go, back to the museum or into someone else's hands, I sit there in the dark or am stared at by strangers."

"Iknokman, when we find Cora, we will make sure you will be safe in the British Museum. I will tell Nicholas about you and we will visit you when we can—as often as you want." Arve paused. "It's the best I can do for you, at least for now."

"Visiting me at the museum when you can would be good enough for me. Truly it would be."

Arve spoke to Ola as she sat with her arms wrapped around her knees and rocked. "Ola, we'll find Cora, I promise." Arve could not bear the look of fear on Ola's face any longer. "If Cora does not find us or we find her by the end of tomorrow, I will call on Nicholas. Yes, but for now I'm planning an idea. If that doesn't work, I will."

"You promise?"

Before Arve could answer, Clyde rolled on his back with a loud snore.

Arve spoke in a much louder voice, "I promise. I believe we are safe here, but certainly our eardrums are not."

Chapter 12

Voices filled the hotel dining room with anticipation of the second day to the England tourists. They sat in groups around small tables, eating and talking as the low morning sunlight peeked in the windows.

Willie sat quietly and sipped her coffee. Cora sat across from her and welcomed the silence to plan her next strategy for Arve's and Ola's recovery. She occasionally glanced out the street window to see if Archie had arrived. No, Archie yet. Where will we go this time? Cora's mind raced to consider likely locations since she had promised herself this would be the last day without Nicholas' help.

"Who do you think might have taken your suitcase?" Willie asked, as if reading her mind.

"Mr. Mitford and Miss Tomlinson are the best possible suspects," she immediately replied without thinking. "Mitford may not have gotten downed to the boat, but I think he knows something."

"But what about Brandon? Have you asked him? Could he have anything to do with this?" Willie said.

Cora shook her head and sipped her coffee. "Everybody is under suspicion in the present moment." She wanted to keep the news of his murder from Willie for as long as possible. "We also have to consider several other items that were stolen from the museum recently. Yesterday's heist was only a part of it."

"Since Brandon works at the museum and was on the ship, he must know something. It all seems too coincidental. And what about Brandon's fiancée, Eve Tomlinson? You mentioned you saw her on the dock. What did she look like?

Was Brandon happy to see her? Did you and Archie ask her if she saw anything? Or did they even meet before he was killed?" Willie put down her cup and leaned forward, eager to hear more details.

Cora did not respond to Willie's questions about Brandon. "I'll ask Archie if we can find Eve today." She sipped her coffee and looked at her watch. "I wonder what Archie has planned for us. I have some ideas, but I really can't be too sure."

"Cora, I think we should talk more about this Archie fellow."

Cora looked up, startled. "Oh? You did say you'd cover for me. All you have to do is to tell the tour guide I'm in the lavatory."

"No, it's not that," Willie gave the same rigid expression as when they had encountered her husband, Roy, in Chicago.

"What's the matter?" Cora said. "I'll be fine on my own."

"You won't be on your own."

"Yes, that's right. I'll be with Archie." She paused. "Are you worried Archie will take advantage of me?"

"No." Willie said, looking down at her cup. "I don't want to see you get hurt, that's all."

"I am not here to look for romance, as I have said many times. I am here only for adventure, and in this case, to search for my case."

"But what if Archie is the one who committed the theft?"

"What? No, of course he didn't. He was with me the whole time."

"Yes, but what if when you were not looking, he talked to those two creeps and told them to steal his case and yours?"

The Missing Jackal Murder

"I'm pretty sure I was with him the entire time. I would remember seeing him talking to the creeps."

"Well, if you see Brandon again, you can ask him if he ever saw Archie talking to those two criminals. Just make sure you take him aside without Archie watching."

"Alright, alright, if I see Brandon, I will ask him. But I doubt I will see him," Cora said in hopes not to give any impression of Brandon's murder.

"Why not? If you and Archie go back to the museum, you're bound to run into him."

"Maybe, look, I did say one more day and I will stop looking." She looked at her watch. It read 7:55. She still had a few minutes. "You liked Brandon, didn't you?" She looked closely at Willie. After a moment of pause, she continued. "Willie, it's perfectly okay to admit you like someone. Brandon was very sweet to you. It's okay to let go of the past and enjoy yourself." Cora paused. "I thought I heard you crying last night. Are you alright?"

Willie's eyes glistened. Then she shook her head. "I had fun with him on the ship. But he's too young for me. He made me feel young and reminded me of the things I've missed since I got married. I'm sure he saw me as someone old and safe; someone who would not try to interfere with his relationship."

"How did that make you feel?"

"He could have been using me, but as I said, I did have a good time."

"What did you two talk about?"

Willie chuckled and looked away. "This and that."

"Sorry Willie, I didn't mean to pry. Did he ever say anything about the artifacts on the ship?"

Willie laughed. "That's all Brandon talked about. As I remembered, he bragged about how he planned to get into the archaeology world and excavate. He seemed so sure of himself that he would make it big in archaeology. He told me he had big dreams that were about to come true."

Cora noticed Willie's sudden expression of concern. "What is it Willie?"

"I hope you won't take this the wrong way. Brandon appeared agitated about Archie not supporting his desire for an excavation. He thought Archie stood in the way of his success," Willie said.

"Yes, Archie did mention something about that. But then I never asked him how one would achieve fame and fortune in archaeology. I'm not particularly sure how one would do that unless an archaeologist made an important discovery."

"He talked about the expedition that found the Prince of Iknokman. He said he would've given anything to hold those artifacts in his hands."

"Did he say anything about what they were worth, dollar value, that is?"

"He said it would be worth a fortune to the right buyer."

Cora was about to ask her if that seemed strange but did not want Willie to think badly of Brandon at this point. Her quote from Brandon's words ran through her mind. "He said it would be worth a fortune to the right buyer."

Willie sipped her coffee again. Her eyes glistened, and she shook her head. "Okay, yes, it was fun spending time with him. But it is time for me to move on. You just promise me you will be careful."

"I assure you, Archie will not hurt me." As Cora thought of another line of questioning, she saw Archie's car through the dining-room window before she could speak any more. She felt a small thrill at the idea of seeing him again.

The tour leader called the group outside to leave.

"He's here," Cora said, and picked up her things from the table and put them into her pouch. "Remember to cover for me, right?"

"Just this one last time," Willie said with a knowing look on her face.

"Good."

"Cora, please be careful."

"I will be careful," Cora said and smiled. She put her hand on Willie's elbow for a moment. They walked to the front door where Archie's chauffer, Mr. Hilliard, was waiting with the door opened and Archie sat on the far side looking out. The group went in one direction, she went in the other.

#####

Bevan's eyebrows rose when Archie and Cora walked in. It was Cora's idea to visit Scotland Yard to see if he had any additional evidence. Bevan shook his head. "You two have become bloody pests. How many times do I have to tell you to let Scotland Yard to sort this out?"

Before Archie spoke, two Scotland Yard 'bobbies' shuffled forward and held onto a shabbily clothed man. "We don't mean to be obnoxious." The arrested man looked down at his feet as he moved forward.

Cora swiveled her head to get a good look at the arrested man. Satisfied he was not one of the two who stole her case, she looked back at Archie and Bevan. "But since you are too busy to search for our missing artifacts, we thought you might share anything you know to help us in our search."

"You do realize I am under no obligation to inform you about anything regarding our investigation?"

"You need not have to tell us anyone's private business," Archie said. "Would it be overly impertinent for me to ask you to share anything you know that could help us with our search for our luggage? You said the theft may have something to do with the murder. I thought this would be an opportunity for us to help each other."

"I don't need help from amateur detectives. You'll get in my way and get yourselves killed."

Cora folded her arms. "It's a chance I'm ready to take."

Bevan glowered at her.

Archie cleared his throat. "What Miss Gudmundson means is that any information you can give us would be helpful." He held up a hand to stop her from making further brash statements like the last one.

Bevan frowned. "If your thieves acted on Williamson's instructions, then they will wait for him to show up with money for the goods."

"Archie and I came to the same conclusion. The reason we visited the questionable pub is hoping to find someone who either wanted to unload or purchase the Jackal of Prince Iknokman."

Bevan gave Cora a stern look. "That type of investigation could get you killed."

"Then if you have any information that will help us stay clear of such places, now would be a good time to share. As you stated, you don't want to form an opinion until you have the facts. I understand, but I am sure you have opinions that could help us find those facts?"

"Very well," Bevan said. "However, my opinions may lead you nowhere and possibly to people who are not responsible for these crimes."

The Missing Jackal Murder

"So, you do suspect some people, but you're not ready to arrest them?" Archie said.

"Exactly. Your Mr. Mitford, for example, according to your suspicions and to our investigation, several artifacts are indeed missing from the museum. He appears to have little concern about them, which makes him suspicious. But that does not make him a murderer or a thief. Possibly, but I need to do more investigating."

"He could've hired those two thugs to steal Archie's case," Cora said.

"Again, my opinion, but I do not think Mr. Mitford would associate with those two, shall we say, gentlemen? I believe he is above that. I do suspect Williamson may have contacted them, but again, it's only speculation."

"So, the thieves may be impatient to get rid of what they have stolen, at least that is if they've learned that Williamson is dead." Archie said. "They may either lie low till the heat if off, or out and about trying to find another contact to unload the goods."

Bevan only nodded. "Just as a detective in your mystery radio stories would put it."

"What have you learned from Miss Tomlinson?" Cora asked Bevan.

"I don't have any strong suspicions about her regarding the murder or the theft. True, she didn't seem to be much in anguish over her fiancé's bloody corpse, but many other things could explain that. Maybe they were having problems. Maybe Miss Tomlinson had second thoughts about marrying Williamson. Maybe with Mr. Williamson in the United States, Miss Tomlinson found another suitor to take his place. Again, these could be reasons to explain why tears did not physically flow down her cheeks."

"But what if–" Cora began but stopped when another officer approached Bevan abruptly with a slip of paper and they whispered.

Bevan nodded at Cora and Archie. "Something has come up that requires my attention."

"Anything you'd like to share–"

"This has nothing to do with your investigation, rather nothing to do with the murder or the theft of your property."

"But what about–"

Bevan nodded at Cora and Archie, then dashed off.

Cora pressed her lips together. "I certainly would like to have a conversation with Miss Tomlinson myself. If she and Brandon were having problems, as Bevan suggested, then why would she have come down to the dock to meet the boat. It makes no sense."

"Hmm, that is a good point. But I doubt she would talk to us. She seemed quite annoyed with me at the dock."

Cora looked toward the door where Bevan spoke with colleagues. "I think he knows more that he didn't share with us."

"That wasn't much," Archie said, shaking his head. "I guess it's back to do what the detectives on the radio mystery programs say and 'pound the pavement' and—Cora, no." He reached out and grabbed her arm as she moved toward Bevan. "Don't interrupt him."

Cora stopped and watched as more men joined Bevan in the hallway outside his office. She glanced at Bevan's desk. A piece of paper with the name Eve Tomlinson scrawled across the surface caught her eye. She glanced over her shoulder to see that men circled around Bevan in conversation. She reached out and plucked the paper off his desk.

"Cora," Archie whispered, "what are you doing?"

"Finding Eve's address," she whispered back. "What else are we to do?"

Archie stepped next to her and glanced down at the desk. "He looks familiar," Archie whispered as he pointed to a photograph of a rough-looking man.

Bevan's voice reached them and it sounded like his conversation was ending. Archie pulled Cora from the desk and toward the door before Bevan returned.

"I know I've seen him before," Archie said as they walked toward his car.

"Who?"

"The man in the photo. I believe it was what you Americans call a 'mug shot'."

"Who is he?"

"I don't know. But I wonder if he's one of those men I saw hanging around Mitford at the museum."

Cora lifted her eyebrows. "Oh, so perhaps Mitford has been associating himself with hardened criminals."

"I only got a brief glance at the photo. But I do not believe it was either of the two men who stole our cases. He looked too refined to be one of them."

They got into Archie's car and Mr. Hilliard sat behind the wheel. "I would wager just about anything you are about to suggest that we find Eve Tomlinson."

Cora nodded with a grin. "Well, I didn't steal her address off Bevan's desk just for fun."

Archie grinned. "Now that's interesting."

"Oh, and there is one more thing."

"What's that?"

"Where can I get some silk stockings?" Cora said, rubbing her knee.

"Silk stockings? Is that part of our investigation?" Archie frowned with a look of confusion.

"No, not really. But it is a part of my new independent life."

Chapter 13

Cora slid her hands down her silk stockings from her thigh to her calf. She caught Archie's eyes as she did so, though only briefly.

Archie turned away. "I was just making sure your new outfit was fitting fine. If not, I can turn around and go back so you can pick out that pink dress you looked at."

"I think I made the right choice with this light robin's egg blue number. I like the ruffles around the sleeves."

"I do as well."

"And my silk stockings?" She lifted her skirt ever so slightly to allow Archie to get a look at her entire leg.

"Fine." Archie said without looking.

She smiled, then looked again at Archie's sister's dress folded on the seat behind her.

"You're certain Evelyn would not want her dress back?"

"Most women, and for sure, your sister, will never wear a dress worn by another, or in this case, it depends on who wore the dress. Still…" she looked again at the folded dress. "I'm not a miser, but if she wants to give up a nice dress like this, who am I to argue?"

"Still, I'm glad you found something at the dress shop."

"You didn't have to buy me a new dress, Archie."

"You know I can afford it, though."

"When I get back home, I'll send you–"

"Cora."

"Well, I wasn't brought up that way. Taking things from people is what I mean."

Archie shook his head, and his lips tightened.

"But I do admit I like these silk stockings. I've never worn a pair before. And I know you like my new silk stockings, Archie. You couldn't stop staring at them."

Archie stuttered. "I merely wanted to make sure you got what you wanted, and that the clerk did not sell you something you did not want."

She put one hand on the knee of her new dress. "I wonder what my mother would say." She also thought about her promise to call for Nicholas by the end of the day. "I do hope I find Arve and Ola today," she said, to change the subject. Her hopes of finding them were beginning to wan. In the meantime, it was wonderful spending time with Archie, getting to know him and enjoying his company.

"I know you do. They are wonderful carvings and I understand your concern about losing them."

"I hope you don't think I am keeping you with me under false pretenses."

"It never occurred to me. But if you attend any of my archaeology digs, you must wear a digger's jumper and possibly a handkerchief wrapped around your head? Not like the beautiful garments you are wearing now."

This surprised Cora. "I thought you were against women wearing trousers."

"I said nothing about—I meant it is merely frowned upon."

"I take it you have no lady diggers, to say lady archaeologists in your expedition?"

"A woman might, shall we say, disrupt the men from doing their jobs." Archie cleared his throat.

She sensed his discomfort and couldn't resist more teasing. "So, you think I would fill out a digger's jumper more curvaceously than the men-folk on your crew?"

The Missing Jackal Murder

Archie gave a sharp inhale. "It's not me, it's the other men. You know how immature some men can be when next to a beautiful woman—I mean a woman. Myself, I would act like a perfect gentleman."

"Of course," Cora smiled. She looked up as they stopped in front of an old apartment building. "Is this where Eve lives?"

"Yes," Archie said. They got out of the car and walked into the building and down a hallway.

Archie knocked on the well-worn door to Eve's apartment while Cora looked up and down the hallway. The building inside and out was incredibly old, but kept up enough not to appear decrepit.

They heard a woman's voice call out on the other side of the door, "Who the bloody hell is it?"

Before Eve's door opened, they heard a door creak behind them. Cora and Archie saw an old lady's eyes and not much more peering out through the crack of the door.

Archie smiled, and the old woman grunted.

Eve's door opened. "Mind your own business, you old beezen," a young woman in Eve's apartments said to an older woman.

The old woman grunted and slammed her door.

"Blimy, you almost caught me starkers. Now, here, what do you want?" the young woman spoke in a tone that suggested she wanted nothing to do with them.

Cora looked at the woman who appeared to be about Eve's age and type, but with short, wavy hair. Her face would have been lovely, if it wasn't for her scowl.

"Is this the apartment of Eve Tomlinson?" Cora asked. She noticed she wore a nightgown and a silk wrapper.

"Yeah, what's it to, you? Have you come all the way across the pond just to see her?" she said to Cora, then looked at Archie. "And what about you? Are you also a nosy American?"

"No, I'm not from the United States," Archie said. "Is Miss Tomlinson at home?"

"No, she ain't. What do you want her for?"

Archie cleared his throat. "I imagine you've heard of Mr. Brandon Williamson. I am his associate, Archie Thorogood, from the British Museum."

"Ahh," the woman said in a seductive voice. She smiled at Archie and moved closer to touch his arm. "So, you came round. Brandon mentioned we should meet some time back." She motioned her head toward Cora. "Who's this, your secretary or summit? Come on in while I finish dressing and we can make plans."

"You misunderstood," Cora said.

"Oh? What are you, his new squeeze? What would a classy chassis like him want with the likes of you? Hey, I'm not into that sort of thing."

"No, no," Archie said as his face turned red. "We are only here to talk to Miss Tomlinson."

She frowned. "And what for? Does this have something to do with those two blokes she's been hanging around with as of late? Especially the one who looks like he should be in a cage at the zoo?"

Cora looked at Archie, then at the woman. "Can you describe the two men?"

"Yeah, sure." She walked into the apartment, and Cora and Archie followed. She reached for a cigarette on a side table and lit it. "One was tall and well dressed and the other looked like an ape." She laughed at her own words. "I said to Eve, 'Brandon isn't good enough for you?' She says to me, 'Brandon is no longer in the picture.' Now why would she dump Brandon out of the blue like that? What did he do?"

"I'm not sure what their relationship is like at the present," Archie replied, staring forward, without mentioning Brandon's death.

"Do you know where Eve is now?" Cora asked.

"Oh, why didn't you ask in the first place? That would have been short and sweet. She has gone to church."

"To church?" Cora said, "It's not Sunday. Why would she go there?"

She glared at Cora. "I know what day it is. I said to her, 'It's not Sunday', but she told me to mind my own beeswax. So, why did she go to church now is her business and none of mine, now is it?"

"Which church?" Cora said.

"You sure are nosy, aren't you?"

"It's important for us to speak with her as soon as possible," Archie said. "I apologize for this intrusion."

The woman looked from Archie to Cora and back again. She took a step towards Archie and leaned into his side. "If you ditch the colonial here and buy me a drink, I'll think about telling you."

"I'm not..." Cora growled. "Archie, say yes to her so we can talk to Tomlinson."

Archie nodded.

The woman smiled, approached Archie, put her hands on his shoulder and kissed him on the cheek. She sneered at Cora. "Sorry, tootsie."

Cora felt her anger rising. "Now the church?"

"Alright, alright, don't get your starchy corset in a knot. She went to the big church a few blocks down there." She motioned with her thumb.

"You mean the Gothic Cathedral?" Archie said.

"Isn't that what I said?"

"Thank you, you have been a great help." Archie stepped through the door.

"Hey, what about our drinks?"

"I need to talk to Miss Tomlinson about something urgent. After that, I shall return to you and fulfill our agreement."

"Alright, I'll get dolled up for you, dearie," she said to Archie. "Lady, you keep your colonial fingers off him, he's mine now."

"Oh, you can count on that."

Cora glanced at Archie with a smile once they were outside again and walked toward his car. "Archie, I would be happy to show you a few of the defensive moves my father taught me for the next time, a barracuda like that goes after you."

He looked back at her with raised eyebrows. "I may just have to take you up on that offer." He cleared his throat. "I was a bit out of my league."

"I'll say. I don't believe I've ever seen a man's face quite that shade of red." Cora laughed.

Archie seemed relieved when they arrived at his car and quickly changed the subject. "The church she referred to is the Gothic Cathedral down the street."

"Oh?"

"It's London's sister to the Notre Dame in Paris. I wonder why Miss Tomlinson would visit the Gothic Cathedral, on such a random day as any."

"She said she saw Eve Tomlinson with two other men. She also said one man looked like an ape. I wonder if it's the same man you saw in the photograph on Bevan's desk."

"Why would Eve associate with men like that and why meet them in a church?" Archie frowned.

Cora considered his questions for several moments as they drove toward the church. "In some dime novels I've read, criminals sometimes exchange information between church pews. I wonder if that's what Eve Tomlinson is doing."

Archie smiled. "Only you 'colonials' use the term dime novels. Here in jolly old England, we refer to them as Penny Dreadfuls."

Cora laughed. "Okay then. In the Penny Dreadfuls, the criminals sometimes meet in church. Don't you think it's possible that's what Eve is doing?"

"I suppose anything is possible."

"Possible, but improbable, is what you're thinking, isn't it?" Cora teased.

He chuckled. "Well, I suppose it's better to look there than dodgy bars. We might luck out and find the ruffians who stole our cases and solve Bevan's case all in one shot."

Cora grinned. "That would be more than luck. That would be magic."

Archie raised an eyebrow and cleared his throat before he spoke. "Is that what you meant when you talked about magic last evening?"

Cora gave him a startled look. "Did I mention magic? Hmm, I don't remember." She frowned. "Let's just hope Bevan doesn't think this is a bad idea and we make a second trip to a jail cell. I suspect that would be too much for my mother to handle."

"We'll be more cautious this time," Archie said.

Hilliard parked the car in front of a large, ornate building. "Don't worry. I'll take care of you." She reached over and kissed Archie on the cheek, then got out of the car before Hilliard could open it. She saw Archie holding a hand to his cheek. He sat immobilized for a few seconds longer. She stuck her head back into the car. "Are you coming?"

"Yes. Of course." He got out of the car, caught up with Cora, and put his elbow out. She took it and smiled.

#####

Cora observed the immense doors of the cathedral's exterior as they strolled to the main entrance. "It's so fascinating to first see an incredible and famous building like this on the pages of the National Geographic magazine and then to see it in real life." She studied the structure. "Imagine the labor and artistry involved in creating this building. It takes my breath away."

"Interesting." Archie stood next to her and inspected the upper walls. "I've lived here all my life and passed by this cathedral many times, but never considered the work involved in creating such a monumental treasure. I truly have taken this all for granted."

They moved forward and Archie opened the cathedral door, and Cora entered.

"What about the pyramids? You must have been inside them." Cora gasped at the enormous interior of the cathedral. "The artwork and high ceiling are amazing." She scanned up and became dizzy, as if she could fall up. She shook her head and looked ahead to the large stained-glass window. Metal frames bonded together held each color, forming a large, colorful six-sided star. The sunlight broke through the stain glass windows to the gray marble pillars lit up with a splash of color. The mesmerizing scene intoxicated her so much she bumped into a chair. She reached to grab hold of the wooden back, then realized the entire floor held rows and rows of chairs and not standard church pews.

The Missing Jackal Murder

Archie looked around. "I believe this is one of the stops with your tour group."

"Yes, it is, but I don't remember which day they schedule us to visit. At least I'm not missing the St. Paul Cathedral part of the trip."

"So, what's the plan?"

They advanced to the back set of chairs. From there, they had a full view of the entire sanctuary. The cathedral appeared almost empty. Occasional parishioners on bended knees and various sightseers with Brownie cameras were the only visible occupants.

After a few moments of silence while she scanned the large chapel, Cora sighed. "I suppose this was a bad idea, like moving from one haystack to another to find a needle. I wonder where she is." She glanced at Archie. "You're so patient to go along with my crazy ideas."

"Yes, well, let's focus on what we know so far," he said. "What is it, Cora?" Alarm came from Archie's voice as he looked between her and the group of people.

"It's my tour group," Cora whispered. The guide allowed the cathedral's representative to describe the splendid architecture of the building.

Archie grinned. "This is most unfortunate."

"It isn't funny." Cora watched the group move closer to the front, then turn when the guide pointed to something interesting in the back. She sank lower and Archie chuckled.

Cora watched as the guide pointed towards the front and all sets of eyes turned except one. The group moved on as Willie stood rooted to the floor. She looked between the back pew and the group moving farther away and then walked towards the back.

"Horse feathers. They'll see her walking back here," Cora whispered. "The tour guide will surely notice me if she does."

As Willie approached, she lifted her shoulders and her hands in a gesture that said, "Why are you here?" She walked to the last row of chairs and sat next to Archie while Cora remained scrunched down.

"What are you doing?" Cora asked in a loud whisper.

"I was about to ask you the same question. It's nice to see you again, Mr. Thorogood."

"Please, Archie is fine."

Willie gave a small, halfhearted smile. Her expression immediately grew annoyed when she looked at Cora on Archie's other side. "Did you know someone murdered Brandon?"

"How did you hear?" Cora asked.

"Listen," Archie said, "I think we should get out of here and talk about this outside. I don't want anyone to hear us." Willie and Archie stood first and walked. Cora slid along with them, then stood up in front of Archie so the group would not see her. They left the building.

Willie sat on the brick wall that bordered the cathedral and watched Cora and Archie sit down. "I hope you are being careful," Willie said. Her face screwed up with fear in a look that reminded Cora of the night they ran into Roy in Chicago.

"Don't worry about us. We'll be fine," Cora said.

"How did you learn about Brandon?" Archie asked.

Willie looked at Cora. Her expression changed from fear to anger. "Why didn't you tell me about Brandon's murder? It horrified me. Do you know how that made me feel? A detective came to the hotel right before we got on the trolley. He asked a lot of questions about what any of us may have seen. Then, he pointed me out—by name. He interrogated me."

"Was his name Inspector Bevan?" Archie asked.

"Yes, how did you–" Willie's face turned white. "You talked to him? You told him about me and Brandon?"

"I'm sorry, he got it out of me," she said. "But I told him that we were sure you had nothing to do with this. He seemed understanding. Did he give you a hard time?"

"No, just a few questions. Since he knew I was with the group, he let me go. It scared me. Her bottom lip quivered as she tried to regain her composure."

Cora patted Willie's elbow. "I didn't want you to be sad. I wanted you to remember the fun you had during our voyage, the fun you had being on your own with another man." She gave Willie a sympathetic look.

Willie pulled out a handkerchief and dried her tears. "Okay, yes. I liked him, casually. So why didn't you tell me that someone killed him? Do you know who did it? Why was he murdered? Is his death related to your stolen cases? What is going on? Could the murderer be after you?" Her voice ended on a high pitch.

"What makes you ask that?" Cora frowned. "How could you have jumped to the conclusion that Brandon's murderer would put us in danger?"

Willie took a deep breath and blew it out slowly. "Our first stop this morning was at the British Museum. I half hoped you and Archie would be there looking for clues about the missing cases. When we got to the Egyptian exhibit, Mr. Mitford, the curator, interrupted us."

"Mitford, that's correct," Archie said.

"Did he do or say anything suspicious?" Cora said.

"Well, yes. Cora, you told me someone had stolen the jackal, but he said it was downstairs being cleaned. Is that suspicious?"

Archie made sure his tone was reassuring. "I'm sure it was more prudent for him to say an artifact is temporarily out for cleaning. He couldn't admit someone had stolen it. Visitors would think the museum could not take care of itself or give the impression visitors could be in danger."

Cora concurred. "Maybe so, if this was a normal case. But since we think Mitford had something to do with the theft, maybe not." She turned to Willie. "What else did he say?"

"He gave a presentation about the Egyptian display. When he finished, our tour guide led us off, and I had a bad feeling about Mr. Mitford. I don't know what came over me, I don't know. Maybe it had something to do with one of the major pieces being stolen, but I somehow got the urge to follow him, to see if he was up to something."

"Oh, Willie, that was quite brave of you. Did you see or hear anything of value? What did Mitford do?"

"It's not so much what he did. It was the two men he was talking with. They seemed too odd to be museum people, though."

"What did they look like?" Cora said as she sat up straighter. "Did they look like ruffians?"

"No. They seemed to be well dressed. One of them was tall and one was a short, squat man." Willie motioned with her hands, giving the impression that the second man was muscular.

"They could be the men who stole our cases," Archie said.

"But Willie said they were well dressed. Our crooks were not," Cora said with her fingers to her lips and her eyebrows lowered in thought. Willie's description did not jibe with her sketchy memory of the two men who grabbed the cases and ran. They were neither well-dressed nor muscular.

"How did they act toward Mr. Mitford?" Archie asked.

"Well, the tall one was a sort of gentlemanly-like, yet devilish and gave me the heebie-jeebies." Willie shivered.

"In what way?" Archie said.

"He was almost sinister. He and the other man kept giving each other these looks, like they had a big secret— well, I got chills up and down my spine."

"What did the second man look like?"

"He was stocky, muscular and looked like someone who would kill you if you even looked at him wrong. He was scowling the entire time like he was mad about something."

"He didn't look stupid or anything like that?"

"No, he looked around like he was suspicious though, and that wanted to make sure no one was listening in. I hid behind a tall Egyptian statue while they talked."

"What else did you hear?" Archie asked.

"I couldn't get all of it. They were mostly quiet. But I heard Brandon's name a few times. Then Mr. Mitford said the Jackal of Prince Iknokman was down in the basement getting cleaned."

"He told those two it was getting cleaned?" Cora's voice rose. "Why would he tell them that if they were the thieves?" She looked at Archie. It now seemed they had two new suspects to consider besides the two thieves from the dock, Mitford, and Eve Tomlinson. How many others would come out of the woodwork?

"Why indeed? I wonder if this means they have already made the deal."

"I think it means there are two different thugs. So now we need to broaden our search and–" she stopped talking as a movement caught her eye. "Look, is that Eve?"

Archie and Willie both turned.

"That is Eve Tomlinson," Archie said as he watched her walk around from the other side of the cathedral without a glance in their direction.

"What is she up to?" Cora said.

"Who is Eve Tomlinson?" Willie asked.

Cora reminded Willie that she was Brandon's fiancée. She told her about Eve's presence at the murder scene and their suspicions about her lack of emotion regarding Brandon's death.

"So that's Brandon's fiancée," Willie said as she stared at the woman. "She doesn't look so special to me. Maybe we should follow her in, get a better look at what she's up to."

"Good idea, Willie. However, if she sees us, she'll recognize us and know we are following her. And if she did murder Brandon, she could be dangerous?"

"She's never seen me. I'm here with a tour group, so she won't be suspicious if I follow," Willie said. Without waiting for an answer, Willie stood and rushed towards the entrance.

Cora and Archie followed behind, more cautiously. She gave a surprised grin at Willie's new nature. They tried to stay out of sight by staying close to the walls. Eve Tomlinson entered one of the confession booths and closed the door.

"I've got to hear this," Cora whispered as she walked towards the confession booth.

Archie grabbed her elbow. "We can't listen to her confession. That's just not right." They caught up to Willie. She lowered her head and shoulders.

"But what if it's her confession to the murder or the theft?" Cora noticed the confession booths. The doors were closed in the right-hand booth, which meant someone was inside waiting for the priest. The center booth was open, and Eve Tomlinson was in the third.

"I think Cora's right," Willie said. "If she killed Brandon, she might be here to confess, and we should listen."

"But what if it's something else that may be private?" Archie said.

"What other private confession would she say that we already didn't know by her character. Archie, in a situation like this, we need to take drastic measures." Cora took a step toward the occupied confession booth and tried to listen through the wall. She stepped back. "The walls are so thick it's hard to hear from out here."

"That's the point, Cora," Archie said in a sarcastic voice.

"Then I guess there's only one way to talk to her," Cora said as she stepped into the far left booth and reached for the handle.

"Cora, no I don't think we should—" Archie began as the priest's door in the right booth opened, and the priest stepped out. The three immediately took a few steps back.

"Now or never..." Cora whispered, but it was Willie who acted, dashed to the door of the middle confessional booth, and walked in. Cora watched over her shoulder as the priest entered the middle booth to hear Willie's confession.

"That's my girl," Cora whispered.

Archie shook his head. "I think we're corrupting Willie. I don't think she should spend so much time with us."

Cora reached for the handle of the left confession booth priest's door and opened it.

"Cora, I really don't think we should—"

"Shh," Cora whispered. "Willie did this so we would have time to talk to Eve. I don't want Willie to think this was all a waste."

"It shouldn't be that much of a waste. I'm sure she has plenty to confess," Archie said.

"Stay out here if you want. I'm going in." Cora opened the door and stepped in and felt Archie step in behind her. They closed the door and sat down close together on the single chair. Cora pointed to the small sliding door that separated the two chambers. Archie shook his head. She rolled her eyes and slid the door open.

"Forgive me father for I have sinned," Eve started, then paused as if waiting. "Aren't you going to ask me when my last confession was?"

Cora nudged Archie. He cleared his throat. "Ah, I apologize. When was your last confession?"

Eve sighed, as if relieved. "That's better. For a minute there, I thought it wasn't you but the actual priest. Like I told you last time, I do not know what Brandon did with the item. You're barking up the wrong tree."

"But you were there. Surely you saw something," Archie said, obviously trying to keep her talking.

"I saw nothing. There was a lot of commotion when those two fools went chasing after a couple of petty thieves. I tried to find Brandon but never did until it was too late, so leave me out of this."

"Ask her if she saw who killed Brandon?" Cora whispered into Archie's ear. The two of them were sitting so close together in the priest's chair that she was practically in his lap.

"Hey, is somebody else in there with you?" Eve asked, trying to peer through the screen covering the opening.

"What makes you think—" Archie started.

"It sounds like there's a woman, there's a woman in there and—you two!" Eve said as she leaned towards the screen.

Cora and Archie stared back.

"I am going to tell the priest you are in here and—"

Cora placed her hands on her waist. "Don't get your rosaries tied in a knot, sister. Go ahead and do that. The worst he will do is throw us out. But as for you, you're going to jail for the murder of Brandon Williamson."

"How dare you accuse me of killing the man I loved?" Her voice grew defensive.

"The man you loved? If you loved him, why didn't you shed any tears for him when you stood over his lifeless body?"

Eve opened her mouth, but nothing came out. She reached for the door handle.

"You know you are a suspect," Archie said. "If you didn't murder Brandon, then tell us everything you know to help us find who did." He spoke quickly as if trying to change her mind before she left.

Eve hesitated.

"You know Inspector Bevan suspects you of Brandon's murder," Cora lied. "It's not just us."

Eve paused. "Alright. Alright. Brandon and I were not doing so well lately."

"Oh, come off it," Archie said. "No matter the state of your relationship, you would have cried over Brandon's death if you had any feelings for him at all."

Eve gasped. "Have you ever lost anyone? Everyone has their own way of grieving. This is mine."

"Bevan won't believe that and neither do we," Archie said.

"I don't care if you believe me or not. I didn't murder Brandon because I'm not the kind of person who would kill just anyone."

"Who were you expecting to talk to here in the confessional?" Archie said.

Eve gasped. "No one. I don't know his name."

Cora tsked. "Why is it that I don't believe you?"

"You've got to understand. You've got to believe me. I am definitely not the one who killed Brandon."

"Then tell us…" Archie said as their door opened and a robed priest peered down at them.

Cora heard Eve's door open and close with a bang. She had left.

Before the priest spoke, Cora and Archie got up. "Our feet were tired, and we needed a place to sit and, I don't know how we got in here," Cora babbled. "So, so sorry. Our feet are fine now—and we're leaving the church now, and we'll leave you to your… duties."

"Make sure that you do leave," the priest said with a stern look. He walked in and sat down.

"Yes, we will. And again, we're so sorry." Cora walked towards the back and saw Willie in a chair pulling down a kneeling bench to pray.

Cora stopped next to the row and gave Willie a questioning look.

"I have to do twelve Hail Marys, which is a considerable feat since I'm Protestant," Willie said, but then rose to follow them out the door. "You know, I feel a bit better about Roy after talking with the priest." She paused. "Did you get any information from her?" They made their way outside.

"Maybe. Evidently, she thought she was talking with someone else. Eve said she didn't know what Brandon did with 'the item', probably the jackal," Cora said. "She sounded frightened, almost as if she were being threatened. She was adamant that she did not kill Brandon."

Willie lowered her eyebrows. "Isn't that what they all say? Who do you think she came here to meet and where are they now?"

"We don't know," Archie said. "No one else showed up at the confessional while we were there. The list of suspects is growing. I'm sorry we dragged you into this, Willie."

"That's okay. Like I said, it was freeing to talk to the priest. I really think I'm unloading all my fears and hostilities about Roy. So at least I got something out of it."

"I'm happy for you, Willie. I have to say you dashing into the confessional booth to give us time shows you really are ready to take the plunge into your new life," Cora said.

"How so?" Archie asked.

"Willie is no longer the little frightened mouse she was when we first met at the St. Paul train station. Now she's ready to jump in when someone is in need and take charge of the situation. I think that shows strong character. Look, I still have goose-pimples just thinking of it."

"Thanks, and—oh look," Willie said and pointed. "That's the tour. I've got to join them before I miss the bus. Are you coming with me, Cora?"

"I can't. I've got to keep looking for Arve and Ola."

"But what if those two men I saw talking with Mitford were going to meet Eve? They were frightening, especially the short stocky fellow—you could be in danger, both of you."

"We'll be fine," Cora said, trying to sound confident when she saw Willie's worried expression. She looked at Archie, then back at Willie. "Please, I promise I will come back tonight."

"You promise."

"Ab-so-lute-ly," Cora said, looking straight into Willie's eyes.

"See you tonight then," Willie said and stealthily made her way back to the group as if she had never left.

Chapter 14

"It's about time they left that damn church," the stocky man said as he observed Archie drive off.

The tall, dapper man started the engine and followed them. "Mr. Kent, do have patience," he said in a smooth voice as he kept his eyes on Archie's car ahead of them.

"Are you sure he's the man we want, Stokes?"

The taller man frowned. "Mr. Mitford was clear in his description of Archibald Thorogood. That was him. Furthermore, I'll do the thinking here. Your job is to follow my orders. Your talents lie in your brawn and not in your brain. That is a muscle you seem to lack." Recently Kent seemed to challenge his authority and perhaps need to deal with him in the future.

Kent scowled at Stokes as his hands formed into fists.

"Oh, don't be like that. It makes you look like a spoiled little brat." Stokes attempted to make his voice sound appeasing. Now was not the time to deal with Kent. They needed to determine what Archibald Thorogood was up to and if he had received the jackal.

Kent cracked his knuckles.

"We'll have none of that. Concentrate on your future earnings when this task is over." Stokes stopped his car two car lengths behind Archie's while he waited for the traffic cop to signal him on. Just as Stokes was about to proceed forward, Archie took a right turn.

"There," Kent said, his finger extended. "He turned right."

"I have eyes, haven't I? How many times do I have to tell you to keep your mouth shut?" He pursed his lips. Mustn't lose control, not right now. He took a breath.

"If it were not for the big pay-out, I would not waste my time with you either," Kent said.

Stokes sighed but did not reply. Archie turned right again, and Stokes followed.

"If you're so smart, then tell me why this Archie bloke is spending so much time with this bird? Who is she?" Kent asked.

"Do I have to explain to you about the fair sex and why men fancy them?"

"No, you don't. I was referring to her getting in our way. She'll ruin this entire operation."

"A little birdie like that? Why are you afraid she will clobber you? If that's the case, it looks like I hired the wrong man."

"You look like the wrong man," Kent shouted.

"Don't shout." They continued to follow Archie.

"Look, since you're so ignorant—" Kent started.

"Shut up. They're stopping." Stokes drove past and parked in a space two cars ahead. They sat in the car and watched Archie and Cora get out and head down the street.

"I wonder what they're after?" Stokes said under his breath.

"It's a pub? Need I say more?" Kent said with a chortle. "He wants to get the birdie drunk so he can have an easier time getting his way. These hoity-toity blokes are just like the rest of us, after all."

"Hmm," Stokes said, as if Kent had not spoken. He looked at Archie and Cora through the rearview mirror. "I wonder why they are at this particular place?"

"Now I have to tell you what men and women do in a pub?"

"Perhaps they're meeting someone," Stokes said, again ignoring Kent's statement. "I wouldn't be surprised if that chap knows where the jackal has gone. Mitford said he was on the ship with Brandon. Maybe he's the one who stole it and is now trying to pawn it off."

Kent snorted and shook his head.

"We need to follow them in and get them to talk to us before anyone else has a chance to. A man in my line of work must be flexible and, like I said, I'll do the talking."

"You always like to talk when I could-" Kent's threat went unnoticed, Stokes left the car. Kent got out and followed behind.

"Again, keep your big mouth shut while I do the talking," Stokes said over his shoulder.

Kent growled and cracked his knuckles.

"I feel like we're being followed." Archie peeked over his shoulder for the third time. He grabbed the handrail of the stairway leading down to another dodgy bar.

"Lively down there, isn't it?" Cora looked down the steps. She didn't pay attention to Archie's words as she chewed her bottom lip and prepared to enter another questionable place.

"Maybe a bit too lively. This isn't exactly a sterling neighborhood." Archie took another quick glance over his shoulder at the people behind him.

Cora ignored his last comment as she considered their next move. "I've been thinking. You did suggest to Bevan that my wood carvings are valuable. Maybe the thieves sold them to Mitford along with the jackal. Mitford would have seen the value of them and paid them a few pennies so he could make a profit from them. Maybe he has all three items hidden away."

"That may be so, but we've found no evidence that Mitford has our pieces. Nor do I have any idea where he stores the stolen items."

Cora looked at him. "I still think he has them. We just haven't found the evidence." They paused before heading into the bar.

Archie let go of the rail and winked at Cora. "Is that why you spoke so loudly to Mitford back at the museum?" He grinned. "So, your carvings would hear you and come running to find you?"

Cora gasped and stared at him. "What? Why did you ask that?"

Before Archie could reply, three drunken men stumbled out of the door and passed them on the stairway.

Cora moved closer to Archie and struggled to compose herself after his question.

Archie laughed. "Sorry, I was just having a spot of fun while I ready, myself for this." Archie pointed to the door. He straightened his spine and narrowed his eyes.

She caught hold of his sleeve. "The reason I shouted," Cora lied. "Was to make Mitford tense, hoping he would slip up and reveal something."

Archie shook his head and looked at Cora. "Did you see any deception on Mitford's part?" His eyes shifted back to the street behind them.

"No. I thought he showed sincere concern when we talked about the missing jackal. And I believe it was a genuine insult to him when you accused him of having the jackal."

"Yes, I suppose it is so." Archie leaned on the rail. Then motioned toward the door. "Which brings us back to this place."

Cora wanted to find Ola, Arve and the Jackal, but she wasn't exactly eager to face another dodgy bar. "It sounds like they have a talented piano player to keep the crowd lively."

"Again, be careful, and also hope there are no undercover agents here."

Cora nodded. They stepped down. He opened the door, and they entered.

The noise and smoke of the crowd took some time to get used to. They grabbed a table when two people got up and left, then ordered drinks from a server. "At least the piano stopped, for now." Cora watched the piano player head to the bar and sit down among others.

When Archie sat down, his back collided with the back of a neighbor drinker. He excused himself and the man grunted in reply.

"Maybe it's time to just dive in and play the part."

"What do you mean, *play the part?*"

"I think you were right about role-playing. You mentioned briefly on the ship that you were in school plays as a kid."

"I did say youth, not nursery," Archie said with raised eyebrows. "No, I aspired to Shakespearean methodologies."

"How did you do?"

"I did receive applause. One time I got a standing ovation." He sat up straighter, as if proud of his accomplishments.

Cora felt a tingling sensation in her stomach as she watched him laugh. Archie tilted his head back when he laughed, as if focused on the moment. She smiled at Archie.

She shook her head. "I keep wondering if Eve and Brandon planned the theft together. After all, Brandon said they were close. If we suspect Brandon was planning the theft, then why wouldn't Eve have anything to do with that?"

"Interesting," Archie said, rubbing his hand on his chin. "But then, if he had something to do with the Jackal of Iknokman, and the other missing artifacts, I believe in order for him to get away with this, he would..."

"Pardon me for interrupting," a voice spoke from above Cora. "I could not help overhearing you mention something I may be interested in, something that could be highly beneficial for all concerned."

Cora looked over her shoulder to find two men watching them. She saw Archie's eyebrows narrow while he examined the tall man. Cora spoke fast and without thinking, "Why yes, gentlemen, please do sit down." The man's voice was smooth and practiced, as if he was well-versed in the art of persuasion. Her senses were immediately on alert.

"Thank you miss," the tall man said. "You are most kind."

The men each took a seat at their table. The shorter, stocky man sat next to Archie without saying a word. He observed them with narrowed eyes.

"This is very nice now, don't you think?" The tall man said. "My name is Mr. Stokes, and this is my associate Mr. Kent and what are your names, if I may be so bold to enquire."

Archie introduced himself and Cora to the two men.

Cora smiled courteously at the stocky man, who grinned menacingly back as if he wanted nothing to do with her. If she could put a description on his expression, she would say he wanted to hurt her. He must be "the muscle" in their association. She shuddered and kept her distance from him.

The Missing Jackal Murder

Cora studied Mr. Stokes. His expression could not be more different from Kent's. He smiled softly at Cora and Archie. He wore a camel colored coat with a dark brown tie beneath. Mr. Stokes sat straight as if he were giving them his undivided attention. He reminded Cora of one of her father's top sales agents, or a door-to-door salesman her mother and sister had to deal with. Her father would have called him a "city slicker." Though Mr. Stokes was far more pleasant than his associate, Cora believed she should be careful around him as well, not knowing what special dangers he possessed. With their description of Eve's roommate, these are the people Eve had to meet. She took a sip from her glass and thought the best way to get information from Mr. Stokes was to pile on the flattery with meaningless pleasantries, hoping to loosen his tongue. She opened her mouth, but Archie spoke first.

"What is it that you want?" he addressed Mr. Stokes, staring into his eyes.

Mr. Kent gave Archie an annoyed scowl.

"Ah, straight to the point, a direct question deserves a direct answer," Stokes said. "Very well, a direct answer is what you should get."

"Thank you, kind sir," Cora said, giving him a smile of encouragement.

"I do not profess to be an eavesdropper, but you mentioned something I am interested in; the Jackal of Prince Iknokman. Is it, perhaps, in your possession?"

"What do you know of—" Archie began roughly, but Cora cut him off.

"I hope you understand the historical significance of the statue, to say nothing about it being quite priceless," Cora said without giving Stokes a straight answer.

"I am aware of both," Stokes said, glancing at Cora.

"And I hope you understand," Kent said sharply and stood, "we will do whatever it takes to get the statue by any means, even if—"

Stokes interrupted as he waved Kent back down in his seat. "Now, now, my uneducated and socially inept friend… we are among friends." He gave Kent a thin smile.

Kent glared at Stokes, as if ready to strike. Stokes looked back and wordlessly sent Kent a message with his eyes that said, 'sit down and shut up'. Kent obeyed and sat back down. He folded his arms over his chest and sneered at Archie's drink as if he wanted the glass to explode.

"Now then, do forgive Mr. Kent's rude interruption. Yes, I am quite aware of its value, historically and monetarily." He smiled at Cora.

"So, I assume you have many antiquities in your collection, Mr. Stokes. Do tell me about your collection," she said sweetly.

"Ah, miss, my collection is miniscule. But to be quite honest, I am more of a treasure locator. I bring together those who possess what my clients are looking for to said clients, with a commission, of course."

"Of course."

"Or I may purchase the item for resale directly to the client. Also, if you wish, I would consider you as a client and sell the artifact and charge a nominal fee." Stokes finished with a satisfied expression.

"Oh my," Cora said, "that's rather disappointing."

Stokes' face changed abruptly as he looked at her. "Miss Cora?"

"Well, you see, I hoped to see, rather inspect your collection, and see where the statue will rest. I like to have the peaceful knowledge that it will go to a suitable home."

"Oh, I assure you that the statue's final resting place will be among a fine choice of antiquities. Are you considering dealing directly with the client? I assure you, I can gain the highest profit from—"

"No, no, no," Archie interrupted, finally weighing in on the discussion. "I assure you that Miss Cora does intend to see the artifact's proper resting place. I do not wish to seem impertinent, but Miss Cora does insist on meeting with the collector and…"

Kent sprung from his seat, grabbed Archie by the collar, and lifted him. "Listen here you slug. I want the statue now or I'll—"

"Mr. Kent, you will unhand Mr. Thorogood now or I will—" Stokes shouted as he sprang up and grabbed Kent's arm.

Other patrons around them fell silent as they sat and watched the struggle before them.

Kent's face reddened. "Stokes, you are plain stupid, aren't you? They've been playing you all this time and you can't see it. You can't give them the name of our client."

"Get off me." Archie pushed Kent to his chair.

"Why you," Kent jumped up and hit Archie in the mouth.

"Tell them to stop it!" Cora said to Stokes, as Archie landed his fist squarely on Kent's nose. Kent landed on another customer.

Someone screamed, and a couple of servers approached as if to stop the scuffle.

"Why you—" the man said to Kent.

"You have been playing me," Stokes stood abruptly and spoke to Cora, "haven't you?"

"What if I have? You stole our suitcases. You tried to get information from us, didn't you?"

"Information?" Stokes said with a look of confusion.

The other customer hit Kent in the mouth and Kent fell over. Kent got back up and went for Archie.

Archie sidestepped him, and Kent stumbled past.

"Yes, information on how you would frame us for your murder of Brandon Williamson," Cora said.

Stokes sighed. "I had nothing to do with his murder."

Kent rose to his feet. "You stay out of this. That is none of your business, bitch. Watch what you say, or you'll end up—"

Archie struck Kent so hard he fell to the ground and had trouble getting up. After a few moments, he rose back up without a word.

Stokes grabbed hold of Cora's arm in a tight grip. "Where is the Jackal?"

"No idea." Archie said as he pulled Cora away from Stokes.

"So, you were playing us," Stokes's voice changed from genteel to vicious in a blink of an eye.

Cora leaned forward. "What is the name of your client, the one you are going to sell it to?"

"Where is the jackal?" Stokes repeated, his voice growing more urgent.

"No idea."

Kent took a step forward and slapped Cora.

She gasped and put a hand up to her cheek.

"What?" Archie clenched his fists and stepped towards Kent.

Cora stopped Archie and turned to Kent herself. "Hasn't your mother ever told you not to strike a lady?" She kicked Kent in the groin.

Kent fell back down to the ground, bent with his hands to his crotch.

The Missing Jackal Murder

Those around gasped at her action.

Kent staggered to his feet. "You better find the jackal and–"

Cora approached Stokes. "As for you–" She reached back and hit Stokes hard on the nose. He fell, tried to get up, but the large man picked him up. He was about to slug Kent, but Kent struck back. They brawled.

Stokes rolled on the floor and did not get up.

Archie looked around. "I think we'd better get out of here, now."

"If any of Bevan's men were here, they would've stopped us by now."

Archie watched the bartender, who spoke to another very large and muscular man, then pointed towards Kent. "Bevan's men are the least of our worries."

Archie grabbed Cora's hand again and pulled her out of the saloon as Kent's body flew. He smashed into a table and broke it in half as he landed. The sounds of screaming clients disappeared as Archie and Cora leaped into the car and drove off.

Chapter 15

"Arve, I really don't think this is a good idea," Ola said, wringing her hands.

"Of course it's a good idea," Iknokman said. "I wish I had thought of it myself. Now remember the plan, Arve. All you need to do is to get a police officer's attention. You yell, holler, or call him names. Do whatever you can to make him think it was Jerry calling out. He'll arrest Jerry, take everything out of his pockets and bring you and him to Scotland Yard. I'm sure your Cora will have reported you as valuable stolen property by now. Once Cora comes to get you and you tell her everything, she will send the police for us."

"But what if you fall out of his pocket and get lost?" Ola asked with a worried look on her face.

"I won't fall out," Arve said reassuringly. His right hand was on the front dresser leg with his eyes on Jerry.

Iknokman also watched for the right time for Arve to cross the room and get into Jerry's coat pocket. "Oh, also, take mental notes of your surroundings as you go to lead her back here."

Though Arve's plan was simple, still anything could go wrong while he hitch a ride in Jerry's pocket on his way to meet with another potential buyer. He ignored Ola's pleads for them to stay together. The rescue from Nicholas, if anything did go wrong, seemed not enough to quell her fears. Now, the first step was to observe the two hoodlums and find a right time and way for Arve to make his way to Jerry's coat before he leaves and without being spotted.

The Missing Jackal Murder

They listened to the two men talking. "Be careful," Clyde said to Jerry, "I don't trust anybody I don't know."

"Are you my wet-nurse? Don't you think I know how to take care of myself?" Jerry said while he shook his head.

"Are you sure I can't come along?" Clyde said as he panned the room, his eyes as if something will come out and attack. "You know, this place gives me the creeps. I'd rather not be here alone."

"Like I said, stop acting like a little tyke and be a man for a change. If you were there, you would ruin everything. Don't you want to get paid, or do you want to hang on to the bloody thing forever?"

Clyde nodded his head to show that he wanted his money just as much as Jerry did.

"Now, if all goes according to plan, we'll have a nice payoff from this bloke."

"How do you know the barkeep was not giving you a runaround?"

"He'll be good on his word." Jerry pointed his thumb over his shoulder. "We go way back, we do. Besides, I flipped him a bob."

"But what about this bloke you're meetin'?" Clyde wrung his hands. "What if he is not good at his word? What if he wants little doggie there and wants to keep his loot?"

"Just in case." Jerry took his coat off and threw it on the floor. "I've got my insurance." He pulled a gun out of his waistband and showed it to Clyde.

The three under the dresser looked at each other. "Now."

"I'll be fine," Arve said, and bolted around the furniture for cover.

"Best be going," Jerry said with a huff.

Arve reached the coat and scrambled for the first pocket he could find. Jerry lifted his coat. Arve grabbed hold and hung onto the opposite side so Clyde could not see him. Ola gasped as Arve moved like a spider towards the front pocket. Jerry got the coat on when Arve grabbed the flap of the top pocket.

Jerry shook the coat by the collar for a more comfortable fit. Arve's left hand broke its grasp and bounced, holding on with his other hand tight. Ola gasped again.

"What the bloody hell! There's that bloody sound again," Clyde said, and moved in front of Jerry.

Ola and Iknokman scurried back.

Jerry swung around to see Clyde pointing to the dresser. The rapid move was enough for Arve to grab the pocket with his other hand and swing inside.

"And have supper ready when I get back. No lying down for any nap, then."

Arve settled into the pocket.

"I'll make my famous soup to celebrate." Clyde spoke in a jovial voice.

"Did we have your famous soup last time when — oh, never mind," Jerry pulled the door open to leave. Arve peaked out enough to see Ola's painful expression as Jerry closed the door.

Arve was on his own, alone. He grabbed hold when the coat jostled up and down as Jerry trotted down the stairs. Jerry hummed his way out the door into the street. This was the first time Arve had ever been completely alone, away from Ola and the rest of the villagers, before-. He cleared his mind. "I can do this—I don't need Nicholas, I can..."

Arve's imagination got the best of him as he remembered scenes with dark trees and wolves baying at the moon. "Stop it," he told himself. "Where am I?" Arve shook himself out of his imaginings. The street sounds filled his ears. "Stop this, think. What did Iknokman say?" Arve's mind cleared. "Look out for landmarks. Get bearings. Find someone or something that will help."

Arve slowly brought his head out. Jerry's right arm pivoted back and forth in front of his eyes and attempt to spot anything between swings. People around him were not aware of him or alarmed at the movements from Jerry's pocket. Arve moved his head out further to get a better view. So far, he had seen nothing different from the view from the third-floor window of the apartment. Jerry turned a corner. What landmarks could Arve spot? The street sign on a building that said 'Fuller' verified their street. As Jerry turned left, Arve saw another plaque that read, 'Brine.'

Fuller and Brine. He'll remember that. But in what direction were they walking? He looked around and tried to determine the direction of the sun. His observations from the shadows of the building, he concluded that Fuller was on an east/west street. So, he's walking north. The shadows ahead with the sun behind told him he was more than likely correct.

"Ah, evenin' miss," Jerry had stopped to speak to someone.

"Beat it," a woman's voice said with strong heels clopping on the pavement as she walked away.

Arve quickly brought his head down.

"Just saying evenin," he shouted. "Just being friendly. I'm headin' for a well-respected drinking establishment. Would you like to join me?"

The distant voice responded, "Get a wiggle on."

"Sheesh, she thinks she's such a swell," Jerry resumed his walk. "But look at those gams."

Arve brought his head out again and looked behind him to watch her. He didn't know what "gams" meant, but her long legs would interest any man as they brought her swaying hips so high and low, which made her butt wiggle. It reminded Arve of what it would look like for two small pigs to wrestle under a blanket.

Arve looked forward and all around. Though he ignored cars that passed by, but one caught his attention when a little girl stared out from the passenger side window. Her eyes caught his, and she watched him as the car moved on. She waved. Arve waved back. She smiled. Before the car moved out of sight, he saw the girl turn to her mother.

He grinned. She's going to have a problem telling her mother what she saw, since the magic prohibited her from giving an explanation. That little girl would sit in frustration. "I must remember to tell Nicholas to bring her one of Ola's wool sweaters for Christmas this year," Arve said to himself. Speaking of remembering, he resumed his attempt to store as much scenery as possible into his memory.

Arve got down in Jerry's pocket when he stopped, walked down a small flight of concrete stairs, and opened a door. A generous wave of voices, aromatic smells, and piano music peaked Arve's interest. Jerry was no longer moving. He was possibly scanning the room for the contact he had mentioned to Clyde.

Arve worried inside Jerry's pocket. Yes, there were obviously many people here which represented many chances for him to get someone's attention and get into danger. He wasn't sure what to do next.

"Ah hah," Jerry said and resumed his trek, then stopped again. "I believe you are the two gentlemen who want what I have in my possession."

"Are you just being cute?" a harsh voice asked.

"A poor choice of words from my uneducated friend," the other said calmly in a more genteel voice.

"Hey," the harsh voice said.

"Yes," the genteel voice said. "We may be interested in acquiring some merchandise you offer."

"I am your man then," Jerry said in an enthusiastic tone. The sudden movement under Arve's feet told him Jerry took off his coat and placed it on the chair to his right. The coat immediately fell to the floor. "First, I need to know you're not coppers."

"Listen," the first reacted. "How do we know that you're not a cop? And if you are—"

Arve lifted his head out of the pocket and ignored the details of the conversation. He suspected Jerry had removed his coat to reveal his pistol, as he had done to show Clyde back at the apartment. It was obviously a show of dominance, and Arve shuddered. Maybe their decision not to call for Nicholas to help had been a mistake. He crawled out and walked a few inches from the coat. He gazed around the saloon for anything that would help him bring the police to the rescue.

As Arve pictured a map to their location in his head, he wished he had a paper and pencil to draw it out. He walked out enough to get a partial view of a couple behind the bar, a man and a woman darting from side to side. If only he could find that paper to write a message.

He returned and passed by the coat to the chair leg under Jerry. He watched his leg move nervously under the table. Then he noticed that the conversation between Jerry and the two men had heated up. Arve ignored their conversation and looked towards the door.

Arve notice a woman's purse on the floor two tables away. A quick glance showed a woman, possibly a barmaid, walking toward Jerry's table. Her foot stopped inches from Arve. He took a few steps back, looked at the woman's purse under the table and thought, "now or never." Arve made his dash across the floor and reached the first table. He stopped and heard Jerry shouting as he roughly dismissed the barmaid and pushed his chair back.

"Did your mama teach you to talk like that?" the barmaid said in an angry voice.

Arve looked at the purse, now one table away, ready for the dash.

"Beat it, Mary," Jerry said and stood up. "You've gone and done it. You wasted my time like any other woman would." Jerry's hand absentmindedly reached for the jacket, not knowing the coat had fallen to the floor. The barmaid approached the table where Arve stood. Jerry's hand moved down to search for his coat, his eyes now joining the search.

Arve dashed back towards Jerry's coat and heard the barmaid shout, "Bloody mice!" Arve rounded the coat with his eyes on the open pocket. When Jerry lifted his coat, Arve dove and missed the pocket. He held onto the area of the coat close enough to the pocket for him to make another move, again like a spider, towards the pocket.

Jerry stomped towards the door with the coat in his hand. He turned and swore at the two men. The force swung Arve closer to the pocket. He held on. Jerry took the collar and swung the coat around, much like a man putting on a cloak. Arve held on, making his body swing parallel to the floor.

Some eyes in the saloon caught the acrobatics, but no one reacted—as they were probably too drunk to care.

As Jerry exited the building, he reached the top steps. His body came to a sharp stop, and he moved sharply to his right. "Pardon me, miss, I seem to have missed the last step."

"Don't worry about it. No harm done," a woman said.

Arve got one foot into the pocket when he heard the woman's voice and could not believe his ears.

"I've got a feeling we'll find something in here," she said as Jerry stepped away.

"I suppose," a man answered. "I've got no other ideas. Maybe you can tell me why we need to stop at all these telegraph offices. You said you wanted to tell me something."

He recognized the man's voice; it was too good to be true. Arve stuck his head out to see the couple begin their descent. Only the backs of their heads were visible.

"It's got to be them," Arve said out loud and looked up to see that Jerry hadn't heard his exclamation. "Should I chance it?" Before the man's and woman's heads disappeared down the stairway, Arve saw the door open and the woman's profile was visible for less than half a second.

"It's got to be Cora," Arve said out loud again. Despite the people around and the chance that Jerry would notice him, Arve made his move. He pulled his foot from the pocket, slid down Jerry's coat and jumped.

Jerry's heel kicked Arve back and into the street. "She has Ola's side pouch." He got up and saw another couple open the door. So many people were around. Surely, someone would see him. But this was a desperate situation. Arve made a dash to the opened door.

"Egads, what was that?" a woman cried out.

"Is that Tom Thumb?" a man said.

"No, it's a mouse you clod," another said.

Arve took each concrete step by running up, turning around, and sliding down to the next. He dashed inside right before the door closed on him.

Conversations inside mingled with arguments outside. The protective magic prevented those who saw Arve from understanding what they had seen. Arve quickly scanned the bar. He saw the two men Jerry had talked to walk out with their heads tilted away from Cora and Archie. Arve dashed under the table to see Archie and Cora look at the backs of the two men with curiosity. They silently looked at each other and shrugged.

They took the seats vacated by the three men. Arve made his way across the floor, under the table and chairs, and hid behind the purse he had aimed for earlier. The purse lifted and Arve scurried towards Cora's and Archie's table. The owner of the purse screamed.

"Pardon, miss," the barmaid said. "I'll have a word with the proprietor about our mice situation here."

"Did that bloody mouse wear a green coat?" one man asked.

"What was that?" Archie said.

"I believe she said it was a mouse," Cora said.

"Pesky things." Archie lifted his foot and looked down, but Arve moved behind Cora's chair before he could spot him. The barmaid approached, got the orders and walked away as Archie played with his coins on the tabletop.

Now the problem that remained was how to get Cora's attention but not startle her, Archie, or anyone else in the room. Arve approached Cora's foot, her toes wiggled slightly. "If I were to climb up her leg and—hold on, is that silk stockings she's wearing?" Arve took a few steps slightly to his left to see the bottom of Cora's face, to verify she was the one he was looking for. Arve shook his head and moved back and looked around again at her leg. "If Marit catches Cora wearing silk stockings, she will…" Arve became mesmerized by the shiny surface and brought his hand up to touch.

"Anyway you were about to tell me what you discovered from the telegraph office."

Cora crossed her leg to the right and placed it over her left knee. Arve jumped back. Cora's feet wiggled. Archie mirrored Cora and placed his right leg over his left knee.

"Well, first, I wanted to tell my mother that I am all right here in London," Cora said.

Arve looked at Archie's pant leg and wondered if he could crawl up without him noticing. The barmaid returned with their drinks. Arve used the distraction to make his move. In one uninterrupted fluid motion, he climbed up Archie's pants leg to his knee, ran to the tip of Archie's right foot, sprang off like from a swimming pool diving board and grabbed the bottom of Cora's dress and clung onto her knee.

Cora squealed, dropped her leg and pushed back her chair.

"Sorry, miss," the barmaid said. "I will talk to the proprietor about the present mice situation."

Cora ignored the woman and gazed at what clung to her knee. Arve and Cora stared at each other for what seemed like several minutes. Arve raised his eyebrows and Cora blinked.

"These pesky mice," Archie said and reached for his right leg. He moved his hand to look under the table.

Cora immediately snatched Arve and quickly dropped him into her pouch. "I need to use the ladies' room!"

"Are you alright?"

"It's not the mice. I need to freshen up a bit. I'll be right back." Cora sprang from her chair before Archie responded.

Cora walked straight to the door, opened it, and hoped that no one was inside. She was alone. She closed, then locked the door, then reached into her pouch to pull out Arve. "Arve, how? Where? Where is Ola? What's going on?"

"We don't have time."

"Why? Is Ola in danger?"

"No, for now she and Iknokman are fine. The two who have us are complete bumbling idiots, but we're not sure how dangerous they could be if the situation warranted it."

"Where did they take you—and did you say they have the statue of Iknokman?"

Arve spoke rapidly and gave an abridged version of their encounters. He explained Iknokman is a live being and told his story. He told her about the two thugs, their impatience to search for another buyer, and Arve's deceptive plan to travel with Jerry.

"Where are they now?" Cora said. Her breathing seemed to return to normal.

Arve told her about the corner of Fuller and Brine and other landmarks on the way. "What about you?" Arve asked.

Cora gave her abridged version of their exploits.

"Yes, the idiots talked about Brandon's murder." Arve said. "Have the police discovered who did it?"

"No, but I believe I do. Everything is making sense and coming together. But now is not the time. We need to get Ola."

"I don't understand?" Arve said. "Why didn't Nicholas come?"

"I didn't call him. Did you?"

Arve shook his head. "No."

"You didn't want Nicholas to show up? He would've been able to get you out of this mess."

The Missing Jackal Murder

"No, I thought you didn't either. Unless we were all in danger, well, serious danger. I knew we could figure this out by ourselves without help from Nicholas."

Cora smiled. "We truly are great traveling companions."

"Now all we have to do is collect Ola and we'll be together again. Then we need to get Iknokman back to the museum. And after that, there's still time for you to enjoy your tour."

"I'm looking forward to that, but first, Archie and I have things to clear up. I also need to think of something to tell him without him-" A knock sounded on the door and a woman's voice interrupted their conversation. "I'll be out in a minute," Cora said. "Arve, we've got to leave. I wish I had time to think. Someone else needs to use the facilities and — that's it." Cora stood up, placed Arve in her pouch and dashed out of the bathroom and approached Archie. "We have to go now." Cora glanced towards the lady's bathroom.

"What's the matter?"

"I know where my case is. Our cases are."

"What? How?"

Again, Cora glanced back at the lavatory door. "I heard two women in the ladies' room talk about it. They were going along with two men, eh, Stokes and Kent. Yeah, that's it. They talked about the location. Stokes and Kent are on their way there now."

"I knew it. I thought those were the two when we entered. We need to get inspector Bevan and the police."

"But Archie?"

"We can't handle this alone. They're dangerous men. And who knows what the people who have our case are like?"

"They said they were—oh, I suppose you're right."

"But we have to go now. Scotland Yard is not too far from here." They dashed out. Archie took Cora's elbow and led her to the door.

As they left, the barmaid called after them. "Please come back when you can. I'm sure the proprietor will have the whole mice situation sorted out by then."

#####

"You've got to believe me Inspector, I heard the women describe where our cases are."

Inspector Bevan cocked his head back. "And you believed the words of some strange woman behind a lavatory door?"

"Why not? Isn't it worth an investigation? Why else would anybody talk about an object so specific?"

Bevan sneered. "Why do you spend your visit in those cheap saloons? Do you plan to clean up our fair city? Or is this the way American women behave these days? I know about your flappers. Are you one of those flappers, Miss Gudmundson?"

Cora glared at him. "We go to these cheap saloons for information to help us find our luggage, Inspector Bevan," Cora said. "Why do you have undercover police in those cheap saloons for refreshments?"

Bevan took a deep breath and put his fists on his hips. "What do you make of this, Mr. Thorogood?"

"Well, I–" Archie paused and looked into Cora's face. "I think there's something to it. After all, Cora is an honest woman, but only she knows what happened in the ladies' room, of course."

Bevan opened his mouth, then closed his eyes and shook his head. He waved his hand. "No, no, I can't see this as possible. I don't have time for this nonsense."

"No time?" Cora sputtered. "What exactly do you have time for then, sir?"

"The apprehension of Miss Tomlinson about the murder of Mr. Williamson."

"She—Look—What?"

Bevan interrupted her. "I had sent out a dispatch to pick her up. Unless your lady friends from the lavatory told you where she is as well."

"Inspector!"

"No miss, I'm sorry. It will have to wait."

"Wait!"

Bevan shook his head again and walked away.

"You yellow bellied—" Archie grabbed Cora's hand and jerked her away. "How could he?" The other officers watched Cora stomp towards the door. "What are you all looking at?"

"Shh, do you want them to think you're intoxicated? You'll get a citation."

Archie signaled Mr. Hilliard to bring the car to the front. They walked out the door and down the front sidewalk.

She stood on the sidewalk in front of the building and took a deep breath. With her emotions in check, her mind shifted gears. "Isn't that Bevan's automobile in front?" Cora pointed to the green car the inspector drove away from the loading dock the day before.

"Yes, I believe it is."

They both approached Bevan's car. "Are the officers still looking at me?"

He glanced back toward the building. "I dare say most are."

"Good." Cora grabbed Archie's hand and pulled him. "Get in."

"I beg your pardon?"

"Get in. You can lead the police to—"

"You want me to steal a car, *the Inspector's car* to be specific?"

"Oh, get in, I'll drive." Cora said as she rounded the front and opened the door. "Oh, that's right. The steering wheel is on the wrong side in England." She stepped next to Archie and opened the door.

Archie pulled the door from Cora's hand. "You can't do this!"

"Why not? I told you I've driven an automobile before." Cora jumped in behind the steering wheel. "My brother has the oldest automobile dealership in Duluth, for crying out loud. Don't you think he taught me how to drive? Jeepers, was Mother furious."

She moved the pouch to her side and looked in to see Arve shifted around in alarm. He whispered up at her, "What are you doing?"

"But Cora," Archie said, his hands above the door, and looked down at Cora.

"Are you coming with me or not?"

"I refuse—I absolutely refuse."

"Very well, I'll have to find Fuller and Brine streets by myself."

Archie pointed to the north. "You go down the street to — what am I saying?"

"Wish me luck Arch, that is, if the coppers don't catch me first and put me in the slammer."

The Missing Jackal Murder

"Cora," Archie said. He looked through the front window to see police officers watching them with alarmed expressions. "Cora, they are becoming suspicious."

"Only suspicious?" Cora asked, and put her forefinger and thumb to her lips to let out a loud whistle. More heads turned. "Here we go." Cora put her foot on the clutch. She pushed the start button, and the motor came to life.

"Here now," a voice called from the doorway of the police station.

"Get in, or get out of my way, Archie."

"I—Oh—" Archie ran around the front and opened the door. When Archie got in and closed his door, Cora shifted a lever and lifted the clutch. A terrible grinding sound sprang from the front. "No, not that lever, the other lever," he yelled.

"Do you want to drive?" Cora said, looking straight into Archie's eyes.

Archie looked in horror at the group of police officers running toward them. Bevan in the rear as they came barreling toward them. "Go, go, go!"

Cora grabbed the other lever and pulled, letting go of the clutch. The car jumped forward, sputtered as if to come to a stop, then picked up speed as the officers and Bevan put their hands on the front door. She put down the clutch again and shifted into the next gear. The car sped up.

"You're on the right side of the road!" Archie said with terror in his voice as cars came straight at them.

"Oh, that's right. The right side of the road is the wrong side of the road here."

Cora swerved away from the car on her left side in time to miss an oncoming furniture truck. The truck swerved and rock dangerously close to tipping over. The driver stuck his head out and shouted at her.

"What did he say?"

Archie reached for the top of his hat and held on. "He said 'have a lovely'—look out!"

Cora mistook the sidewalk as the road and turned right back onto the street. She approached a young couple on the sidewalk. The man grabbed the woman's hand and pulled her sharply out of the way as the car narrowly missed them. The woman screamed.

"Don't tell me," Cora said after straightening herself and almost hitting another car coming on her right, "she's wishing me a lovely day as well."

Cora heard police bells behind her. "It's about bloody time they got going."

"You know we are in big- no, this street here," Archie said, pointing forward. "Turn right when we get to that intersection."

"Right, right or left to right? I'm not too sure if—"

"Right, right—now, before you miss it." Cora took a sharp turn and ran up the sidewalk. Pedestrians scattered. She knocked over a newsstand and got back on the road.

"Left lane. I said left lane," Archie said, pointing to his left.

"Oops," Cora spun the wheel before another oncoming truck. He put on his brake to avoid her, but the car behind him smacked into his rear end. "I said oops, sorry. You think he's alright?" She said, reaching up to look in the rearview mirror.

"Look out," Archie said, and pointed forward. Two horses' eyes widened as they saw Cora's car almost on top of them. Both whinnied and reared up on their hind legs. She spun the steering wheel as the horse on the left came down and stepped on Bevan's landing board by Cora's door. She

The Missing Jackal Murder

let out a small shriek. The car rocked and Archie looked at the horse.

"Are the horses alright?" Cora reached up to glance at the rearview mirror again.

"They're fine. Eyes front, eyes front."

"I hope we didn't lose our posse. Nope, they're still there," Cora said after she took another quick glance in the side mirror. "You know, I think I'm getting the hang of this, oh!" She swerved quickly to the right to avoid a crossing pedestrian. She narrowly missed yet another car. She swerved sharply back into the left lane.

"Sure, you're getting the hang of it," Archie said sarcastically while holding his hat down.

"Thank you, Archie," she beamed a big smile.

From Cora's pouch, Arve shouted up, "Are-you-sure Eric taught you how to drive?"

"Shh," Cora said and returned to her driving.

"Eric, you mean your brother? What does your brother have to do with this?"

"Oh, never mind," Cora said as she spun the wheel, narrowly missing yet another pedestrian on the street.

#####

Iknokman's ears perked up at the sounds of distant police bells. He lifted his head from his paws and looked toward the window. Iknokman saw Ola asleep, her head against his right flank. He looked towards the window again.

"Is that copper getting any closer?" Clyde said after swallowing a mouth full of soup.

"Now, just shut up and eat," Jerry said, clanking his soup spoon into his bowl.

"Sounds like it, doesn't it?"

"How would they know we were here? Did you tip 'em off?"

"Get off, Jerry. Why would I tip off a bobby?"

"So, you didn't, so I didn't, so shut up and eat or I'll take yours."

"Alright, alright, you don't have to be so mad. You're always angry with me."

Iknokman listen to the men, then looked back at the window. "The stupid bloke was right. Maybe we should at least get near the window, just in case they are coming for us." He heard a loud tap on the door and sprang to his feet, shaking Ola awake.

Ola lifted her head from Iknokman's side. "What's going on?" She sprang to her feet as the rap on the door echoed again. Iknokman saw a broken bowl of soup spilled on the floor.

"Who is it?" Clyde asked Jerry.

"As if I would know, it's probably bloody Santa Claus for all I care. Open the door and keep your knife in your pocket ready."

Iknokman and Ola walked close to the edge of the dresser. They watched Jerry and Clyde lean on opposite sides of the door, both with their hands in their pocket. Iknokman listened to the police bells getting louder.

Ola put her hands to her mouth. "What should we do?"

"Get to the window."

"But—"

A third knock sounded. Jerry and Clyde stared at the door but said nothing.

"They're staring at the door," Iknokman said to Ola. "Go now. If they look in your direction, I'll distract them."

"Who's there?" Jerry said.

"Now!" Iknokman commanded.

The Missing Jackal Murder

"Mr. Stokes and Mr. Kent," a gentle voice sounded from the other side of the door. "We have thought about your offer and are ready to make a deal."

Ola reached and grabbed the dusty curtain and climbed up. She reached the window ledge as the door opened.

"Good evening. May we come in?" Stokes asked.

"You may entrée," Jerry said in a pleasant voice.

Ola held onto the curtain behind her as she moved to the window latch in the center. She grabbed hold with her free hand and pushed.

"May I have a look at the merchandise?"

"Right here," Jerry said. He bumped Clyde aside, walked to the box on the top of the dresser. Iknokman backed away from the front edge and moved to the left edge to get a better look at Ola. The curtain moved, but the latch of the window would not open.

"Wait," Jerry said, "you're not the police, are you now?"

Iknokman understood Jerry's suspicion. The clanging bells got closer.

Kent grabbed Jerry's collar. "Listen, you maggot. Hand over the jackal or I'll thrash you."

"Er, hey now," Clyde said, "get your filthy paws off my friend."

"Mr. Kent," Stokes spoke in a curt voice.

Kent let go. Jerry rotated his shoulder. "Now, there is no need for that." Jerry placed the box on the table, opened it, and gasped. "What is this?" Jerry said and took a step backwards.

"Where is the merchandise?"

"I don't understand. Clyde, did you do anything with the merchandise?"

After a few profane words, the men's fists hit faces. Legs scuffled as if in a dance. Ola grunted and attempted to open the window. The curtain let loose to reveal her completely exposed while the fight continued. The two men came dangerously close to the window. Now exposed, Ola ran back behind the curtain.

Clyde managed to get Kent onto the floor, his left foot kicked Iknokman. The Prince rolled, then stood back up and growled. He leapt forward and bit Clyde on the ankle just as he was about to get up.

"Ouch!" Clyde screamed, lost his balance and dove forward from the pain. His head rammed into the curtain near where Ola stood. The force of his motion smashed the window and pushed Ola outside, hanging onto the curtain. Ola screamed. The sound was loud enough to distract Stokes, so Jerry could punch him hard enough to knock him to the floor.

Ola screamed again as Iknokman saw her silhouette hanging onto the curtain outside the broken window. Stokes rolled and looked underneath the dresser. Iknokman and Stokes gazed at each other. Stokes reached, but Iknokman bit Stokes' hand. "If you touch me again, I'll crawl down your throat and eat your in-sides."

Stokes froze as Jerry lifted him from the floor to continue their dance.

#####

"Here!" Cora said as the car jerked to a stop over-turning a trash can.

"Are you sure?"

"I'm sure. You did say this is Fuller and Brine?" They got out.

As Cora and Archie size up the building and plan their strategy, they heard a woman scream from the third-floor window. Without hesitation, Archie leapt through the door and ran in.

Cora looked up to the widow where she heard the familiar voice. She walked underneath and stepped on broken glass. The curtain shifted and her mouth opened in a gasp.

"Ola!" Arve shouted from the pouch.

"Ola!" Cora shouted.

Ola stopped screaming and looked down.

"Ola, let go," Cora said with her hand outstretched.

"I can't," Ola said while she and the curtain flapped. Her dress and belt flapped in the breeze.

"Yes, you can," Arve said, then turned to the sound of the police bells enter the area.

"I can't," Ola said.

Cora saw the police car stopped behind her. She looked up again. "You have to trust me. I will catch you."

"I can't!"

"Ola, it's now or never. Just freeze."

Ola closed her eyes and let go. She returned to her wooden form with her hands behind her back and her dress and belt no longer flapped in the breeze.

Bevan stomped behind Cora. "You are under arrest."

Cora reached out and grabbed Ola with both hands. She put Ola in her left hand. As she spun around to face Bevan, she reached into her pouch with her right hand and grabbed Arve, who also had returned to the wooden form and pulled him out. "There," Cora held her two wood carvings in front of Bevan's face. "I told you the truth. These are mine, from my case. Archie's upstairs right now with the thugs who took our cases." Then she pointed up with Arve in her hand.

Bevan followed Cora's point. Just then Clyde stuck his head out, saw Bevan and the police and said, "Oy," and pulled his head back in.

"Go," Bevan commanded his officers. They ran inside.

Cora counted the men, "One, two, three, four, five... Five officers?" Cora asked in shock. "You brought five officers to apprehend *one* woman?" Cora shook her head and looked at the vehicle they used to get there. "A paddy wagon? Five men and a paddy wagon?"

Bevan could only babble, then found his voice. "See here, now. You stay down here and let us handle this." He ran inside.

"Not on your life." As Cora spun around to follow, she saw Hilliard exit Archie's car. She then faced the door Bevan entered, paused, then entered herself. She signaled Hilliard to follow. As they reached the second floor, Hilliard jumped in and stood next to Archie.

Stokes, Kent, Jerry, and Clyde each had an officer behind them, holding onto their elbows. The fifth officer was holding onto Archie. "Where is my statue?" Archie pulled away to grab the empty box from the floor. He scanned the room and found the suitcase.

Cora remembered Arve mentioned they had hidden under a dresser. Upon spotting that piece of furniture, her eyes found the floor underneath and a long snout with an eye on Cora. She winked, lifted Ola out of the pouch. Ola came to life for a moment to wave at Iknokman. The prince smiled as she put Ola back in her pouch, then Cora put her finger to her lip to tell him to be quiet.

Blood dripped from a cut on Jerry's mouth, and he had a swollen eye. "Like I said, I don't know what you're bloody talking about. We don't have this gentleman's statue, do we Clyde?"

The Missing Jackal Murder

Clyde shook his head, then whispered loud enough for everyone to hear. "It bit me, Jerry. Right here on my ankle, he did, right here."

Archie saw Clyde's head tilt towards the corner of the dresser. "Here, clear the way." He bent down on one knee and stared under the dresser. He slowly reached both hands underneath and said in a quiet, almost loving voice, "There you are." He dragged his arm out with the motionless sitting Jackal of Prince Iknokman resting in his hands. "Back to the Museum we go. Yours too?"

Cora nodded, patted her pouch and gave a sigh of relief.

Cora peeked over her shoulder, then whispered to Iknokman. "Don't worry, it's only for a short while." Cora watched Iknokman move his eyes towards hers.

"What?" Archie said and gave her a confused glance.

"Nothing." She watched Kent give another jerk to get himself free from the police who held him.

He stood and carefully placed the statue back into the opened box, closed it and placed the box in the case.

She looked at the two black cases. They were identical. Hers now lay open with her clothing scattered about higgledy-piggledy. "Oh," she gasped. "Which one of you fungi rummaged through my things?" She held up a pair of panties and watched all the men blush.

Bevan ruffled. "Put those bloody, I mean your bloomers away."

Cora scrambled to put all her clothes in her case. She inspected the room to see if she missed anything.

Jerry shook his head. "Here miss, we didn't know it was a lady's case, now did we, Clyde?"

Clyde shook his head vigorously. "Jerry and I didn't think we could get much for those lady things, did we, Jerry?"

"Shut up, you buffoon."

"Why? We couldn't have?"

"Shut up!"

"All is fine and dandy," Bevan said. "You have your property and I have my murderers." He looked at Jerry and Clyde.

Jerry stretched his back. His voice rose in panic. "No, wait, you think we knocked off Williamson?"

Clyde wiggled to break away. "We didn't kill no one".

Bevan folded his arms. "Save it for the magistrate."

"But we didn't. We weren't near the bloke. We hired us to take the statue. Why would we want to kill him?"

Cora turned to Clyde. "He hired you via telegraph?"

Clyde nodded his head rapidly.

"Shut up."

"But we were to sit right here, pretty as you please. Then the telegraph kid came knocking at our door."

"Yeah," Jerry said. "Yeah, we were to just sit here minding our business. So, we are innocent, you see. Tell them Clyde."

"Yes, innocent until we took those–"

"Shut the hell up." Jerry tried to kick Clyde.

"As I said, save it for the magistrate." Bevan began.

Cora folded her arms and shook her head. "You're making a big mistake."

"Now see here, I've had about as much as I can handle of you, both of you."

"Go ahead, make another big mistake. As for Archie and me, we got our treasure back. But if you want to make another mistake, then go right ahead."

"And I suppose you suggest these two did not steal your belongings?"

"Oh, I didn't say that. They did steal the cases. We saw them do it with our own eyes."

"We didn't steal. We found these cases, yes, we did. Didn't we, Clyde?"

Clyde nodded his head vigorously. "And we didn't know which one we found, so we had to take both."

"Shut up!"

Bevan's head bounced from Jerry to Cora. "And I suppose you know who killed Williamson, someone that isn't these two."

"Yes, I believe I do."

"And I suppose you are going to tell me?"

"I could, but you won't believe me if I tell you now."

"Why not now?"

"I really don't have the proof here and now."

"And when will you?"

"Inspector, if you really want me to tell you who the murderer is and why, we all need to go to the museum—now."

"The Museum?"

"Now."

"I assume all of us?" Bevan said, looking around the room, then sighed.

"All of us. And you need that officer to bring Eve Tomlinson and drag her to the museum as well."

"So, you think Miss Tomlinson is the murderer? So, I was right, then."

Cora's voice rose. "Inspector, to the museum, please."

"I should have my head examined. You heard the lady." Bevan pointed to the fifth police officer. "And you can *escort* these two downstairs."

"Sir," Hilliard said to Archie.

"If you don't mind, Miss Gudmundson and I have a ride to the museum."

After Bevan gave Archie a disbelieving stare, Cora spoke out. "Oh, Jeepers creepers, you can follow us if you're that suspicious about us."

Bevan growled. "Right, then." They all left the room, some with reservations. Kent's scowl, but safe, with his hands bound.

Cora walked down the steps with Archie as they followed Stokes.

Archie chuckled at Stokes. "Why do you look so scared, Mr. Stokes? I thought you were always cool under pressure."

Stokes gazed with boredom at the case in Archie's hand. "You do not know what I saw."

Cora laughed. "I have a pretty good idea."

Chapter 16

"I hope you're not wasting Scotland Yard's time," Bevan said in a huff.

"Patience, sir," Cora said as she led the parade through the halls of the ornate, brown pillared and brick-walled display rooms of the British Museum. The late afternoon light faded, and the interior was dimly lit by small incandescent bulbs overhead. The shadowy displays felt eerie as she passed by, as if the stuffed animals and mannequins could come to life at any moment. She exited one archway into the glassed roofed cathedral-like room that housed the Egyptian exhibit. As she led the parade, Archie signaled museum employees to clear out on-lookers.

She saw Archie give her a sideways look of concern, possibly worried she might lead them into deeper trouble. Bevan would no doubt have words to say to her for stealing his car. Hopefully, it would only be words and not charges.

The way Archie carried the Jackal of the Prince of Iknokman amused her. He held the case tightly clutched to his chest, as if someone would reach out and snatch it again. He clutched to it so tightly it appeared no blood could circulate through his fingers.

As they reached their destination, they could pick up Eve Tomlinson's screech. Her voice echoed through-out the Egyptian display. "If you don't cough up my part of the money, I will make things unpleasant for you. We had a deal. It's not my fault Brandon failed in his task."

"Quiet down before someone hears you," Mitford said, tilting his head to the police officer. "I don't have the money. Had my people came through, I have hopes."

Archie came forward and held his black case high. "Are you looking for this?"

"What? You found it?" Mitford said. He turned away from Eve, and Cora watched his scowl turn into a phony smile. "How fortunate. Here, I'll take that for safekeeping." He approached Archie with his hands extended.

"No, you will not," Archie said and sidestepped Mitford.

"I beg your pardon. I am the curator." Mitford stopped when he saw Bevan. "Inspector Bevan, do I have you to thank for finding our missing artifact?"

Bevan did not reply and did not look away from Mitford.

Archie set the black case down, opened it and the box, and lifted out the wooden statue.

"Ah, lovely." Mitford walked towards Archie with his hands extended again.

"No, you don't." Archie reached over the barrier and placed the Jackal of Prince Iknokman on its presentation stand and turned.

Inspector Bevan moved in front of Eve Tomlinson and turned to Cora. "Now, speak before I run you and Miss Tomlinson in."

"What? I didn't kill Brandon!" she screeched and took a step back. Her shabby fur stole slid off one shoulder. "Keep your hands off me," she said to the officer. He ignored her and held onto her arm.

Out of the corner of her eye, Cora saw Iknokman adjust his head towards Bevan. She cleared her throat. Iknokman looked at her and she shook her head slightly, then returned to his statue form.

Archie looked at the statue of Iknokman, then back at Cora with a look of confusion.

The Missing Jackal Murder

Bevan spoke to Eve. "Tell me why I should trust you. Were you about to leave town?"

"My, my grandmother is ill," Eve said with a fake snivel. She lifted a handkerchief to her eye to wipe away nonexistent tears.

"Save it for the magistrate," Bevan said in a stern voice.

"But I didn't kill Brandon, I tell you," her voice grew more desperate.

"She is telling the truth," Cora said. "Miss Tomlinson didn't kill Mr. Williamson, but she certainly had a hand in all of this."

"Now see here," Bevan shot a glare at Cora. "My patience is growing thin. Do you know who killed Mr. Williamson or not?"

"If you'll be patient a little longer, I'm sure we'll be able to clear up any doubts."

Stokes spoke up. "I do not see why Mr. Kent and—"

"I didn't kill him," Kent said, snapping out the words. He took two steps towards Cora, one hand in a fist, the other lifting toward her throat.

Archie stepped forward to block him.

"See here, Mr. Thorogood. I will have no violence in my museum," Mitford said.

"Is theft tolerated in your museum? Is theft tolerated by a supposedly respected curator?"

"That accusation will get you in trouble, Mr. Thorogood."

"Stokes is your go-between, Mr. Mitford, isn't he?" Archie said. "He's the one you used to handle your sales of stolen artifacts from the museum. I remember seeing you in conversation with him and Kent before I left for New York."

Cora stepped forward. "And the money for the jackal of would have been a nice wedding present for Mr. Williamson and Miss Tomlinson, wouldn't it, Mr. Mitford?"

Bevan bristled. "Wait, are you implying Mr. Mitford is responsible for the theft?"

Archie took a step to Bevan. "Yes. Mitford had Williamson steal the jackal for him." He looked at Mitford. "What were your plans, to give him money for it or split the take after they sold it to a high-end collector?"

"Neither. This is ridiculous," Mitford said. "Why I would never-"

"Why have other treasures gone missing from the museum, never seen again?"

"I assure you I took nothing from the museum, Mr. Thorogood. I would never—wait. What about Mr. Neubauer? He works in the lower level and had plenty of opportunities."

Archie stiffened in shock. "What! Freddie? That is preposterous."

"Of course," Mitford sputtered back. "He is a young man, possibly in need of money."

"Where is Mr. Neubauer?" Bevan asked.

Archie lifted his hand to stop Bevan while he focused on Mitford. "You and I both know Freddie wouldn't ever take anything from this museum for profit or otherwise."

"Archie's right," Cora said. "In my brief acquaintance with Freddie would take nothing from this museum. He is very thorough in his record keeping. He wouldn't even misplace a sewing pin." She looked at Bevan. "You can ask Freddie to come up from the basement to interrogate him, but I assure you, it would be a waste of your time."

Bevan sputtered. "I will make that decision. I shall interrogate Mr. Neubauer if I am not satisfied as to whom the museum thief is."

"Fair enough," Cora said to Bevan, then turned to Mitford. "Where were we? Oh yes, Archie was discussing your involvement in the jackal's theft."

He nodded. "You used Williamson's desire for fame and fortune to lure him to help you steal artifacts."

Bevan raised his hand. "One thing at a time. We'll check out the stolen property later. Right now, I am concerned about the murder of Williamson."

"Mitford did have Williamson steal for him, but he didn't kill him," Cora said.

"What makes you so sure? Means, motive, opportunity, it's all there," Bevan said.

"Why would Mitford be on the ship in order to murder Williamson if he was also meant to be waiting for the delivery of the jackal here at the museum? He knew Williamson would bring him the jackal. Therefore, why would Mitford hire these two buffoons?" She pointed to Jerry and Clyde. "They would not be necessary if Williamson and Mitford's plans were to have gone smoothly."

Bevan turned to Jerry and Clyde. "Did you two have dealings with Williamson before?"

Jerry shook his head. "Never saw the bloke before in my life."

Bevan turned to Cora. "If they are not the murderers, who is?"

Cora locked eyes with Eve.

"What? Why are you looking at me?" Eve's eyes were now on her.

Stokes took this opportunity to run. His heavy footsteps pounded on the museum's wooden floor. The officer in charge of him hesitated. Bevan shouted, "What's the matter with you, go after him?"

The officer ran out. The sound of a whistle drifted through the window.

"I hope you are not going to tell me Stokes was the murderer." Bevan gestured to Cora as his shoulders drooped.

"No, but I'm sure Eve can tell us who killed Brandon. I believe Eve was about to tell us only moments ago."

"So, you did murder Mr. Williamson." Bevan reached for her.

Eve put her fist on her hips. "Listen, you'll not pin this one on me."

"You lied to us before," Bevan accused. "You were jealous and confronted Williamson. He denied it but you kept on him. He continued to deny it, so you stabbed him."

"I—I, would never, no. But I did see someone kill Brandon," Eve whimpered unconvincingly.

"What?" Bevan said. "Who?" The room grew quiet.

"It was..." Eve paused, tilted her hips, crossed her hands, and smiled as she looked at Cora. She spoke rapidly. "It was your friend from the ship. She was mad because Brandon told her he wasn't interested and was engaged to me. She did it." Eve stared at Cora, pressed her lips together, and nodded her head.

"Willie did not kill Brandon," Cora said. "You're lying. Willie didn't know about his murder until the next day when the tour guide told the group. If you saw Willie kill Brandon, what did she look like?"

Eve gave Cora a dirty look. "I don't remember. I was distraught. You're covering for her because she is your friend." She pointed her finger at Cora.

The Missing Jackal Murder

"Do you deny it was your friend?" Bevan said to Cora with raised eyebrows.

"No inspector, it was not. Miss Tomlinson overheard us talk about Willie spending time with Brandon on the cruise. She has never seen Willie."

"Then did Miss Tomlinson kill Mr. Williamson in a jealous rage because he was with another woman?" Bevan asked.

"No inspector. The fact that Miss Tomlinson made a beeline to the cargo hold pretty much tells us about their relationship."

"I don't understand," Archie said.

"Isn't it obvious, Archie? If Eve and Brandon had a bona fide romantic relationship, they would have met on the upper deck, not in the cargo hold?"

Eve stepped forward. "We did meet on the upper deck. Brandon said he wanted to show me something and we—"

Cora held up a hand. "Stop. The timing was wrong for you to first meet elsewhere, then go to the cargo hold. Brandon would have told you that the heist had already taken place."

Eve moved her mouth silently like a fish, then found her voice. "I didn't kill Brandon."

"First you admitted you were in the cargo hold and witnessed the murder. Now you say you were not in the cargo hold. Careful."

"How, how dare you?" She appealed to Bevan. "I told you what happened. It was that woman—and her husband. That's right. There was a man with her. He took a knife and—"

Cora shook her head. "Impossible. The Chicago police arrested Willie's husband. He was said to stay 72 hours before they were going to release him, giving him no chance

to board our ship bound for London. And if Roy
miraculously had boarded our ship, he would have hunted
Willie down the first day."

Bevan grunted at Cora. "How do you know the Chicago
police released him?"

Cora reached into her pouch, pulled out two pieces of
paper and handed one to the Inspector. "This is a message
from the Chicago Police Department, second precinct. It
states Roy, Willie's husband, remained in jail for three days
before being released. There was no time for him to board
our ship."

Archie put his hand on Cora's wrist. "So, you spent so
much time at the telegraph offices for messages like this?"

"Exactly. That's what I wanted to tell you at the saloon
before, before I overheard the women in the lavatory." Cora
took in a deep breath and turned to Eve. "You've admitted
you saw who murdered Brandon. Now would be a good
time to tell us who."

Eve shot another look to her right and back at Cora,
then pointed towards Archie. "It was him. He was the one
who killed Brandon."

"Excuse me?" Archie said. "How could you make up
that outlandish lie?"

"It's because you would not let Brandon go on any
expeditions.

"The museum assigns expeditions, and Brandon knew
that and would have told you. Furthermore, I dashed off the
ship during the time of the murder, with a police officer as a
witness."

Bevan nodded. "This is true. I have spoken to the
officer Mr. Thorogood is referring to." He then turned to
Cora. "If you know who the murderer is with means and
motive, now is the time to tell me. My patience is at an end."

Cora nodded. "Very well, Inspector, here is how I see it. The British Museum assigned Archie and Brandon to transport the Egyptian artifacts from New York to England. Mr. Mitford assigned Brandon to accompany Archie, much to Archie's chagrin. Brandon was a very ambitious man who desired to come with or take charge of an expedition. But this was not for archaeological reasons, but for glory and riches. He became, shall we say, employed by the curator, Mr. Mitford, to lift artifacts, contact a buyer through a go between. But this latest planned heist with the Jackal of the Price of Iknokman. Everything was going according to plan."

"Was going?" Bevan said. "I take it something changed?"

"Oh yes, Inspector. That very change led to Brandon's murder. Again, if everything had gone according to plan, Brandon would have stolen the jackal and presented it to Mitford, or his go-between."

Archie put his hands on his hips. "I suppose I became the one who upset that plan."

"How?" Bevan said to Archie.

"During the voyage, I grew suspicious of Brandon and told him I planned to carry the jackal off the ship myself."

"I see," Bevan said. "Was that the change you were referring to?"

"Only partially," Cora said. "One telegram Williamson received was the key. I've discovered some man named Founder had sent him the message."

"Again, your time at the telegraph offices?" Archie said.

"Exactly." Cora handed the second piece of paper to Bevan as she explained to Archie. "I feared you would've thought my ideas to be ridiculous. I wanted to keep it quiet until things fell into place. Don't you see? It all makes sense.

The telegraph Mr. Williamson sent was to hire these two here." She motioned to Clyde and Jerry. "Perhaps this Founder gave Brandon a better offer. Thus, I believe he no longer had any intention of bringing the jackal to Mitford. He directed these two to steal the black case, then planned to meet them later for the payoff. That was the telegraph he had in his hand when Archie saw him on the cargo deck."

"Though we did not find a telegram on his body," Bevan said, and squinted his eyes to read the contents. "Who is Founder?" The room fell silent when no one answered.

"I do not know," Cora said to Mitford. "Is that your code name for a collector of stolen artifacts?"

"How did you know about a code name?" Mitford sputtered, but quickly closed his mouth and looked at Kent.

"I didn't tell anybody anything."

"Actually you did," Cora said to Kent. "You reacted to Archie's statement when we met you in the saloon. Just after he used the phrase 'The collector' in his statement, you shot up and said we used your buyer's codename."

Kent swore.

"If you check the telegraph office on the ship, they can verify the message from Founder," Cora said, tilting her head towards Bevan and the paper in his hand. "Having a new buyer changed everything, and it made some people mad as it changed their financial side of things slightly."

"Is this so?" Bevan spoke to Jerry and Clyde.

"You got nothing on me," Jerry said.

"I caught you with the cases," Bevan said, shook his head. "Now this makes perfect sense. Kent and Stokes, acting on their own, approached Williamson. They didn't believe Williamson when he told them he did not have the jackal. They struggled. Stokes killed Williamson. Am I correct?" Bevan looked at Kent.

The Missing Jackal Murder

Eve broke in. "It was Stokes. I tried to stop him. Stokes killed Williamson."

"No," Cora interrupted. "That's not so. And your outburst pretty well clinches it."

Archie spoke up. "In our brief acquaintance with Stokes, I can't believe he would be... a blade man. He wouldn't have done the dirty work himself." Everyone looked at Kent.

"Now see here, you stupid bloke," Kent said and took two steps towards Archie. The officer behind Kent held him back. "I saw Stokes kill him, and that is the truth." He looked at Eve with narrowed eyes. "You tell him, you tell him, missy."

"Ah, yes," Eve said nervously. "He did. Stokes, that is, I saw him."

"No Eve," Cora said, shaking her head. "You saw Mr. Kent kill Brandon."

"See here, you hussy little American," Kent said, and pulled away from the officer to take two steps towards Cora. The officer leapt forward and grabbed Kent's elbow. Archie lunged between Kent and Cora, making sure to keep him away from her.

"Quiet you," Bevan said and nodded at the second police officer. He took out his club and smacked Kent on the cheek. Kent settled down.

Cora stepped towards Archie and stood beside him. "Kent did kill Brandon, but for his own goals. Whether to steal the Jackal for himself, or to present the booty to Mitford to disgrace Stokes, either way, it was Kent who murdered Brandon."

"Look here, I didn't kill him," Kent shouted. "Yes, I hated Stokes, always pushing me around like a dog on a leash. He only looked at me like a frog, like I was like these two slugs."

"Hey," Jerry said."

"Did he call us names?" Clyde asked and clenched his fists, ready to attack, but then he saw the second police officer's club and stopped struggling.

"So what?" Kent continued. "That doesn't mean I killed him. You have no proof."

"When did you first suspect Kent?" Archie said.

Cora suppresses a chuckle. "It was what he said in the saloon that made me suspect him."

"What did he say?" Archie said.

"Well, if you recall, Stokes thought you had the jackal. He tried to bribe you. If you didn't have it, both Stokes and Kent wanted you to continue to search while they monitored us, ready to move if we found it."

"But what did Kent say?" Bevan asked.

"When Archie and I mentioned the murder, Mr. Kent told us to butt out, leave it alone or 'We would feel his blade'—isn't that what you said to us, Mr. Kent?"

Archie straightened. "Yes, I do remember those words."

"So, what if I did say that?" Kent said.

"You didn't want us to stop looking for the jackal. But you warned us not to investigate the murder. Why would you say that? Why would you care if Archie and I took an interest in the murder? How would you know someone stabbed Brandon and not shot or strangled unless it was you? Only Brandon's murderer would've said that." She turned to Bevan. "I saw the newspaper about Brandon's murder. I believe you intentionally left that out—just for this."

Bevan turned to Kent. "Just for that."

The Missing Jackal Murder

"Anyone could have used the blade. You have no proof that I killed him." Kent said.

"But that would make you the prime suspect." Cora said, pressing her lips together. "I suppose it would be nice to have more proof, unless you care to confess." Cora turned to Eve. "Don't let me stop you. Please continue."

Eve shook her head. "You have no proof. You have no proof at all."

"Oh well," Cora said, turning to Archie. She placed her hand on his right arm. "I guess I can admit when I'm licked. But then again, Archie and I got our cases back in the end. What difference is it to us who killed Williamson? That leaves you and Kent alone to discuss things—privately, at that. Sure, discuss it with Mr. Kent. He knows you will keep quiet, especially when you squawk about not getting your cut, like he promised."

Archie put his fingers to his chin. "You're right, Cora. I see what you mean. No evidence means they'll be free so they can discuss the situation alone."

"Wait," Eve said with a look of panic as she looked at Kent.

"Yes?" Bevan said.

"Don't you say anything," Kent said, his fists clenched.

"I believe when Archie said 'alone', he meant with no witnesses," Cora said.

"Wait," Eve said, and her eyes widened. "Don't leave me here alone with him."

"I said shut up," Kent said, clenching his fists.

"No, I will not let you kill…."

"I said shut up."

"You shut up!" Bevan said. "Don't interrupt a lady— yes, Miss Tomlinson."

R. M. Scott

"If you say one word." Kent lunged towards Eve. The officer pulled Kent back.

Eve looked at Kent. "You would kill me, just like you killed Brandon. Yes, I'll testify. I did see him kill Brandon.

"You bitch, you ruined everything." Kent's eyes burned into Cora's. He jumped forward, grabbed the Billy club out of the officer's belt and pointed it at Cora. "You'll pay."

In the confusion of grabbing Kent, Iknokman shouted, "Look out!".

She stepped backwards. Before Archie reached her, Kent flung the Billy club as the officer smacked him in the head with his fist. She stumbled, fell backwards and heard the club whiz past her right ear. She looked down at her pouch flattened on the floor. Arve and Ola had spilled out.

"Ooh," Ola said, then she and Arve stiffened at their wooden forms. Cora immediately scooped them up and quietly stashed them back inside her pouch. She looked to see what she had stumbled over. It was Nicholas, rubbing his side. He gave Cora a wink and disappeared.

Archie leapt forward. "Cora darling, are you okay? Did he hit you?" Archie leaned over and she reached for his arm. He lifted and examined her.

"No. The club passed my ear and—oh dear." She pulled at a torn corner of her sleeve. A nearby display tore through the shoulder of her dress.

Archie grabbed Cora, held her in a tight embrace, and kissed her hard on the lips. Cora did not protest and was hardly aware when her arms reached up and around his neck. Her heartbeat fluttered, and she was not sure if it was from the whizzing club or being in Archie's arms.

"And as for you," Bevan said to the other two officers, "lock them all up."

Cora took a step back. "Us too?"

The Missing Jackal Murder

"You did take my car?"

"In order to lead – you didn't listen to me, and Archie, and here we were right. If I hadn't, yes, take that drastic action, they would have gotten away, with the Jackal, continue to clean out the museum and, yes, Kent would have gone free and would have murdered Thomlinson. I see my actions justified, in the name of public safety, don't you agree, Inspector?"

"What about your interference with Scotland Yard?"

"Interference," Archie jumped in. "We were…" He glanced at Cora, then back to the inspector, "we were not interfering with Scotland Yard, we were merely conducting research."

"Research," Bevan said as he folded his arms.

"Yes, research on the anthropologic level. As you know, I am an archeologist."

"Then I suggest you leave your research on dusty bones and leave the investigating to Scotland Yard." He paused, then shook his head as each officer put their hands on Cora's and Archie's shoulder. "Ah, leave them. It will just be more paperwork." He pointed at Archie and Cora. "Beyond my better judgment," he muttered, looked in the Jackal's direction, and scratched his head.

They did what the Inspector told them.

Archie brought his arm around Cora's waist and held her close to his side. "Yes and, oh, Mitford," Archie turned to his now old boss. "The keys, if you'd please, I will lock up tonight." Mitford's sudden move to his pocket caused Bevan to reach for his pistol.

"Really now, Inspector." Mitford tossed the keys to Archie. "After all, I'm not a murderer."

Bevan led him out.

Archie wrapped his arms around Cora's waist. "Are you sure you're alright, my darling?"

"Yes, don't be such a worrywart."

"With your well-being I—"

"Oh Archie, really now," Cora reached up to kiss him again. She broke away after a moment. "Are you really concerned about my well-being?"

"Always, my dear."

"Well then, don't forget. You promised me dinner."

"Quite right. But I'm glad all of that's over." Archie stepped up to the Jackal. He leaned over the barrier and adjusted the wood sculpture to a better viewing angle, then leaned back.

She stepped closer, reached into her pouch, and lifted Arve and Ola. "I suppose I should let these two say goodbye to Iknokman." She reached over the wooden banister and put Arve and Ola on either side of the jackal statue. As she tried to stand back, she came close to falling headfirst into the Egyptian display.

Archie reached out, pulled her forward and looked back at the three wooden figures, then at Cora with a perplexed expression.

Cora saw the jackal's head turn to look at her. She stepped in front of Archie to focus on her and not the three figures. "Before we go, I'd like for you to finish the rest of the story about Prince Iknokman."

"I suppose this is a good time and place to complete the story," Archie said and glanced over his shoulder at the statute. Iknokman froze. Archie once again focused on Cora. The three figures came to life. "I told you most of the story already."

The Missing Jackal Murder

"Yes, but do you think that Prince Iknokman tried to kill the King in order to gain power? I mean, it was a terrible accusation by his brother and mother."

"Things like that happened many times throughout history," Archie said, and waved his hand around the room.

Iknokman stared deep into Archie's back. His eyebrows lowered in anger.

"But this is different, isn't it?"

"Quite, and sad as well."

"Oh?"

"As I've explained earlier, Iknokman's mother was the King's second wife. The older brother, Smenkhankur, was born to the first wife. As they were growing up, they competed for power. At first the King loved his two sons equally, without prejudice."

"At first?" Cora asked.

Archie nodded. "The King favored then his first son and virtually ignored Iknokman. However, in the long run, it was clear that Iknokman was the better son."

"Why? How do you know all this?"

"From Iknokman's best friend, Haromaheb. He was both a loyal friend and tutor. Remember him, I will explain at the end. The king suspected his first son to overthrow his throne and blame his attempt on Iknokman. Then a greater force attempted to overthrow the king. Then, the evidence of Iknokman's guilt became overwhelming, but Iknokman completely denied involvement. The king did not believe him, especially when his mother also denounced him. The king pronounced and carried out Iknokman's sentence."

"What happened from that point?"

"Most believe he was—shall we say—dismembered and his remains thrown to the jackals." Archie pointed his thumb behind him. "This symbol was a warning to others that who tried to overthrow the king—a jackal was an animal that would steal and kill mercilessly. The jackal, however, also had many outstanding qualities."

"Most believe? Is there another story?"

Archie nodded his head. "There is a legend that the chief priestess cast a spell and turned him into this jackal figure. The idea was to cast a punishment that would cause Iknokman to suffer forever as the jackal the king believed him to be."

"That is a sad story indeed."

"But that's not the worst of the story."

"There's more?"

"Remember his friend, Haromaheb?"

"Yes."

"Haromaheb truly was a good friend. Haromaheb left the city not only because he feared the king would also charge him with treason, but because he learned who truly incited the uprisings. He left for safety to preserve the knowledge and make sure history would learn the truth—the truth that Iknokman truly was innocent."

"How did Haromaheb preserve the knowledge? I've read that if leaders in ancient Egypt did such horrible things, all knowledge erased from history. The next ruler would scratch off writings from stone hieroglyphs, leaving no trace that the last leader ever existed."

Archie grinned. "Yes, that is exactly what they did."

"But how do you know Iknokman was innocent? How did you know for sure?"

"Again, Iknokman's friend Haromaheb sought to that," Archie said.

Cora glanced over Archie's shoulder to see that Iknokman's head turned completely to watch Archie. His neck was outstretched, and his ears perked.

The Missing Jackal Murder

"You see," Archie continued, "to preserve these facts, Haromaheb wrote everything down on papyri and wrapped it in a tight metal container. Earlier, he watched the jackals pick over Iknokman's bones. He saw the priestess bury the bones, along with this jackal wooden carving preserved in the case and buried in an unmarked and desolate grave. Haromaheb's last words were that he attempted to dig up the jackal carving, hoping he could revive his good friend, Iknokman. However, he could not find the exact spot or dig deep enough. He laid the container there on top and in proximity to his burial, then covered it up. He hoped Ra would read his message and bring Iknokman into the afterlife. But in reality, we learned the accurate history of what happened to Iknokman."

"It's a good thing you found the container with the scroll," Cora said.

"As it is, farmers or builders did not destroy it through the centuries. Though they discovered the scroll first, I led the expedition, after I researched the scroll, to dig for the grave to see if the message was true. And here he is." Again, Archie pointed his thumb over his shoulder.

"But what did the message say exactly about Iknokman?" Cora asked and wanted Iknokman to hear this firsthand.

"Haromaheb wrote that, moments before the coup, he heard those responsible planning the attack. Unfortunately, they discovered Haromaheb. He fled, afraid they would kill him."

"Double trouble," Cora said, "but who planned the coup? Who really was responsible for the attack?"

Archie paused. "You must understand that Iknokman was second in birth. His mother encouraged him to grow up as a powerful man, physically and intellectually, to prove to the king he would be the best for Egypt. The first son rested on his birthright. He didn't follow Iknokman's genuine growth and strength but became a weak, spoiled brat."

"Oh boy, I can guess where this is going."

"Yes, it was Iknokman's mother who created the uprisings."

Cora watched Iknokman stand up on all four legs and turn completely towards Archie. His eyes widened and his jaw dropped. "But I don't understand. Wasn't Iknokman aware of this?" Cora's eyes bounced between Archie and Iknokman.

"According to Haromaheb, he was not. Haromaheb believed Iknokman had shown such loyalty to the king, to please him and gain in preference to his first son. Iknokman did everything to prove himself so his father would be proud of him. Therefore, I believe Iknokman didn't pay attention to what was happening behind him. Iknokman's mother did not tell him about her plans. If the coup was successful, his mother would be the queen of Egypt, with Iknokman as her puppet king."

Cora glanced at Iknokman. He was so still and unmoving that she thought he had returned to his hardened, wooden form. "So, what happened?"

"After Iknokman's punishment, his mother attempted another take over which was squashed. It became obvious to the king that Iknokman's mother handled everything. He realized Iknokman was indeed completely innocent, and he grieved for his lost son. According to Haromaheb, the king pleaded with the priests to undo the magic and bring Iknokman back to life. They couldn't, because that magic could not be reversed. Sad, his father was so grieved he could not dig up his beloved son, but just left him there."

The Missing Jackal Murder

Cora saw Iknokman sit and return to his original shape, but not quick enough.

Archie looked at Iknokman and stared, his eyebrows lowered in confusion.

"How sad," Cora said and reached for Archie's arm.

Archie shook his head. "Shortly, very shortly after the king's death, his first son became king and Egypt fell into bad times. I won't get into details now. Most of it was the first son's fault, as again, he was the weaker man after all." He paused. "After this research, I wondered what would've happened if Iknokman had become king. He was stronger and smarter, and likely cared a lot more about the people. I'm sure Egypt would not have gone through such turmoil. Who knows, perhaps under Iknokman's rule, under his lineage, the Egyptian Empire would've lasted much longer than it did. But that is only my speculation."

"But for now," Cora said as she reached over the railing to touch the sitting still Iknokman. "In our eyes and now the world's eyes, will remember Iknokman as one of Egyptians' greatest leaders."

"Ab-so-lute-ly," Archie said again.

"And Iknokman is free," Ola said loudly.

"Yes," Archie said. "He is free, quite right Cora."

"And he will have trusted friends in us, right Archie?" Cora reached over the rail again, grabbed Arve and Ola and struggled back to her feet.

Archie nodded. "Oh, of course, my dear, quite right." He put his arm around Cora's shoulder and both stared at Iknokman.

Cora placed Arve and Ola back into her pouch. "Archie, let me take a photograph of you with Iknokman, please."

"I'd like that. Perhaps you will share a copy with me." He stood at the railing and off to one side so Cora could snap a photo of them with her Kodak.

She had to take two as Iknokman winked at her the first time, and she definitely could not share that with Archie.

After a few moments, Archie leaned close and whispered to Cora, "I'm famished as well. Let's get out of here before we turn into statues."

Cora laughed and raised one eyebrow. "Oh, you never know what can happen with a little magic." As they walked away, Cora glanced at Iknokman. Then she turned to her pouch to assure that Arve and Ola remained inside. She paused, looked back at Iknokman. "Do you think he'll be safe there tonight?"

"Certainly, that is his pedestal. Besides, Mitford, Kent and Thomlinson have been taken away."

"And what about Stokes?"

Archie stopped, "Oh, my. That would be reckless of me." They turned, he picked up the Prince and held him with great care, like he would a baby. "Let's take him down to the basement for tonight."

"Why, Mr. Thorogood, you're not using the Prince as a way to bring me down the basement, to…"

Without catching Cora's humorous tone, he interrupted, "Why Cora, I would never take advantage of you or any other lady in the basement of the museum, or anywhere else."

"Oh, you wouldn't?" Cora said in a disappointed tone.

"No, and, besides, we have Freddy as a, a chaperone."

"Do we have to? I mean, we do?"

"Ad-so-lute-ly"

"Oh, jeepers creepers," Cora said as Archie led her as what seems he didn't catch her disappointing tone.

Chapter 17

The morning sun and haze warmed the seaside docks. Passengers and well-wishers strolled the deck, filled with the buzz of excitement. Cora and Willie strolled around a man pushing a cart who was not watching where he was going.

Cora peeked into her pouch to insure Arve and Ola remained in their places, with another glance over her shoulder to see their departing tour group remain in sight. Though her luggage moved safely up the loading ramp, she had decided not to place them in the case again. Ola knit safety belts and side handles to prevent the pouch from upending itself. After completion of the remodification, it was Arve's idea to shake the pouch upside down with the two to prove Ola's alterations would work safely in their hotel without prying eyes, of course. Seeing the two snug and secure, she agreed they could stay in the pouch during boarding.

Cora and Willie looked over their shoulders, both anxious. "I'm sure he'll be here shortly," Willie said. "It was kind of him to pay for the taxi."

"I know. I'm sure he'll be here soon." Cora scanned the pier to search for Archie's familiar hat, among the many men milling about. Archie could not escort Cora to the pier due to work related conferences.

Willie wrapped her arm around Cora's elbow.

"He did apologize when he told me the governors of the museum wanted to speak with him immediately," Cora said and remembered his words. *'If the governors want to introduce me to the new museum curator, I need to be there. The governors are in control of the museum's future expeditions, many that I*

*have proposed. However, I shall inform them that a lady waits for me
and I must break away. I'm sure they will not keep me longer than
necessary."*

After the excitement of ferreting out a murderer and
searching for Arve and Ola, Cora agreed to rejoin her tour
group. The tours and excursions of London delighted Arve
and Ola after their frightful expedition. But Cora had found
the scheduled tours mundane after her grand and dangerous
adventures with Archie. Of course, she enjoyed learning
about England and its history and culture, but her thoughts
had frequently wandered to him and his whereabouts.

She had never felt this way about any man. Archie was a
true gentleman and had a genuine concern for her happiness.
He had joined her several times during breaks in the tour,
but it had never been for very long. Cora sighed. Now that
she was about to depart, she realized how much she would
miss Archie once she left the country.

She tried to shake off her feelings of sadness and told
herself, *"No, my plan is to travel and experience adventures on my
own terms. I won't be someone's mousy little wife or maid. It will be
good to get back home and plan the next big adventure."*

But then she remembered many of the embraces and
kisses she and Archie had shared. She sighed. He was just a
passing exploit, it seemed. That's what adventures are about,
new sites, new people and new experiences, then move on.

Cora scanned the crowd for Archie once again, but her
eyes stopped and fixated on one man, a man she feared to
recognize. He stood and scanned the crowd. A face in the
dark came to mind, along with a painful feeling. Then she
remembered. The shock wave reverberated up and down her
spine. But how could it be? Here—in England.

Cora pulled Willie closer.

The Missing Jackal Murder

The sudden movement made Willie look at Cora, then in the direction she was staring. Willie gasped. "He's here. Roy is here. What am I going to do?"

Cora took a deep breath, then let it out in a snort of impatience. Since she had become involved with a vicious murder case, and almost murdered herself, she will not shrink before a domineering bully like Willie's husband, Roy. "Come on, Willie. We've got to nip this in the bud now, once and for all."

Roy stopped when he saw Willie and then made his way through the crowd in her direction.

Cora's mind conjured an idea that was devious, but in her opinion, necessary. She looked down at the carefully stitched patch on the shoulder of her blouse caused by the Billy club thrown in the museum. She sighed. "Oh well, there goes my nice stitching." She grabbed the material on her shoulder and pulled to re-create the rip.

Willie grasped Cora's arm. "What are we going to do?"

"Scream," Cora said.

"What?" Willie's voice came out in a high-pitched moan. Roy was now only a few arm-lengths away.

"Scream and run!" Cora spun Willie around, grabbed her wrist and pulled her into a sprint as both let out loud a scream. "Louder." Cora screamed as loud as she could and kept Willie into a run.

Willie screamed again.

"More. Louder."

Willie looked back as Roy reached for her shoulder.

Cora pulled Willie into a faster run as the crowd separated and watched in horror. She saw three constables talking together. One officer casually waved his stick around until he noticed their plight. He grabbed the handle of his stick in midair and signaled the other officers to follow.

"One more time." They both let out their loudest screams.

The three constables approached and put themselves between Roy and the ladies. The officer with the nightstick held it with both hands and pressed it against Roy's throat. Another came behind him and grabbed his elbows and held tight. "Now what's this bloke up to, ladies?"

A second officer grabbed Roy's shoulder. "I hope you have a good explanation for chasing these fine women."

"Good heavens." The third officer was staring at Cora's ripped blouse. "Tearing a lady's dress, that deserves a clubbing indeed."

Cora pointed to Roy with one hand and tried to cover her lack of tears by wiping her eyes with the other hand. "This man tried to reach for me. He wanted to take us with him. I said no, but he—he–" she tried to bring up phony tears and hoped the officers believed her deception despite the lack of wetness.

"Grabbing a lady. That was not nice, now was it?"

A woman in the crown called out, "Take him in the back and pulverize him. I say it will do him a bit of good."

"No," Roy pointed towards Willie. "That's my wife."

"Now look here," one officer said. "Is there any truth to what this bloke said?" He stared directly at Willie. She looked at Cora, then back at the officer.

Willie glanced at Cora, took a deep breath, and spoke in a phony southern accent. "No, heavens, no, I cannot believe this is happening. I do believe I have the vapors. Yes, the vapors, something fierce indeed."

"Now you listen to me, you filthy bitch. When I get you home, I'm going to take the belt to you. And this time I won't be so light on you," Roy threatened as he struggled to break away from the officer holding him back.

The Missing Jackal Murder

Willie screamed, put one hand on her forehead and waved the other in front of her face like a fan. She turned her back to Cora and collapsed. Cora caught her before she hit the ground.

"Look what you've done!" Cora shouted at Roy.

"Listen here, you little bitch, you stop giving my wife ideas and mind your own business."

"That's enough. Take him away." The two officers holding Roy dragged him off.

"When I get a hold of you, I'll kill you I'll…"

"That will be all," one officer said, and prodded Roy to keep him moving.

"Will you be alright here? Can I bring you to a hospital?" One officer kneeled next to Willie, peering anxiously at her face.

"No," Willie said. She sprang back up to her feet. "I'll be just fine."

Cora thought Willie had recovered from her ordeal a little too quickly to be convincing.

"And what have you two been up to?" A man's voice said from behind.

"Archie!" Cora said and hurried into his open arms.

"And you are?" one officer asked suspiciously.

"Oh," Cora answered, "he's my cousin. Yes, this is my cousin, cousin Archie, here to see us off."

"Yes," Willie said, "and what took you so long, cousin Archie?"

As Cora stood back, Archie placed his hands on his hips and lifted one eyebrow. "I'm sorry, I'm late. However, I did arrive in time to see… everything."

"Oh, you did?" she said and glanced at the police officer. "Thank you, officer, for your help. We'll be fine now that my cousin is here."

"Very well. Sir. Misses." The officer nodded and walked off.

"Did you really have to rip your dress?" Archie reached out to tug at the torn fabric.

Cora thought Archie was staring at her bare shoulder a little longer than he should. She pulled the loose flap of fabric up and held it in place. "I'll mend it later, on board the ship."

Archie's eyebrows remained raised. "Now that was quite deceitful. The law may be lenient in Chicago, but here in London that man could stay behind bars for years—for a crime he did not commit."

"In a way he did," Willie said. "He belted me too many times. I was his wife, for Christ's sake! He had no right to treat me that way."

Cora frowned. "I guess that's what women get when they get married."

Archie made a strangled sound, and Cora glanced in his direction. "What's the matter, Archie? Oh, don't look at me like that. When we get out to sea, we'll telegraph Scotland Yard and tell them it was a misunderstanding, despite his threats."

Willie chuckled. "I say we wait until the ship reaches New York. Or maybe when we get off the train in St. Paul. Or, after the long voyage home, I may just—well, just forget about it."

Cora laughed. "Willie, you're devious."

"He deserves it. Maybe by the time I get home my father will have good news for me about my divorce." Willie's eyes darted between Cora and Archie. "Perhaps I should get on board. They've loaded our trunks. The ship will leave soon."

"Good idea," Ola said from the pouch.

The Missing Jackal Murder

Willie glanced at Cora, smiled, then reached for Archie's hands. "The last few days have been delightful. I am so grateful that you took Cora and I on a personal tour of London and invited us for dinner at your family's home. It was absolutely…"

"Educational," Archie finished her sentence with a smile of understanding.

"I was about to say—magical." Willie gave a deep, what Cora thought, a longing sigh.

Cora frowned. "We only had one dinner at the Thorogood's though."

"Yes, but Marcus was so charming." Willie sighed again and gave a dreamy look.

Archie shook his head. "That's my brother for you. He does like to charm the ladies."

"Still," Willie said with a glowing smile, "to be admired by a wealthy English playboy—isn't that every woman's fantasy?"

Archie nodded. "If it's only one evening. A memory to bring home, I suppose, as long as you realize he has at least twenty-five other women on a string."

"But twenty-sixth in line for that handsome, rich English playboy is not so bad for a girl from Moose Lake, Minnesota."

Archie smiled at Willie. "You should now realize there are other men out there who find you worthy."

Willie smiled, then chuckled. "I'll also never forget when you came with us on our tour through Buckingham Palace. The guide became so angry when you knew more about the palace than he did."

All three laughed.

"And the best part was after he ejected you from the group and you gave us a personal tour. Many other guests came along. I am exceedingly blessed to have met you, Archie. I hope that if you ever come to America again, we will meet you again." Willie pulled Archie into a hug and kissed his cheek. She looked at Cora and winked, then walked away.

Cora watched a couple saying their goodbyes in a long passionate kiss, then looked away nervously. She checked her pouch to see if Arve and Ola remained. They clutched on to the fabric as they gazed through the peepholes at the surrounding crowd.

Archie reached for Cora's hand, placed it on his elbow, and lead her away from the crowd to a quieter spot. "This has been quite a trip for you."

"One I will never forget."

"Will you forget me?" He was looking at her intently, and she grew uncomfortable.

"Archie, I will never forget about you." Saying goodbye seemed so hard, but why? They hardly knew each other. It was almost like they were passing strangers.

"I suppose you're wondering why the governors called me to the museum?"

Cora cleared her mind. "Of course, why?"

"The governors and board members concocted an absolutely ridiculous idea that—I should take over as museum curator."

"What? That's wonderful—isn't it?"

Archie took a deep breath. "I am not sure I want to take the job."

"Why not?"

"I asked if the job meant I could no longer lead an expedition. Some suggested caretaking of the museum is a full-time job, others disagreed. I got the impression my expedition days would be over if I take the position. I asked for time to think about it. Then I strode through the museum and found myself in front of the Egyptian exhibit. I stared at the Jackal of Prince Iknokman and asked him for advice." Archie gave a nervous chuckle.

Cora watched him with great interest. "Really?"

"I talked over the entire prospect; the museum, expeditions and…" Archie stopped abruptly and looked uncomfortably at Cora.

"Well? What did he say—I mean, did he help you to a conclusion?"

"Strange. As I walked away, clarity struck me."

"Clarity?"

"It seemed like my subconscious mind spoke out loud to tell me what I should do."

"You heard a voice?" Cora nearly strangled to hear if Iknokman spoke to him.

"So clear I had to turn around to see if anyone was there talking to me—funny, isn't it?"

"Funny, yes." Cora smiled.

"I think you should take Iknokman's advice," Ola said loudly from Cora's pouch. Cora pulled the bag shut to ensure no other advice leaked out.

"You're right. You know, I walked straight back to the governors and refused the job."

"Oh, Archie, are you sure?"

He nodded. "I don't want to stop my archeological research and historical writings. I'm doing what I've always wanted to do. Before I had a chance to leave, the governors gave in. I can be curator for special exhibits and still do expeditions. Those who wanted me to lead an excavation already had plans for me to go in the next season."

"Oh Archie, that's wonderful. Where will you go?"

"I've proposed an expedition to Norway."

"Norway?"

"Of course. A Viking village was just discovered in northern Norway."

"How did you know about the discovery? Wait— Freddie?"

Archie nodded his head. "He did as I asked when you first visited the basement. I wonder if Freddie would like to come along. I plan to assemble a crew to join the adventure."

"What did the governors say about that?"

"They were excited. I told them I would get back to them in a few weeks. I am in the middle of another project."

"Really. What project is that?"

Archie's response became lost in the ship's whistle, reminding passengers the ship would depart soon.

"I've got to go." She paused at Archie for a moment. "Good luck to you." She moved around him and dashed off toward the gangplank.

"Cora, wait!"

"I've got to go," she said, panting. "I'm sorry we didn't have a chance to…"

"Cora, wait!" Archie caught up and grabbed her elbow to spin her around. "I've got to ask you something."

"Can you talk while we run?" she said, hurrying. Archie caught up.

"This is quite irregular," Archie said, gasping for breath.

"Goodbyes are always irregular."

"No, Cora," Archie said.

Cora raced to the gangplank with Archie on her heal.

"Wait," Archie said as they raced up the gangplank.

She spoke over her shoulder. "Archie, this has been the most wonderful experience I have ever had. And you were sure such a great friend."

The Missing Jackal Murder

"Is that all you see me as, just a friend?" Archie's words caused her to slow down halfway up the gangplank. He grabbed her elbow and brought her to the side rail, allowing others to pass. She stood higher on the plank. Archie looked up. "Cora," he looked around at the other passengers and moved his lips, but nothing came out. He then shouted, "Cora—will you marry me?"

Cora took two steps back. She did not know how long she stared at him. They both stood motionless and silent. Her instinct was to run, and she did just that.

Without a word, she dashed up the gangplank to find herself on the ship's deck. She wasn't sure what made her stop. She didn't want to look back at Archie. A firm hand on her elbow and the breath on the back of her neck made her listen.

"I know we've only known each other for such a short time, too short. But I do know if we spent more time together, you possibly could have fallen in love with me, like I have with you. I know you're afraid of being trapped by marriage, but I promise you here and now I will never trap you. Being with you makes my heart sing. And I want my heart to sing for the rest of my life because of you. I wish you could feel the same for me and..." Again, the boat whistle masked Archie's plea.

"I can't, I can't love you. I can't..." Cora shouted.

"Yes, you can," a faint woman's voice emerged from her pouch.

"I'm sorry." She broke out of Archie's grasp and dashed around a corner without looking back. Once she reached the safety of their cabin, she burst into tears.

Chapter 18

"Duluth, Duluth in five minutes. Duluth," the train conductor shouted. Cora felt the train decelerate and found its way near the depot. Clacking sounds slowed with the hissing of the air brakes. People around her were gathering their belongings and prepared to depart.

"It's good to be home," Ola whispered loudly.

Cora looked out over Lake Superior and said nothing.

"It will be good to see everyone," Arve said, looking up at Cora. "Won't it?"

"I'm sure everyone is eager to hear your story, Cora," Ola said.

Still, Cora said nothing. The entire return trip ran through her mind. Ever since the ship left England, she had thought about it over and over. Now, the train trip home ran through her mind, almost as if the scene taunted her, laughed at her. She held back her tears. Had she made the right decision?

"I know I said Archie was a catch Cora," Willie's voice rang in her head, "but it's good you are careful about these things. These things may come from the heart, but your head needs to decide."

Marriage certainly was not in her plans. She assumed going to England would open doors; visits to big cities, meeting new people and having endless adventures. But every time she repeated that mantra, Archie's face came to the forefront of her mind. His voice, his smile, his touch. When the memories of his embrace and the heavenly kisses crept into her thoughts, Cora squashed them as far down as they would go.

The Missing Jackal Murder

Even the splendid Fourth of July celebration on the Brandenburg did little for Cora's spirit. When the fireworks lifted off the ship to celebrate America's 150th anniversary, only Arve and Ola, from on top of their deck table, enjoyed the spectacular fireworks. When all eyes focused on the rockets and firecrackers, Arve and Ola came to life and applauded. Willie looked at Cora frequently, as if checking to see if she would respond.

When Cora saw Arve's and Ola's excitement, she joined in the merriment and promised to remember this night as one of the vacation's greatest moments. After that, she had tried to keep her spirits up for the remaining journey home. But the first sight of the Statue of Liberty squashed all her joy.

The train from New York was the last leg. At the train stops, Cora and Willie ventured out and frequently came dangerously close to being left behind. At the stop in Milwaukee, they had to run and jump to catch the moving train. It was her way of savoring the last moments of adventure the trip offered.

"You're always welcome to come and stay with me in Duluth," Cora said to a tearful Willie at the St. Paul Union Depot. "We have plenty of room at the house." She unsuccessfully tried to hold her tears. "You can stay as long as you want."

Cora promised to stay in touch with Willie. The sight of Willie embracing her father, who came to St. Paul to meet her, and his delight at learning Roy was now in a London jail cell, cheered her. He told them how thrilled he was to see how Willie, a frightened woman when she left, had learned to smile once again.

"And it was Cora's influence," Willie said to her father. He invited them to lunch while they waited for Cora's train to leave for Duluth. Willie had to take a different train that rerouted through the Minneapolis depot to go to Moose Lake. They said goodbye and Cora cried at the last sight of Willie. Her vacation was over. The train trip to Duluth was torture, as her memories made her sad. The adventures she had enjoyed would always remain important. When she got home, she would continue her journal to chronicle everything she had experienced.

The train jerked to a stop. People got up. Cora remained seated. She looked out the window and saw her father waiting in the crowd. She remained seated and waited for the last passenger to leave.

"Cora, are we home?" Ola asked from inside the pouch.

"Yes." Cora wiped her tears and composed herself. "It certainly is good to be home." Now safe from prying eyes and ears, she opened her pouch to speak without whispering. "I did miss everyone."

"But Cora," Ola said. "Who will you miss the most from our trip?"

"Ola!" Arve said sternly.

"Like I said, Cora could always change her mind. I mean technology today. She could send a telegraph across the ocean. She can even ask Nicholas to bring a message to Archie."

"How could Nicholas bring a message back?" Arve argued.

"Well, he could just leave the message on…" Ola said. She frowned as she thought and put her finger to her mouth and not come up with a reasonable solution.

Cora sighed, stood up and walked off the train.

#####

The Missing Jackal Murder

The shiny black Ford Model T came to a squeaky stop. Cora looked out at the familiar house. So wonderful and yet so depressing. She had relayed to her father the true story of her trip; the theft of Arve and Ola, the club that had just barely missed her head, and, of course, her time with Archie. She hoped it didn't make him think less of her ability to be an independent and responsible woman. "You won't tell mother about this, will you?" she asked him.

"If you wish, but I think there is nothing wrong with telling your mother about this Archie fellow. Though I think it would be sensible to keep the misadventures of Arve and Ola quiet, at least for the time being."

Cora looked at her father when he said, "for the time being."

Knude took a deep breath and stared into his daughter's eyes. "I know you and your mother don't always see eye to eye. However, I want you to understand your mother does love you. You don't have to be afraid of her. You mean more to her than you could imagine. Also, I happen to know something about her that you don't know. Before I married her, she had a wayward spirit, much like you."

"Really?" Cora could not imagine her always proper mother daring for adventure. She seemed such a homebody.

"Yes, there were times she wanted to put on her father's boots and go trampling through the woods. But her mother, your Grandmother Sarah, would not allow it. When your grandmother came to America, her mother died while in the middle of the Atlantic voyage and left her as Keeper at a very young age. I met Sarah when she was about as old as your mother is now. She was stern and seemingly unmoving, like your mother seems to you. But I could see in her eyes a tiny spark of adventure, something that had been denied to her because of her duty."

There it was again, the curse that drained all those who longed to be free, to express adventure—the Keeper's duty.

As if he read Cora's mind, Knude continued, "Do you remember the story about how the title 'Santa Keeper' came to be?"

Cora chose not to respond.

"Sigrid, Agar's wife, called the title 'Datter som tar seg av landsbyboerne,' phrased in Norwegian, of course. The direct meaning is 'Daughter who takes care of the Villagers.'" Knude paused, Cora said nothing. "Since that title had remained for over 600 years, it was Sarah's brother Jacob, hoping to Americanize the family, who translated the Norwegian phrase into 'Santa Keeper'. He got that idea after Clement Clarke Moore's, 'The Night Before Christmas' poem. Since Nicholas used magic to continue his Christmas Eve gift-giving journey, Jacob thought the Americanized title would suit perfectly."

"Yeah, yeah, Nicholas visited Moore's house. He spotted Nicholas. The magic prevented Moore from telling people about their encounter exactly, so he concocted a poem the best way he could. So, what does this have to do with anything?"

"Everything," Knude replied. "Each Santa Keeper, or Legend Keeper—your mother, grandmother, all the first-born women in our family from Norway and in America got this opportunity to do something grand, something incredible."

"Incredible? Jeepers creepers, you've got to be kidding."

"No, I'm not. Just because you can't see it... look Cora. Each woman who carried the title not only accepted the responsibility but decided to take on the responsibility for the Village. Some things in their lives may become lost, but not their freedom."

The Missing Jackal Murder

"You're kidding," Cora said.

Arve climbed out of the pouch. "Do you regret taking Ola and I along, Cora?"

She looked down and saw Arve standing straight up with his hands on his hips, with Ola standing next to him.

"Well, no, of course not. I didn't mean you were a burden."

"You took care of us. Did we disappoint you? You walked through the streets of London and saw everything, experienced everything. Though we were missing for a short couple days, we made the rest of the trip together. Were we in your way? Did we ruin your trip?"

Cora said nothing.

Knude took Cora's hand. "Being in charge and involved in caring for the Villagers is a thrill for your mother. I have never seen an ounce of regret. You consider the job a curse, but those sparks, those flickers of light for adventure from your mother, grandmother, and their ancestry are all bunched up in you, and how. You may be worlds apart from your mother, but she is your mother, and she loves you dearly. Remember that."

"I will," Cora said and looked at her father.

"I was glad when you finally purged that silly notion of being dumped on us because you were born late. That notion was what your generation would call—applesauce!"

Cora shook her head in embarrassment. "Well, that was stupid of me. I acted like a spoiled brat."

"You, a brat? Leaning more towards a typical teenager, perhaps."

"I'm not a teenager anymore."

"What about us?" Arve said quietly.

Cora's eyebrows lowered. "I don't think you are a nuisance."

"Or a curse?" Ola asked.

"No, it's just that I've been thinking too much about myself lately. I did have a great time with you as my traveling companions."

"What about future adventures?" Arve asked.

"Depends," she said and looked at her father, "depends on what adventures may come."

They both looked through the windshield but said nothing. Arve returned to the pouch.

"Still," Ola said, "what are you going to do about Archie?"

Cora said nothing.

Knude opened his door and looked at Cora. "Welcome home. We better get in before they look out the window and wonder what's wrong."

"I guess Mother knows everything about what happened to Arve and Ola. I suppose Nicholas told her by now."

"I don't believe so. I didn't see any sparks flying."

Cora got out.

"What about Archie?" Ola called out.

"Shh," Cora said. Cora and her father walked toward the house.

Knude stopped. "Seriously? Did you really steal a police officer's car and drive dangerously through the streets of London?"

Cora smiled and nodded her head.

"That's my girl," Knude said as he reached for the doorknob, stopped and continued. "Not the stealing the police officer's car part, of course."

"Oh no, of course not." Cora grinned.

The Missing Jackal Murder

The front door had not fully opened before Alice jumped into Cora's arms. She picked her up and Alice squeezed. "I missed you. Did you miss me?"

"Of course I did." She had never received such a welcome, and it was a great comfort.

Anna came into view with Agnes in her arms, who let out a loud screen. "Agnes missed you too."

Cora put Alice down. Anna gave Agnes to Alice. The older sister struggled to carry the younger as she walked off. Anna hugged Cora. "I'll bet you wish you were back in London."

"You have no idea."

"So, what was he like?"

"He who? Wait, who told you?"

"You just did. I knew you would fall in love with someone while you were there. So, what's he like?"

"Let's change the subject. Where's Hans?"

"He's upstairs arguing with Stian about whether the University of Minnesota gopher football team will be any good this year."

As if on cue, footsteps flopped down the stairs. "And, if there were any time I wish I was wrong," Hans said, "now would be it. But then I, oh Cora, welcome home. We missed you." He hugged her and kissed her cheek.

"Oh, Cora sweetie," Marit interrupted, and banged her way through the kitchen door. She hugged her daughter ever-so tightly, the two of them surrounded by the scent of roast beef and potatoes.

The scent reminded Cora of her first dinner at the Thorogood's home, and she felt an overwhelming sadness.

"How was your holiday?" Marit said.

"Fine, fine." Cora lied.

"Now, I hope you've got all of this adventure stuff out of your system. Charlie Dalton asked how you were. You remember Charlie, don't you?"

"No, really, I don't," Cora said, halfheartedly.

"Now let Cora catch her breath," Knude said.

"Of course," Marit said. "We can discuss Charlie later." Cora sighed and looked at her father with raised eyebrows.

"Cora, why don't you bring your suitcase to your room and take Arve and Ola to the attic," Knude suggested. "I'll get your trunk out of the trunk later. Trunk? I believe the English call it the boot."

"You did take care of Arve and Ola, didn't you?" Marit asked. "Where are they? I shouldn't have let you keep any of the Villagers with you. I'll have another word with Nicholas. You could've lost them, or worse."

"Who's Charlie Dalton, mother?" Anna said to stop her mother's tirade. "Really, you throw a man at Cora before you even asked about Arve and Ola and whether they had a pleasant trip or if they're alright?"

Cora reached in and pulled them out and placed them on the small round table next to the hallway lamp.

"Arve, Ola," Alice shouted and ran back to the front hallway, leading Agnes behind in a sitting position. Agnes flopped over to one side and cried.

"It's great to be home. It was an incredible trip," Ola said as Anna made her way back into the living room and picked up Agnes.

"What all did you see?" Hans asked.

"Everything," Arve said. "Big Ben, the Parliament, and the changing of the guards, the St. Paul Cathedral—and stops in New York and Chicago."

"Yes, all that, but my favorite is Cora with Archie," Ola said.

Arve bumped Ola. "Oops."

"Who's Archie?" Marit asked from the hallway.

"Who's Archie, Momma?" Alice asked.

"Someone I met and said goodbye to," Cora said quickly, before anyone could make something more out of the reference to Archie.

"Why?" Marit asked. "Did he make trouble for you?"

Knude put his hand on Cora's shoulder. "Maybe you should go upstairs and unpack, sit and clear your mind and join us for dinner."

"Good idea," Cora said. She reached for her case.

Marit put her hand on Knude's elbow. "Wait, who was this, Archie? What did he do?"

Alice stepped up to Anna, close enough so that her head tilted back for her to look straight up to her mother. "What did Archie do to Cora momma?"

"I'll unpack. I'll tell you about Big Ben, the Parliament changing of the guards, and the second trip to the St. Paul Cathedral," Cora said.

"Wait!" Marit commanded.

"Go ahead," Knude said.

"I agree, I'm starving," Hans said.

Marit gave Hans a harsh look.

"We'll see you at dinner," Anna said.

"Isn't Cora going to eat dinner with us?" Alice asked.

Halfway up the stairs, Cora heard the conversation heat up, beginning with her mother. "I hope this is the last time Cora's damnable adventures lead her off alone."

"Mother, the children," Anna said.

"Well, she certainly is not taking Arve and Ola along again."

"What's wrong with Cora taking Arve and Ola along?" Anna asked.

"Yeah," Ola said, "what was wrong with Cora taking me and Arve along?"

"Don't worry about your Mother," Knude said to Anna, "being the Keeper puts a lot of strain on a person."

Marit put her fists on her hips. "That has nothing to do with this."

"Yes, it does Mom, you have been in charge for so many years," Anna said.

"Maybe Ola and I should go back to the attic," Arve said.

Cora stopped on the first landing, put her case down, sat and listened. Not that she wanted to hear what they were talking about, but how they argued without hardly any regard to her feelings. Her fears that everything would return to the same and always on her. Next, they would argue about her marital status and wanted to go here and there instead of settling down. Cora looked up the stairs and wanted to dash to her room and shut the door, but knew she would find no comfort there either. She sighed.

A shadow emerged from the hallway floor. Cora wanted to stand up and dash before they spotted her. Hans came into view. He had Arve and Ola in his hand. They looked eager to leave the discussion.

Hans and Cora looked at each other for a few seconds until he broke the silence. "Let me guess, you're sad your adventure is over and asking yourself why you returned to hear the same arguments all over again." He climbed the stairs next to Cora.

Cora said nothing.

"I know it seems everyone is making lots of noise and nobody's listening."

"Yes, exactly."

"I try not to take sides, though I partially understand your struggle for independence."

"Partially?" Cora said.

Hans sat down a couple of steps below Cora. He placed Arve and Ola next to her.

"I'm sure they'd...," Ola started. Arve silenced her with a gesture. They looked at Cora.

"I know what your family thinks of me," Hans said.

"What do you mean?" Cora said, trying to sound surprised.

Hans smiled and continued. "I know your family thinks I'm a joke, that perhaps Anna should not have married me. That's the way it's always been. My father enjoyed life, but married a stern woman who complained about everything. She literally drove him to his grave. I adopted his good nature as my mother turned against me."

"Why haven't you mentioned anything about your family to me before?"

Hans gave a phony smile. "Despite my attempts to stay positive, I felt alone. My self-esteem faltered until I met Anna. I loved her from the start, though I believed she would not want me. But she did, and I couldn't believe my good fortune. Anna is my adventure. That's why I understand your plight—at least partially."

"I don't understand."

"I know you will get what you want. I know you'll be free from here. You will not have the responsibility for the Villagers to trap you. You will see the world. Experience places you've never thought you would ever visit. Yes, Cora, I fear you will get your wish and go anywhere you want—alone."

Cora looked at Hans as he emphasized the last word.

"Be careful what you wish for. You might get it." He got up and walked down the stairs.

"Maybe there's something in what Hans said," Ola said.

"We only want you to be happy, Cora," Arve said.

Cora took a deep breath, shook her head, picked up Arve and Ola and went up the steps, leaving her suitcase behind.

Chapter 19

Hammer tapping filled the foyer to the attic as Cora arrived and opened the attic door. Villagers worked on, and at first were unaware of her entrance. The scene filled her senses to make her feel at home again. The Villagers were as much her family as the people downstairs.

"Look," a small girl shouted, "it's Cora, she's back." Everyone turned. Little Uda ran out to the front. "Did you bring me something from London?"

"Yes, I did!" Cora said and placed Arve and Ola down on the Village platform. Stian, Ola's father, leapt forward and embraced his daughter.

Gunda approached the edge first. "Did you have fun?"

Her husband Nils sighed. "I hope she did. We're way behind in woolen things. I don't know if we'll ever catch up."

"Oh Nils, stop beating your gums. We're not too far behind."

"Where's Kel?" Cora asked Uda, surprised to see only one twin.

Uda giggled and pointed to her hut.

"I'm in here," Kel shouted from inside, grunted, then dashed out with toilet paper trailing behind him like streamers.

Uda giggled again. "I wanted to see how long it would take for Kel to escape. I tied him up like a mummy. Shoot, I guess not very long. Let me try again."

"Hello Cora," Kel panted, "did you bring me something from London?"

"Yes, I did. It was Arve who picked it out. Where's Nicholas?"

"He's down in storage with Astrid," Nils said. "Oh, here they are."

Astrid appeared with Baldur and Berthina, all carrying leather pieces as Nicholas brought up the rear and carried a load of wood.

"Hello, Cora," Baldur and Berthina said in unison.

As the three dropped their armfuls of leather near Baldur's station, Berthina spoke first. "Did you have a pleasant trip?"

"Cora said she brought us something, Mother," Uda said, jumping up and down.

"She did?" Berthina said.

Baldur stood next to Berthina. "You look exhausted."

"I am," Cora's eyes shot to Nicholas.

Nicholas stacked his armful of wood next to Nils' station. "I know that you're more than exhausted."

Cora said nothing.

Kel's voice pierced the silence. "Now it's your turn to see how long you can stay tied up, Uda."

"No, it isn't."

"Yes, it is."

"I have to speak with you in private, if that is okay?" Cora said to Nicholas.

"Back to work," Nils shouted.

"Sometimes your voice sounds like one of those noisy factory whistles," Gunda said to Nils.

"Of course," Nicholas said to Cora.

"It is your turn, too, Uda."

"I think not, Kel."

Cora lifted Nicholas, then thought she needed Astrid's motherly touch. "Astrid?"

"Of course, dear."

Cora picked up Astrid in her other hand.

"Yeah-ha," Kel said.

"You-na," Uda answered.

"Yeah-ha."

"You-na."

Cora spun around and closed the Village door with her hip. Kel and Uda's argument muffled through the door as she carried Nicholas and Astrid to the foyer. She placed the two on the small round table next to the window and chair, then sighed. "Thank you for not saying anything about what you saw in London."

"What is she talking about?" Astrid asked Nicholas.

"Our secret," Nicholas said and winked at Cora.

"Actually, I don't mind if you tell anyone in the Village, just don't tell my mother. In fact, don't tell Anna either. They will raise the roof…"

"Arve and Ola were safe with me at the beginning of your stay in London. You needn't have worried."

Cora stiffened her shoulders. "Why were you spying on me?"

Nicholas gave a secret smile. "I do have a good sense about these things, when the Villagers or the Keeper's family are in danger."

"So, you really knew what was going on?"

"Remember, Arve and Ola were not in danger because you were there. You were and are concerned about their safety. You filled your mind with their well-being."

"Yes, but I'm not the Keeper."

Nicholas pointed at Cora. "No, but you are a granddaughter of Agar. And that's magic enough for you." Nicholas paused. "Now, however, I sense you're sad."

"This has nothing to do with the young man you met, does it?" Astrid said. "That Archie fellow that you fell in love with?"

Cora looked at Nicholas and then back to Astrid.

"How did you know about Archie? Besides, I don't love Archie."

"Are you sure about that?" Astrid asked. "Seems to me he's in love with you."

"Why do you say that? How could you possibly know if that's true?"

"My dear," Astrid said with a sympathetic smile, "we've been around for a long time, in case you've forgotten. We've seen it all—and how."

Cora dropped into the chair and slumped back. She stared at the wall and noticed the rays of sunshine dancing around because of the swaying of the trees. Nicholas and Astrid walked closer to her left ear.

"You've never been in love before, Cora," Astrid said. "The first time can be very scary."

"I'm not in love." Cora raised her voice. She looked to Astrid, then back to the wall. "My parents have paraded men in front of me to marry me off for years. Do you think I would fall for the first man I met on my own?"

"They didn't introduce you to those men to marry you off," Nicholas said. "Your parents want you to be happy. Yes, there are financial implications, but mainly they want you to be happy and find someone to share your life together."

"They want you to be in love and for someone to love you," Astrid said.

"First, do you admit you love Archie?"

Cora's mouth opened and closed. She wrapped her arms around her but did not reply.

"You didn't say no," Astrid said.

"Cora," Nicholas said. "Archie is different. That spark is there. The very spark you have been looking for."

"What do you mean?"

"His light of magic is dim. It's trying to shine out. And when you are next to him, he feels it, he sees it for the first time in his adult life."

"How would you know that? Every time I talked to him about magic, he thought it was poppycock. And he would... What do you mean adult life?"

Nicholas reached into his side pocket and pulled out a piece of paper and lifted it to Cora. She reached for it and the paper grew to full size in her hand. She recognized it as a 'Dear Santa' letter and read it aloud. *"Dear Santa. You don't have to bring me anything. Whatever you have for me, you can bring it to a poor girl. I have a Mommy and Daddy and I am happy. Hope you are fine. Happy Christmas—Elizabeth. P.S. I believe in you."*

Cora returned the letter to Nicholas. "What does this have to do with Archie?"

"Little Elizabeth's letter intrigued me. That year I brought her one of Vidor's silver necklaces. The next year I brought her one of Ola's sweaters. I found her sleeping on the couch next to the fireplace. After I finished placing her present under the tree, I saw she was not only awake but watching me. We talked about magic, we talked about the poor, and she asked me to make sure I made stops for them. We talked about Lars' eight tiny reindeer and the tiny sled. We talked about how much I loved making my Christmas Eve trips and how I looked forward to them every year. It was a delightful conversation until I heard her father's footsteps walking down the stairs and I made my way out. And every year there was Elizabeth, awake and waiting for me, ready for our next yearly chat."

"So, what does this have to do with Archie?"

"Even when she married and had children, still, she waited up for me while her husband and family slept. Even when her family told her to stop acting like a child and stop waiting for Santa, still I stopped by and we talked for a moment. Every year I stopped by her large mansion, the Thorogood mansion in London."

Cora's eyes widened, her jaw dropped. Her mind flashed to the spot in the hallway where she had looked up at an old woman looking down. Their eyes had connected as if the old woman was greeting a beloved granddaughter.

"Yes, you know her as Grandmother Elizabeth. Every year she wanted me to bring something for her family and her husband's family. Of course, as high and mighty as they are, they all turned their noses up on the humble gifts and sent them to charity. But that was exactly what Elizabeth hoped would happen—their gifts would go into the hands of the poor and into the hands of those who would appreciate them. And as for the Thorogood family, that's one reason I don't believe this notion of 'Santa's nice list, Santa's naughty list' bit. Those who miss out and do not see the magic in their life go through life in a state of spiritual death as its own punishment."

"So, you knew—"

"Archie's grandmother? Yes, where do you suppose his love for family and adventure came from? Certainly not his mother."

Cora's eyes glistened.

"The spark is there, Cora. Archie and you met entirely on your own, mind you. No help from your parents, me, or anyone else. I know it's your decision. But when someone like this enters your life, I suggest you hang on and don't pass him by. But unlike the Thorogood's who never gave a second thought to the precious gifts we gave, I know in my heart of hearts, if you pass up this gift you may regret it. I hope not, for your sake."

Cora's tears gave way to defiance. "I will not be someone's-" Cora got up and left the room with her hands over her face.

#####

Cora slammed her bedroom door behind her, dropped to her bed, and leaned back against the headboard. She wrapped her arms around her bent knees, closed her eyes and rocked to help soothe the pain. Did she truly love Archie? She had never willingly spent as much time with a man as she had with him. No one had ever proposed to her. No man had ever told her he loved her. No man had ever promised to let her stay free, to be herself.

But the idea of marriage felt like a trap. Once entered, there was no escape. She thought about Willie and the hardships she had experienced in her marriage to Roy. Cora lowered her legs and silenced her mind. So much had happened. She took deep breath and felt nothing. Even the sounds of the downstairs chatter that usually found their way through her bedroom door grew silent.

Thoughts churned in her mind. "*I am home. But what is home? No one is to push a man on me, one who will domineer over me. No. Archie is not like that. He is so open and understanding. But no, forget him. I'm here, he's there.*"

A tear rolled down Cora's cheek. She wiped it away. "*Ease the pain. What pain? I have no pain.*" Cora's mind drifted. She felt nothing, only the rise and fall of her chest with every breath until even that grew silent. She floated, she flew in the sky, in the clouds, then alongside a large black bird, a giant crow. They were going somewhere, but she didn't know where. The sounds of drums, distant and calling softly, echoed in her mind. The sun's brightness seeped through

Cora's eyelids. But the position of her bed would not allow her to receive sunlight in the way she craved it. She frowned, the bright sun, the sounds of soft drums became sharp.

Cora opened her eyes, and the drumbeats fell silent. No longer in her room and no longer laying but standing in a field of tall green grass and thick green trees surrounded most of the area. "This looks so real. How could it be?" She lifted her arms and flattened her hands and smoothed the tops of the tall grass as if to test its authenticity. They were real, yet not alarmed by this strange and sudden transportation. Peace filled her soul.

Cora became aware she was not alone. First, she noticed the wooden houses with thatched roofs stood one hundred yards away. She gazed at a picturesque scene of an old Scandinavian village. She belonged here.

She walked to the village, entered, but all seemed abandoned. The voice of a man who spoke on the other side of the village found its way to Cora. Upon passing the last hut, she found people, perhaps the residences of this village, who gathered in a circle holding hands. Three people stood in the center. Their clothing fit the historical time of the village, ancient, yet magical. Everything was so peaceful, everyone so happy and yet familiar.

Cora approached and stood behind the circle. Those who's back to her, she hoped would not notice her but afraid those on the other side who did face her would react to her presence. They causally glance at her as if she were part of the group. The old gray-haired, long-bearded man raised his hands and spoke both to the crowd and to the young people, the two with their backs to her. "As always, it is my pleasure to link two people who began their journey alone, now together, in love, to give their promise, for now and all the future has for them."

The Missing Jackal Murder

It was a marriage ceremony. She could not see who the couple were as they stood with their backs to her. Their attire was familiar. The woman wore a green dress and had braided brown hair in one strand down her back. The man had blonde, shoulder-length hair and a thin beard. When they looked at each other, their profiles were familiar to her. Cora moved closer. A man in the circle saw her and smiled. His wife let go of her husband's hand and took hold of Cora's hand to draw her into the circle.

A girl on the other side of the woman leaned forward and looked at Cora. "Who is that mama?"

"Shh," the woman said.

"Is she an auntie?" A boy standing next to the girl also leaned forward to stare at her.

"Kel, Uda, quiet," the woman said.

A lightning bolt of realization shot down Cora's spine.

"My children are quite a handful."

Cora looked into the mother's eyes. "Berthina?"

The woman smiled and looked at the man. It was Baldur, and he also smiled at Cora.

As the old man spoke, Cora gave him her attention. "You entered the circle apart, yet you found each other," he said to the two in front of him. "You two will leave the circle together, but not separate from the circle you have entered and will walk as husband and wife, never to separate, never to be alone again."

The old man nodded, and the young man spoke. "Ola, my life was empty without you. I have searched for you. I was lost until I entered this village where you were born, where you grew. You accepted me as one of the villagers. I knew you were the one for me. Our lives together will not bind us in chains but bound by love and respect. I wish to spend the rest of my life with you."

The old man looked at the young woman and nodded. "Arve, my happiest moment was the day you entered our village and my life. Then, as now, I have found that our hearts beat as one. We will be together forever. I fear nothing about you as my husband. I know you want what is best for me, and I want what is best for you, now and forever."

The old man lifted his hand. "They have found each other and pledged to each other. They will live together in love, happiness and freedom, for no one has the power to separate these two who have now become one. Only death can separate what I have joined and that time will be a long…" The old man stuttered. For a fleeting moment, his face shifted from complete joy, to horrified sadness and fear, then resumed its joyful pose and continued, "—a very long time."

The couple embraced and kissed. The circle released their grip, then collapsed around the couple in applause. Cora stood still and watched the greeting.

After a moment, Arve stepped away from the crowd toward Cora and embraced her. "Thank you for joining us at our wedding." He released her.

Ola followed and embraced Cora next and kissed her on the cheek. "Thank you for having faith in us." The bride and groom gave her a long look, smiled, then walked toward the village. The crowd followed, walked past her, gave their greetings till they left her alone.

"Why are you here?" a man spoke sharply behind her.

She spun around to find the old man facing her, his eyebrows lowered as if angry.

"I'm sorry; I really don't know how I got here." Cora found it hard to speak.

"You are intruding on something sacred," he said.

"I would leave if I knew how."

"Interesting. You are intruding, yet you do not know how you got here and don't know how to leave. If I didn't know any better, I would say that sounds like you're *trapped*." The man made a snorting sound and walked towards the village. Cora, not knowing what else to do, followed him. He walked past the village, past the place she found herself here and to a small hill and continued to follow.

As the old man reached the top of the small incline, Cora turned back to the village. Arve and Ola looked at her and waved their hands over their heads. She lifted her hand halfheartedly, smiled, then saw the old man disappeared behind the hill. "Wait!" Cora shouted and ran after him to catch up. From the top of the hill, she watched him on his way toward a small hut with smoke lifting from the chimney. Next to the hut were a metal sundial and other movable devices. She remembered stories about the shaman who had saved the village from death because of a plague. "Wait, are you, are you Agar?"

He stopped, his back to her, but the profile of his long hair bearded face was enough to speak to her. "I am surprised you know anything about me. I know you are a granddaughter, but you're not the one who protects the Villagers. I asked before, why're you here?"

"I don't know."

Agar grunted and walked on.

"I don't know. But I'm glad to be here." Her answer surprised Cora unexpectedly, but true—she was glad to be there.

"Glad to be here? Why are you glad to be in a place that makes you feel trapped?"

"I'm not trapped."

"You're not, then why don't you leave?"

"I don't know how to leave."

"Oh?"

Cora looked to her right. Somehow, she knew that was the way out. She didn't know why she knew, but that way was the exit. But she had no feelings of being trapped.

Agar turned and watched her closely.

"Well," Cora said, folding her arms, "maybe I'm not trapped. Maybe I want to be here."

"You want to be here?"

"Yes, I do."

Agar opened his mouth to speak, but Cora interrupted, "Here's what I see. The idea of marrying Archie and the fear of being trapped scare me. Somehow after the voyage home, I was magically transported here and blessed to witness the marriage of Arve and Ola, along with the entire village, in human form. Now, after the ceremony, I find myself here, with you and ready to receive your wisdom to help me see the problem more clearly and in hopes of making the right decision."

Agar looked astonished and folded his arms. "My, but you are a clever miss."

"I have been told that a lot lately. But I guess I really am not. Also, let me make myself clear, Mr. Agar. I don't say this to mock you, but…" Cora let go of her crossed arms and placed her hands behind her back. "I will listen to you with an open mind and an open heart. I realize you are one of the wisest men I will ever know, and I am happy you can help me with this."

Agar first stood silent with an expression Cora can only surmise as surprised and confusion. He then smiled. "Very well. What is it that you need my help with?"

"I love Archie, and he wants to marry me, but I don't want to be, um, trapped."

The Missing Jackal Murder

"Do you believe Arve and Ola feel trapped? Are your parents trapped? What about your sister and her husband? Do they look as if they made the wrong decision?"

"That's not the point."

"Oh?"

"I'm different from them."

"How so?"

"I want adventure. I want to go places, to visit other countries and other people. But I believe that if I marry Archie, or anyone else, I will lose my chance. I understand marriage is a big step. To have faith, you will remain in love to the day you die. You see, I'm happy—now."

"So how do you know you will remain happy as you are now? Can you guarantee yourself you will have no regrets? What about regret for living a life—alone?"

Cora felt a shiver down her spine when Agar put the emphasis on the last word. She again looked in the direction she knew would lead her out and back to her family. Her mind shifted to Archie. She remembered his smile and his proposal. "I don't know. That's what I'm afraid of. What is the right answer? How can I make the right decision? Please help me."

"Do you not have all the information to help you make the right decision?"

"What information is that?"

"You said you are afraid of being trapped and your days of adventure would be over."

"Yes, basically that's it. A man wants a wife who will stay home and take care of the house and children."

"But is this what you expect from Archie? Did he not promise you adventure? Was there any evidence he was lying, or he would stop you from doing what you want? Is there any evidence that if you marry him, you'll be trapped?"

"He did say if I ever wanted to go..." Cora remembered Archie's proposal. There was nothing in Archie's proposal to prove Agar wrong. "Maybe I should reconsider..."

"When Arve and Ola came and asked if they could travel with you, did you refuse them? No. You brought them along, not to satisfy them but to satisfy you. You brought them along as traveling companions. Is there the possibility Archie asked you to be his traveling companion? Would you still be afraid to marry him when your happiness is all that matters to him?"

"Maybe, maybe it is time for me to... At least maybe I should consider marriage if—"

"Do not look into the eyes of Arve and Ola as wooden figures. Look into their hearts. They do not know what the future holds for them. They do not fear what will happen to the others. They do not fear they will forget their lives or their love. They are happy because they have faith, they will be happy in the future—together. Despite the horror that lies ahead of the village, despite the life after that horror, they are happy together. And as for you and Archie, you need not to seek the advice of an old man. You need not to seek the advice of my trusted friends Nicholas and Astrid. You need to seek here." He pointed to Cora's heart. "You have always known the answers. Do not let doubt or fear ever cloud the warmth of the sun inside you. Do not listen to the words of doubt and fear telling you to live your life. You command. You love. You live. So whatever direction you choose, your heart will guide you and keep you happy."

Cora paused.

"Now, clever miss, what will your decision be—do not tell me, tell yourself and only let those you love know what you will do and what you will be."

The Missing Jackal Murder

Cora leapt forward and wrapped her arms around Agar. Agar lifted his arms around Cora and patted her shoulder. "Now if you will excuse me, granddaughter, I choose to spend the rest of this day with the newlyweds. You know what to do."

Agar released Cora and walked towards the village. She had a strong desire to follow him, to be with Arve and Ola, to spend the time in their joyous moment. But she looked back at the path and knew what she wanted and had to do.

She took one last look at the back of Agar's head as he disappeared over the hill. She looked again at the path that would bring her back. The hill disappeared along with the trees and grass. A flap of crow's wings, a quiet beating of a drum, and Cora opened her eyes.

The blur faded. Her room came into focus. Saliva drooled down her chin. Her body lay limp, dangerously close to falling off the bed. She sat up against the headboard and re-familiarized herself. The sounds of the family discussing her situation seeped into her brain. She was home.

Cora swung her legs over and sat on the side of the bed. She wiped her chin and blinked several times. She then let out a deep sigh, jumped up and bounced across the room in two steps, yank open the door and charge down the steps. Her suitcase remained on the first landing. "Good," she said to herself, and picked up the case as she marched down the stairs. The room grew silent when she entered. She marched to her father. "I'm going back to England. I'm going to find Archie. I have to."

"But you just got here," Marit said.

"I don't care, I'm leaving. I will come back once I find Archie. Father, I need to borrow some money and I need a ride to the station."

"Well, I'm not sure that's such a good idea," Knude said, giving a startled look toward Marit.

"If you can't, I will," Hans said.

"You stay out of this," Anna said.

Hans shook his head. "No, I won't. Cora has finally found someone, and I think we should support her."

"This is ridiculous," Marit said. "There are so many men available here and…"

"No mother," Cora said.

Hans stepped to Cora. "We have some money, and we will loan all of it to you Cora."

"Oh Hans, how sweet," Anna said.

"Does Daddy have candy?" Alice asked.

"This is ridiculous," Marit said, "I don't want you to go. It's stupid to go all the way back to England. Over some boy that likely hasn't thought twice about you since you left."

"No, it's not stupid," a man's voice said from the table in the living room. Cora looked to see Arve had come down to join in the commotion with Ola at his side. Cora looked at them and smiled.

"Can we go too?" Kel said, dashing onto the table next to them.

"No," Berthina said, as more of the Villagers appeared on the table.

"We don't get to go anywhere," Uda said.

"What's going on?" a man's voice shouted from on top of the living room bookcase. "We need to get back to work."

"Nils, it's alright," Nicholas said. "We're here for Cora."

"What are you all doing here?" Marit said, "Nils is right. We can handle this."

Nicholas placed his hands on his beard and murmured, as if to himself. "I could pop over to London and place a letter on his desk at the museum…"

"That's not what Nils said," Anna said. "Nils just wants everyone to go back to work."

"Maybe I could speak to Elizabeth…" Nicholas said, pointing his finger in the air.

"As they should."

"They don't always have to work," Gunda said.

"Yes, that's it, Elizabeth, but will Archie listen," Nicholas said placing his hand back to his beard.

"Now see here," Nils said.

"No, you see here," Anna said.

"Look until I hand over the responsibility to you…" Marit said to Anna as she put her hands on her waist.

"Can we go?" Kel said.

Nicholas raised his hands. "Ah, but then I don't need to do anything."

"Where's Cora going?" Alice asked.

"Why can't we go?" Uda asked.

Cora sighed and rolled her eyes. "This is ridiculous." She saw Hans smiling and giving her an approving wink. Cora smiled at Hans and said, "I'm off." She grabbed the doorknob and pulled the door open, then gasped at the figure in front of her, standing dumbfounded. "Archie!"

The room instantly fell silent, including the Villagers who had resumed their wooden form. Arve, in the middle of expressing himself while he became his wooden form, rocked dangerously close to tipping over. Anna reached to steady him.

Cora's jaw dropped to see the man, big as life, standing at their door, one hand lifted ready to knock, the other hand with a small suitcase. He stood motionless and stared into her eyes. His mouth moved as he tried to speak. Words slowly formed. "I thought I had a speech prepared. Now I can't even…Cora, may I come in?"

Cora paused, then nodded and stepped aside for him to enter.

He removed his hat, put it under his arm, and held out his hand to Cora.

They connected. Sure enough, he was real. She half expected to see Agar but found only the stunned eyes of her family watching them.

"Cora," Marit whispered sharply, "let the gentleman in."

"Oh, yes, yes Archie, do come in." She pulled him inside, and Hans closed the door behind him.

"Cora," Marit said again. "Aren't you going to introduce your gentleman friend?"

Her eyes stared into Archie's. She nodded, cleared her throat, and introduced him. After everyone gave short, 'not knowing what to do' responses, Cora turned to him. "How did you get here so fast? I only arrived home moments ago. And how did you know my address?" She glanced toward the Villagers to make sure they were in their wood carving form and stood still.

"Well, you see, it's like this…"

"Would you like to sit down?" Anna asked, motioning for Archie to step into the parlor.

"Yes, well, no, actually, not right now." Archie looked at Cora. "You see, after you left I dragged myself back home and I thought—no—blast it all, oh, I do apologize," Archie said looking at Alice.

She looked back at Archie with a blank face.

"I thought, well, after our journey together, in good taste, of course," Archie said to Knude and Marit. Archie took a deep breath and pushed on. "I boarded what they advertised as the fastest ship, bound for Philadelphia. Then I took a train to St. Paul. There I boarded the train to Duluth. I may have seen you, I rehearsed a speech, yet everything I

The Missing Jackal Murder

thought I would say left my foolish brain, and I thought more time is what I needed to prepare myself. Before I caught up, I saw you enter your father's car and off you went before... Well, as you Americans would say, 'I grabbed a cab' to follow you, not too close of course. I certainly did not want you to think that I was stalking you. Well, I lurked around to bring up enough courage to knock, and so here I am, wanted or not."

Archie stopped chattering. Cora was unaware she still held Archie's hand. They stood looking into each other's eyes. She realized everyone would think she looked like a love-struck teenager.

"And so, to the point. Cora, I am here to ask you—again—the same question I asked before you parted and—I–"

"I think we should leave these two together, alone," Hans said.

"No," Archie said, "no, I would like for you all to witness this, for better or worse, and well..." Archie took a deep breath. "Well, blast it all, Cora will you..."

"Yes, I will marry you Archie." Cora pulled Archie into a deep kiss. The room erupted in applause. They broke away. "That is, if you promise adventures are still in our future."

"Of course, wherever you want to go, I will take you there, including expeditions, and we will go on excavations and explorations, of course." He gave her an enormous smile.

Alice tugged on Archie's pants. "Grand-mummy said you did something to Auntie Cora." Her voice was full of anger and bewilderment.

Archie smiled and got down on one knee. "What I did was I fell in love with your auntie. I hope that was not too bad for me."

"Oh no," Alice's face cracked into a smile, "I'm sure that would make Auntie Cora happy. That would make grandpa and grand-mummy happy. It would make Nicholas and Astrid-"

Anna reached unnecessarily for Alice's mouth as Cora recognized the protective magic.

"But I thought now they're going to marry, he could see Nicholas…"

"Shh," Anna said

"That's right. He, they would." Cora gazed into Archie's eyes. "Archie, if you agree to another condition."

"Name it."

"That you fully and totally approve of my family."

"But of course." Archie scanned the room with a smile.

"Not just them, but the rest of my, uh, *unusual* family."

Archie paused with a puzzled look. "Where are they? I would love to meet them."

Anna spoke up. "Just to put your mind at ease, Archie, Cora's not going to introduce you to criminals or other unsavory people. On the other hand, they're the most wonderful people you'll ever meet."

"You're right. In fact, they are the best part of our family," Cora took a deep breath, exhaled, turned, picked up Arve and Ola and presented the woodcarvings to Archie. "Here."

Archie took both carvings. He frowned in confusion.

Cora exhaled another deep breath. "Now, Arve and Ola, you know."

Still, there was no reaction, but confusion, from Archie.

"Arve and Ola, do you think Archie is a good pick for me? A good pick for our family?"

Arve and Ola instantly came to life. Ola spoke first. "Oh yes, Cora, I agree he is the one."

"Indubitably," Arve said.

Archie dropped the two, who froze, bounced off the floor, then came back to life. "That went well," Arve said sarcastically, rubbing his posterior.

"Oh, men," Ola said.

Hans reached for Archie's arm and pulled him back to prevent him from stomping on Arve and Ola.

Cora picked up Arve and Ola and placed them on the table next to Nicholas and Astrid.

"Welcome to the family, Archie," Nicholas said.

"I know you will make Cora thrilled," Astrid said.

"Can we go to London too?" Kel asked.

"Shh," Berthina said.

"We don't get to go anywhere," Uda said.

Baldur put his hands on his waist. "Quiet you two."

"But we don't—" Kel said.

"Your father said to be quiet," Berthina said.

Stain peeked over the other villager's shoulders. "What's going on? Are we going somewhere?"

Nils stood on top of the bookcase. "Now, can we get back to work?"

"In a while," Gunda said, standing with the rest of the villagers at the table. "We need to welcome Archie to..."

"Archie?" Nicholas said in surprise.

"Archie!" Cora said.

"Oh, my!" Astrid said.

Cora saw the bottom of Archie's shoes as he lay unconscious on the floor. She groaned and wondered what his reaction would be when he became conscience again.

Nicholas pointed to Archie. "We need some of that smelling salts."

R. M. Scott

"I do believe there is still some in the table drawer underneath Nicholas," Knude said. He opened the drawer and pulled out the small container.

Anna chuckled. "Oh yeah, I remember the last time we used those."

Hans said as he rubbed his nose. "Oh boy, I sure do too."

"Here." Cora gave a small wave under his nose.

Archie sat up.

Hans patted Archie's back. "Oh boy? So that's what I looked like when I fainted when I met the Villagers. In fact, I believe it was this same spot."

Archie sat dazed and confused, staring at the Villagers as they moved around and talked all at once. "How? What?"

Cora knelt by Archie. "I understand if you want to change your mind about marrying me. I did try to warn you about magic. At first, I thought it was a curse, a trap to take care of the Villagers, but now I realize I am blessed. We're blessed to have them in our life. If you are still interested in marrying me, I will tell you all about them, how they came to be here with us. It may take time and if you are patient -"

"This may take some time to sort out." Archie sputtered, sitting cross-legged on the floor as he shook his head.

"I understand," Nicholas said. "I remember you as a child every time I visited your grandmother on Christmas Eve night."

Archie looked stunned as he observed Nicholas. "You were at our house?"

Cora wrapped her arm around Archie's elbow. "Yes. And again, I will tell you everything about the Village if you still want to hear, if you still want to marry me."

The Missing Jackal Murder

"Marry you? Of course I want to marry... they won't bite or jump out or anything like that, will they?"

"Of course not. Well, except for those two mischievous hoodlums," Cora concluded as she pointed to the twins.

"Me," Kel said, "you mean Uda."

"Me? Na-ah."

"Na-hah."

"Quiet you two," Berthina said.

Archie laughed. "Yes, yes, I do, and I promise I will accept your family—even though there is so much for me to understand in the present moment." Archie got up and moved into the living room.

Nils grunted. "Now can we get back to work?"

Archie stopped and stared at Nils.

"Oh, don't mind Nils. It is his way," Gunda said. "Anna, could you bring me up to Nils? I'll handle him."

"Oh sure, Gunda." Anna did as she asked. Gunda and Nils argued their way into the tunnel until they couldn't hear their voices.

Cora shook her head. "Nils is sort of like—like Santa's head elf. But don't tell him that. He'll tell you in no uncertain terms why he isn't."

"Santa?" Archie said.

"Eh, no, not a good opening. But we'll get there."

"And don't forget our friend Prince Iknokman," Ola said as the Villagers found their way to the living room.

"Iknokman," Archie said in surprise. "Is he one of these also?"

"No," Cora said to Archie, then turned to Ola. "One thing at a time."

"We like the way this couch bounces," Kel said when he and Uda bounced on the couch after Archie sat down.

"As for you two," Cora grabbed both and placed them on the floor.

"And you two be quiet," Marit said.

When Archie settled down, he saw Alice with a large smile approach with her hand out. "My name is Alice." Archie took her hand and smiled. "The Village is really nice. Well, sometimes Kel and Uda are naughty. I'm sure you will like them all. And they will like you too."

Archie smiled.

The rest of the Villagers walked on the floor and stood next to Kel and Uda.

"I said you two be quiet," Baldur said.

"But we want to go to London," Uda said.

"Shh," Berthina said.

Cora sat, picked up Nicholas and placed him on her knee. "Nicholas tells the story the best."

"I may have before, but not this time," Nicholas said. "I think it's your turn to tell the story, Cora."

Cora looked at Archie. "Are you sure you want to stay?"

"Ab-so-lute-ly," Archie said and placed his flat, trembling hand next to Nicholas. He walked on Archie's hand and held on to his thumb. "This is the most interesting feeling."

"You've got that Christmas feeling," Hans said. "Again, we, now Cora, will explain."

Cora cleared her throat. "It's like this. — Many centuries ago, in the small town of Northland, in northern Norway, lived a great and powerful shaman named Agar, who loved the villagers very, very much."

Epilogue

Tobacco smoke rose towards the ceiling. Voices and clinking glasses vibrated throughout the London saloon. "This seems a bit more agreeable than the sleazy pubs I usually have to visit," Peter Stokes said to himself. He closed the door behind him and scanned the clientele. To his left stood the bar and stools with drinkers guzzling from their mugs. Patrons filled tables and chairs with customers who sat and drank. But the booths against the right wall interested Stokes the most. "That's where he will be."

He took two steps forward and halted when the door opened behind him. Stokes froze. A man and woman came through and passed by, not giving him a moment's glance. Stokes gave a sigh of relief and scanned the booths again.

"I hope all the clues were right. He should be here. Am I too early? Or perhaps I'm too late, maybe—His mind froze, then reengaged when he saw an arm and tobacco smoke rising from a back booth. The tall panel covered the man. Obviously, he did not want anyone to notice him or become disturbed.

Stokes adjusted his tie and looked over his attire to make sure he looked presentable. He cleared his throat, took a deep breath, and moved forward. He did not stop until he reached the other side of the booth, spun, and faced the man. "Excuse me, am I interrupting?"

The man casually glanced at him, then returned to his relaxed pose as if Stokes did not exist. "May I join you?" Again, the man only lifted his mug. Stokes took his silence as his answer and did not speak until after the man lowered his mug. The man was a fairly well-dressed gentleman, with long black hair and sporting a large black beard, of which was well kept. His eyes were half closed, as if this was his way of presenting a relaxed and non-threatening stance.

"Yes." Stokes cleared his throat and sat opposite the man. "Yes, I wanted to introduce myself and to offer my services to you. My name is—"

"I know who you are, Stokes, and of your qualifications too," the man interrupted.

"Yes sir, Mr. Founder, I—" Stokes stopped when Founder glanced up at the mention of his name. "Oh, pardon me Governor, as I mentioned, if you have any use of my kind of-"

"You were sloppy," Founder interrupted, "you and your partner."

"Yes, Mr. Kent was sloppy. I know I should have kept him under control."

"I wonder what kind of information Mr. Kent is spilling about you now, as we speak."

"Yes, I have learned from my mistakes, and I have obtained a new assistant who is…"

"Yes, I do believe she will be more useful." Founder said, squinting while he stroked his black beard. "She will prove useful indeed."

"Yes, I believe so. Now I want to tell you that my financial requirements are quite reasonable. However, if there are any tasks that…"

"I do not tolerate mistakes, Stokes. Mistakes usually prove to be… dangerous."

"Yes sir, I understand."

"I will contact you shortly." He brought his pipe back to his mouth.

"Yes, sir," Stokes said. He understood the message that it was time for him to leave. He got up and took one step, stopped, and looked at Founder. "How shall I? —"

"I will contact you, Mr. Stokes."

"Yes, sir."

Stokes took another step when Founder took his pipe out of his mouth. "Stokes."

"Yes, sir?"

Founder stared into Stokes' eyes. "Do not contact me again." The dark black eyes warned Stokes he should be cautious with this man.

"Yes, sir."

Stokes walked gingerly to the door, took one last look at the man's arm and a cloud of tobacco smoke, then left the building.

About the Author

R. M. Scott is a woodcarver and author from Minnesota who has carved so long the wooden figures came to life and asked her to write their stories. That makes her either crazy or enlightened—you decide. She holds a bachelor's degree in journalism from the University of Minnesota and the MBA from Concordia University. R. M. Scott lives in Minnesota with her woodcarvings and her cats.

More books in the Santa Keeper Mystery series featuring the magical Villagers will follow *–Elsie's Secret Life, and Alice's Secret Message*. Now available is *Christina's Secret Family* on Amazon.

Cora Chronicles Mystery series, *The Missing Jackal Murder, The Hollywood Honeymoon Murder and The London Wedding Murder*. [With more coming] Each standalone story features Cora's adventures around the globe in 1926-1927. Each story includes a devious and twisting murder mystery.

Thank you for reading. I invite you to share your thoughts and reactions.

Author Website: https://www.rmscottwriter.com/
Website: www.santakeepers.com
Facebook: https://www.facebook.com/rmscottwriter